LEAD ME
home

JAN 17

CH

// the winds of change series //

LEAD ME
home

a novel by

stacy hawkins adams

ZONDERVAN®

ZONDERVAN.com/
AUTHORTRACKER
follow your favorite authors

ZONDERVAN

Lead Me Home

Copyright © 2013 by Stacy Hawkins Adams

This title is also available as a Zondervan ebook.
Visit www.zondervan.com/ebooks.

This title is also available in a Zondervan audio edition.
Visit www.zondervan.fm.

Requests for information should be addressed to:

Zondervan, Grand Rapids, Michigan 49530

Library of Congress Cataloging-in-Publication Data

Adams, Stacy Hawkins, 1971-
  Lead me home / Stacy Hawkins Adams.
    pages cm
  ISBN 978-0-310-33403-3 (trade paper)
  1. Terminally ill--Fiction. 2. African Americans--Fiction. I. Title.
  PS3601.D396L43 2013
  813'.6--dc23
                                          2013002812

Printed in the United States of America

13 14 15 16 17 /RRD/ 20 19 18 17 16 15 14 13 12 11 10 9 8 7 6 5 4 3 2 1

*This book is dedicated to you, wherever you are
and whatever your circumstances.
May you not only be entertained by this story, but also inspired to
recognize and embrace the blessings borne from your life's broken
places. May your soul be refreshed and your spirit filled with peace.*

For God did not send his Son into the world to condemn the world, but to save the world through him. . . . But whoever lives by the truth comes into the light, so that it may be seen plainly that what he has done has been done through God.

John 3:17, 21

one

Shiloh Wilson Griffin blew into the delicate instrument one last time, and its mournful notes curled through the air like white smoke snaking its way into oblivion.

The music flowing from the recorder was hollow and wistful—a perfect reflection of her emotions today, and every year on this date, August 13. "Her Song," as Shiloh had titled the piece, wasn't long. It was a repetitive melody she played over and over, until it seeped into her soul and settled in her bones, where the pain had been lodged for what felt like forever. In many ways, eighteen years could be considered forever. So it caught her off guard when she stumbled over a few notes this morning. That had never happened, not once since she wrote and played this song on the first anniversary of this date. The simple mistake rattled her.

Shiloh lowered the instrument to her side and peered into the inky darkness of her backyard. Minutes later, she turned away from the wall of windows and laid the recorder on an ottoman that doubled as a coffee table. She glanced at the small round clock hanging above the entrance to the sunroom. Great. She had fifteen minutes before alarms began pinging and chiming, feet hit the floor, echoes of "Mommy" or "Mom" filled the house, and everyone simultaneously needed her.

Shiloh sidestepped the ottoman and knelt in front of the sofa. She lowered her head onto her clasped hands. Her shoulder-length, charcoal black hair swung forward and framed her round ebony face like a stage curtain. She wanted to pray but couldn't focus. The familiar questions kept intruding.

Will this be the year I stop feeling guilty? Or lose the shame?

Shiloh sighed and silently answered herself in the same breath: *No, and no.*

No matter how much restitution she paid with every word and deed, her blood-stained hands could never really be clean, even if no one else knew they were dirty.

First she had stumbled over the notes to "Her Song." Now, she felt tongue-tied. What could she pray differently, or more persuasively, this year than she had all the years before? Did she really have the right to be burden-free—forgiven for her ancient decisions? The answer came as readily as it should for a preacher's wife and pastor's daughter: God forgives any sin that one is truly sorry for committing.

Her heart wanted to accept that truth, but her mind kept circling back to the reality that life, and a person's choices, didn't always yield cut-and-dried conclusions.

What if I knew I was wrong? What if I didn't care about anyone but myself?

Those questions looped through Shiloh's mind, and no matter how much she willed the words that matched her persistent regret to flow, they eluded her. Shiloh rarely noticed the tick-tock of the clock, but this morning, it sounded like a gong, pressuring her to hurry. In five minutes, the once-a-year opportunity she gave herself to plead for God's peace would be a wrap.

Before she could nudge herself into action, the faint beeping of one of the boys' alarm clocks forced her surrender. She lifted her head, sat back on her heels, and scanned her surroundings to pinpoint everything she needed to tuck away. The recorder had to be put in its case and returned to the corner with her flutes; the candle must be extinguished and placed in its usual spot on the kitchen counter; and the three-by-five frame next to the candle, which bore seven words she couldn't risk anyone else ever reading, should be hidden until this time next year, when she pulled it out for the nineteenth annual commemoration.

Shiloh pushed herself up by the palms of her hands and swiftly put things away. Within minutes, she'd have coffee percolating and oatmeal simmering for Randy, various cold cereals on the table for her four hungry boys, and a cheerful smile fixed on her face when all of them came trotting downstairs and delivered the hugs and kisses she demanded. Good thing they couldn't see her heart this morning; it would give her away. Her silent tears would go unnoticed, as usual, and she was thankful.

Two

By the time Shiloh shooed Lemuel, Omari, Raphael, and David out of the house and to their summer camp carpools, she had decided what to wear to breakfast with Dayna.

She placed the last bowl from the boys' morning meal in the dishwasher and grabbed an apple to stave off the hunger her rumbling stomach announced. Usually, she ate with the family; if she didn't munch on something now, she'd be gobbling up everything in sight by the time she reached downtown Milwaukee.

Shiloh trotted upstairs to her bedroom and, mindful for the second time this morning of the ticking clock, strode to her closet to find the dress she had in mind. Dayna probably had a marathon slate of workshops and receptions to attend, and Shiloh had no doubt that the eldest Wilson sister would be looking her best. Her personal status of stay-at-home mom, part-time flute teacher, and Baptist church First Lady didn't require tailored business suits, and Shiloh feared that her Sunday best might be out of place in a corporate setting. Even so, she located her tried-and-true black sheath with cap sleeves and grabbed a pair of black, two-inch heels from her shoe rack.

After a quick shower, she pulled her hair up into a long, sleek ponytail and stepped into the knee-length dress. Her full hips and rounded backside caused her to tug a little, but according to Randy, there was nothing to complain about. As if on cue, he entered the bedroom while she was trying to zip the back of the dress with one hand.

"Well, where are you headed this morning, Mrs. Glamorous? You can't be meeting with the ladies from the prayer ministry, dressed like that."

He approached her from behind and finished the job, then encircled her in a hug and kissed her neck.

"Watch it, Reverend," Shiloh teased. "You've already got four sons to send to college."

The joke she uttered to keep things light between them stung, given the anniversary she'd commemorated before sunrise. She forced herself to focus.

"Breakfast with Dayna, remember? She flew in last night for the hospital association conference I told you about."

"Remind me why she isn't staying with us?"

Shiloh shook her head.

"Too many meetings to commute out here. She has a full schedule, which is why I'm going downtown to meet her. She may try to sneak away tomorrow evening to come out and see the boys, though."

Randy released his grip.

"Well, tell her I said hello, and welcome to Milwaukee. I'm heading over to the church. Got a meeting with Vic in an hour."

Shiloh peered at him through the dresser mirror, but his expression left her clueless.

"Everything okay?"

Randy shrugged. "Same as usual. He doesn't like being second in command or being told what to do, instead of doing the telling. I keep reminding him that we are working on the same team, for the same God."

Shiloh stretched past Randy to grab a coral shawl from a nearby chair, and patted his arm. Who knew competition like this existed among pastors, especially two who were supposedly leading a congregation together? Daddy had pastored his church in Atchity, Alabama, for so long, Shiloh couldn't recall him feeling threatened or challenged by other ministers under his charge. Randy kept reminding her that despite their nearly two-year tenure at St. Stephens Baptist Church, he was still considered "the new guy." Vic had an advantage as a lifelong Milwaukee resident and member of St. Stephens Baptist. It didn't seem to matter that Randy had overseen long-awaited renovations or that since his tenure as senior pastor, attendance and membership had increased significantly; some in the already-large congregation were still upset that their beloved Vic remained the full-time second in command.

"Hang in there, babe." Shiloh kissed him before grabbing her purse off the bed and trotting down the stairs.

"You do the same," Randy called after her. "Don't come home after breakfast wanting to change who you are. You are perfectly fine."

Shiloh didn't respond, but she cringed at the realization that Randy knew most of her insecurities well enough to head them off before they took hold of her. She appreciated his support, but what if he had seen her this morning, before sunrise, trying to pray away her demons? She had a feeling if he knew about that Shiloh, he wouldn't be referring to her as *perfect* or *fine*. The words that he'd likely use instead made her want to cry again.

Three

Minutes later, Shiloh headed south on Interstate 43 and maneuvered her silver van through a steady stream of traffic. The drive was punctuated by fits and starts, stemming from pockets of congestion and the three accidents she passed along the route.

"Thank God I don't have to navigate this jungle every morning," she muttered, only to acknowledge seconds later that the traffic was a good distraction. She'd rather focus on the road than lose herself in her thoughts, ambling down the trail her memories liked to travel.

Dayna texted her just as she pulled into the Frontier Airlines Center parking garage.

On 1st floor, near section C. In café called Birdie's.

Shiloh backed the van into a parking spot and turned off the engine before responding.

There in 5 min.

When she strolled into the cozy restaurant, Shiloh immediately spotted her sister sitting at a small round table, chatting with a waiter. Who could miss her? Dressed in a black pinstripe suit that looked as if the material had been cut to her frame, and wearing tasteful yet dramatic makeup and a flawless smile, Dayna appeared ready for a *Black Enterprise* magazine cover shoot.

Dayna had worn her hair in a short, layered 'do for years, but this new, chin-length bob made her look younger, and prettier, Shiloh decided. Marriage was definitely agreeing with her. No fifteen pounds after the wedding for her. And since she and Warren had decided to devote themselves to raising his twin boys rather than having a child together, no baby weight, either.

A familiar jealousy trickled through Shiloh's veins, but Dayna's warm response staunched its flow. She rose from her seat and gripped Shiloh in a long hug.

"How are you?"

When Dayna released her, Shiloh smiled to indicate that all was well. "I'm fine, Dayna; how are you?" Shiloh slid into the seat across from her sister, hoping she looked more composed than she felt.

Dayna settled in her chair and placed a cloth napkin across her lap. "Doing well. And excited to see you, since it's been a minute. How are Randy and the boys? Are you guys liking Milwaukee?"

Shiloh hesitated. How much did Dayna need, or even want, to know? That it had been a challenging twenty-one months since her family left Atchity for Randy to lead one of Milwaukee's historic Baptist churches? That she was still finding it tough to make friends and call the place home?

She couldn't tell the well-traveled Dayna that she was homesick for their native Alabama. Dayna already considered her a country bumpkin clone of Mama. Why contribute to that notion?

Shiloh summoned a smile. "It's going pretty well. The boys are doing great in school and have friends in our neighborhood. I love the house. It has a spacious sunroom facing the backyard that I use for teaching flute lessons—and sometimes just to hide out from all of the testosterone in the house." Shiloh chuckled and took a sip of the water the waiter placed in front of her.

"You're teaching flute lessons? Good for you," Dayna said. "I know you loved doing that back home. I'm glad you've been able to pick up some students."

They each ordered an omelet and coffee, then Shiloh turned the conversation to Dayna. "How's married life treating you and Warren, and the twins? How's the new house coming along? Are you building it to be hurricane proof?"

Dayna smiled. "I don't know if anything is really hurricane proof," she said. "But when you live in central Florida, you have to at least try, so yes, we're adding some beams and other building materials to the frame to strengthen it against high winds. That's all you can do."

Shiloh nodded. "That's smart. Always good to be prepared. The house you've lived in for years isn't far from the hospital; where will this place be?"

"It's on the outskirts of Calero, but it's close enough to Chesdin Medical Center for Warren and me to get to work within fifteen minutes," Dayna said. "The good news is that it's nowhere near Calero's tourist community. The bad news—or at least it sometimes feels this way—is that Warren is serving as the general contractor for the house. He's driving me crazy." Dayna sighed. "Even worse, he's driving the workers crazy! He leaves the hospital three times a day—that I'm aware of; could be more—to drive by and monitor their progress and to make sure they're not cutting corners. I told him I'm going to change his title from vice president of marketing for Chesdin Medical Center to chief button pusher for the Florida Home Builders Association! I guess it's good to be so involved, but if he gets them to add one more thing, or change one more thing, I may give up and lease a three-bedroom apartment instead."

Shiloh laughed. She couldn't recall the last time they'd chatted so freely, and it surprised her how pleased she was to see Dayna happy. "Looks like you sold your house too soon, huh?"

Dayna took a few seconds to swallow the sliver of omelet she had just popped into her mouth. "I still drive by my old home sometimes just to wave at it," she said and laughed. "I loved that place! But I love being with my honey and the boys even more. There's actually enough space in Warren's house for us to comfortably stay there; we just think an important part of solidifying our new family structure is to start building memories together in a neutral space—one we've purchased together. We're hoping that once we move into the new house, his current place will sell as quickly as my home did. My house was only on the market for two days."

"In this economy? Wow," said Shiloh. "Well, it will happen at just the right time for Warren's place, too. Did he skip the conference because of the house?"

Dayna took the final sip of her coffee.

"Our boss decided to send just three of us to Milwaukee because another important conference is taking place in Vegas next month. Warren gets to go to that one. I'm here with a colleague who works in accounting." Dayna peered over Shiloh's shoulder and grinned. "Well, look who I talked up!"

Shiloh turned in her seat. She smiled as a petite, cinnamon-hued woman with flowing hair and a protruding belly waddled toward them. Dayna's colleague paused dramatically when she reached their table.

"Whew, that was a long walk from the registration area. Good morning, Mrs. Avery! Is this your baby sister?"

"Yes, this is my sister Shiloh; but she's my middle sister, remember? Our sister Jessica is the baby of the family."

Dayna shifted her gaze to Shiloh. "This is my friend and coworker, Audrey. I've mentioned you and Jessica to her over the years. As you can see, she's expecting!"

"Nice to meet you, Audrey, and congratulations on the baby; have a seat." Shiloh motioned toward the third chair at the table.

"Thanks, but I'm fine," Audrey said and patted her stomach. "Baby here was hungry first thing this morning, so I ordered room service before coming over. I just wanted to stop by and say hello, because Dayna told me you live here and she was excited about getting a chance to see you. I'll catch up with you in the session, Dayna. Nice to meet you, too, Shiloh."

Dayna and Shiloh watched her disappear around a corner, her purple dress swaying with her shifting weight.

"She seems nice, and she looks cute pregnant."

"Yeah, she does," Dayna said. "She got married seven months ago to a great guy who works in my office. This baby is her and Chas's honeymoon gift. First child for both, and they're thrilled. I'm thrilled for them, too. She's getting big, but as you see, she's not letting it slow her down."

Shiloh smiled. "That's really nice. Still don't want any babies yourself?"

Dayna raised an eyebrow. "Thanks, but raising Michael and Mason is job enough, with girls calling, sports practices every day, and all that. My hat goes off to you, having four! Plus, I'm sure I'll have my chance to babysit for Audrey and Chas; that will fix any maternal longings that sneak up on me. Any more for you?"

Now it was Shiloh's turn to look incredulous. "David is nine, girlfriend; if it ain't happened by now, it ain't gonna happen. He will remain the youngest child."

They laughed and settled into an easy silence while they finished what was left of their meals. Her initial twinges of jealousy had dissipated, and Shiloh was enjoying this time with her sister. She and Dayna hadn't been this comfortable with one another in a long time—longer than she could pinpoint. She wasn't sure if it was because Dayna was in such a happy place with Warren and her stepsons, or because they were away from their parents' critical eyes. The resentment that usually emanated from Dayna for reasons she didn't understand wasn't palpable this morning.

"We've got to bring the boys to Disney World. I keep saying that, and I mean it. Lem will be a senior next year, and I want to come before he goes off to college, while all of my boys are at home."

"Definitely," Dayna said. "The house should be ready in a couple of months. Maybe you all can come for Christmas? Or the boys' spring break? Michael and Mason want to know their step-cousins better—the soul side of their family."

They laughed.

"How have they adjusted to introducing you as their stepmother? Do their friends think they're joking?"

Dayna smirked. "Their friends seem okay with it; it's the friends' parents who struggle with this tall black woman showing up to cheer them on or pick up two blue-eyed, freckled-faced Caucasian teenagers. More than once, I've been asked if I'm the housekeeper or the family's driver, since the boys are too old for a sitter. Michael and Mason seem to take it in stride, though. They love me, and I love them. Warren has done a good job with them."

"And the whole interracial marriage thing—that hasn't caused any issues?"

She and Dayna had never been the kind of sisters to dish like this, but for the first time ever, Dayna seemed open.

"Let's be for real, Shiloh; marriage is hard work, period. We've had to adjust over the past two years to living together, co-parenting, merging our finances, and learning how to keep communicating when we hit a rough patch—all those kinds of things. That needs to happen in any marriage. Add race to it, and it's just another bridge we've decided to cross together. We don't let it become an issue between us. Warren and I know that Mama and Daddy aren't comfortable with him being white, so we don't go to Alabama that often. We also don't hold a grudge. His parents, on the other hand, have embraced me, so we see them regularly.

"We just deal with life as it comes. The most important thing we've decided is to do it together, and I can honestly say that the work and the challenges that have come with this new role have been worth it. I'm very happy. No—I'm very blessed. Great husband, who happens to be fine, too; great kids who love me; a career I love . . ." Dayna sat back and smiled.

Shiloh leaned forward and mirrored her sister's expression. "You are glowing. I'm happy for you, Dayna. You deserve it."

Those sentiments were heartfelt, so why were they accompanied by a swell of resentment? She had her own handsome husband, four loving sons, plus a beautiful home and no need to work outside of it. What gave?

Struggling for an answer right now would be a waste of brainpower, she decided, as would comparing herself to her superstar big sister.

Despite the devastation of a long-ago divorce and their parents' reservations about her interracial marriage, Dayna clearly was choosing to live on her own terms. Shiloh's heart quivered. Did this mean her own existence could be considered little more than tracing the dots of a pattern someone else decided was her best fit? She fixed a smile that she hoped looked more authentic than it felt. Pretending to be content continued to be hard work.

four

Dayna insisted on paying for breakfast. She laid a bill on the table that covered both the meal and the tip, then held Shiloh in a long hug. They strolled out of the café together, but went in different directions—Dayna striding confidently toward a sea of similarly dressed executives and she, back to her domestic sameness. She was returning home to be the wife of, mother of, First Lady of, but what did that really mean?

Dayna had Warren and two stepsons, but she still got a chance to just be Dayna, to hang out with colleagues and friends, to pursue goals she loved. So did baby-of-the-family Jessica, who routinely spent time with some of the nation's noted celebrities and always had an amazing itinerary of professional speaking engagements. Shiloh mentally ran down her personal checklist of pluses again—the husband, children, home, community respect—with no change of heart: it was still, as always, middle-child nice. Problem was, it was also middle-child boring. And unimportant.

Shiloh's thoughts turned to this morning's secret, predawn commemoration, and she chided herself. *You chose this path, Shi. You gave up your dreams to prove to God that you were sorry. You willingly offered to sacrifice for him. Don't complain now. Honor your word.*

"Yes, Lord," she said aloud and sighed. "I will. I am."

But her mood sank further when she remembered the laundry and bills awaiting her, and the closet in desperate need of a summer cleaning. Shiloh stepped out of the elevator, into the parking garage, and plodded to her van. When she slid into the driver's seat and cranked the engine, Mary Mary's latest hit song filled the air: *"It's your tiiiime. Go get, go get, go get, your blessing!"*

She didn't necessarily have a fancy new blessing awaiting her, but that song made her feel like she'd better try and find one. Shiloh sighed. This attitude was silly. She increased the volume and sang along for the next half hour to the upbeat songs flowing from the radio. By the time she reached North Shore, she was feeling better. She pulled into her driveway and decided that parking in the garage would be a waste of time, since she'd be in and out this afternoon, running errands.

Shiloh stepped out of the van and strolled to the end of the driveway to check the mailbox. Ms. Betsy across the street was engrossed in her weekly weeding. Her floppy yellow hat bounced about her ears when she paused and raised her head to wave at Shiloh.

Shiloh smiled. "I see you're tending the garden before the temperature climbs."

Ms. Betsy nodded. "I'll spend the rest of the day inside, sipping iced tea and enjoying the flowers from the window. You look nice this morning. Coming from a funeral?"

"No, just got a little dressed up to go downtown for a breakfast meeting."

Shiloh didn't feel like getting into a long conversation about her sister the successful hospital executive. Better to immerse herself in her chores, until this mood passed.

"I'll catch up with you later, Ms. Betsy," Shiloh said. "Tell your husband I said hello."

"Alright, dear! You enjoy the rest of the day."

Once inside, Shiloh changed clothes, removed the breakfast dishes from the dishwasher, and began the first of several loads of laundry.

The phone rang the minute she grabbed an armful of Randy's shirts. She dropped them in front of the washer and dashed for the cordless handset. Her breathless hello was embarrassing. Even more so when she realized that the caller was a member of St. Stephens Baptist.

"Well, hello, Dr. Carter, how are you?"

"I'm doing well, Mrs. Griffin. How is pastor today? And those smart young men?"

"Everyone's great," Shiloh said. "If you're looking for Pastor Randy, he's not here. He went to the church office several hours ago. If you can't reach him, just leave a message and he'll call you back."

"Actually," he said, "I'm calling for you."

"Oh?"

"I know you've heard me talk about my work for Milwaukee Public Schools. Well, the school year will resume in three weeks, and I found out yesterday that one of my music teachers will be out until late October. Her mother had a stroke last month and she thought she'd have everything settled before school starts. Turns out she's going to have to oversee her mother's care long term, and for now, help her mother transition into rehab. That means we'll be one teacher short, and I've got to fix this immediately."

Shiloh was intrigued. "How can I help?"

"I've seen you play your flute and recorder, and even the piano on some Sunday mornings, and you're quite talented. You indicated when you and Pastor first arrived that you studied music education. Is that correct?"

Shiloh didn't realize she was holding her breath until he nudged her. "First Lady . . . you there?"

"Um, yes, I'm here, and yes, that's correct. I majored in music education." Should she tell him she never graduated?

"The two substitutes we usually hire for the music department are not available right now for long-term positions. I don't think it's wise to bring in a sub who doesn't know music and can't quickly build a rapport with the students, especially since an official part of the high school calendar is a fall concert for which the students will need to prepare. I was about to place an ad on the school district website when you came to mind. Would you be willing to serve as our long-term sub, until Mrs. Helmsley returns from family-care leave? You would receive a nice daily rate during that period, and if any students ask for private instruction, there wouldn't be a conflict with you doing that."

Shiloh was stunned. "You want me to apply?"

"Yes," Dr. Carter said. "And if you'll take the position, it's yours. I'm the hiring director—no need for an interview and all that. I'm not sure if you've taught a group of students before, but I hear good things about the individual flute lessons you offer in your home. Your ability to play multiple instruments is an asset. We have an orchestra teacher on staff, so you'd primarily be working with the band students, and filling in for Kristina, our orchestra instructor, only as needed."

Shiloh was honored, but she knew better than to get her hopes up. "What other qualifications are needed? I studied at Birmingham-Southern College for two years, but I didn't return after my sophomore year. I married Pastor Griffin instead, and not long after, had Lem."

Dr. Carter chuckled. "Can't have a better excuse than that, can you? Under normal circumstances, teachers must have a bachelor's degree and a teaching license, and both of those would still be required. Since you wouldn't be teaching a core subject, like math or science, the No Child Left Behind mandates don't apply. I can bring you in under a provisional emergency license, with the understanding that if you plan to sub for the school district in the future, you'll finish your degree and pursue full certification as soon as possible. To help out in the short term, you'll need to attend a substitute teacher workshop before school begins. One is scheduled for next week—Thursday through Saturday, from nine a.m. to noon. Can you make that work?"

"I think so . . . but my not having a degree doesn't bother you?"

Dr. Carter fell silent, and Shiloh's stomach quivered. She didn't know if this was something she even wanted to do, but the fact that she could be turned down because she lacked a piece of paper made her ill.

"From what I've seen, First Lady, your experience makes up for your not having a degree," Dr. Carter finally said. "And it's not too late, you know? You could go back to school anytime to finish up the credits you need to graduate. There are some great universities right here in Milwaukee to choose from."

The door wasn't closing. Shiloh's spirit opened up as she considered the possibilities. She had been teaching flute lessons for years one-on-one, and had occasionally taught piano, too. Working with high school kids could be a challenge, but if it was anything like what she'd experienced so far in raising her two oldest boys, it also could be amazing.

"How soon would I need to start after the substitute training next week? And would the state require me to enroll in college right away to work on completing my degree? That's something I'd need to talk to Pastor about. Also . . . what would the teaching schedule look like?"

"We'd like to have you onsite before the school year begins, so you'll be ready to hit the ground running when the students return," Dr. Carter said. "That means after the training, you could visit the school as early as the following Monday to get acclimated and meet other teachers. You would be working a normal school day, for the most part.

"Our school doesn't have a marching band, so you don't have to worry about a band camp or after-school field practices. There are two band periods Monday through Thursday—one just for students who are in jazz band, and a combined class for all band members—ninth grade through twelfth grade. You'd need to teach each of those, and also be available during students' study hall periods in case they need help with their instruments, perfecting a piece of music, or help with college applications. During the time you're not actually teaching, you'll have plenty of planning time—coming up with strategies to help them learn better or finding new music to consider teaching them. Usually, this time would also be used to schedule opportunities for the orchestra to play in the community, but I wouldn't worry about that this semester. In fact, since this is a modified schedule, I'd consider having you do the job part-time, and leave by one-thirty each day, if that's best for your schedule. The most important aspect of the job will be to follow Mrs. Helmsley's curriculum outline and be a presence for the kids. You're a mom of four; I think you'll be great. And I'm not pressuring you to go back to school, but if after the experience at Sherman Park High you decide you've enjoyed it, then you'll be on track to do what you need to get the degree, and stay on our substitute teacher roster."

A smile coursed through Shiloh until it reached her face. She'd have to talk this over with Randy, but it was short-term and extra income. Plus, it would be helpful to Dr. Carter; how could he object?

"Why not, Dr. Carter? Why not? Sign me up."

five

Shiloh was still euphoric over her good fortune when her youngest student, Naima, arrived later that afternoon with her mother, Jade, for a weekly flute lesson.

The striking mother-daughter duo were dressed impeccably as usual, with Jade in a periwinkle blue capri set and wedge sandals, and ten-year-old Naima in a crisp white and blue tennis outfit with a pair of pristine white Keds. Her long, fine hair was secured by a headband and flowed past her shoulders, like her mom's. If Shiloh wasn't used to the pair regularly dressing with head-turning fashion sense, she would have questioned whether they'd just left a photo shoot.

Jade had been a walking, talking magazine cover from the day Shiloh met her, in the weeks before she and Randy moved the family to Milwaukee. She quickly let Shiloh know that while she was technically the "second lady" of St. Stephens Baptist, given that her husband Vic had been passed over for senior pastor, in the eyes of many, she should—and would—be treated with the respect of a leading lady in the church.

Shiloh had been surprised when, not long after that conversation, Jade entrusted her precious Naima to her for flute lessons. Was it a peace offering after her diva introduction? Or was Jade simply looking for an excuse to come into the Griffin home each week, to get a first-hand look at what was going on and keep tabs on her competition?

Despite Randy's insistence that she was paranoid, Shiloh continued to believe the latter, which meant she didn't trust Jade for a minute. Randy was a loving and faithful husband, but he had eyes: Maybe he was unintentionally blinded by Jade's face and figure, like other men in their congregation, regardless of whether they'd admit it. Or maybe the coy innocence Jade had perfected really had him fooled. Still, Shiloh had never turned away a child who expressed an interest in music and was willing to practice. She wouldn't begin now, even if that child's mother challenged her patience.

Shiloh had to admit it, though: Jade had reasons to always bring her "A" game. Reverend Vic wasn't hard on the eyes, and a fair number of women at church fluttered about him and flirted with him every chance they could. Whatever Jade's motivation, seeing her today in full diva form deflated some of Shiloh's joy. She knew she'd have to spend the next forty-five minutes listening to sweet little Naima practice while being forced to eavesdrop on Jade's cell phone conversation about some aspect of her fabulous life. Or, instead of making a call, Jade would try to carry on a conversation with her about someone in church, while Shiloh sought to instruct Naima and listen to ensure the girl hit the right notes.

Today, however, it seemed Shiloh might be spared. Jade didn't give the house her usual sweeping glance or graze any surfaces with her fingertips, as if checking for dust. Surprisingly, she remained in the foyer, without inviting herself to roam into various rooms.

"Would you mind if I run out for a little bit while Naima's with you?" she asked. "I should be back by the time she finishes; I just need to take care of one thing I didn't get to earlier today."

Shiloh hoped her expression didn't reveal her relief. *Two blessings in one day? Thank you, Lord.*

"Take your time! Naima is good with me," she told Jade. "I'll listen to her practice, then introduce a new song I'd like her to begin learning. By the way, where is little Nicholas?"

Jade tossed her loosely curled dark brown hair over one shoulder, gave Shiloh what Shiloh secretly called the Jade Smith TV Personality Smile, then sauntered out of the front door, down the steps, toward her shiny black SUV.

"He's home with Vic this afternoon. They're having some daddy-son bonding time!" she said and giggled. "Can you imagine Vic changing diapers? He wants to know when Nicky will be potty-trained. I told him that at two years old, that's still near the bottom of Nicky's list of 'firsts' to accomplish, unlike when Naima was that age. Boys just aren't ready to learn as quickly as girls—you know from having four of them." Jade slid behind the wheel of the SUV, covered her eyes with a pair of oversized shades, and waved before driving away.

Shiloh wanted to roll her eyes, but was mindful that Naima stood beside her, taking it all in. She pasted a smile on her face and turned toward the girl. "Now, young lady, tell me how often you practiced last week."

They chatted for a few minutes, and as usual each time this week, Raphael strolled past the sunroom on his way outside. Shiloh had been waiting. He didn't have football practice on Mondays, and once he'd figured out that was Naima's day to come for lessons, he always made a point of being seen. Any other time Shiloh's students were around, the soon-to-be seventh grader disappeared, but this particular "client" yielded the opposite reaction.

Each time it happened, Shiloh suppressed a laugh. Yet the thought of her twelve-year-old expressing an interest in girls pricked her heart. She wasn't ready for him to grow up. It was cute, however, to consider that a "younger woman" had caught his eye, and to watch his efforts to make the crush mutual. Naima was indeed gorgeous, but unlike her mother, she didn't yet seem to understand her effect on the opposite sex.

The girl played a few scales without missing a note, then sailed through a youthful version of "Zelda's Lullaby." When Shiloh handed her sheet music for a longer composition, Naima's eyes grew wide.

"That looks hard."

Her soft voice made her sound more vulnerable than Shiloh knew she was. Shiloh patted her shoulder.

"That's only because you haven't heard it yet, or tried to play it. That's not unusual, though. Sometimes we look at a mountain in front of us and convince ourselves we'll never get to the top. The key is to take it hill by hill, and before you know it, you're there. It's the same with music. We are going to take this section by section, and as you learn each section, you'll move on to the next one, until you're ready to play the whole song. You'll have it down by recital time, okay?"

Naima mustered a hint of a smile. "Okay."

Shiloh removed her flute from its case and walked over to the stand Naima and her other students used. She played the song all the way through, with Naima standing next to her, reading the music and listening.

"That's so pretty," Naima said. "I'm gonna be able to play that?"

"Yep," Shiloh said, "you'll be able to play it and leave your parents and the audience feeling great and saying, 'Wow.'"

She leaned over and hugged Naima. She was a sweet little girl. Hopefully Jade wouldn't guide her to become so focused on her appearance that Naima forgot the importance of her inner beauty and her relationship with God. Shiloh knew she had no right to judge Jade and that worrying was sinful. She would plant seeds about discipline and hard work while she had Naima for forty-five minutes each week, and trust God to water what he saw fit for Naima's life. Despite what Jade did or didn't do, God had the final say.

six

"Why would you want to spend your days in a classroom with a bunch of high schoolers?"

Randy's response that evening to Shiloh's announcement that she'd been offered a temporary teaching position was unsettling.

"You don't need to work," he continued. "You're busy enough around the house, and what will the folks at St. Stephens think? That they're not paying me enough to support us, or that you're not happy at home?"

This was a first. When had he cared so much about what other people thought?

"Now you're sounding like you-know-who." Shiloh criss-crossed from the oven to the kitchen island to wrap up dinner preparations. "We're not in Atchity, and this is not my daddy's church. Many pastors' wives work; why would that cause raised eyebrows? Plus, it's temporary. I'd have to go back to school and get my bachelor's degree to turn it into a full-fledged career. But I think it's a great opportunity, and it will give me something to do during the day while you and the boys are away."

"Don't you have your hands full now, though?"

"Yeah, I do."

Shiloh thought about the laundry and other chores she had completed today before her Monday student, Naima, arrived for her flute lesson. She placed a plate of baked chicken, rice, green beans, and baked sweet potato in front of Randy, who was sitting at the kitchen table, then proceeded to prepare her own.

"Boys! I'm not calling you again. If you're going to eat dinner, you'd better come down before your dad says grace. Otherwise, you can stay where you are for the rest of the night!"

She heard feet shuffling and the sounds of boys making pit stops in the bathroom to wash their hands. While she and Randy waited for them, she resumed her response.

"I do stay busy here, but the boys are growing older. They can help more around the house for a couple of months, and besides, it will be good for them. Any girl they marry these days is going to want their help with cooking, cleaning, and caring for the kids."

Randy took a sip of soda and peered at her. "So glad you aren't one of the 'girls these days,' babe. You take good care of me."

So could a maid.

That sarcastic reply didn't slip past Shiloh's lips, but she gifted Randy with a smirk. Truthfully, she loved taking care of him and their family, but she didn't like feeling as if that was all that gave her value.

Randy shrugged and grabbed a roll from the bread basket in front of him. The boys filed in, fixed their plates, and sat in their usual spots—the two oldest boys across from each other and the two youngest facing each other, with Randy and Shiloh at each end of the table. Randy blessed the food, and they dug in like they hadn't eaten for days.

"If ya'll are so hungry, what took you so long to come?" Shiloh sighed. She knew she'd never figure them out. They ate in silence, until Lem launched into another update on his recent visit to Alabama, where he'd stayed with Shiloh's parents for two weeks. Since returning home, he'd been keeping the family abreast of the latest news with friends he met during a summer science camp for high school students hosted by Alabama University, including frequent announcements about a young lady named Lia.

"She's thinking about becoming a civil engineer, instead of studying electrical engineering," Lem said. "Either way, she's going to do well."

Shiloh gave Randy a knowing glance, but spoke to Lem. "What colleges is she considering?"

"Alabama U, Spelman, Vanderbilt, Emory, Howard, Georgia Tech . . ."

"You sure do seem to know a lot about her plans, son," Randy said and grinned.

Lem blushed and lowered his eyes. His close-cropped haircut framed his face nicely, and with that chiseled chocolate jaw and super-bright smile, he was the spitting image of his dad. Sometimes when Shiloh looked at him, she remembered Randy at that age, just as eager and optimistic as Lem was now.

"Careful, son," Randy continued. "She's all the way in Alabama and you're here. How's that going to work?"

Shiloh took a bite and watched Lem's face contort as he sought to articulate his perspective. It was clear he'd thought it through.

"There's Instagram, ooVoo, texting. It's not that hard to stay in touch these days, Dad. Besides, we're just friends, okay?"

Randy and Shiloh traded smiles, before returning their attention to their meals. After cleaning his plate, Randy sat back with a satisfied smile and raised the topic that had never left Shiloh's mind.

"Let's ask the troop here what they think about your going to work."

"What was that?" Raphael's twelve-year-old voice still hadn't changed, and the squeakiness of it was sweet music to Shiloh's ears. He was as cute as a button, but she knew she couldn't tell him that. At least not before bedtime, when she had him alone and they could review the highs and lows of his day and share other things on their minds.

"What do you guys think about your mom working for a while? At a high school in Milwaukee?"

Eight eyes grew saucer-sized.

"Really?" David asked. "Doing what?"

"Teaching music," Shiloh said. "The band director at Sherman Park High, near downtown, is out for a while caring for her sick mother, and they need a temporary replacement, through the end of October."

"You'll be teaching high school students?" Lem said. "I don't know, Mom. Some of those kids can be rough on substitute teachers. It ain't pretty."

Shiloh shook her head and gave him an amused smile. "It ain't 'pretty' how ya'll try to be rough on me, either. I'm flattered that you're worried about me, but I think I can handle it. The question is, can you guys handle stuff around here while I'm doing this? You'll have to pitch in with dinner, laundry, and other chores more than usual."

Her two middle sons, Omari and Raphael, frowned.

"We have to do girl stuff?" Omari groaned.

Shiloh restrained herself from glaring at him. She had created some monsters. She glanced at Randy, who strategically avoided eye contact by reaching for the plate of fresh-baked cookies in the center of the table. No—she corrected herself—*they* had created some monsters.

"Let's just say you'll have a chance to practice some skills you need anyway, to take care of yourself once you go off to college," Shiloh said. "And for your information, none of the things I mentioned counts as 'girl stuff.' They are life skills." She waited several seconds for that truth to resonate. "I'll take your silence as evidence that you'll fully support me and will be on board with helping out more. Thank you!"

The boys opened their mouths to protest but fell silent when Randy raised his palm. "Let's chill, guys." Randy looked down the long table and locked eyes with Shiloh. "I can tell this means a lot to you. It will inconvenience the family for a while, because we are used to you doing everything, taking care of the house and us. But if this is something you feel strongly about, we are going to support you."

Shiloh blew him a kiss. "Thank you, babe."

"Now, we don't want fast food meals for dinner every night just 'cause you're working." Randy winked at her. "But if you want to give this teaching thing a try, go for it."

Shiloh rubbed her palms together and looked around the table. "Chick-fil-A, here we come!" she said and laughed, before softening her expression. "Seriously, though, we'll get through this fine. Lots of families have two working parents. I'm excited!"

"What happens if you get into the classroom and hate it? Is there an out clause?" Randy asked. "Or will you be forced to stay the entire term, even if it isn't working out?"

Why is he thinking it won't work out? Shiloh felt irritation creeping up her spine, even though she knew he didn't mean any harm. She responded with a shrug. "Dr. Carter and I didn't get that far. I'll ask him about that, and also ask him to email the contract so you and I can go over it together."

Shiloh sat back and smiled. Maybe it was premature, since she didn't know what she was getting herself into, as Randy was wisely pointing out, but for the first time in a long time, she was enthusiastic about something more than her cherished roles of wife and mom. This was for her, and it felt good.

seven

Shiloh held her cell phone at arm's length and glared at it. *Should have known better.*

Still elated after the call from Dr. Carter two days ago, and their first formal meeting this afternoon, she had taken a few minutes before Wednesday night Bible study to check in with Mama. Now she was kicking herself. What made her think Mama would be imressed by her opportunity to teach? Mama was the perfect Southern Baptist minister's wife for her generation; she had never done anything that would take her away from Daddy and the church. Why had Shiloh thought she'd celebrate her plans to manage her First Lady role differently?

Mama was in the middle of a lecture about the proper care and nurturing of preacher husbands and their families, and refused to be interrupted. In a single breath, she had imagined Shiloh's four sons in delinquency, Randy with another woman—or two—and Shiloh homeless and forced to work to survive. Shiloh shook her head. This was the twenty-first century—most women she knew were working to survive, making her role as a stay-at-home pastor's wife somewhat of a luxury these days, not the other way around. When Shiloh no longer heard the shrill tone coming from the receiver, she brought it to her ear again, just in time to hear Mama's question, "Do you understand what I'm saying, Shiloh? This is important."

"Mama, it's an eight-week substitute teaching gig, not a tour of duty in Afghanistan—really. Everyone will be fine. The boys are sixteen, fourteen, twelve, and nine. No one is in diapers and all of them can read. They're capable of helping prepare meals, wash clothes, and whatever else needs to be done if I'm tied up. They need to begin learning how to fend for themselves.

"Plus," Shiloh continued, "I'll be working school hours and should be home by three each afternoon, if not earlier, on some days. That's plenty of time to oversee homework, cook dinner, and get the younger boys to football practice when Randy and Lem can't help out. This is a new generation—women work. You know that; two of your daughters go to a job every day."

"Uh-huh," Mama said.

Shiloh pictured her on the other end of the phone, scowling or pursing her lips.

"Those other two girls of mine don't have kids. And they aren't married to a prominent minister. Your role calls for different choices, Shiloh. You can't do like everybody else. You have to be Randy's biggest supporter and his always-available helpmate. That's the only way your daddy and I have made it all these years. I've put his needs before my own."

And he put the church's needs above yours and his daughters.

That silent retort bubbled forth before Shiloh could staunch it. And Mama wasn't quite right; Dayna actually was a mother now, given that her stepsons' biological mother was deceased.

"Mama?"

"Yes, Shiloh?"

"What did you want to do—what were your goals—before you married Daddy? Didn't you dream of doing something special, something just for you?"

Mama didn't respond for so long that Shiloh thought the call had dropped. "Hello?"

"Well, what kind of question is that? My life is the life I'm living—loving your daddy, loving you girls . . . taking care of God's business. That's what is important. Are you getting your priorities mixed up?"

Shiloh didn't have a ready response. Was Mama right? Was she so busy trying to be like her sisters that she was about to mess up a good thing? Shiloh glanced at the clock and was startled by how late it was. She leapt from her comfortable position on the sofa.

"Gotta run, Mama! I've got to get to Bible study—the ladies will be waiting on me. Thanks for sharing your perspective. Pray with me that all will go well, and that none of the terrible things you're worried about will happen."

Shiloh didn't want to end the call before Mama said goodbye, but the clock was ticking. *Father, please don't let her launch into another mini-sermon.*

"Tell my grandsons I said hello, okay? It was such a joy to have Lem here this summer. I hope next summer the other boys will come, too."

Shiloh smiled. It had been good for Lem to have his grandparents all to himself those two weeks in July. He'd come back talking about them as if they were real people, people he had an interest in spending time with, rather than doing so out of obligation.

"We'll have to arrange that, Mama," Shiloh said. "I've gotta run now. Love you."

"Love you, too, Shiloh. You take to heart what I said. Don't go getting all distracted. That's what cost Dayna her first husband. You keep your eyes on your family—all the rest will come and go."

Is that what Mama really thought? Dayna's first husband, Brent, had cheated on her because Dayna had a life beyond their marriage, and a career? Really?

Shiloh shook her head. "Bye, Mama; I'll call you later in the week."

"Shiloh . . . God be with you, sweetheart. Talk to you soon."

Mama sounded sad, but Shiloh decided not to fret. She placed the cordless phone on its base, then grabbed her empty glass from the tray on the ottoman and headed for the kitchen. Thankfully, she was already dressed appropriately. The black slacks and sleeveless teal blouse she'd worn to her afternoon meeting with Dr. Carter to formalize their agreement were perfect. In fact, she might be considered overdressed to the ladies who showed up in jeans and shorts tonight. She'd run a comb through her hair and dab on some lipstick during the fifteen-minute drive to Brown Deer, the nearby suburb that served as home to St. Stephens Baptist and the majority of its parishioners.

"Lem! I'm going to Bible study," Shiloh called on her way out. "Get David from football practice in half an hour, okay?"

"Yes, ma'am!"

Despite her determination to disregard her mother's perspective, Mama's words hovered over Shiloh like a cloud during the drive to church. She turned off the radio and traveled in silence, playing over and over in her mind the various pitfalls Mama had presented. By the time she pulled into the church parking lot, Shiloh had gone from second-guessing her decision to substitute teach, to trying to figure out how to tell Dr. Carter now wasn't a good time.

Marlene Givens turned into the parking lot just as Shiloh was locking the van. Shiloh stood by the vehicle and waited for Marlene to park so they could walk in together.

"Well, good evening, First Lady!"

Marlene, who was at least two decades older than Shiloh and recovering from knee replacement surgery, toddled over and kissed Shiloh on the cheek. She was one of the members who had genuinely embraced the Griffin family, and Shiloh loved her exuberant spirit, her energy, and her kind heart.

"I was all prepared to come tipping in this evening and explain to you why I'm late, and it looks like we'll be explaining together!"

Marlene laughed, but Shiloh blushed. She should have been there to open the meeting with prayer and get things started, but because of that lengthy lecture from Mama, she was ten minutes late. The ladies would be murmuring about this for sure. Hopefully they had started with refreshments, instead of waiting until the end of the meeting.

"I don't have a good excuse," Shiloh said and shook her head. "Pray for me, okay? How's that knee?"

"Better every day, praise the Lord! You know I'm picking at you. No one's on time all the time. Life happens, right? Let's get in here and see what we need to do." She peered at Shiloh while they walked toward the church. "Everything alright? You seem distracted."

Shiloh hesitated. Pastor's wife rule No. 1 was to never tell a member of the congregation your personal business. Whatever you said about yourself also went for your husband, and no matter how accurate the story started out, by the time it reached the hundredth member of the congregation, or wound its way through a community's rumor mill, it had been altered a hundred times. Shiloh had honored this unspoken rule since marrying Randy, but this evening, she was desperate for a second opinion. Mama had shaken her confidence.

"I'm fine, just considering whether to take on a long-term substitute teaching job."

"Oh?"

"Yes—Sherman Park High School in the city needs a temporary music teacher for eight weeks, and I've been asked to fill in. I'm just not sure how it will work with the family's schedule, and I need to let the school know ASAP what I'm going to do."

Marlene held open the side door of the church so Shiloh could enter. "I understand," Marlene said. "I'm sure God will lead you to the right decision. Just ask yourself how the opportunity came to you in the first place. If it was something you sought out, then maybe you do need to reflect and see if your priorities are in the right place. If it was something that just came your way, then that may be a sign that this was meant for you."

Shiloh squeezed her hand and nodded. "Thanks for that wisdom, Sister Marlene. Let's get inside."

They walked at a comfortable pace toward the church's educational wing and heard voices as they drew closer. Shiloh entered the Bible study classroom first, expecting to find the women socializing while they waited for her. Instead, they were seated with their Bibles open, reading along in unison with Jade, who sat near the center of the circle, guiding them through a passage in Romans.

Shiloh wanted to shake herself. Surely she was imagining things. Not because the Bible study was moving forward without her; that was resourceful. But being led by Jade? *The* Jade, whose interests leaned more toward Michael Kors and Ralph Lauren than Matthew, Mark, Luke, and John? Clearly, there was a first time for everything.

eight

Maybe Shiloh was thrown off guard because she'd rarely seen Jade read aloud from the Bible, let alone guide other women through its passages. Or maybe it was the way Jade sat in the chair Shiloh usually occupied, looking so at ease and confident. Whatever the reason, Shiloh wasn't thinking godly thoughts toward her spiritual sister right about now.

Jade and the other women wrapped up the reading of the eighth chapter of Romans, then she looked up, and into Shiloh's eyes.

"Oh, hi, you made it."

Members of the group turned toward the door, and a few looked relieved when they saw Shiloh. She was embarrassed again.

"Hello, everyone. I'm sorry I'm late this evening. Looks like Sister Jade has you on the right path. I'll just sit here and listen."

Jade pointed to two seats just outside of the formal circle, behind two members of the group. Shiloh bit her tongue. If Jade had been coming on a regular basis, she'd know that Shiloh usually arranged the chairs so everyone could fit into the circle. Nevertheless, she followed Marlene and took a seat next to her in the back row.

"Anyone want to expound on what we just read?" Jade's eyes swept the circle.

When Sister Adelaide raised her hand, Shiloh grew nervous. She was one of the eldest women in the church, and didn't hide her feelings. Everyone—including Jade—knew how much Sister Adelaide disliked Jade and considered her flashy with no substance.

"No, I don't think so, Sister Jade," Sister Adelaide said. "But thank you for warming us up this evening with devotions. Since First Lady Griffin is here, she can go ahead and teach us what she prepared for tonight."

The other women nodded in support of her suggestion, but Jade seemed defiant. Funny how they had twin feelings tonight, Shiloh mused. Why hadn't Jade called to ask if Shiloh wanted or needed her to start the meeting? That might have defused the tension they were experiencing right now. Despite her feelings, Shiloh realized she needed to do the right thing.

"No, we're not going to interrupt one lesson to start a new one," Shiloh said. "I'll save what I have for next week, and I'll do my best to show up on time. Go ahead, Jade. Where were you?"

Now Jade seemed flustered. "Um, well, I was reading Romans, chapter eight. Does anyone want to share their thoughts on that passage? What does it mean when Paul writes that we are heirs of God and coheirs with Christ?"

Jade's wide eyes and quivering lip told Shiloh that for once, sister girl's confidence was shaky. She clearly had expected Shiloh to take over the Bible study when she arrived; now Jade was stuck with actually having to teach.

"What does it mean to *you*, Sister Jade?" Shiloh knew Marlene's query was also a challenge.

Jade squirmed and tucked her hair behind one ear. "Good question, Sister Marlene. Very good. Let me see . . . well, to me it means that because we can call God our Father, and because whatever we're facing he's there with us, everything is going to work out for us in the end. It means that as an heir to God's kingdom, we really have nothing to fear, as long as we are trusting God and living in a way that pleases him. We want to run from the negative and uncomfortable things, but God may have placed us in that particularly tough season for a reason that only he truly knows. Sometimes the things that we think are going to harm us . . . sometimes those things come into our lives to strengthen our character, draw us closer to God, or in some other way shape us for the better."

Shiloh tried to conceal her surprise. Jade was actually making sense. The women settled down and seemed ready to connect with her, in spite of her perfect hair and nails, designer outfit, and flawless skin.

Shiloh raised her hand. Jade hesitated, then nodded, giving her permission to speak.

"Thanks for that insight, Sister Jade," Shiloh said. "I'm wondering, how many of you can sit here and in two minutes name five things that you think are wrong with you?"

"Inside or outside?"

The ladies chuckled at Sister Benita's question.

"You decide," Shiloh said.

"I can name ten things, rather than five," Benita said. "I'll start with these: My thighs are too big, my hair is too short, my nose is rather prominent."

"Not that I agree with you, but great examples, Sister Benita," Shiloh said, and everyone laughed. "Thanks for sharing. Now, I'm wondering if you, and any others, can name five things that are right with you, in two minutes?"

Silence enveloped the room.

"Come on, ladies," Shiloh said. "See how we treat ourselves? I know some of you here realize how fabulous you are. This isn't just about looks—it's about your heart. That's what that passage Sister Jade read means to me. I have to remind myself of that every now and then, and coming here tonight was perfect timing. All of us can lose confidence if we're relying solely on ourselves to be that Proverbs 31 superwoman."

Members of the group had turned away from Jade and were giving their full attention to Shiloh. She looked up, into Jade's eyes, and saw what resembled anger.

"I just wanted to chime in," Shiloh said, motioning for everyone to turn back to Jade. "You've got the floor again."

Jade cleared her throat and looked at her Bible. "No, you were doing fine, Sister Shiloh, just fine. I don't have much more to add."

The ladies spent the next half hour sharing their personal experiences with trusting God, or with struggling to trust him. Jade did her best to facilitate their banter and answer their questions, and with each positive response from one of the ladies, Shiloh saw her sit a little straighter in her seat. Yet she couldn't help but question Jade's newfound interest in serving the women. Was Reverend Vic prepping for a Sunday morning pulpit takeover, similar to the one his wife had engineered tonight?

Shiloh's chest tightened at the thought, but in an instant she remembered who she was and where she was—a child of God and in his house. She had to let go of that worry, to focus on what mattered most. Right now, that was getting herself ready to lead a public high school band, and keeping her family together in the process.

nine

Just as she had the two previous weeks since Jade had commandeered Bible study, Shiloh made sure to leave home early tonight so she'd reach St. Stephens Baptist well before the ladies began arriving.

For the third day in a row, she'd spent several hours at Sherman Park High, getting her classroom ready for the start of school next week, and she was weary. Training the week before had gone well, and she felt prepared to give these students what they needed. When she turned into the parking lot of the church and noted it was empty, she was tempted to lower her seat and take a five-minute power nap. Instead, Shiloh said a silent prayer for energy and patience, grabbed the shoulder bag that held her Bible, study worksheets, paper, and pens, and stepped out of the van.

She hoped she didn't look as raggedy as she felt, but if she did, she knew she couldn't complain. Millions of women worked outside of the home every day, and she had merely organized a classroom and sat in on staff meetings with other Sherman Park teachers this week. It was time to admit the truth: she was a wimp who had been spoiled for nearly twenty years.

She chuckled at her confession. She wasn't sure why God sent her this teaching position in this particular season, but she was still excited about it, and she intended to learn whatever lessons he had in mind and hopefully use the experience for good in other ways down the road.

Shiloh was entering the church when a beeping horn caught her attention. She paused and turned toward the sound. Jade waved as she whipped her SUV into a parking space next to Shiloh's van.

She leaned out of the driver's side window before turning off the ignition. "Wait for me—I'll walk in with you!"

Shiloh roused a smile.

Jade jumped out of the car and trotted toward Shiloh in her skinny jeans, a loose-fitting beige linen top, and bronze sandals. Shiloh grudgingly made another confession as she approached: If Beyoncé had a fraternal twin, it would be Jade.

Why, Lord, why?

Jade opened her arms and hugged Shiloh, who loosely reciprocated.

"Thought I'd get here early again, in case you need my assistance," Jade said. "You did well tonight, though—got here on time!"

Shiloh had a ready retort, but decided to behave. "Where are Naima and Nicholas this evening?"

"Hanging out with my mother. She's visiting from California, and was happy to have some time alone with her grandbabies."

Shiloh and Jade stepped inside the church's rear entrance hallway. Jade kept pace as Shiloh moved about the building, turning on lights throughout the education wing, in anticipation of men's Bible study taking place, too.

"No youths are coming tonight, right?" Jade asked.

Shiloh shook her head. "They've moved their Bible study night to Tuesday, right before youth choir rehearsal."

Jade nodded, then paused as Shiloh turned on the last light on her route, in the room where their group would be meeting.

"You know, I've been thinking," Jade said. "Week before last went well, and I enjoyed leading the women in a discussion. It might be good if you and I co-facilitate the Wednesday night Bible study. That way, when you're running behind, I can pitch in. Especially since I hear you're going to be working now."

Shiloh, who had begun rearranging chairs, stopped and peered at Jade. "Who said I needed help?" What she really wanted to know was who had told Jade she'd be working? The only one she'd mentioned it to at church was Sister Marlene.

Jade put a hand on her hip and leaned her head to one side. "You're not being territorial over how God's Word gets delivered, are you?"

Score one for Jade. Shiloh didn't have a ready response, and she knew she sounded defensive. The real issue was Jade inviting herself into this role. And her lack of grounding in the Bible, despite having been married to Vic for twelve years. Or maybe she did know the Bible well, but most people considered her an expert in hair and makeup, rather than prayer and meditation. She still hadn't shared what had sparked her sudden interest in the Wednesday Bible study, and Shiloh continued to have questions about her sincerity.

"I'm not being territorial, Jade," Shiloh finally responded. "I just want what's best for the women. Let's talk to Pastor Randy about this later, okay?"

Jade pursed her lips. Shiloh knew she was offended that Shiloh hadn't suggested asking both of their husbands.

"I'll see what Vic has to say tonight," Jade said softly. She moved past Shiloh to take one of the seats in the circle Shiloh had formed with the chairs.

Shiloh felt small and petty for taking this stance, but she took the stewardship of God's Word seriously. Participating in discussions was fine at every level, but if Jade wanted to help teach, she needed to show herself ready to study and ready to meditate on what she was reading, so she could discern God's will and confidently lead the women through the lessons. Many of them were informal Bible scholars themselves; they came on Wednesday nights eager to learn more than the basics, to help them grow.

Members of the Bible study began arriving minutes later, and Shiloh hustled to make a few extra copies of her worksheet when she saw she didn't have quite enough. She returned to the classroom at exactly six-thirty and found the women sitting in silence. The change was so dramatic from the laughter and chatter that had filled the room minutes before, Shiloh wondered if someone had shared bad news.

"Everyone okay?"

She placed her worksheets on an empty chair in the circle. No one responded, but the women peered at her uncomfortably. "Well, good evening, ladies. I'm on time tonight, so why the funny stares?"

Shiloh chuckled at her self-deprecation, but no one joined her.

"They're taking in our news," Jade said and smiled. "I just informed them that as of tonight, you and I are co-leaders of this Bible study—the First Lady and Second Lady of St. Stephens Baptist. Awesome, isn't it?"

Shiloh took a step back. Had this grown woman come into this church and pulled a fast one? Mere minutes after they'd been discussing these roles?

Shiloh's eyes narrowed and her lips parted, but before her unedited thoughts tumbled out, someone coughed. She shifted her gaze from Jade to the other women and saw Marlene shake her head. That silent instruction brought Shiloh back to her senses. Regardless of how Jade behaved, she wouldn't reciprocate. Shiloh surveyed the women's expressions. Young adult, middle aged, older, they were all doing the same—peering at her, waiting for her reaction. Shiloh was certain that a few, including Sister Adelaide, wanted her to declare Jade's announcement inaccurate. Her only response wound up being a strained smile, and an arrow prayer—short, sweet, and to the point.

This is all about you, Father. Keep me focused on that.

Shiloh picked up the worksheets and gave a stack to each woman on the end of the semicircle, to take one and pass inward.

"Ladies, let's get your Bibles out, and after I start us off with prayer, my um . . . co-leader . . . Sister Jade, will lead us in reading tonight's passages of Scripture. We are going to learn together and have a glorious time in the Lord, amen?"

The women were slow to echo her, but they did.

"Amen."

Ten

Shiloh was still so undone by Jade that ninety minutes later, she sat in her van and called Randy from the church parking lot.

The men's Bible study had wrapped up early tonight, and since the church janitor was there to lock up and make sure the women got off safely, Randy had gone home to check on the boys. Shiloh estimated he should be pulling into their driveway any second now. She waited until her last Bible study member drove away before calling him.

Randy picked up on the third ring, and she heard the garage door lowering in the background. Before he could say hello, she spewed.

"And then, Randy, she purposely dashed into the classroom ahead of me and announced her new role—seconds after we'd had a conversation about talking to our husbands about it. Girlfriend is sick!"

"Calm down, Shi."

Randy's tone angered her, but she also felt a twinge of shame. Had she really led the women through a study tonight about God's grace while holding a grudge against a fellow pastor's wife? Randy didn't want to frustrate her more by calling her out, she surmised, and he didn't have to. She was wrong, and she knew it.

Shiloh released a deep breath and felt her temper cooling.

"You don't have ownership over God's Word or who teaches what, sweetie," Randy said after a long silence. "We don't know Jade's heart, or why she suddenly wants to be involved in this way. Maybe she—"

"Nearly two years after I began teaching the Bible study? She had plenty of time to do it before we came to St. Stephens, and time to ask to be my co-teacher when we were settling in." Shiloh knew he hated when she interrupted him, but he didn't call her on it.

"For whatever reason, she's coming now, and she's trying to get involved, Shiloh," he said. "She may not be perfect at it, but God's Word never falls on deaf ears, as long as his truths are being accurately delivered. Something she says during her teaching time is going to hit home to someone in the study. I guarantee it. Just let it go."

Shiloh bit her lip. Randy was right. She had to leave this with God. And Jade knew she would. Shiloh had to give it to her—sister girl had picked a battle she knew she could win.

She sighed and started the van. She was going to go home, make sure the boys were straight for summer camp tomorrow, take a bubble bath, and call it a night. She'd also ask God to forgive her for this bad attitude . . . after she let it simmer a little while longer.

eleven

Shiloh had just given Randy his nightly banana split and snuggled next to him when his cell phone rang.

"I'll be there in half an hour," he said after listening for a few minutes.

Randy placed the ice cream on the coffee table and headed out of the family room.

"Deacon Wray's wife has had a stroke. I need to get over to St. Luke's. You coming?"

She glanced at the clock and groaned inwardly. It was nearly ten p.m. Her body said no, but Randy's posing of the question meant he wanted her to go. She did a mental rundown of what the boys were up to, to gauge whether she needed to give them further instructions before leaving. When she'd checked a few minutes ago, the three younger boys were in bed, reading, and Lem, who had his own room, was listening to music on his iPod and hanging out with friends via live video feeds on ooVoo. If only she had half his energy! She tried to shake off the weariness that gripped her this time every night and nodded.

"I'll grab my purse and tell Lem we're heading out."

Shiloh took the time to shed her sweatpants and slip into a clean T-shirt and a pair of fat woman jeans (at least that's what she called them) and sandals before trotting to the door. She grabbed the car keys off the credenza in the foyer and called for Randy.

"Come on, babe! I'll drive."

Once she'd settled behind the wheel of Randy's car, Shiloh turned down the radio so they could chat during the forty-five-minute drive to the hospital, just south of the city.

"What happened?"

Shiloh knew from the brevity of his conversation with Deacon Wray that he didn't have a lot of details; but the call reminded her that Sister Wray hadn't been at Bible study tonight, and she wasn't one to miss.

"They were having dinner and she slumped over. He called 911 right away. Fortunately they live half a mile from a fire station, and the rescue squad was there in minutes."

They rode the rest of the way to the hospital in silence, each lost in thought, and Shiloh uttered a prayer for Sister Wray. Her sudden illness would be upsetting to all of the older ladies in the congregation, especially to Sister Adelaide. They were more like sisters than friends, so she'd be worried sick. Shiloh made a mental note to call Sister Adelaide and send an email to the rest of her Bible study members tomorrow, to share the news and ask for their prayers.

She steered the car into the hospital entrance and gripped the wheel for comfort. The anxiety that always raced through her body in medical settings surfaced, as if on cue. Her throat tightened. Her shoulders tensed. Her heart thumped against her chest. How she hated hospitals. Always had since that horrible day years ago. Her procedure hadn't taken place in a full-fledged hospital; still, most medical facilities, with their sterile whiteness and antiseptic smells, took her back in time.

Randy walked a few paces ahead of her as they entered the foyer. Shiloh took several deep breaths and shifted her focus to the cute toddler a woman walking in front of her bounced in her arms. The boy's big brown eyes followed Shiloh until the woman stepped into an elevator and the doors closed behind them.

"You coming?"

Randy was waiting at a first-floor intersection. She pursed her lips and decided not to react to his impatience. Clearly neither of them had felt like leaving home this late in the evening, but his mood didn't need to be contagious.

Randy's regular visits to church members in the hospital made him an excellent navigator. He strode the hallways with confidence. Shiloh kept pace with him, and within minutes, they turned a corner together and found Deacon Wray standing outside of what must be his wife's hospital room. His eyes were closed and his chin was touching his chest.

Shiloh's heart sank. Were they too late? Was he praying or grieving?

Deacon Wray lifted his eyes. "Pastor, you came. Mrs. Griffin, thank you for coming, too." He shook Randy's hand before spreading his arms to give Shiloh a hug. The elderly man clung to her in what felt like a combination of fear and frailness. When Deacon Wray finally pulled away, Randy rested a hand on his shoulder, and Shiloh knew he was waiting for Deacon Wray to share his wife's status before speaking and possibly uttering something inappropriate. Shiloh had seen her husband in this position many times over the years, and she still marveled at how masterfully he communicated compassion to his worried or grief-stricken members.

"She's going to be okay, the doctors say." Tears flooded Deacon Wray's eyes as he whispered that news. "Thank God, thank God. She had me scared."

"I can imagine." Randy matched his tone to Deacon Wray's. "Thank God."

Deacon Wray lowered his head into his hands and sobbed. "I thought I'd lost her, Pastor," he said when he had composed himself. "What would I have done?"

He was five to six inches shorter than Randy, and he leaned into

Randy until Randy embraced him and let him cry. This was the first time Shiloh had seen the stoic Deacon Wray show such deep emotion. It was obvious he'd been terrified to witness the stroke. Shiloh approached him and rubbed his arm.

"It's going to be okay."

She looked up to make eye contact with Randy, just as Vic and Jade emerged from Sister Wray's room, hand in hand.

Shiloh glanced at her husband as surprise clouded his expression for a split second. She wished for the thousandth time she were half as good at masking her emotions. Jade and Vic could probably read all over her face her curiosity about why and how they had finagled some private time with Sister Wray.

"What a surprise."

Randy's tone conveyed Shiloh's sentiments.

"Brothers in the pulpit, brothers in service," Vic said.

He produced one of those megawatt smiles that routinely left female worshippers at St. Stephens Baptist weak-kneed. When Randy didn't return the Colgate offering, Vic's grin faded, and he cleared his throat.

"Well, Deacon Wray called us right after talking to you, and I figured it would be appropriate for us to come down. This sounded serious. Jade and I were in there praying over Sister Wray as she slept. I figured you'd do the same when you arrived. The more prayers, the better."

Randy's smile was fixed. "I see. Well, you're right about that— the more the better." He turned to Deacon Wray. "Is it okay if I go in?"

Deacon Wray nodded, and seemed oblivious to the exchange that had taken place between the two ministers.

Randy glanced at Vic but didn't make eye contact. "You want to join me?"

Vic didn't hesitate. He headed toward the room. "Of course."

Randy motioned for Deacon Wray to join them. "The prayer is for you and Sister Wray."

The men disappeared, leaving Shiloh with Jade, who was dressed to turn heads, even this time of night.

"This is late for you to be out, having little ones at home. Good thing your mom is here." Shiloh made the statement for lack of anything better to say. If she brought up the women's Bible study, the conversation might shift in a direction that wouldn't be pretty.

"Both of the kids were fast asleep when Vic got the call from Deacon Wray," Jade responded. "Mom can handle anything that comes up, so I felt comfortable tagging along. I need to do more outreach like this."

Suddenly Shiloh was grateful she had accompanied Randy. Jade, who could have conveniently stayed home because of her two young children—and usually did—had volunteered to come. Were she and Vic waging one-upmanship war? And had Jade ever spoken to Sister Wray in church, or during her recent visits to Bible study? This diva's eagerness to come to the hospital tonight was part of an agenda. Something was up, but Shiloh couldn't figure out the "what" or the "why."

If Vic had been selected senior pastor of St. Stephens Baptist over Randy, he wouldn't be making that much more money; but was that what Jade was vying for? She already seemed to have her material needs met. Vic earned a handsome wage as full-time assistant pastor of their large church; and Jade had no qualms about strategically mentioning that her deceased father had left her a sizable inheritance. Plus, Vic having grown up in this city, in a tight-knit, well-to-do family, already provided Jade with a level of respect and prestige that Randy and Shiloh, as newcomers, were still working to earn. Shiloh wasn't expecting any answers tonight, but she hated having to wait here with Jade and pretend those questions didn't matter.

Shiloh and Jade lingered outside Sister Wray's hospital room, eyeballing each other for a few minutes before Jade ended the awkwardness by whipping out her cell phone.

Shiloh was dying to know who she was calling this time of night to chat about what seemed to be her favorite interests—an upcoming Saks Fifth Avenue sale or her new designer bag. But instead of dialing a number, Jade leaned against the wall and scrolled through her emails or texts.

Shiloh decided to find the waiting room and call her boys. She peered in both directions until she noticed a sign indicating there was one down a hall to the left.

"I'll be back," she told Jade. "I'm going to grab a seat for a while."

Jade lowered her cell phone. "Wait—I'll come with you."

Shiloh paused and silently recited the Golden Rule. *Do unto others as you would have them do unto you . . .*

Jade tossed the phone into her satchel bag and motioned for Shiloh to lead the way. "Bible study went well tonight, don't you think?"

Here we go. Shiloh couldn't help but frown. "Do you?"

Jade seemed confused. "Well, yes, I thought it was great. I'm going to enjoy co-teaching the class."

"After inviting yourself to do so, I would hope you would."

There, she had said it. Shiloh had kicked political correctness to the curb, but she felt better.

Jade stopped walking and put a hand on her hip. "What was that?"

Shiloh wished she could pull out her iPhone and hit record. This woman deserved an Oscar for the innocent facade she could master at a second's notice.

"Nothing, Jade. Are you coming?"

Jade stayed put for a few seconds, and Shiloh knew she was debating whether to respond. When she resumed walking beside Shiloh, she changed the subject. "So, are you looking forward to the public school teaching you'll be doing soon?" Jade asked. "Why were you looking for work anyway? And are you still going to give Naima flute lessons?"

Here we go again . . .

Shiloh's reply was purposely measured. "Actually, I wasn't looking," she said. "I was presented with an opportunity to help out in a pinch as a substitute music teacher for a while, and it just so happens that I'm going to give it a shot, that's all. And yes, I'll continue teaching all of my private flute students, including Naima. I would have told you right away if I were planning to stop."

Shiloh fixed her face with what she hoped was a sweet smile. Why did she allow this woman to bring out the worst in her?

They entered the waiting room, and Shiloh spotted several seats near the flat-screen TV mounted to a wall in the far corner. Besides those few chairs, every seat was filled with anxious, bleary-eyed, sleeping, or tearful men and women. Half a dozen squirming kids rounded out the hodge-podge of occupants.

Shiloh slid into the cushioned chair closest to the TV and fixed her gaze on CNN. Medical correspondent Dr. Sanjay Gupta was reporting, and Shiloh hoped her obvious interest in his description of childhood brain trauma would limit conversation. Then again, wishing Jade wouldn't talk was like wishing water didn't pour when it rained.

Jade sat next to her and leaned close. "Well, however it came about, congrats on your job. I haven't worked for someone else in so long, I probably wouldn't know how to behave. Plus, my schedule stays full these days, with taking care of Naima and little Nick. So . . . to my first question of the night: How do you think our Bible study sessions are going?"

Shiloh noted Jade's terminology. After just two meetings—one of which Jade took over, and the other of which she declared herself co-leader—she was already referring to the weekly studies as a mutual project.

"I really don't know, Jade. What do you think?"

"I think we've got to gel, to figure out how we work best together, but I think it's going to be good for the members of St. Stephens Baptist to see their First Lady and Second Lady partnering, one with the perspective of an older woman and mother, and the other a mom of younger kids."

Shiloh glared at her. There was a six-year difference in their ages; surely Jade wasn't calling her old. Regardless, Shiloh felt every inch the thirty-eight-year-old hag when she sized herself up next to her "Second Lady," a term she was convinced Jade had coined. In all of her years as a preacher's kid, she'd never heard another assistant or associate pastor's wife refer to herself this way, or called by this title by others in a congregation.

"Since you're wanting to help lead, I think you're right; it's going to take some time for us to figure out the best way to work together and support the women we're serving," Shiloh said.

As she offered the olive branch, it struck her that maybe Randy was right; maybe she was wrong for resenting Jade's desire to get more involved with the Bible study. She had no right to act as if she owned the role. Maybe God was using Jade's newfound interest to help some of the women in ways only he understood.

Jade leaned in closer as the chatter around them grew. "What was the last part of what you said? Couldn't hear you over the TV."

Shiloh shook her head and glanced at the screen. "Nothing worth repeating."

Jade shrugged and fell silent and fixed her gaze on Headline News report. Shiloh texted Lem and Omari to see if they had gone to bed yet. Lem replied seconds later.

In bed, listening to music. Lights out soon. Everything ok?

Omari's lack of response meant he had fallen asleep, Shiloh surmised. She updated Lem on Sister Wray's condition and suggested that he soon follow his brothers to dreamland.

Even grown teenagers need rest.

Lem replied with a smiley face.

Shiloh glanced at the time on her cell phone and wondered how much longer Randy would stay. It was nearly midnight. Her schedule wasn't as flexible these days as it used to be. She needed to get to bed so she could rise early for work. There wasn't much left to do to get the band room ready for school next week, but she still had to be there by nine a.m. At this point, it was inevitable that she'd have to down more than one cup of coffee in the morning to stay alert.

When Randy and Vic appeared in the doorway of the waiting room about fifteen minutes later, she wanted to cheer. Randy motioned for Shiloh and Jade to join them.

"Thank God," Jade said. "I was about to curl up in this seat and call it a night, and you know that would have been a hot mess for my hair and mascara."

Shiloh couldn't help but chuckle. Somehow she had wound up with a sidekick who served as her personal version of Whitley Gilbert, the character from the TV sitcom *A Different World*. The Whitley on the show seemed bearable, compared to Jade, but maybe that was because one could watch for half an hour or change channels. Jade wasn't planning to go anywhere, and in fact was becoming more entrenched in Shiloh's world.

Shiloh, Randy, and the boys had been in Milwaukee for nearly two years, yet Jade had become more interested in her family in the past two weeks than ever before. Randy thought nothing of it, but Shiloh believed in the wisdom Mama had always shared, to keep your friends close and your enemies closer. Firsthand experience over the years had made this one of her personal truths.

The two couples left the waiting room and paused in front of the information desk in the lobby.

"See you at the church tomorrow, Rev," Randy said to Vic. "That's assuming that we don't get any more calls from members tonight."

"Don't speak that into existence, man!" Vic shook his head and draped his muscular arm around Jade's shoulders, maneuvering her out of the sliding glass doors. "See you in the morn."

When Shiloh and Randy reached their car, Randy extended his hand for her keys. "I left mine at home. I don't mind driving."

She handed them over and walked around to the passenger side.

"What did you think about Vic showing up like that?" she asked on the ride home.

"I don't know, babe," Randy said after a long pause. "Not sure what that was about. I've got my eyes open, though. I'm watching and listening."

Shiloh was glad to hear it. She hated for church to be about politics and competition, but she also knew this was Randy's livelihood, as well as his life's purpose. He needed to be both prayerful and alert.

Oprah was right: When you were passionate about something, doing what needed to be done didn't feel like work. Shiloh was certain that was the only reason she didn't give in to the temptation to stretch out in her bed this morning and repeatedly hit the snooze button.

She and Randy had returned home after one a.m to find all four boys asleep, and while Shiloh had been eager to follow suit, her romantic hubby had other ideas. By the time she closed her eyes it was nearly three a.m. She wasn't complaining then, but she wept when the alarm clock sounded less than three hours later.

To his credit, Randy slid out of bed and made coffee while she dressed. He even nudged the boys to get moving on time, so she didn't have to lose her cool or her religion yelling them down to breakfast and out to their summer camp carpool spots.

"When are you going to let me start driving?" Lem asked between bites of cereal. "Basketball camp is just twenty minutes away."

"You haven't had your license that long. Plus, what are you going to drive—my van?" Shiloh asked.

Lem swiveled his head from Shiloh to Randy and back. "I thought you guys were planning to get me a used car next year, when I'm a senior."

Randy kept reading the sports section of the morning paper and took another bite of oatmeal. "If we do, you'll earn that privilege by figuring out how to pay for gas," he said.

"Huh?" Lem frowned and left the table to place his bowl in the sink. He grabbed his swim trunks from the back of the chair he'd been sitting in, and slung them over his lanky shoulder. Shiloh chuckled to herself. He might forget some things, but not those swim trunks. Breaks at basketball camp offered opportunities to swim at the gym's indoor pool, and he never missed. "I don't have any money. Or a job."

"Not yet," Randy said. "We'll talk."

"Lia doesn't have to do any of that," he muttered on his way out of the door. "Her grandparents gave her a car over the summer, and they put gas in it, too."

Lem must have recognized the warning in both of his parents' eyes. He waved and disappeared to join his carpool before they could respond.

Shiloh rested her elbows on the kitchen island. "He's still talking about this Lia girl in Alabama. He can't find a girlfriend at his school, or at least in the Milwaukee metro area?"

Randy shrugged. "Virtual dating is in. I'm sure he's got something up his sleeve. He told me yesterday it would be great to spend Thanksgiving in Atchity, and he definitely wants to return to Atchity for the science camp next summer. Apparently Lia lives about an hour away, just outside of Birmingham, and they're cooking up a way to see each other more often."

Shiloh shook her head. "They think we've forgotten what it's like to be young and in love. But what about the Davis girl at church? I thought she had a crush on Lem and was trying to convince him to hang out with her."

Randy grinned. "She hasn't given up. She just doesn't know she's competing with a girl eight hundred miles away. Omari, on the other hand, has four or five different girls in the congregation swarming him every Sunday, and he stays on that cell phone."

Shiloh grabbed her tote bag and strolled over to Randy to give him a kiss. "What are we going to do with these teenagers?" she said.

"Don't forget to keep checking their Twitter and Instagram pages. I've had to slack off since I've been preparing for the school year."

Randy's raised eyebrows told her he had forgotten already.

She feigned frustration and pinched his arm. "Do it today, Reverend Daddy. We've got to stay on top of what they're up to."

He lightly pinched her back and kissed her again. "Don't be late. Have a good day."

"Sounds like you're trying to get rid of me so you can go back to bed. No fair."

Randy gave her a sly smile. "If you weren't going off to school, *we* just might do that. But that's not my plan. I'm heading back to the hospital this morning to check on Sister Wray. I'll go to the church from there, for the quarterly trustee meeting."

Shiloh waved goodbye again and stepped into the garage, where she settled in the van. It was a sticky-hot morning, and by the time cold air was flowing full throttle from the vents, she was already sweaty. She cranked up the radio and sang along to the songs in rotation this morning on Tom Joyner's syndicated radio show.

Her ringing cell phone interrupted the private music fest. Dayna's number surfaced on caller ID, and she slid her Bluetooth device in her ear while at a stop sign.

"Good morning; to what do I owe this call?"

Dayna chuckled. "Do I touch base that infrequently?"

They both knew the answer was yes, but neither commented. Normally Shiloh wouldn't take a call while she was driving, but hearing from the ever-busy Dayna was unusual, so she'd give her a few minutes.

"I'll have to do better," Dayna acknowledged. "I wanted to let you know it looks like we're on track to have the house finished by late October. We'd love to have the family join us for Thanksgiving, and I've even convinced Mama and Daddy to come. Of course, they're going to want to be home by Saturday morning, so Daddy can preach that Sunday, but they're willing to come."

"Shut the front door." Getting Daddy, and as a result Mama, to change their plans and leave Atchity during a holiday was huge. They must really want to see this house.

"Randy and I were just discussing Thanksgiving plans and how Lem is trying to convince us to go to Alabama so he can see a girl he met during his summer camp," Shiloh said. "He's not going to go for changing the family gathering to Calero, but I think the rest of us would love to visit sunny Florida. Now, Randy may have the same issue as Daddy, as far as needing to return home to preach on the last Sunday of the month. Will that be okay?"

"I haven't forgotten that Randy is Daddy's clone," Dayna said.

Dayna laughed, but Shiloh knew she wasn't really joking. Shiloh wasn't oblivious to the looks Dayna and their sister Jessica exchanged whenever Daddy and Randy were together; she knew they resented the relationship between the two men. Truthfully, she'd had her moments, too.

From the time Randy had begun spending summers with their family at age sixteen, Daddy had unofficially adopted him, and Shiloh and her sisters had, each in her own way, felt pushed aside. Randy was the son of Daddy's best friend and comrade from Vietnam; but in some ways, Randy's bond with Daddy became stronger than the one he shared with his own father, and Daddy tended to seek out Randy over his daughters when he had some down time or needed a confidante other than Mama. Randy returned home to Buffalo, New York, at the end of that first summer with the Wilson family, but his heart remained in Atchity. It had merged with Daddy's, and he visited as often as his father allowed—a few days during Christmas break, during spring break, and every summer thereafter.

Shiloh would never admit to Dayna or Jessica that she sometimes wondered whether Daddy had encouraged Randy to marry her, to make him an official part of the family. Her husband's genuine affection and caring always overshadowed that nagging fear. As she did whenever the fretful musing arose, she shook it off this morning, and forced herself to refocus on the conversation with Dayna.

"Anyway," Shiloh said wryly, in response to Dayna dubbing Randy their father's clone. She turned into a grocery store parking lot so she could chat without distraction. "I'm going to ignore that comment and keep it moving this morning."

"I'm sorry," Dayna said and chuckled. "But you need to get some swag about you, girl; that was your perfect chance to tease me about bringing 'a brother from another mother' named Warren into the family."

Shiloh laughed. "Since when did you, the corporate executive, begin using slang?"

"When? Let's see . . . soon after tying the knot two years, five weeks, and six days ago, and moving in with two rambunctious teens who consider themselves Drake's biggest fans and who try to out-rap each other every chance they get."

Shiloh pictured Michael and Mason in action and doubled over with laughter. She was thankful she had taken time to park. An older woman had returned to the car next to Shiloh's and peered at Shiloh with concern as she unloaded her groceries.

Shiloh waved and pointed to her ear. But the woman looked even more confused. Shiloh realized she either didn't see the Bluetooth device or didn't know what it was. The woman placed the third bag in her trunk, slid behind the wheel, and sped away without looking back.

Shiloh laughed harder.

"I've got to go, Dayna. This is too much for me this morning. When I start teaching next week, I'll ask my students to show me some swag."

"Bye, girl," Dayna said. "And if you have to get them to 'show' you, don't worry about it."

She hung up before Shiloh could respond, and Shiloh smiled. The formality between them seemed to be thawing a little more each time they talked. She could share a laugh with the sister who had kept her at arm's length for nearly a decade. Shiloh hoped Randy would be open to spending Thanksgiving in Florida so the positive trajectory could continue. The more often she and Dayna chatted, the more she realized what she'd been missing. If Dayna was offering a way into her heart, Shiloh was ready to take it. When the time was right, God would bring her closer to Jessica, too.

fourteen

Two hours into her new gig and so far so good.

Shiloh perched on the stool at the front of the band room and waited for the next round of student musicians to breeze in and take their seats. This group would be the full band—grades nine through twelve—and if they were as focused as the jazz band students had been, she might do okay at this teaching thing.

Shiloh was reviewing a note with instructions from Mrs. Helmsley when an afro distracted her. In fact, she saw the hair before she saw the rest of the girl. A soft, flowy affair at least six inches high filled the doorway, attached to the body of a tall, thin, fair-skinned teenager with delicate features. Shiloh wasn't sure whether to laugh at the first-day-of-school joke, or take the young lady's 'do seriously. The girl perched on the first seat in the flute section and smiled at Shiloh. Shiloh could tell from this close proximity that it was no prank—the afro was real, not a wig, and this student was wearing it with confidence.

Another bold frame filled the doorway, and this time it was a tall girl with an asymmetrical bob and one of the brightest smiles Shiloh had ever seen.

"Monica, why did you leave me?"

The second girl's voice filled the band room as she strode toward the woodwind section, where she took a seat and began opening her saxophone case. Her afro-wearing, flute-playing friend, who Shiloh now knew as Monica, giggled.

"Don't mind us. That's my silly best friend, Phaedra," Monica said. "She'll behave once class starts."

Shiloh nodded, but in an effort to maintain her authority, suppressed the smile that wanted to escape.

Phaedra raised a tenor saxophone to her lips and blew one note in Monica's direction, as if taunting her. The other students laughed, but kept preparing for class, which let Shiloh know they were used to the banter between these two. Without Shiloh having to utter a word, the students pulled out their flutes, saxophones, clarinets, trumpets, and other instruments, and by the time the bell rang, everyone was ready to play.

Shiloh was speechless. She hadn't expected this level of maturity from a group of high school students. But Dr. Carter had reiterated after she'd completed the substitute teacher workshop that she was starting in a great place—a magnet school with kids who wanted to be there and were eager to learn. He had been modest.

"My goodness," Shiloh finally said, after the bell rang. "Looks like I'm the one who's not ready. I'm Mrs. Griffin, and as many of you know from the letter your parents received, Mrs. Helmlsey won't return until late October, due to a relative's illness. I'm looking forward to working with you until then. I'm a trained flutist and pianist and have taught students of all ages for years. I also have four children, ranging in age from sixteen to nine, and all of them play instruments. Let's take attendance, and then we'll get started on the music."

A young man in the drum section raised his hand.

"Yes?" Shiloh responded.

"You have an interesting accent; where are you from?"

Shiloh smiled. "I should have warned you all. I am from Alabama, and you'll have to forgive my thick accent. I've lived in Milwaukee for almost two years, but I still say 'waaata' for 'water' and 'ya'll' or 'you all' instead of 'you guys.' I'm working on it!"

The students laughed.

As with the first period of the day, this hour whizzed by, and before Shiloh knew it, it was time to send this group of kids on their way. While everyone else dashed off to the next class, the girl with the afro, Monica, took her time packing up, then approached Shiloh.

"Thanks for giving us a great start to the school year," she said. "I love playing the flute, and would love to talk to you more about it, since you say that's one of your primary instruments. I think I might want to make a career of it."

"Anytime, Monica," Shiloh said. "I studied the flute extensively and can show you some helpful breathing techniques and tongue methods, as well as some practice drills to strengthen your tone. Since you say you're considering this as a career, are you also taking private lessons?"

Monica nodded. "Yes. I've had the same teacher since fifth grade, and she's great. But I'm always looking for mentors."

Shiloh was impressed. "I'll be happy to help," she said, appreciating the girl's forthrightness. "What grade are you?"

"I'm in the tenth," Monica said.

"Okay," Shiloh said. "I was just wondering how much more time you have to prepare for college auditions and special summer programs."

"I'm already starting," Monica said. "It would be great to get an early acceptance into a good school, so I'm giving it my all, every chance I get. Thanks again for being willing to help me. See you on Thursday. Better get to my next class!"

Monica trotted out of the room with her flute case tucked under her arm. Shiloh hadn't seen her friend, Phaedra, standing in the doorway until now. Phaedra waved, then took Monica by her free arm and pulled her from sight.

Ah, teenagers. To be young and carefree again.

Shiloh chuckled at that notion. Why was it that one always remembered their high school days wistfully, forgetting all of the awful parts?

She slid off the stool and tucked away her notes. This would be a free period, so she could relax in the teacher's lounge and meet a few more of her temporary colleagues. Shiloh smiled as she walked through halls filled with pockets of plotting, giggling, whispering teen girls, and with boys doing the same just out of earshot. This felt right. She had made a good decision, and Mama shouldn't worry. Instead of going home tired every evening, Shiloh had a feeling this group of kids would energize her.

fifteen

The teachers' lounge was as lively as the hallway had been.

Shiloh entered just as someone shared something funny, and everyone was in stitches. They looked her way, and a petite Asian lady with thick, shiny black hair approached her with an extended hand.

"You must be Shiloh, Thelma Helmsley's sub. I'm Eva, and I teach world history. I wasn't here when our principal introduced you at the faculty and staff meeting last week; welcome. If you have any questions or need helping figuring out something about the school or with the students, I'll be happy to help."

Shiloh smiled and shook her hand. The tiny lady was only as tall as Shiloh's shoulder, but she didn't seem fazed by her petite stature or by Shiloh's height.

"Thanks for the warm welcome, Eva. It's great to meet you."

"Come on in and find a seat. Greg here—Mr. Chartowsky to the students—was just regaling us with stories about his weekend outing on Lake Michigan. Apparently his tiny boat tipped over on a first date with his dream woman, and she swam to shore, soaking wet and mad."

Shiloh looked from Eva to Greg, unsure of how to react.

Greg chimed in. "Yes, that really happened, and I'm still trying to get back in her good graces. But you don't want to hear all of that on your first official day here. Welcome, Shiloh. How's it going?"

Shiloh glanced at her watch. "Given that it's just 10:30, so far so good. The students have been attentive and really into their music.

Surprising for a first day of school, especially just after the Labor Day holiday. Seems like all of them actually practiced over the summer."

Eva nodded. "I'm sure they did. This is a school full of dedicated kids. They like to play and goof off like everybody else their age, but on the other hand, they take what they do seriously. You've landed in a good place. Any students stand out yet?"

Shiloh sat next to Greg and grabbed a banana from the bowl on the table in front of her. "I had two students in the class that just ended that I'd like to know more about. Do you know Monica and Phaedra, two sophomores?"

"Yes," said Eva. "I had them in my history class last year. According to Thelma, both of them are gifted. Phaedra is the outgoing risk-taker, on that sax and otherwise. Monica is pretty quiet. She's a good girl. Her mom died a little over two years ago, and she's being raised by her dad, with help from her grandmother. Pretty mature for her age."

Learning about her students' backgrounds was helpful. Shiloh knew that inevitably, it would make teaching them easier.

An African American woman with a short, layered hairstyle that reminded Shiloh of her sister Dayna's former 'do, stepped into the lounge. Her bright red lipstick, large hoop earrings, and colorful flowing skirt were a magnet for attention. She waved hello to everyone, then paused when she saw Shiloh.

"Welcome again, Shiloh. We met last week during the staff meeting, but I'm sure your mind is full of various names and faces. I'm Kristina Banks, or Kris for short, and I teach orchestra. I left right after our meeting last Monday for a last-minute vacation, and wasn't around when you and everyone else were organizing your classrooms. Just in case you weren't told, the orchestra practice room is right next to the band room; holler if you need me."

Shiloh grinned. How did this vivacious lady think anyone could forget her? "I remember you, Kris," Shiloh said. "Especially since you and, temporarily I, comprise the music department. Things are going well so far, but thanks for your support. I'm sure I'll have questions for you over the next eight weeks. How long have you been here?"

"Ten years, and I love it," Kris said. "The kids are great, the faculty is great, and so are the parents. The pay could always be better, but what teacher doesn't complain about that? How long have you been teaching?"

Shiloh hesitated. "I'm . . . I haven't been in a classroom setting, but I have taught one-on-one lessons for years."

Kris raised an eyebrow. "I see. Well . . . I hope this works out for you. Welcome again." She sauntered over to the refrigerator and retrieved a Diet Coke. "My morning caffeine fix is necessary," she said, and filled a mug she was carrying with ice from the teachers' lounge freezer.

Shiloh fixed a smile on her face, but she wished she were invisible. That had not gone well. What was she going to say when they asked where she'd received her degree, or how long she'd had her teaching license?

She spent the rest of the break listening to her new colleagues trade stories about their Labor Day activities, praying that they'd stay on topic, rather than inquiring further about her background and training. When the bell finally rang, Shiloh hoped her relief wasn't palpable. Everyone finished what they were doing and left quickly. Shiloh headed for her classroom, too. She didn't have to teach another class, but she was required to be present during this period in case a student came in seeking additional help.

When she reached the band room, she sagged in relief.

That bothered her, though. Why was she so concerned about

fitting in and wanting them to like her? Why was she allowing concerns like this to mar her first day with her students? Shiloh made a mental note to call Dr. Carter this evening to make sure her teaching colleagues would be okay with her lack of credentials if they found out, especially since she was subbing at a magnet school. She didn't want any surprises or drama. If her lack of a degree and teaching experience were going to be a problem, better to end this now before she, or her students, got attached.

Part of her wished she could snap her fingers and zap herself to the safety of her home. Usually on a weekday morning she'd be in her sunroom practicing the flute, or completing some of her household chores. That was familiar. That felt comfortable. Being in the classroom with the students had been exhilarating, but teacher politics might be the end of her.

sixteen

Lack of sleep left Shiloh less perky this morning than she had been on Day One.

She had tossed and turned most of the night, fretting over her inadequacies. What if her informal teaching style meant she wasn't giving students what they needed? What if the other teachers protested her presence? Not only would she be embarrassed, so would Randy.

She wanted to talk with him about her concerns, but feared he'd tell her she should have thought about all of that before taking the position. Yesterday, he and the boys had celebrated her first day of teaching by preparing dinner and surprising her with a cake. Their thoughtfulness made her feel special, but the butterflies remained, even after a brief chat with Dr. Carter, who assured her that she had received a full endorsement from officials at the state Board of Education.

"Dr. Singleton, Sherman Park's principal, is well aware that you are two years away from completing your bachelor's degree," Dr. Carter told her. "She also knows you are a talented musician with one-on-one teaching experience, and that you have a way of connecting with students. You aren't the first non-degreed person we've had in the classroom. We don't do it often, but on occasion, there's good reason for exceptions, and with the school year so close to starting, we needed your help."

He reminded her that he'd already received a glowing letter of reference from the current dean of the music education department at

Birmingham-Southern, who had reviewed her undergraduate records and reported that she left the college in good standing, with high honors. A letter was also en route from the university in Paris, where Shiloh spent the summer after her sophomore year, studying with master flutists.

"How many people can say they've done something spectacular like that?" Dr. Carter asked. "Don't worry about anything; you're good to go."

Shiloh clung to those words this morning, half an hour before the first period, as she wrote scales on the chalkboard that she wanted her students to practice as a warm-up. Mrs. Helmsley had provided a range of ideas, and this was one of them.

There was a light tap at the door, and Monica poked her head inside. "Good morning. You're here early."

"Good morning, Mrs. Griffin," Monica said. "May I come in?"

"Sure. Grab a seat and give me a minute."

Shiloh scribbled the rest of the musical notes on the board before sitting next to the girl, in the front row of the C-shaped setup.

"I just wanted to follow up on what I mentioned yesterday, about becoming a professional flutist, and ask how to go about doing that. I know I should go to a school with a good music program, and I've looked at a few online, but I have no clue which ones are really good, outside of the famous ones we all know about, like Juilliard and Berkeley. My private teacher keeps talking about those, and I'll probably apply, but I wondered if you could give me some guidance on some other good programs, too."

"Have you talked to your guidance counselor?" At Lem's high school, part of the guidance counselor's job was to help juniors and seniors plan for college; Shiloh was certain the counselors at a magnet school like Sherman Park would offer that kind of assistance, and more.

Monica nodded. "Yes, but he doesn't take my flute idea seriously. He keeps telling me to stop treating a hobby as a career path, plus I'm just in tenth grade, so he says I'm rushing things. But when I search online, I see there are flutists playing in orchestras, collaborating with recording artists, and performing in other arenas. I really want to do something like that, and I'm afraid if I wait until my junior or senior year to get focused, I won't be adequately prepared."

Shiloh was impressed again by this soft-spoken girl, and by her tenacity. Monica was right. The professional musician world was competitive, and it required a lot of focus and sacrifice. She sat back and folded her arms.

"I see you have your flute," she said to Monica. "Would you play something for me?"

"Sure."

Monica opened the flute case and quickly assembled the instrument. After a few puffs to tune it, she closed her eyes and launched into a fast-paced version of an R&B jazzy classic, "Just the Two of Us."

Shiloh's eyes widened. This girl had to be kidding. She waited until Monica reached the end of the piece and was preparing to play something else, before stopping her.

"Where did you learn that?"

Monica gave her a shy smile. "I taught myself. Actually, Phaedra and I both did. We play this song together at different events people invite us to. It's great to combine my flute with her saxophone on this number."

Shiloh was floored, but Monica seemed to be just warming up. "The next piece I'll play is something Mrs. Helmsley gave the class to learn."

Monica launched into "November Song," and her delivery was flawless. Shiloh shook her head. This girl had "it." Beneath the big hair and tiny frame resided a gift.

"Wow, young lady. I don't know what to say."

"Do you think I could play professionally?"

Before Shiloh could enumerate to herself all the reasons to be cautious in encouraging the girl, she blurted a response—the kind she had longed to receive years ago, when she felt just like Monica— passionate about music and eager to make it her career.

"Absolutely. You have the talent. But making it a career is going to take a lot of drive and hard work. Hours of practice. More private lessons. That's what you have to ask if you're ready for. I'm not an expert since I've never played professionally, but I'll do what I can to guide you in the right direction."

Monica's eyes lit up and a grin spread across her face. "Thank you, Mrs. Griffin. I'm so glad you came this year. I'm so happy right now."

Shiloh held up a finger. "Remember what I just told you; it's going to take a lot of effort to get where you say you want to go. It's not all glamorous and fun. Keep that in mind, okay? Why don't you continue to research careers for a professional flutist, and also review all of the pros and cons? You're wise to start looking at colleges offering what you want to study so you can apply early. I've got a few good ones in mind to share with you, but I will explore a little more before giving you my recommendations."

Shiloh couldn't believe Sherman Park's guidance counselor had not given the girl more help. But maybe it was because Monica was still a sophomore, with quite a few seniors in need of assistance first.

"Where did you attend college?" Monica asked.

Shiloh hesitated, not because she was ashamed of having studied at Birmingham-Southern; to the contrary. It was noted as one of the best liberal arts colleges in the nation. But mentioning the university triggered a lot of regret, and a flood of memories she still yearned to forget.

Right now, she wanted to stay in this moment with young Monica, and steer this girl down a path on which her musical talent could shine. She told Monica about Birmingham-Southern, while simultaneously praying that the girl would consider Alabama too far from Milwaukee to put on her list of options. The college wasn't the problem, nor were the people. It was a personal symbol of pain for Shiloh, and admittedly, she couldn't separate her reality—or someone else's—from that fact.

"If you start working on your applications and preparing audition pieces with your private teacher, you should be okay. You plan on taking the SAT or ACT, right?"

Monica nodded. "I'll take the SAT this fall, just to see how I do, and again next fall, to see how the scores compare. That still gives me my senior year to take it a final time."

Shiloh patted Monica's hand. She barely knew the girl but was already falling in love with her.

"You'll be fine. Do some research and narrow your list of potential colleges and let me know what you come up with. I'll help you find an audition piece that will blow an audition panel away, if you nail it. Since you play by ear too, you may want to prepare a traditional piece, which I'll help you find, as well as something contemporary—maybe a jazz or classical piece—that showcases the range of your talent."

The bell rang and Monica disassembled her flute with record speed so she could be on time for her first-period class. "Is it okay to leave my flute here, since I'll be back in a couple of hours?"

Shiloh nodded and pointed to her desk in the corner of the room. "Put it over there. See you soon."

Monica seemed giddy as she dashed out of the room. Shiloh felt a part of her heart go with the motherless girl. Whatever Monica's hopes and dreams, Shiloh was now invested in helping birth them.

seventeen

The end-of-class bell rang today before any of them were ready. Shiloh had been teaching only two weeks, but already had grown fond of her students, and was delighted to see they were warming to her as well.

"Aw, man; I just got the notes right!" Evian quickly blew through the melody on his trumpet one last time before tucking away his music and packing up the instrument.

"Keep practicing," Shiloh encouraged him. "You nailed it, and it will only get better."

"Are you going to come and see the performance, Mrs. Griffin?" Tedra asked.

Shiloh smiled at the petite girl with wiry blond hair and copper-rimmed eyeglasses. She played the clarinet and rarely talked, but it was nice to realize that just as she was aware of the countdown occurring with her long-term sub status, so were they. Shiloh had been pleased with their progress and had high hopes that Mrs. Helmsley would find her students fully prepared for the fall recital, which was scheduled for the first week in November.

"Of course I'm coming, Tedra," Shiloh said. "After seeing you guys work so hard, I wouldn't miss the recital. I'll be here sitting front and center, peacock proud."

Drew, one of the drummers, snickered.

Shiloh grinned at him. "I know, I know," she said. "Old-lady, Southern language. I've already been told I need to get some swag."

The class erupted in fits of laughter over her use of "their" cool word, then most of them ducked out to make it to their next class.

Phaedra and Monica trotted over to hug Shiloh.

"We love you, Mrs. G! You are hilarious," Phaedra said.

Shiloh hugged them both at once and chuckled. "Ya'll just feel sorry for me."

"Ya'll?" Monica said and giggled. "I love your accent and the funny things you say. You are so cute!"

Shiloh smirked. "You girls are going to be late for your next class. Get out of here."

Phaedra took off with a wave goodbye. "Happy Monday!"

"One more thing," Monica said as she headed toward the door. "I read online last night about a summer music competition for young musicians at Columbia College Chicago. The students who audition and win a spot will work with professional musicians for four days to prepare for a weekend performance. Winners will be selected in various instrument categories to compete for a partial college scholarship and a chance to attend a national musicians' conference, where they can network with professionals and learn more about music-related careers."

"Wow—you applying?" Shiloh asked.

Monica nodded. "I have to audition, though. Will you help me find a really good piece?"

Shiloh felt a knot forming in her stomach, but the smile never left her face. She of all people being asked to help this sweet girl with something as life-changing as this.

Lord, you have a sense of humor. You really do.

"You bet, Monica. I'll bring some ideas to class tomorrow. Or if you want me to email you some pieces to consider, shoot me an email so I'll have your address, and we'll go from there."

Monica gave her a thumbs-up before scooting from the classroom.

Shiloh smiled as she disappeared. The girl's lanky frame reminded Shiloh of herself at that age. So did Monica's hopes and dreams. How had one fateful summer killed hers?

eighteen

Jade's call canceling Naima's flute lesson came that afternoon right after school, and as far as Shiloh was concerned, it was right on time.

"I . . . I'm not myself tonight. I'm going to stay home and take some medicine," Jade said. "Naima's disappointed because she loves spending time with you, but we'll pick up where we left off next week, okay? I'll plan to see you Wednesday night at Bible study, and I'll lead the session, like we discussed."

Shiloh hadn't wished an illness on St. Stephens' "Second Lady," but she was grateful for a break from the scrutiny Jade's visits to her home always yielded, and from hearing about Jade's fabulous life. Shiloh believed that she wasn't feeling well, though. Jade had seemed distracted at the last two Bible studies, asking members to repeat their comments, then still giving idiotic replies to whatever they shared, as if she hadn't accurately heard them. Nicholas had just turned two, but Shiloh was beginning to wonder if she was under the weather because she was pregnant again.

Whatever the reason, tonight's reprieve was perfect. Not having Naima this afternoon would give her a chance to start dinner early and begin researching flute solos for Monica's audition. While David worked at the kitchen table on his fourth grade art project and the tilapia baked, Shiloh sat across from him, in front of her laptop, and searched for musical scores in an appropriate level of play for Monica. There were the traditional and lovely flute solos the judges were likely used to hearing, but she also searched for some contemporary pieces the girl might like. "Ribbon in the Sky" or "Somewhere Over the Rainbow" might be nice surprises.

When Shiloh wrapped up her research, she checked her messages and saw that Monica had followed through with forwarding her email address. Shiloh sent the girl links to the various musical scores she had selected and suggested that Monica play around with each of them to pinpoint her favorite few.

That task accomplished, Shiloh closed the laptop and left the table to check on dinner. The baked tilapia smelled delicious, and a quick check of the pot on the stove indicated the rice would be ready in minutes.

Raphael burst through the kitchen door with a water bottle in one hand and his football in the other. Another blessing tonight had been having him ride home with a teammate rather than having to be picked up.

"Hey, son," Shiloh said. "How was practice?"

He had reached the age where he could now play for his school, rather than in a community recreation league, and so far he loved his coach and teammates.

"Good," he said, and put his bag and ball in a corner.

"You know you have to take those things up to your room," Shiloh said without looking his way. "And when you're done, you can help me get the salad ready."

"Aw, Mom," Raphael said.

"Aw, son," Shiloh said.

She strolled over and hugged his waist, marveling at the fact that at just twelve, he was already her height. Five-seven or not, she was still mama.

"You'll thank me when you're all grown and you know how to take care of yourself and prepare your own meals. David is trying to finish his art project, but I'll have him set the table to make it all fair.

Your older brothers have been doing their part, too, since I've been working."

Raphael shook his head. "You and Daddy don't have to do anything anymore."

Shiloh poked his arm. "Careful. I did all the work in having you knuckleheads."

He picked up his bags and headed to his room. Shiloh rendered a final instruction while he was still within earshot. "And don't take forever—dinner will be ready in ten minutes."

Shiloh returned to the kitchen table and looked over David's shoulder. He was engrossed in the papier-mâché animal he was creating and hadn't uttered a word, not even his usual, "How much longer before we eat?"

She smiled at the hard-to-decipher creation and could tell he was proud of himself. From the looks of it, he was nowhere near finished. They would have to eat in the dining room tonight in order to leave David's workspace as he needed it. She rubbed his shoulders. "Looking good, son."

David grinned. "I'm glad I chose to do this, because not many people take time to create an actual replica of an animal. They like to draw and paint, but this takes more work, and it looks more life-like."

Shiloh returned the smile. He was the youngest, but he was also the most intellectual of the bunch. She slid into the seat across from him and opened her laptop again. She clicked on her computer screen and saw that Monica had responded to her email.

Thank you, Mrs. G. You are the best! Can't wait to try out these songs to see which two will help me win a spot in the program. If you have any advice about what might be best for me, let me know!

Also, I see in your email signature that you attend St. Stephens Baptist Church. I used to go there when I was a little girl. I loved it. My family doesn't go to church that much these days, but I'd love to visit sometime . . . Anyway, thank you again. See you in class day after tomorrow.

Sincerely,
Monica

Even this girl's emails made Shiloh smile. Monica's voice and personality shone through regardless of the format. Shiloh was convinced that her positive attitude and willingness to work hard were going to take her far. And she loved that Monica had asked about church. Shiloh had lost count of how often people asked her about St. Stephens Baptist and received a personal invitation from her simply because her email signature served as a conversation starter. It included a phrase indicating that she was "Planted at St. Stephens Baptist, in Milwaukee's Brown Deer suburb, to love and serve all who cross my path."

Everyone from personal acquaintances to her sons' teachers had asked her more about the church and had visited as a result. Some had even become members. Since Monica had inquired on her own, Shiloh decided she deserved the same warm welcome anyone else would receive.

It's my pleasure, Monica. Truthfully, I think any of the songs I've sent you will go over well with the judges, and I think you can play each of them masterfully. Why don't you listen to each one carefully, give it some thought, and go with the two songs that feel right? Regarding St. Stephens, I'd love to have you visit anytime—and your family, too. If you all are former members, you know where we are located. Services are at 8 a.m. and 11, with Sunday school in between at 9:45. We are laid back and loving, so come on by, anytime. FYI, our youth Sunday is always the fourth Sunday, and our youth leaders hold Bible study for teens on Tuesday nights, when "y'all" can have the building to yourselves. LOL You don't have to be a member to participate. See you at school. Let me know if you need more help, or if you have more questions—about music or church. Off to finish dinner! Have a good night. Mrs. G.

Shiloh hit send and sighed. She peered at David, whose head was lowered, chubby cheeks dimpled, and shoulders hunched as he worked on his art. How thankful she was for him and for each of her boys. Every now and then, however, she wondered what it would have been like to raise a daughter. Tonight was one of those times . . .

nineteen

Despite Jade's awkwardness during the past couple of meetings, Shiloh couldn't recall ever seeing her squirm in Bible study quite as much as she was tonight. If Shiloh didn't feel so guilty for enjoying it, it could have been a treat.

Jade had simply chimed in on the past two studies, even after declaring herself a co-leader; but tonight, Shiloh had handed over the reins. Though she had been under the weather earlier in the week, Jade assured Shiloh she was ready for tonight's session, and she had chosen the subject of trusting God through storms. Problem was, the women in the group were having a hard time relating to the message, and to Jade's manner of teaching it, with her sitting before them dressed like a celebrity housewife who had never set foot in Wal-Mart, requested emergency prayers, or struggled for anything other than to fix a chipped nail or bad hairdo right before her next big occasion.

Jade was doing her best to draw the women in, and Shiloh could see that she didn't seem to understand why they weren't warming up to her.

"Um, let's talk more about Naomi, the mother-in-law of Ruth, and all that she suffered while living in a foreign land. First her husband dies, and then her two sons. Wouldn't that make any of us despair? Have any of you gone through a trial so severe that you thought God had forsaken you?"

A few women nodded, but no one expounded.

"Well, it's during those times, when we feel the loneliest or most afraid, or most deeply hurt, that we must remember God is there with us."

The silence was palpable, and uncomfortable. Jade seemed to want the women to launch into a discussion, and Shiloh was certain the women were waiting for Jade to lead them there, by sharing from her heart, either a personal experience or that of someone else, that would make her comments more relevant. Instead, she chose to move on.

"Let's turn to 1 Samuel 25 and read about Abigail and her marriage to the evil and foolish Nabal."

Sister Marlene volunteered to read the passage aloud, while everyone else followed along in their Bibles.

"I'm reading from the NIV version," Marlene began. "'Now Samuel died, and all Israel assembled and mourned for him . . .'"

By the time Marlene reached the end of the chapter, which detailed Abigail's longsuffering with her foolish husband and the wisdom she used in dealing with David, many of the women were murmuring with excitement about Abigail's victory over dire circumstances.

But Jade lost them again. "Amen to that, sisters, right? Abigail handled her business! How have we handled our Abigail moments?"

The women fell silent, and Jade shot Shiloh a glance that she read as a plea for help. Shiloh cleared her throat and scanned the circle of twenty or so women.

"You know, I think we've all been there, whether we've had to deal with an unfair or downright terrible boss, struggled in a personal relationship like Abigail, or simply didn't see how we were going to make it through some other tough situation, like a job loss, divorce, or death of a loved one," Shiloh said. "I think the message in Abigail's experience is that wherever we find ourselves stuck, frustrated, or hurting, God sees and hears us. Isn't it fair to say, though, that sometimes when we are in the middle of our valley experiences, we can't see God for all of the 'stuff' cluttering our vision?"

"Amen, First Lady!"

That affirmation from Sister Clara set off a round of copycats, and a few women began sharing their personal experiences, including Sister Sarah, whose seventy-three-year-old face was marred by the burns she suffered sixty years earlier, when her family home caught fire and left her trapped inside. Sister Carlita shared the devastation of losing her brother in recent months, and how she didn't understand why God allowed him to die in a car accident just before the birth of his second child. Even Sister Marlene chimed in and shared how watching her spiritually strong mother lose her leg to an infection five years earlier had strained her faith.

"I couldn't understand how this woman, who would have done anything God asked of her—who *did* do anything and everything she felt God was leading her to do—had to suffer like this; why God didn't heal her and let her keep her leg," Marlene said. "Mama never felt the same after that loss; she just went downhill. When we buried her five months later, I stopped going to church for a while. Now I know I should have followed Abigail's example and remained steadfast when I didn't understand; but for a long time, I felt like Ruth's mother-in-law Naomi, like God had forsaken me."

Shiloh glanced at Jade to see if she wanted to respond, but a slight smile was fixed on her expressionless face, and Shiloh wondered if Jade had let her mind wander, because she didn't seem to be in tune with Marlene's sharing.

"What led you back to God, Marlene?" Shiloh finally asked.

Marlene leaned forward in her chair, and her voice softened.

"Honestly, it was Mama. It took me forever to go through all of her stuff, and about two years after she died—that will be three years ago this month—I finally decided to clean out the chests of drawers I had moved from her home into my attic. In one of them, I found a journal she had been keeping the last year of her life . . ."

Marlene's eyes watered and she choked up.

"It was the journal I had given her the Mother's Day before her death. I sat on my living room sofa on that Saturday afternoon and read all of her entries. In the last few pages, I found some truths that shook me to my core. Mama wrote on the day after her leg was amputated just five words: 'Thy will be done, Lord.' And then later she wrote, 'You are my joy, Heavenly Father.' And her final entry said, 'Your love is better than life. I love you more each day, and in you I find my peace and rest.'"

Marlene sat back in her seat and wiped her cheeks. "I will never forget those words; they're stamped in my heart and mind," she said. "Mama loved God anyhow. So why did I think I had the right to hold a grudge when she had accepted his will? I returned to St. Stephens Baptist the very next day and rededicated my life to God."

"Wow. Amen." Jade offered that double-word feedback and turned to Shiloh. "You go ahead and finish us out, okay?"

Shiloh wrapped up the discussion, and about ten minutes later, ended with prayer.

When everyone was gone except Shiloh and Jade, and they were walking through the education wing shutting off lights, Jade paused and turned to her.

"Thank you for tonight, Shiloh. I guess I'm not as ready as I thought I was to lead this study."

Shiloh touched her arm, but she didn't know what to say. Tonight hadn't gone well, and Shiloh was concerned that if the awkwardness continued, the women might stop coming and dissuade others from participating, too. At the same time, she remembered Randy's admonition, and also what God had dropped into her spirit a few weeks ago: Jade's interest in being here and helping lead the study might be him doing something in particular with her, or through her.

"Don't worry about it, Jade," Shiloh said. "We all start somewhere. But you do seem a bit perplexed by how to get the women talking, or engaged in the topic you've presented. Maybe we can think about how to lead the study together, with me covering certain parts and you handling others—at least until they get used to both of us teaching."

Jade was on the verge of tears, but instead of allowing them to fall, she inhaled and mustered a smile. "Didn't you know? I'm only comfortable with makeup, fashion, shoes, and shopping."

Shiloh's eyes widened, and Jade nodded. "Yeah—I know that's what the ladies of St. Stephens Baptist think about me and say about me behind my back. They think I'm shallow and dumb. I'm not, you know; but I admit that I don't know my Bible like I should. Vic and I have been married twelve years, but he has never required me to study. He does his thing and I do mine. We pray together, but we read the Bible on our own. I guess I need to do a little more studying before I lead our Wednesday sessions. It's important for me to be a part of this group, Shiloh."

Shiloh wasn't sure how to take this vulnerable version of Jade. She was convinced more than ever that Jade's hormones were raging and she must be expecting. When Jade wanted her to know, she'd tell her.

"You *are* a part of this group, Jade," Shiloh said. "Don't feel obligated to lead the group just to belong. Chime in when you want, or sit there and soak in the wisdom and the Word. Just come and be you."

Shiloh hoped Jade didn't think she was nudging her toward a lesser role to regain sole leadership of the Bible study. She was sincere about Jade getting acclimated, and maybe once she began reading her

Bible more, and got used to the format of the study, she'd feel more confident about teaching.

Jade sighed. "You're right," she said. "I need to come for a while to get to know everyone better, and what you all do. Our church is so large that it's easy to see people Sunday after Sunday and not really know them. It's better to take it slow, for that reason alone. I guess I was jumping the gun in trying to step in stride with you right off the bat."

Shiloh was tempted to remind Jade that she'd been at St. Stephens Baptist for nearly two years and teaching the Bible study that entire time. The fact that Jade had chosen to come to a few studies before declaring herself a lead teacher of the class was only part of the reason Shiloh and some of the other women had become resentful; her sudden interest in even attending after all these years had also left them questioning her motives.

"Plus," Jade continued, "you've known this Bible stuff since you could talk; you're a PK, which makes you the perfect preacher's wife. I'm learning on the job."

She flipped her hair and in the process, seemed to switch on her confidence. "So thanks for moving forward with the Bible study class as you have been," Jade said and gave Shiloh a light hug. "I'll pop in as often as I can, but only as a student for the time being."

Jade's megawatt smile returned, and Shiloh marveled at the transformation. This woman was a work of art, and certainly not a piece that could be easily understood.

Monica strolled into class the following morning and almost made it to her seat before Shiloh recognized her.

Shiloh strode over to the girl and bent low, to peer into her eyes. "Who are you?"

Monica giggled. "What?"

Her usually mile-high soft afro had been replaced by copper brown straightened hair that flowed past her shoulders to the middle of her small back. She had one side swooped across her forehead for a dramatic bang, and the other tucked behind an ear, which bore a small pearl earring, and she wore a hint of sheer lip gloss. She could pass for the teenage sister of Jada Pinkett Smith, in a taller, but otherwise just as petite, package.

"Wow."

Shiloh had noted the girl's beauty when she met her on the first day of class. With this transformation, Monica was stunning.

"Who are you? Where is Monica?"

Monica laughed. "Did I look bad before or something? You didn't like my afro?"

"I loved your afro," Shiloh said. "It was beautiful and artsy. This is the sophisticated, grown-up version of Miss Monica, I guess. And you look great either way."

Monica smirked. "Hmm, hmmm. You adults like this straightened hair, corporate look, don't you? The other is just so much easier to take care of. But I could get used to this."

Phaedra sidled over. "And especially all of the attention you're getting from the fine boys, right?"

The girls grinned at each other.

"Did you see Trey Holloman checking you out?" Phaedra whispered the question in amazement.

"You're kidding!" Monica whispered back.

The girls leaned toward each other, and into their conversation, forgetting that Shiloh completed their circle. Though they were oblivious to her presence, Shiloh tried to mask her surprise. This was a first, too. Both girls were lovely, but they had always seemed more focused on their music and their studies than on the routine teenage socializing and romantic drama that often came with it. Maybe they had been interested all along, she surmised, but had used their other interests to mask what they thought they were lacking.

"Girl, you should have listened to your grandmama a long time ago," Phaedra said. "That straight hair and lip gloss is the truth! Got the men trippin' over you!"

"Men?" Shiloh raised an eyebrow and folded her arms.

The girls turned toward her, startled that she was still standing there.

"Oh, you know what we meant, Mrs. Griffin. Young men— boys," Phaedra said.

Shiloh shook her head and walked away. Monica's grandmother may not know what she had started. That statement-making, but unassuming, afro may have kept sweet little Monica a little more focused. And safe. With the reaction she was getting this morning, she might never go back.

Twenty-one

That day, Shiloh struggled to maintain discipline in class for the first time, and it was her favorite student's fault.

Monica's new look was the talk of the entire band period, among the girls and the guys. Half the girls were hating on her, while the other half were trying to figure out how she had gone from thick and poofy one day, to straight and sleek the next.

The boys couldn't focus, notes were being missed, and chatter ensued like never before. If Shiloh weren't trying to get the group prepared for the upcoming fall recital, their reaction to a simple style change might have been laughable. Instead, she was frustrated.

She rapped on her music stand to silence them, and tried to do so without bringing any more attention to Monica.

"Okay, everyone. We have to pay attention. Let's get it together!"

They managed to practice three songs, but none were up to par, as far as Shiloh was concerned.

Monica seemed both self-conscious and exhilarated by the stir she had caused. She and Phaedra exchanged glances and giggles the entire period. Shiloh prayed that the inner beauty and sweetness she knew Monica possessed wouldn't get lost in her new outer fabulousness. But if this look that her grandmother had convinced her to try wowed the summer camp audition judges like her grandmother was hoping, more power to her.

Later that morning, as Shiloh strolled to the teachers' lounge, she saw Monica in a position she hadn't witnessed before—staring into the eyes of a boy, who seemed to be saying just what she wanted to hear. Shiloh fought the urge to walk over and snatch her away, and her reaction surprised her. She was fretting over this girl like an overprotective aunt. What was the big deal? What teenage girl didn't want to have a high school romance? Many did have them, and Monica wasn't doing anything inappropriate.

Still, when she saw Monica take the guy's phone number and walk away with a grin as wide as a half moon, Shiloh knew the rest of the girl's day, and semester, were going to take on a life of their own. When the boy turned and walked in the opposite direction with a smug grin of his own, Shiloh understood.

He wasn't just any boy. This was Trey Holloman, Sherman Park's handsome star quarterback and citywide Student Athlete of the Year. And, according to all of the girls Shiloh had overhead talking, also the school's most eligible bachelor.

Shiloh was excited for Monica on one hand to see what must be her high school dating dreams come true, but on the other, fearful that a distraction like this might take her way off course. She told herself to relax; her eldest son was dating occasionally, despite his continued interest in Lia from Alabama, and balancing his school work, and so did many other teens in their church. For some reason, she felt extra-protective of Monica, though. Shiloh wasn't sure if it was because of their twin interest in the flute, because the girl's mother was deceased and couldn't monitor and shepherd her, or because she didn't want Monica's sweet spirit marred by boy drama and issues of the heart before she was ready.

She made a mental note to call Columbia College Chicago when she returned to her desk and find out how soon they would alert students about their acceptance to the summer music program. If Monica made it in, at least she'd have a reason to focus on that, more so than on Trey Holloman.

Jade showed up for Bible study the next Wednesday, but sat in the back and didn't say much. The week after that, she didn't come at all.

Shiloh considered giving her a call the morning after she missed, but what she learned over breakfast—or rather, what Randy discovered as he read the morning paper—stunned her into inaction.

The two oldest boys were teasing Randy for continuing to read the print version of the *Milwaukee Journal Sentinel* every morning rather than going online like most modern people, when he held up his palm to interrupt them.

"Well, I'll be," he said. "Reverend Vic has a beauty queen on his hands again."

Shiloh paused midstroke in brushing David's hair and frowned.

"What was that?"

"Jade Devereaux Smith has won the Mrs. Milwaukee pageant and will compete for the Mrs. Wisconsin title and ten thousand dollars in prizes next month, in Fond du Lac."

Lem and Omari exchanged glances.

"Well, Dad," Omari said, "she *is* fine."

Lem nodded and sat back in his chair. He folded his arms and grinned. "I think she can win."

Shiloh couldn't believe them, or the news itself. "Maybe that's why she missed Bible study last night. She's focused on the beauty pageant scene again. With a busy husband and two young kids? What on earth?"

"Wonder why Vic didn't give me a heads-up," Randy said. He folded the newspaper and set it aside. "That couple is something else. Oh well, if that's what she wants to do, all the best to her, and to their family."

Shiloh shook her head, and because of the boys' presence, decided not to utter what she would have otherwise shared with her husband: She could have sworn that Jade's recently erratic behavior was due to her being pregnant. If she had entered a pageant, that clearly wasn't the case. Now Shiloh was even more curious, though, about what was going on with Jade. She was too young for a midlife crisis, and young Nicholas was too old for her to just now be suffering from postpartum depression. What gave?

Twenty-three

A busy day at school relegated Shiloh's questions about Jade to the background until dinnertime. When the family gathered around the table that evening, Randy shared that Vic had shrugged off questions about Jade's pageant preparations, but seemed proud of her victory. Lem turned the conversation to the family's Thanksgiving plans just as Shiloh placed a peach cobbler on the table for dessert.

"So . . . ," Lem said, and dipped a healthy spoonful of the cobbler into a dessert bowl, followed by a scoop of French vanilla ice cream. "When were you thinking we'd leave for Alabama this year? Right after school on the Tuesday before Thanksgiving, or on Wednesday morning?"

Randy and Shiloh looked at one another. Although Dayna had made the invitation to Florida weeks ago, in the rush of the new school year they had forgotten to tell the kids that plans for Thanksgiving had changed. How was Lem going to take this? He had a serious case of puppy love. Better to break the news now, Shiloh mused, rather than allow him to continue making plans to see Lia in November.

"Lem, we're doing something different this year," Shiloh began. "Aunt Dayna and Uncle Warren will be moving into their new house soon, and they're inviting the family to come to Florida this Thanksgiving."

"Yes!" David pumped his fist in the air and Raphael replicated the move.

"Disney World, here we come!" Raphael beamed.

Randy shook his head. "Don't get your hopes up, son. We are going for a quick holiday visit. We may not make it to the theme park this time around. I haven't ruled out going back for spring break, since we'll be able to stay with family, but we may only be able to enjoy Thanksgiving dinner and to see the family this time. I've got to get back by Saturday, so I can preach on Sunday."

David and Raphael's faces fell.

"Can't someone else preach for you so we can stay longer and go to the park?" Raphael asked. "How about Reverend Victor?"

Randy took a bite of the cobbler Shiloh placed in front of him. "Hmmm, good stuff, babe," he told her before responding to Raphael. "Raphie, Reverend Vic's wife will be busy competing in a pageant the week before Thanksgiving. I don't want to add to his responsibilities."

Raphael contorted his face into a sour-lemon expression only a pre-adolescent boy could muster when it came to talk of a married mother participating in a pageant.

"I thought that kind of thing was for young people—ladies in their twenties or something," he said. "How old is Mrs. Smith, and can she do that if she's married and has kids?"

Shiloh laughed out loud. "Obviously she can," she said. "For this pageant, you have to be married; it's the *Mrs.* Wisconsin pageant, so all of the contestants have husbands, and I'm pretty sure that quite a few of them have children."

This time the practical eighth grader, Omari, chimed in. "What sense does it make to have a Mrs. Whatever pageant? Sounds to me like something for old ladies who think they still got it and need to be pumped up. Is she paying to participate?"

Lem frowned. "Didn't you just say she was fine? That means she does still have it, dude."

Omari shrugged. "Why does she have to prove it to everyone else, though? Especially if it's costing money."

Randy beamed and bumped fists with Omari. "That's how you're supposed to think! What's the cost here? You, my son, are going to be my millionaire."

Omari grinned.

Shiloh rolled her eyes. "Ya'll are something else," she said. "Enough talk about Sister Jade; we're bordering on gossip."

Shiloh didn't share that she agreed with Omari's assessment—for some reason Jade must need to feel good about herself. The article in the paper said the winner would receive ten thousand dollars in prizes, including five thousand in cash. Unless Sister Jade was using pageant dresses and shoes she already owned—which Shiloh knew was unlikely—girlfriend might on her own spend up to the cash gift amount getting prepared for the competition.

"Back to what we were originally discussing—our family trip to Florida," Shiloh said. She turned to Randy for support, but he was scarfing down more cobbler.

"Lem, it's settled; we're going to Florida as Dad said, not Alabama," Shiloh said. "I'm not sure when we'll visit Atchity, since your grandparents are coming for Thanksgiving and we'll get to see them at Dayna's."

A range of emotions crossed Lem's face. Shiloh started to respond, but waited, knowing any platitudes she offered right now would rub him wrong. She didn't know much about this girl Lia, but Shiloh had never seen him this upset. He finally nodded to indicate that he accepted the decision, and ate the rest of his dessert in silence.

Later that evening, when Shiloh was upstairs loading the washer, she heard Lem chatting and laughing, and also the voice of a girl. She paused to listen more carefully. Surely he hadn't snuck someone into his bedroom . . .

She tiptoed down the hall and peeked inside his door, which was slightly ajar. Lem's back was to her, and he was sitting cross-legged on his bed peering at his computer screen, at a lovely, honey-brown girl with long, spiral-curled hair that fell just below her chin. They weren't on Skype, but it was obviously a similar program.

She shifted accidentally and the door creaked open, startling Lem. "Mom . . ."

Shiloh opened the door all the way. Might as well enter now, since she'd been busted. She stepped inside and walked over to his bed, to get a better glimpse of the girl, who must be Lia.

The teenager saw her approaching and waved. "Hi, Mrs. Griffin. How are you?"

Well, now. How polite.

"Well, hello . . ." Shiloh looked to Lem, not wanting to assume who she was and be completely wrong.

Lem fidgeted with embarrassment, but his home training prevailed. "Uh, Lia, this is my mom; Mom, meet Lia."

"Hi, Lia. I've heard nice things about you. Did you enjoy the summer science program as much as Lem?"

Lia nodded and smiled. "Yes, ma'am. It has made me rethink my whole career path. I'm still going to be an engineer, but now I can make a decision about the best form of engineering to pursue, since I've had exposure to all of the options."

"That's great, young lady," Shiloh said. "Keep up the good work."

"Thank you, Mrs. Griffin. Lemuel just told me that your family won't be coming to Alabama for Thanksgiving, but I hope to meet you at some other time."

"Do you have family in Atchity?"

"No, ma'am," Lia said. "My family lives in a small town near Birmingham, and I attend a magnet school in Birmingham. I enjoyed the summer program at Alabama U, though. I'm applying again next year."

Shiloh was about to mention that she had attended college in Birmingham and ask more about Lia's magnet high school, but Lem shifted on his bed—her cue that she had stayed too long.

"Nice to meet you, Lia. Take care."

She waved goodbye and when she was out of the girl's line of view, winked at Lem, who blushed. Shiloh closed the door but left it cracked, as it had been before.

So that was Miss Lia, she mused, and headed downstairs to the family room. Not bad at all.

Twenty-four

The clarity of the flute solo was so sweet and pure that Shiloh almost wept. She sat at her teacher post in the band room this morning and listened with her eyes closed as Monica perfectly played every note of "Russian Dance," one of the pieces the girl had chosen for the summer program audition.

When she blew the final note, her best buddy Phaedra erupted into applause. But Monica shushed her. "Be quiet! I want to hear what Mrs. Griffin has to say!"

Shiloh could tell the girl's nerves were on edge, and truthfully, because she was rooting so hard for Monica, hers were, too. Monica's life would change for the better if she were selected for this summer program. Both of these girls' lives could change, because Phaedra had decided to audition, too.

"Wonderful and sassy, Monica. Way to go. I think you'll nail it. Just stay focused. And keep practicing every day between now and the audition. You will be great."

Shiloh swiveled her chair to the right to face Phaedra, who was strapping on her saxophone so she could play her audition pieces.

"Show me what you got, missy," Shiloh challenged her.

Phaedra grinned. With a toss of her head, which was covered in spiky natural curls, she launched into the first of two sax solos that were bluesy and filled with personality, just like Phaedra herself. Shiloh closed her eyes as she listened. Wouldn't it be awesome if both of these young ladies were accepted? Both were worthy.

"I know Monica plans to turn her love of music into a career; you're just as good," Shiloh told Phaedra. "Do you want to major in music in college as well?"

Phaedra shook her head. "No . . . I'm thinking of sitting out the first semester of college, so I can figure what I love most and where I want to be."

Shiloh was shocked, and the pronouncement seemed to catch Monica off guard, too. The girls traded stares, and finally Phaedra nodded.

"That's right—I said it!" Phaedra said. "I've been trying to tell you, and my parents, for a while that I need to spread my wings. Why waste money on a year of college when I have no idea what I'll do with it?"

Phaedra turned to Shiloh. "Aren't I being wise in doing that?"

Shiloh pursed her lips and prayed that the right words would come. "In some ways, yes, my dear," she said. "But look at the big picture: If you enter college ready to learn, and take all of the classes you want, not just those that are required, you'll be arming yourself with information about a variety of subjects and potential career paths that can help you understand yourself better and figure out what you're passionate about. Sometimes that can happen inside a classroom, on a college campus. Otherwise, unless you're planning to travel the world or do something else out of the norm, you won't be exposing yourself to anything new and different to help you figure out what you might want to do long term. Understand what I'm saying?"

Phaedra nodded.

"Well, that's just my two cents' worth; I'm sure you and your parents will decide what's best. You just keep practicing these audition pieces for now so you can get into this summer program. Even that is going to make a difference in how you see the world; you just wait. Don't rule out college yet, though. It's definitely not for everyone, but it can be a good path to find your way."

Phaedra laid the saxophone on a seat next to her and approached Shiloh for a hug. Monica pouted.

"She was mine first!" she said and dashed over to flank Shiloh on the opposite side.

Shiloh laughed and opened her arms to encircle both girls. With the three of them nearly being the same height, it was a perfect Kodak moment.

"My girls," she said. "I'm going to miss you when I leave soon."

"We don't want Mrs. Helmsley to come back," Phaedra said. "She's nice and all, but you make this class much more fun. You get us. I don't even mind practicing."

"Yeah, yeah, yeah," Shiloh said. She smirked, but inside she was smiling, grateful that in this short time, she had managed to bond with these sweet girls, and make an impact on the students in both of her classes. Several students had told her so after the principal announced last week that Mrs. Helmsley would be returning in time to lead the fall concert.

"We mean it," Monica said. "You're the first person who hasn't laughed at my dream or told me to focus on majoring in a 'real' subject so I can get a real job. I've begun researching colleges where I can study music, and some of them have great fellowship opportunities just for flutists. I would love to travel abroad and spend a whole summer just playing my flute, and thanks to you, I've found programs that could make it possible."

Monica's eyes glistened as she ran through the options, and Shiloh's heart soared and sank. *Please God, don't let her follow in my exact footsteps.*

"See?" Monica tapped her cell phone and pulled up a website featuring a list of colleges and universities with respected music programs. There in front of her, eighth on the list, was Shiloh's almost-alma mater, Birmingham-Southern, and listed in italics just beneath the college's name was the Leake Memorial Fellowship that had afforded her with ten weeks of flute studies in Paris, France. That trip had been life-changing in more ways than one, both beautiful and tragic.

"Which schools do you think would be best, beyond the well-renowned ones everyone knows?" Monica asked. "Where did you go again?"

Shiloh turned away and pretended to sort through the sheets of music on her stand. "The one in Birmingham. It's a good school, but you don't want a program that far away from home, do you?"

She hoped her voice wasn't trembling and that the girls couldn't see her shaky hands. Shiloh took a few deep breaths, then praised God for allowing the bell that served as a pronouncement of the start of the school day to ring. She wasn't sure she would have been able to fake her excitement for Monica much longer—not when the dream Monica was chasing was the one that had simultaneously inspired and derailed her life.

Twenty-five

Most of the St. Stephens congregation had read the newspaper article or heard through the church "gossipvine" that Sister Jade was back on the beauty pageant circuit by the time Reverend Vic made a formal announcement the first Sunday of October.

He strode to the pulpit after Randy's sermon and invited Jade to join him.

Shiloh wondered why they had waited until after the Mrs. Milwaukee pageant to share her involvement. Whatever the reason, he stood next to Jade this afternoon appearing proud and thrilled.

"I just wanted to let you all know that my beautiful wife has decided to keep our family on our toes this fall. Many of you know Jade once competed in pageants, and looking at her, we can still see how and why."

Vic grinned at Jade, who blushed and lowered her eyes. Shiloh stifled a laugh, and for once, wished she were in the pulpit or the choir, so she could see the reactions of the women seated behind her. As much as they doted on Vic, they could barely tolerate Jade. She knew they weren't being polite.

"After two children, she is still fit and fabulous enough to grace a stage."

Randy cleared his throat, and Vic got the message to hurry along.

"It is my honor to introduce to you the new Mrs. Milwaukee! She was crowned last Wednesday evening!"

The news was greeted with healthy, but staid applause. Vic accepted it.

"Her ride is not over: The new title will afford her the opportunity

104 / LEAD ME HOME

to compete in the Mrs. Wisconsin pageant the weekend before Thanksgiving. If you're so inclined, please give her your support and your prayers."

Vic passed the microphone to Jade.

"Good afternoon, everyone. As Reverend Vic indicated, I'll be representing Milwaukee and our church family in the Mrs. Wisconsin pageant. My talent will be singing and I'll also do an oratorical speech. It has been a whirlwind, but exciting, journey, since I decided to enter at the last minute. But I'm enjoying meeting other wives and mothers from around the state, and many of them are people of deep faith, so they have been a blessing to me. Please keep me in your prayers, and if you're interested in coming to the big night, see me after service, and I'll give you some information about purchasing tickets."

"Yaay, Mommy!"

Naima's show of support yielded laughter, and another round of applause—this one much larger than Jade or Vic had been able to garner on their own. Jade blushed and gave the mike back to her husband, before stepping down from the pulpit with his assistance. Shiloh knew Jade was glad Nicholas was in the nursery; otherwise he might have chimed in, too.

Minutes later, when the congregation circulated row by row to the front of the sanctuary to place their gifts in the offering plate, Shiloh felt a light touch on her arm and turned to peer into a set of hazel eyes she recognized. Monica gave her a light hug, and the woman behind her smiled and took Shiloh's hand. She was tall, thin, and coffee-bean brown, and her features hinted at what an age-progressed, tanned version of Monica might look like decades from now. The man right behind her wore a suit and a bright smile that mirrored Monica's. His skin was honey yellow like hers, and his wavy, silver hair added to his distinguished aura. He, too, shook Shiloh's hand and squeezed it gently, as if in recognition of who she was.

Randy blessed the offering, rendered the benediction, and encouraged everyone to spend the week making a difference by showing God's love. Seconds later, Jade positioned herself near a rear door of the sanctuary with Naima to distribute flyers about the pageant. Shiloh avoided the spectacle by making her way to Monica and her family to officially welcome them.

The woman who had accompanied Monica leaned toward Shiloh and offered a hug. "Hi, I'm Eleanor. Thank you so much for helping my granddaughter prepare for the summer music camp. She is so excited, and she's feeling pretty confident, thanks to you."

Shiloh smiled and hugged Monica. "You are very welcome. You have a very sweet and talented young lady here. I'm sure she will do whatever she sets her mind to, and do it well."

The man with Monica extended his hand. "I'm Claude, Monica's dad," he said. "Thanks from me as well. My wife died about two years ago, and since then, I haven't seen Monica come home excited about anything until now. You've really helped her, Mrs. Griffin, more than you know."

He looked past Shiloh before she could respond, and when she followed him with her eyes, she realized Randy was standing behind her.

"This young lady hugging my wife must be the student she's always talking about, and you two must be her lucky parents. Randy Griffin."

Claude shook his hand.

"Nice to meet you, Reverend. Yes, this is my daughter Monica, and this other 'young' lady is my mother, Eleanor Garrett. We were blessed by that message today. I have to admit, we haven't been here in a while . . . but we'll be back."

He looked at his mother, and Eleanor nodded. Monica looked from one to the other, and still embracing Shiloh, seemed happier than Shiloh had ever seen her.

Twenty-six

The month of October flew by, and Shiloh's countdown to the end of the week was growing more bittersweet by the hour.

In three more days, she would no longer be a faculty member at Sherman Park High. The job she hadn't thought she was capable of succeeding in would come to an end way before she was ready. These eight weeks had awakened a desire to finish the music education degree she abandoned all those years ago. She enjoyed teaching more than she had expected, and for the first time in a long time, she regretted dropping out of college. Her reasons had made all the sense in the world at the time. She and Randy had finally gotten serious after she returned from France, and he proposed before her summer break ended. When he suggested they get married right away, she decided to give up her studies. Mama and Daddy had been ecstatic. Neither had even asked what that decision would mean for her dreams of playing the flute professionally, or of graduating from her well-regarded college.

Shiloh thought about that now and willed the rising resentment to dissipate. She couldn't blame Mama and Daddy for the decisions she'd made in an effort to gain God's mercy for the awful things she'd done over the course of her sophomore year. Did her current frustration with those long-ago choices mean she wasn't truly sorry for what she had done? She sat at her desk this afternoon and frowned as she mulled over this question.

Maybe the issues she was pining over were the thorn in her side that she'd live with forever, as a reminder that despite God's grace, one's actions always mattered. Everyone faced consequences, good or bad.

She kept returning to the reality that her lack of a degree hadn't seemed to matter as she helped her students perfect their pitch, learn a particular passage of music, or nail a musical score's pacing. Passion and practical experience seemed to make up for what she would have learned in a theory or educational instruction course, but to be fair, she was making that judgment on emotion. She had not assessed her skills in relationship to Mrs. Helmsley's.

Even so, Dr. Carter had assured her that he would keep her on his substitute teacher list. Because she didn't yet have a bachelor's degree, she would always be called last, and only to fill in for music teachers, after all certified substitute teachers passed on the opportunity. That was fair, and she was grateful he was willing to work with her. The message she often preached to her older sons was hitting home: Ultimately, that piece of paper did matter, and as much fun as she was having, she'd never be able to do this long-term if she didn't someday finish college. What would Randy say if she hinted that she wanted to try?

Twenty-seven

Somehow during her tenure at Sherman High, Shiloh never got around to telling her colleagues about her lack of a degree, and by this point, it didn't make sense to bring it up. The students raved about her to their other teachers, and Kris and Eva, the two teachers she spent the most time with because of their mutual breaks and downtime in the teacher's lounge, hadn't asked or seemed to care.

She hoped her friendship with them would last, and she was excited when on Thursday morning, the day before the end of her tenure, the ladies invited her to dinner.

"We're going to miss you," Kris said. "Let us take you out and treat you. Next time you come to sub, we'll just wave and treat you like nothing special. But your inaugural eight-week stint has made you one of us."

Shiloh grinned. "That's sweet, Kris. Let's see, tonight my sons Raphael and David have Little League football practice . . . But maybe I can get my husband to take them, just this once. Let me check with him and let you know before lunchtime."

Six hours later, after preparing dinner for her family and teaching a private flute lesson, Shiloh was sitting in a cozy restaurant in Racine, a nearby suburb, eating a huge plate of pasta and laughing at Kris and Eva's anonymous stories about their students' antics.

"I look at the kids I'm teaching, and then at my overconfident four-year-old daughter, and I wonder what happens between those ages that causes us to stop dreaming, to stop trusting that our true selves are okay, and to put on a mask to fit in with the world," Kris said and sighed. "I mean, I have at least three intelligent and thoughtful young ladies in orchestra, and a couple of young men, who clearly lack the self-confidence to speak up for themselves when the other kids tease them or put them down. They know their stuff and can run circles around entire classes. If they could believe in themselves, they could go so far. It's sad, really. Some of them could ace college, but if they stay where they are now, they'll go, but either limp to a degree or not finish at all. They'll drop the ball on the blessing that awaits them."

Kris took a sip of her drink. "Sorry—didn't mean to get on my soap box, but that kind of stuff just eats away at me."

Shiloh and Eva shook their heads.

"No, sista, we are with you!" Eva said. The "sista" sounded quirky in her Vietnamese accent, but she said it with such passion that Shiloh wanted to hug her.

"I see it with my history students, too," Eva said. "They don't live up to their potential, because it isn't cool to excel academically or to go the extra mile in other ways. Even at this magnet school. It's troubling."

She furrowed her brow. "Then, three nights a week, I go over to the local community college and teach English as a second language and see immigrants from Myanmar, the Sudan, Nepal, and other places working two or three jobs, going to school, and taking my class so they can succeed. It perplexes me!"

Shiloh didn't have school stories to relate, and in truth, the conversation led her back to her own youth, and to the summer she had given up her flute scholarship and her degree program and settled for the role of wife and mother. She had gotten pregnant with Lem soon after she and Randy wed, and that was the way both of them had wanted it. Listening to her colleagues, she wondered what they would think of her choices, especially if they knew what had led her to them. She sipped her tea and fixed a smile on her face.

It was so easy to make judgments, from the outside looking in, she thought, and become frustrated with others' actions or lack of action, especially when one wanted so much for them. But what if those students who seemed on the verge of greatness were dealing with a dying relative, an abusive home life, or a secret illness? From her own troubling experiences, Shiloh had come to understand that smiles could hide a lot, and so could seemingly perfect choices.

She decided to chime in on the conversation when she realized there was an awkward silence that Kris and Eva were waiting for her to fill.

"I can't say much about the school setting since my students are so new to me, and I love them all," Shiloh said, "but raising four sons with four different personalities and sets of needs has been my own mini-classroom. So has working with my private flute students one-on-one. Some of them come to me bringing nothing but their eagerness and determination to learn to play. A few seem to have this natural ability, and can even play a little by ear, but their motivation is mediocre. If I could get my naturally talented students to practice and to care as much as my hard-working beginners, they would amaze themselves. And make me look like a rock star instructor!"

The women laughed long and hard.

"Tell me about your husband's church," Eva said and leaned forward. "St. Stephens is a pretty big congregation, right? I attend the Korean Christian Church around the corner from where your church is located; I should come and visit sometime."

Shiloh graced Eva with a "yeah, right" stare. This was one of those times she had to take the risk of offending, to gain some clarity.

"The Korean Christian Church? I thought you were Vietnamese, Eva. Did I miss something?"

Kris and Eva looked at each other and erupted in laughter again.

Shiloh shrugged and joined in, certain they'd fill her in on the punch line in a few minutes.

When Eva caught her breath, she sat up and reached for Shiloh's hand. "It's alright, Shiloh. You are right. I am Vietnamese—born and raised. But when I moved to Milwaukee, I stumbled upon the Korean church, two days after moving into my new neighborhood. I decided to worship there until I got connected to the local Vietnamese community. They gave me some strange looks when I walked in and explained as best I could that I couldn't understand a word of the Korean they spoke to welcome me. But they accepted me anyway. That day I got so 'connected' that I fell in love with the members of that little church, and with their style of worship, and I never left. I was a duck amid a lake of geese, and I was happy as a lark."

She grinned and shook her head.

"Even after I settled into the Vietnamese community, I stayed at my new church. It offended some of my new friends, especially the older Vietnamese folks, but I decided it was home. So yes, as odd as it sounds, I am Vietnamese American, worshiping a Christian God who was born a Jew, at a Korean Baptist Church, located in a predominantly black neighborhood in a Milwaukee suburb. Welcome to America."

Shiloh was speechless. In two minutes, several ingrained stereotypes had been shattered. It was a wake-up call that she might need to step outside her comfort zone of accepting a segregated Sunday worship experience. Even with Warren as a brother-in-law, she hadn't shaken that notion.

Shiloh raised her palm and held it out to Eva, who responded with a light slap. "Amen, my sister," Shiloh said. "When you visit St. Stephens Baptist I want you to stand up and repeat that story word for word."

"Deal," Eva said. "I'd love to visit soon. Especially since I won't get to see you at school on a regular basis anymore. It will be great to have Thelma back, and I'm so thankful that her mother is doing much better, but you will be missed, Shiloh."

"Aw, thanks, Eva. Thanks to both of you," Shiloh said, including Kris, who sat there and nodded in agreement with Eva's sentiments. "You guys are so kind and smart and open. I've learned a lot about teaching and about education and how to care for students by getting to know you. I'm nowhere near as good as you are, but you still accepted me, and I thank you for that.

"I would love for you to visit me at St. Stephens Baptist. You both are welcome anytime. Kris, I don't know anything about your background, but Eva, I'll warn you that a black Baptist church is totally different from what you've probably experienced."

Eva nodded. "I watch T. D. Jakes, though; I have some idea."

Kris shook her head and her dreads flew in both directions.

"Unh unh, honey. Watching T. D. Jakes ain't shown you nothing. You've had tip-of-the-iceberg exposure. Go to a service in person if you want to see God's people get their shout on, dance in the aisles, or sing at the top of their lungs, as if God is hard of hearing."

Shiloh pursed her lips. "Don't you think that's a little stereotypical?"

Kris shrugged and perused the dessert menu. "I haven't been to church in five years, but I could tell you like it had been yesterday what all goes on. My grandfather was a church trustee, my dad was a deacon, and one of my uncles was an evangelist. I grew up around all the pomp and circumstance and finally decided to have some quiet time with the Lord on my own terms, without pastors, or busybody parishioners who want to run the church and everybody's lives."

Shiloh picked up her dessert menu and pretended to scan it, unsure of how to respond on such a serious matter of faith with someone who was a coworker. Regardless of Kris's perspective, she wasn't going to judge her, nor did she feel it was her place to make her friend feel uncomfortable about her position. When conversations like this arose out of the blue, Shiloh always took it as a sign that God was stirring a pot for whatever reason, and in his time, the seeds that had been planted today would be watered as he saw fit.

"Is dancing and shouting all you got?" Eva's fifty-two-year-old attempts at swagger were killing Shiloh.

"Please stop, Eva," she said and held up a hand. "I can't take anymore. The kids at Sherman Park have ruined you!"

Eva's eyes twinkled. "Just picture me going home and translating all of this American slang into Vietnamese for my parents," she said and laughed. "It makes for some very interesting conversations!"

By the time the evening ended, with all three ladies enjoying the largest slices of chocolate cake Shiloh had ever feasted on, they were satisfied and mutually sleepy. It was half past eight, and each of them needed to get children settled at home, so they could be up and at it again tomorrow.

Kris, Eva, and Shiloh agreed to not let this be the last time they hung out, and Kris even agreed that their next meet up could possibly be at a St. Stephens worship service.

"If Eva's woman enough to come, I'll join her," Kris said.

Shiloh left the restaurant certain about one other thing: This was an experience—from teaching to forming friendships outside of her role as First Lady—that she didn't want to become little more than a memory. Based on the cursory online research she'd conducted this afternoon, she had at least eighteen months of study plus a student teaching assignment before she could officially become a teacher.

Is this where you are leading me, Lord?

He seemed to be saying yes, because the desire to return to school and eventually obtain her teaching license was mushrooming. Now God had to do just one other thing: Let Randy in on the plan, and maybe even allow him to think it was his idea.

Twenty-eight

Shiloh hadn't heard from Jessica in several months, so when her younger sister's number popped up on the cell phone, she answered on the first ring, despite her weariness after a day at school and a lengthy dinner with her colleagues.

"How's the life of a busy world traveler?"

"Great," Jessica said. "How's the life of Florence Brady, minus the maid and the stepchildren, with a little Mother Teresa thrown in?"

Shiloh paused from her kitchen cleanup and smiled in spite of herself. She usually bristled at Jessica's biting wit, but over the past eight weeks she had honed her ability to deliver comebacks that left the instigator speechless. Had she known that's what working at a high school could do for you, she might have tried her hand at it sooner.

"Careful," Shiloh said. "The man upstairs has my back. After all, I'm one of his First Ladies."

Jessica was silent for a few seconds. "Shiloh?"

"Yes?"

"Okay . . . I'm just checking to make sure it's really you. Doesn't sound like the meek and mild sister I know."

That's because we don't talk often enough to really "know" one another.

Shiloh bit her tongue. What good would it do to alienate her sister further? At least Jessica was calling.

"I've been working in a high school for two months, and let's just say the kids there have helped me find some swagger I didn't know I had."

Another lengthy silence was followed by a simple reply: "Wow."

Shiloh smiled. "You okay?"

"The question is, are you? Do Mama and Daddy know you've been working? And on top of that, have a whole new attitude?"

"Alright, alright," Shiloh said. She was doing her best not to let latent resentments surface. She had never said anything all of these years, but Shiloh wasn't blind or dumb; she knew her sisters talked about her behind her back for quitting college to get married, and for starting a family before taking time to really live her life.

She knew they judged her for following in Mama's footsteps and marrying a preacher—Randy at that, rather than someone she met on her own. They whispered about her being too kind and too soft, and for trying to please her husband and let him lead. Shiloh knew it all. Even when she didn't have details about what was specifically said or how they were ridiculing her, she felt their disdain. For all of these years, it had hurt.

It stung to now hear Jessica all but admit some of her unwarranted opinions. Yet she felt ready with a comeback, grateful that her recent experiences had equipped her with a little more confidence, and a stronger sense of herself.

"What led you to call me, Miss Superstar? And how is my brother-in-law?"

"Keith is doing well," Jessica said. "He just got a promotion that keeps him pretty busy, which is good since I'm traveling quite a bit these days."

Shiloh wondered how they managed to have a solid relationship with Jessica's increasingly hectic speaking schedule, which had her crisscrossing the United States at least twice a week, and visiting foreign countries twice a year. They'd been married for several years, but Jessica had never hinted at wanting to start a family. This seemed to be working for them, but it was another sign of just how different the three Wilson sisters were: Dayna seemed to want the career and the stable family life; Shiloh had opted for family life instead of a career; and for Jessica, the career seemed her be-all and end-all. It made sense to Shiloh that she and Mama had the closest relationship of her three siblings; she was the one to whom Mama could most comfortably relate.

Surprisingly, Jessica said she was calling tonight with Mama and Daddy on her mind. "Dayna told me we are all confirmed for Thanksgiving at her new place, and that's great," Jessica said. "I thought it would be nice while we're all together to present Mama and Daddy with a joint gift for their upcoming wedding anniversary—a cruise, which is something they've never done before."

And something they probably had no desire to do. Mama hated water, and Daddy had to be in control. Didn't Jessica know that? Shiloh caught herself before the question crossed her lips.

"Well, what a nice idea," she said instead, employing the diplomacy she'd honed all these years as a preacher's wife. "Do you think we can convince them to get on a boat and stay for more than a two-hour dinner cruise? Mama acts like she gets seasick from that brief excursion alone."

Jessica chuckled. "You make a good point. I was trying to think of something special and different for them to do. And what I didn't finish saying was, I was thinking that as part of the gift, we could send them on the cruise, but also go ourselves, to make it a family vacation they'll always remember."

"Whoa, little sis," Shiloh said, putting away pots and pans while she talked. "You've forgotten I have four sons. That's six tickets for my household. Plus chipping in on the fee for Mama and Daddy. It sounds exciting, but unrealistic, with Lem going into his senior year next year and the expenses that will entail."

"That's even more of a reason to do it," Jessica said. Shiloh heard the familiar intensity in her voice that surfaced when Jessica became a bulldog about an idea and refused to let it go. It was the same intensity Shiloh had seen her use to inspire her audiences and leave them convinced that they could achieve whatever goal they set.

"Again, you didn't let me finish," Jessica said. "I know it would be asking a lot of your family, and truthfully, Dayna's too, having just built the new house. Keith and I have discussed it, and if you guys would be willing to pay for Mama and Daddy's airline tickets to the cruise port in Florida, Keith and I will pay for everyone else."

Shiloh pulled her phone away from her ear and stared at it. "Come again?"

"You heard me."

"Did Publishers Clearing House coming knocking at your door?"

"No, but Oprah did."

Shiloh loved and hated how Jessica trickled out information. "Jessica, you're killing me. Just tell me everything, okay? Save the dramatic effects for later."

"I've been selected to cohost a talk show on the OWN network, based on my work with college students, designed to help them successfully navigate young adult life—job hunting, success in the corporate world, and work-life balance. Oprah hosted a national contest about a year ago, looking for people with ideas for shows on her network. I kept it to myself when *LifeBound* was chosen as a finalist because I didn't want to jinx myself. We signed the contract last week, and it included a signing bonus—a very nice one. I'm making a donation to Daddy's church, but outside of that, I want to use this windfall to bring us together. I thought you and Dayna would feel better helping with the tickets for **Mama and** Daddy's flights to Miami, where we'll board the cruise, and the rest can be a gift from me. A gift for our family, to our family."

Shiloh was stunned. First, because her baby sister was about to become a national TV star, and second, because she was unselfish enough to surround herself with family before she began this amazing ride. This wasn't the Jessica Shiloh knew; God must be working on her, too.

Twenty-nine

Shiloh was still marveling over Jessica's generosity when she sauntered into the family room to find Omari and Raphael leaning forward on the sofa, ogling the flat-screen TV—or rather what was on the TV.

Shiloh was about to ask which action flick had captured their attention when she heard Jade's high-pitched voice. She trotted deeper into the room and paused behind the sofa, which floated in the middle of the room. Her ears hadn't fooled her; there was "Second Lady" Jade, doing a TV interview on the local Fox news station.

"It's an honor to represent Milwaukee in this manner, and I'm glad our citizens will have an opportunity to see and understand that beauty doesn't end in your twenties. We are seasoned women, some mothers, ranging in age from twenty-something to forty-something, and we are all representing our state well. I hope to walk away with the title of Mrs. Wisconsin next month, but mostly I want to make my husband and children proud."

The boys were transfixed. Shiloh shook her head at their unrepentant drooling. She had to grudgingly admit, though, that Jade was actually pretty good at public speaking, and as usual, she looked stunning. She wondered how and when Jade had landed the interview, and why she hadn't bragged about it.

Jade had shown up on Monday as usual to bring Naima for her private lesson, but as had been her practice lately, she disappeared to run errands rather than linger. Shiloh took in the fabulous teal dress Jade wore and wondered if a shopping spree had been one of her tasks that day. The color looked great on her.

Shiloh went to the computer desk in the family room and plugged in her cell phone to charge it, before texting Jade.

Good job. You are pageant ready. :)

She had been feeling smug about Jade's recent spotty attendance at Bible study, certain that Jade had decided to cop out rather than do what was needed to deepen her knowledge and teach effectively. It was clear that Jade had given up and moved on to something that felt more comfortable, and at which she could succeed. However, Shiloh knew she'd be wrong if she didn't pray about how Jade was feeling and keep encouraging her to return to the study. The few times she'd seen Jade at church and invited her back to the study, Jade promised to come in one breath while making an excuse in the next—no childcare (something she'd never had an issue with before), feeling under the weather (which seemed all too convenient lately), or a conflict due to the looming pageant.

Shiloh couldn't stop asking, though. She felt compelled to keep the door open, for reasons she couldn't articulate.

When she didn't receive an immediate reply to her text, she wondered if Jade was sitting somewhere, feeling smug. Wherever she was, Shiloh prayed that God would give her peace and an interest in studying the Bible more often, like she had indicated she would. Shiloh couldn't see a change in her through the brief television interview; but she had detected subtle changes in her attitude when she dropped off Naima for practice—no more scanning the house to gauge its cleanliness, nor chatting loudly on her cell about social events or impressive activities the everyday person didn't know existed. She'd even taken on some extra nursery duties at church lately, an indication that she was trying to do some things differently.

"Is Mrs. Smith famous?"

Shiloh leveled her eyes at Omari. "If she is, what are your plans?"

Omari gazed at the TV and shrugged. "I was just asking. I wonder how many people from church will actually go to the pageant to support her. We should go, you know? Her husband works with Dad; it's the right thing to do."

Shiloh raised an eyebrow.

"And I suppose the 'right thing to do' would include taking you and your brothers along, for support?"

David, who had gone unnoticed on the bean bag in the corner of the room, where he sat comfortably playing with his hand-held video device, piped up without looking Shiloh's way.

"Yeah—our family needs to support their family!"

"Which one of you bribed your brother to make that pitch?"

Shiloh put a hand on her hip, not wanting to believe her two middle sons had a crush on the married mother, with one of them routinely trying to nab the attention of Jade's daughter. Where did that leave Lem?

The silent question brought him top of mind. "Where is Lem?" Shiloh asked Omari and Raphael.

Raphael shrugged. "He was here a few minutes ago, until his phone rang. I think that girl from Alabama was calling. He always leaves the room when she calls."

Shiloh leaned over to rub the top of his head. "You just wait, Mr. Seventh Grader," she said. "I'm going to remind you of this complaint when you are sixteen and girls are calling you."

Shiloh stayed a few minutes longer to catch the weather report for tomorrow, and decided not to tell the boys yet about their aunt Jessica's grand plans for the family, or her talk show gig. None of them would get any sleep if she revealed all of that exciting news at this hour. Plus, she needed to discuss the cruise suggestion with Randy, to see if he would even go for it.

For now, she would prepare for her last day at Sherman Park High tomorrow, then call it a night. Bidding her students goodbye wasn't going to be easy. She hoped Mrs. Helmsley knew how fortunate she was. This first taste of a newfound passion wouldn't be her last.

Thirty

Shiloh would remember this day forever.

Her jazz band students started her waterworks by ending their first-period class with an instrumental serenade of a song they had been secretly practicing to play just for her: "It's So Hard to Say Goodbye to Yesterday" by Boys II Men. Students in her full band class showed up with balloons and a giant greeting card that one of the drummers, who happened to be artistic, had created so everyone could sign. Her seniors wrote personal notes of thanks in which each student shared at least one way she had helped that person grow as a musician. By the end of the day, Shiloh had emptied a box of tissues.

Kris and Eva strutted into the band room after the final bell rang that afternoon with three surprises: a red velvet cake, Sherman Park's principal, and Dr. Carter.

"I'll see you at church on Sunday, but I wanted to come out today and personally thank you for all you've done to help our students get through the start of school without missing a beat—no pun intended," Dr. Carter said. He was beaming. "I've received nothing but high praise about your teaching style and your professionalism, and you've been an asset to Sherman Park and to our school district."

Shiloh smiled in gratitude, because she had no words to convey how much this experience had meant to her. She wanted to hug him, but decided to save it for Sunday, when they'd be in a less formal environment, outside of their colleagues' watchful presence.

Sherman Park's principal did offer Shiloh a hug, and gave her a lovely plant as a parting gift.

"You have been a delight to have on staff, and Mrs. Helmsley is going to be so grateful for how you've kept the students on track," she said. "From listening in this week, I can tell that they'll be ready for the fall recital, and that's an accomplishment. If you ever need a letter of reference, don't hesitate to let me know."

Shiloh nodded her appreciation. Her thoughts immediately turned to the need for a recommendation for whatever university she applied to for her degree. She decided not to mention it now, but she'd soon be making that call.

Kris stepped forward with her cake, and Eva produced the napkins, paper plates, and forks.

"We thought we'd have a recap of dessert, since that went so well last night," Eva said.

Shiloh laughed. "You ladies are something else. Thank you— thank you so much."

She truly felt special, and almost undeserving. They didn't know what a big favor they'd done for her, by welcoming her so warmly and letting her jump right in to help the students. In stepping outside of the wife, mom, and church roles she loved, Shiloh had awakened some long dormant hopes and dreams, along with a few doubts. Why had God given her this opportunity, at this time in her life? On the anniversary date of a choice she'd be forever ashamed of making? Maybe, her heart told her, he was trying to replace the ashes of that day with a beautiful memory. That possibility gave her chills.

Kris passed her a hunk of cake and a fork and nudged her to dig in. Just as Shiloh took her first bite, Monica and Phaedra peeked into the room. They hesitated when they saw the other adults, but Shiloh motioned with her free hand for them to join her.

"Come on in, girls. It's okay," Shiloh said. Then she turned to Kris. "This cake is more than okay. It is amazing. Did you bake this?"

Kris grinned. "Stayed up half the night getting it ready for you, Miss Music Lady. A teacher's work is never done."

"Well, I am thankful, my friend." Shiloh took another bite and shook her head. "Something this good should be against the law."

Monica and Phaedra exchanged glances and giggles.

"We love that Southern 'foreign language' you speak, Mrs. G," Phaedra said.

Shiloh gave them a mock frown. "Watch it. Let me see you try this cake and talk straight."

Monica laughed. "No, thank you. We just wanted to stop by and get a hug, and . . ." She glanced at the principal before continuing. "If it's alright, find out how to get in touch with you when we learn whether we made it into the summer music program. Are we allowed to have your phone number?"

The principal swallowed her cake and shook her head. "That's not permitted, but you can come to me and ask me to relay a message to Mrs. Griffin for you. I'll make sure she gets it," she said.

Shiloh peered at the girls. Had the principal not been standing there, she would have whipped out her cell phone and plugged in their numbers without hesitation.

"All I know is that you better track me down when you get in," Shiloh said, trying to sound stern, and remembering that she already had Monica's email address, and had used it to forward her music for her audition. "The minute after you tell your parents and grandparents, I better be the next person you inform."

"You will, we promise!" Monica said.

"Especially since you're threatening us, and in front of other adults, too!" Phaedra laughed.

Shiloh set the plate she had used for her cake on her nearby desk and walked over to the girls to gather them in her arms.

"Group hug!" she said. "You two young ladies make me proud. Keep being who you are and living on your own terms, not someone else's."

She raised her head and looked into Phaedra's eyes. "For you, that may mean you choose to go to college to find your life's path, rather than sit out. I don't know. But don't miss the forest for the trees, okay?"

Phaedra half nodded and half frowned. "Okay . . . I think I know what you mean by that. I'll give it some thought."

Shiloh wished she could say more, but she knew the girls had to make their own mistakes and with God's help, create their own successes. It was hard not to lecture them, though. Who knew when she took this assignment in late summer that she'd leave this school with her heart walking around outside of her body, as it had with the birth of each of her sons, but this time for these two girls, and several other students. She had assumed that nerve-wracking feat only occurred in motherhood, but love didn't have those kinds of parameters.

She wished as much success and happiness for these two young ladies as she did for her own flesh and blood. And somehow, regardless of the school's policies, she would continue to be there for them, however they needed.

Thirty-one

Shiloh was still basking in the glow of her Sherman Park send-off when she reached home that evening, prepared to dash inside and cook a light dinner before her only Friday afternoon flute student, a sixth grader named Timony, arrived.

She had stopped on the way home to pick up a few groceries, and that had led to a full shopping cart and three bags to now unload. Rather than make several trips to the van, Shiloh juggled two bags in one arm and carried the third by its handle. Where were those boys when you needed them? She managed to open the garage door leading into the kitchen and set the bags on one of the granite counters without making a mess. She dashed back to the car to retrieve her gifts from her school colleagues, including the remainder of the red velvet cake and her balloons.

This time when she entered and closed the door behind her, the scent of spaghetti shocked her speechless. There, atop the stove, was the simmering pot and next to it, a pan of uncooked, buttered garlic bread waiting to be put into the oven and toasted.

"Hello!" she called. "Who's been in my kitchen and where is my family?"

After a few minutes, David came running and hugged her around the waist. "Hi, Mommy! Daddy cooked dinner; are you surprised?"

Shiloh's eyes widened. "Your daddy? All by himself?"

David looked up at her and grinned. "Yes, ma'am, he did. Well, mostly. I helped butter the bread, and Omari helped make the salad."

Shiloh scanned the counters in search of a salad, before noting that it was likely chilling in the fridge. "Oh, my," she said. "What's the occasion?"

Randy strolled into the room and jokingly shoved David out of the way so he could lean into Shiloh for a kiss.

"Daddy!" David protested, but grinned at his parents' display of mutual affection.

Shiloh stepped back after the kiss and closed her eyes to do a quick memory check: She hadn't missed a birthday, or anniversary, or holiday. Was there something she'd forgotten?

Randy was smirking when she opened her eyes. "No, there's no special occasion, other than the fact that you've ended your substitute teaching stint, and I know it was a special time for you. I thought rather than wrapping up on a "back-to-the-same-old, same-old" note, I'd cook dinner for the boys and take you to dinner and a movie."

A slow smile spread across Shiloh's face, and through her heart. "Really? That is so sweet, babe. Thank you."

Randy kissed her lips again. "Let me unpack these groceries, and if you want to change or freshen up, hurry up; we have to grab dinner in the next hour so we'll have time to catch a late movie, too."

Shiloh strode toward the foyer so she could trot upstairs and change, when she remembered Timony. She turned back with a frown on her face and Randy gave her a thumbs-up.

"I checked your calendar on the side of the fridge and saw that you had Sister Shepherd's granddaughter scheduled for a lesson this evening. I looked her up in the church directory so she could get word to the girl's parents that you needed to cancel tonight's lesson."

Shiloh wanted to check this man's DNA. Randy was occasionally thoughtful, but this was more than usual.

"Is there something you need to tell me over dinner? Did you get another job offer? Are we moving? Or do you want something else?"

Randy glanced at David, who was putting the bread she had purchased in the pantry and had his back turned. He nodded at Shiloh
and gave her a naughty smile, but kept his voice even. "Oh yeah, I
want something alright, a little later. But that's not the sole reason
for taking you out. We just haven't had a date night in a while, and I
think the end of your teaching experience is a good time to celebrate
and reconnect."

Shiloh grinned at him. "I couldn't agree more, babe. Give me a
few minutes and I'm all yours."

She trotted up the stairs and tried to think about what she could
quickly change into that was chic and ready to wear. She wanted to
look cute for her hubby tonight to show him she was proud to be his
wife, and she appreciated him. She wasn't an official beauty queen
like Jade, but if he wanted to treat her like one, she'd happily assume
the role.

Dinner was fancier than Shiloh had anticipated, but it didn't matter. Tonight was all about being in the company of the man she loved.

Randy had taken her half an hour outside of Mequon, the suburb they lived in, to Port Washington, to try out a new seafood restaurant that had received rave reviews. They both loved oysters and clams, and whenever an opportunity arose, they sampled new spots that included those items on the menu.

This evening, they sat inside a softly lit spot with a fireplace nearby and a tuxedo-clad gentleman on the piano, playing show tunes and other numbers.

"And this isn't even rated five star," Randy said, impressed with both the atmosphere and the food.

They had just completed their meals and were waiting for the waiter to bring the slice of key lime pie they had agreed to share.

Shiloh had twisted her long hair up into a chignon, put on her diamond pearl drop earrings, and donned a sleeveless silver silk top with her slacks and heels. Randy was gazing at her as if she weren't the mother of his four sons and were really hot, and she was enjoying the attention. She reached across the table for his hand, and he placed his palm in hers.

"We need to do this more often," he said and squeezed her hand. "You look gorgeous tonight, and you are glowing." Still holding her hand, he glanced at the charm bracelet on her arm and tapped it. "I think I'm going to have to buy you another charm. Or maybe two."

Shiloh glanced at it, puzzled. The only charms she had now were a heart, representing her love for him; one with the birthstones of each of their sons; and a flute.

"What's missing?" she asked.

"I think you know," he said and looked into her eyes. "One to represent your college diploma. And another to represent your new career as a high school music teacher."

Shiloh's heart beat faster. Was he actually telling her she could pursue her degree and a teaching career? She really did love this man.

"You know, I have a confession to make," she said, completely changing the subject. The switch caught Randy off guard, and he frowned.

"Yeah?"

"Yeah," she said, and pursed her lips, trying to figure out the best way to articulate what she wanted to convey. She sighed and decided not to try and frame it a certain way, just to say it.

"You are a good man, Reverend Randolph Griffin, and when you just sat here and acknowledged that you know I want to add a teacher charm to this bracelet, because I've fallen in love with the profession and with my students, I realized without a shadow of a doubt that you not only know me, you love me."

"Come again?"

"Randy, we've known each other since I was twelve and you were sixteen, when you came to Atchity for the first time to spend the summer with our family. Daddy and Mama fell in love with you and anointed you as the son they never had, and it seemed to me that you didn't mind assuming that role, since your father was struggling with his own issues."

Randy continued to hold her hand, and listened.

"Before I knew it, you were coming for spring breaks and more summers and sometimes for other special occasions, and then you were professing before the church that God had called you to preach. And then, the summer after my sophomore year, when I came home from France, trying to get re-acclimated to the real world and figure out what I wanted to do with myself, you were there, ready to join Daddy's ministry, and great marriage material."

Her heart beat faster the more she talked. Was she really going to say this and possibly shatter their beautiful evening? She took a deep breath and decided to take the plunge. At this point, if she didn't finish what she'd started, she knew deep down that she'd never again have courage to seek out the truth.

"What are you trying to say here, missy?" Randy squirmed in his seat.

Shiloh looked him in the eye and continued softly, lovingly. "I knew that summer when I came home that you were looking for someone special to settle down with, and while you and I had dated off and on for a year before you proposed, I always wondered whether I just happened to be in Atchity at the right time and in the right family, or whether Daddy asked you to pursue me, or whether you looked up one day and decided I was the one for you. I know you love me, but I admit, that has always been a question."

Randy seemed surprised, but not stunned. "Why are you bringing this up?"

His response left her cold, but she pushed forward. "Because your actions tonight, including understanding that I want to finish my degree and teach, touched me deeply. I felt like for the first time in all these years that our marriage wasn't just something convenient, because I happened to be your surrogate father's single daughter and perfect preacher wife material. I felt like you love *me*, because of me, and I love you for that. Thank you for offering to add those charms to this bracelet someday. I've been worried about whether I'll have your support in wanting to return to school. I appreciate your being willing to let me take this journey, babe."

Randy stared at her for a few minutes before raising her hand to his lips and kissing it. "I have always loved you, Shiloh. You are the mother of my four sons, my helpmate, my lover, my most trusted friend. I didn't choose to marry you on a whim, and I've never regretted it. Have you?"

Randy didn't deliver an eloquent speech or the warm and fuzzy response that countless romantic movies had conditioned Shiloh to expect, and she was a little disappointed. Was it true that her dad had suggested they marry and he didn't want to admit it? Was his marrying her a calculated move? This conversation wasn't allaying those doubts. But what she heard her husband saying was that he was here, and he was hers, and he loved her, and regardless of what had been his motivation all those years ago, he was thankful that she was his queen, and he would honor her.

Shiloh filled in with words what her heart told her his eyes, and his actions, were conveying. She wanted to lean across the table and kiss him. Instead, she did the next best thing—utter a gift to him.

"I have never been disappointed, Randolph James Griffin, and the day I married you is a day I will never regret. I love you, baby, more than you know."

Shiloh's weekend had started off memorable, with the send-off from her students and colleagues on Friday, capped off with a special night out with Randy, and she thought it couldn't get better. This morning, however, she realized the last Sunday in October would go down in history as well.

When Monica, her father, and her grandmother approached the altar to become members of St. Stephens Baptist, Shiloh wept as if her own kin were being saved.

"We live together, do everything else together, Pastor," Monica's dad, Claude, said to Randy and the congregation. "It's time that we come back to church and worship together. Your wife isn't a minister, but she has been such a blessing to my daughter over the past two months that I've seen a change for the better in Monica. Mrs. Griffin didn't talk a lot about God at school, but she invited Monica here to St. Stephens Baptist, and she always took time out to show she cared. That was God's love in action, and we want to fellowship here so we can begin to do the same."

The congregation reacted to Claude's comments with tears and a standing ovation. Some of the male church members left their seats and came forward to personally welcome him and his family.

"We all welcome you, Brother Claude. Your daughter, your mother, and you will be led closer to God and loved on by his people here," Randy assured him. "We embrace all three of you with open hearts and open arms. We aren't a perfect church, because imperfect people abide and worship here. But we are trying to bring light in the midst of darkness, and so we live, love, learn, and hopefully encourage each other along the way."

Randy turned toward Shiloh, who was sitting in the second row still dabbing her eyes with a tissue. He stretched his hand toward her, and Shiloh rose from her seat and approached him and Monica and her family. When she reached his side, Randy clasped Shiloh's hand in his.

"Most of you all know my wife is a gifted musician, and some of you know that in September and October, our own Brother Carter gave her an opportunity to serve as a long-term substitute teacher in one of the schools in his school district."

Shiloh was taking deep breaths to compose herself while Randy expounded.

"I hope my wife won't mind me saying this, but that brief experience changed her life."

Shiloh smiled at him, and felt the tears threatening to erupt again.

"In a good way. She not only fell in love with this little lady here," he said, pointing to Monica, "she also fell in love with teaching. And she is in the process of applying to several area colleges so she can obtain her teaching certification."

The congregation rose to its feet again, with Dr. Carter leading the way, and rendered cheers and applause. Jade, who sat on the opposite side of the aisle from where Shiloh had been sitting, was holding her sleeping son, so she didn't rise. She pasted a smile on her face.

"I share this to follow up on what our new brother in Christ, Claude, was just saying," Randy continued. "Shiloh didn't go to Sherman Park every day and quote Scriptures or lecture her students about how to do things God's way. She just listened, and loved on them, and accepted them where they were—just like Jesus did in his day. And when we do that, God will do the rest! This family standing here today, after spending years out of the church, is evidence of that. So this week, when you're at work, or socializing, or doing routine errands, remember that you carry God's glory with you everywhere you go. That 'glory' is God's love, power, strength, light, spirit of forgiveness, and pure love, people. When we say, or sing, that we need his glory, that's what we're asking for, and the Garrett family is showing us that it is effective."

Instead of a swell of "Amens," Randy's unintentional second sermon seemed to have struck a chord. There was silence, weeping, and a mood of reflection. Randy ended the service then, instead of collecting offering.

"Instead of giving monetarily today, this week, give an offering out of your spirit, out of the glory of God dwelling within you. See how much that costs you, and make the sacrifice with a willing, joyful spirit. Some of you will see results right away. Others of you will be planting seeds that you may never personally see sprout and grow. Just know that you are doing your part, and be ready to be ministered to yourselves. Amen, family? Amen."

That afternoon, the pot roast and green beans Shiloh had left simmering on the stove at home went uneaten. Monica's father had insisted on taking the Griffin family to dinner after service, despite Randy's and Shiloh's repeated protests. The two of them finally yielded when Monica stepped in to make the case.

"Please, Mrs. Griffin? I really consider you to be like a surrogate mother to me, and it would mean a lot for you to get to know my grammy and my dad better."

Monica, who had abandoned her neo-soul afro without looking back, had her hair pinned up in a side-swept ponytail today, and she looked as cute as a button. She was still drawing attention from the opposite sex, including Omari and Raphael, who suddenly appeared at Shiloh's side and were urging her not to disappoint Monica.

"We'll join you, my friend," Randy said and clapped Claude on the back. "But I cannot let you do what you're getting yourself into."

Claude looked confused.

"You can buy my wife's meal if you want, but you don't have a clue how much these four greedy, er, growing sons of mine can eat. I'll cover the Griffin men. If we can agree on that, you choose the place and we're on for a family meal."

Claude threw back his head and bellowed. "I think I'm going to like you, Pastor Randy. It's a deal."

On the way to their van, Shiloh leaned toward Omari and Raphael, who walked in front of her. "Sorry to burst your bubble, boys, but don't get your hopes up about Monica," she said. "First of all, she's fifteen and not interested in younger boys. And didn't you hear her? We're family. You couldn't date her if you wanted to."

The boys' faces fell and for a split second Shiloh felt guilty for shattering their fantasies.

Only for a second, though; they were too young to be getting hung up on girls anyway. Now Lem, on the other hand, might be just the right fit, Shiloh mused. But just as quickly as the thought flitted into her hopes, it fled. Lem's heart was still in Alabama, with his friend Lia, and maybe the only thing that would change that would be another summer at camp, where they couldn't dress up their flaws or annoying habits or spots of immaturity as well as they could online or in a video chat. Shiloh wasn't worried yet, but if Monica caught his eye, she just might look the other way.

Thirty-four

On her first Monday morning in weeks that she didn't have to teach, Shiloh heard God loud and clear, and although she had a million excuses that she knew were valid and sensible, none of them could stand up to his command.

She lay in bed after her morning devotion, praying and listening, and when the notion dropped into her spirit that she needed to reach out to Jade, she opened her eyes and stared at the ceiling. She must have interrupted God's flow and unintentionally interjected Jade into her thoughts. What else could have put Miss Diva on her brain?

The already-gorgeous woman had lost ten pounds—"For TV," Jade explained, since the pageant would be televised. She had added human-hair extensions to give body to her naturally long mane, and she put Naima's flute lessons on hold so she'd have more time to devote to preparing for the pageant. Shiloh missed spending time with Naima each week and made a point of searching for her on Sundays. What she hadn't missed were Jade's uncomfortable visits to Bible study. She wasn't complaining, though, and neither were the other members of the group.

It became clear to her this morning, however, that God was complaining. As much as she tried to ignore it, she knew he was disappointed in how she'd handled the situation, and he wasn't going to let it slide. Too much was at stake.

Shiloh knew better than to play dumb, especially when her heart told her what she needed to do. It felt unfair, but how did you argue with God, especially after meditating on his Word, spending time in prayer with him, and promising to do his will?

"Ugh!" she sat up in bed and said aloud. "Okay, then, okay!"

It was before dawn, and Randy shifted under the covers. "You okay? Who you talking to?" He mumbled the questions without lifting his head or opening his eyes.

"The Lord," she said and sighed.

"Better obey, then," he said and rolled back over, into sleep.

Shiloh wanted to swat him with her pillow, but she couldn't be mad at him because of a directive God had given her. Regardless of whether she liked it, she would be paying Ms. Jade a visit today, and urging her to return to the women's Wednesday night Bible study. As the co-leader.

Thirty-five

Shiloh had welcomed Jade into her home many times because of Naima's flute lessons, but it struck her this morning as she drove to Cedarburg that she'd been invited to Jade and Vic's home only once. The couple had her and Randy over for dinner right after he was named senior pastor at St. Stephens Baptist, and spent the entire evening asking him about his interview process and what he believed had led to his being chosen for the position.

This morning, as she cruised up a long driveway that led to a white brick home with rows of two-story columns in the front, she admired the large maple trees that surrounded the perimeter of the property. Their few remaining golden, red, and orange leaves provided a breathtaking contrast to the bricks, and shielded the house from the view of neighboring properties. What a wonderful sanctuary from the rest of the world, Shiloh thought.

She had come with the intention of finding a Bible study topic she and Jade could teach together. Shiloh knew Jade was going to call her insane for suggesting they come up with something at the last minute, but Shiloh had lost the argument with God this morning, so here she was.

If you want her to do this, Lord, you've got to make it happen. I don't have the right attitude, the right words, or even the right passages of Scripture yet. And did I say I lack the right attitude?

Shiloh strolled to Jade's front door, enjoying the flowers that bordered the winding, cobblestone path leading from the paved driveway to the house. Only the hardiest of mums were still blooming, but Shiloh imagined how colorful and lovely this path must be in the spring. She rang the doorbell, fully expecting to be greeted by a maid, or maybe one of Jade's babysitters. When Jade herself answered, Shiloh tried to shield her surprise with a smile.

"Hey, Shiloh. Come in." Jade, impeccably dressed as always, ushered Shiloh inside and gave her a hug.

Shiloh was surprised by her graciousness, given that Shiloh had called just an hour earlier, asking if she could come right away, to discuss Bible study. There had been a long pause before Jade responded, but her yes had sounded sincere. Still, Shiloh felt the need to apologize. "I don't usually spring requests on people at the last minute like this, but I felt strongly this morning that I shouldn't proceed with this Wednesday's Bible study without you."

Jade nodded. "I understand; don't worry about it. Naima is in school, and Vic is upstairs with Nicholas, so we're okay."

Shiloh nodded. "I hope I won't be long. I don't even know where to start . . ."

"First let's get comfortable," Jade said. She led Shiloh into a spacious family room and directed her to one of two brown leather sofas. "Sit anywhere. Can I get you some tea, coffee, or juice?"

Jade serving her tea? Shiloh had to witness, and experience, this. "Any of those would be fine. I'm usually a coffee drinker, but I'm always open to trying something new."

She sat on the sofa and flipped through a stack of magazines stationed on one side of an expansive, square coffee table made of mahogany or cherry, Shiloh couldn't tell which. There was a copy of *Style*, *People*, *Essence*, and, tucked in the stack last, a *Daily Word* devotional. Shiloh picked it up to flip through it, and was surprised to see that several pages were dog-eared.

She wondered whether this was Reverend Vic's contribution to the pile, or if Jade had been reading this one, too.

Jade returned with a tray of options that included steaming hot water, a miniature chest of various teas, instant coffee, and mango peach orange juice. There were also bagels, danish, and small biscuits.

"How did you pull all of this together with an hour's notice?" Shiloh couldn't help but show how impressed she was.

Jade grinned. "My mother was a California corporate executive wife for thirty years, until my stepfather retired. I adopted a few of her secrets: Always keep coffee and tea on hand, store a few cans of frozen juice that you can quickly thaw, and keep a selection of your favorite pastries or desserts in the freezer, ready to be popped into the oven or microwave for a delectable treat."

Shiloh laughed. Who knew? "My own mother would be proud of you!"

They settled into eating the light pastries and warm beverages and chatted about their kids and Shiloh's teaching gig.

"That's awesome that you're going back to school soon," Jade said, referencing the announcement Randy had made in church yesterday. "I don't know if I could start a new career at this stage. You have a lot of courage."

Shiloh frowned. "What do you mean 'at this stage'? We're in our thirties—we have plenty of time to change our minds and try something new and different. I will admit, though, I didn't go searching for the teaching opportunity. When it came my way, I just happened to seize it, and discover how much I love it. You're doing your thing too, with the beauty pageant. Who knows where that will take you?"

Shiloh was surprised by the wistful smile that crossed Jade's face.

"That's a whole 'nother story, but we'll talk about that shortly, when we get into our Bible study discussion."

"Well, let's go there now," Shiloh said. "Would you be willing to help me teach the class on Wednesday? Since that's two days away, I don't mind leading the discussion and dissecting the Scriptural passage we choose. I just know that you are supposed to help me out, as co-leader, like you first offered a few months ago. I know you haven't made it to the studies recently, and I hope that's mostly due to your busy schedule, but if you have felt like you weren't welcome, I want to apologize right now for the role I've played in that. Instead of questioning whether you were ready to help lead the study, I should have been asking how I could help you feel more prepared. I'm sorry for not doing that, and for maybe feeling threatened by your presence. There's enough room for both of us to share the leadership of this group, and to do things in our own way."

Jade gave Shiloh a wry smile. "God woke you up this morning, too, huh? Thanks for saying all of that. If nothing else, I know why we're supposed to lead this week's Bible study together and exactly the message to share, at least my part of it."

Shiloh didn't try to hide her shock this time.

Jade chuckled and leaned over to pat her hand. "Yes, Shiloh, believe it or not, I've been talking to the Lord, too, lately. And he told me this morning that it's time to come clean. I told Vic this morning over breakfast, and then you called out of the blue and asked to come over. I'm scared out of my mind, but I'm going to do what he's asking, and I'm thinking a passage from the book of Isaiah might be helpful. . . ."

Thirty-six

On the surface, this seemed like it was going to be Bible study as usual.

Shiloh had come in early and set up the room. There were handouts on each seat for anyone who wanted to follow along with the Scriptures and take notes. The biggest difference was that instead of one seat being positioned in the lead spot near the center of the circle, there were two chairs. Shiloh had purposely chosen a black one and a white one.

The women already were aware of just how different Shiloh and Jade were from each other; and during their Monday planning session, they had decided to capitalize upon that, in every way possible. Shiloh wasn't sure why, but she was nervous. Would the women react to tonight's lesson with love? Or would they keep their guards up? Jade's reassurance from their Monday meeting echoed through her mind: It didn't really matter what happened during class; their tasks were to share what God had led them to teach, and to encourage the women to walk out their faith in their own, God-inspired way.

"That's what I've been learning how to do these past few months," Jade told her on Monday. "People can't always see what's going on behind my clothes and makeup and smile, but God is having his way with me."

Shiloh looked up from her notes this evening and was greeted with a smile from Eleanor, Monica's grandmother. She trotted over and opened her arms to envelop Eleanor in a hug.

"Well, hello!" Shiloh said. "I'm so glad you decided to come out. Where is Miss Monica this evening?"

Eleanor shook her head. "You know where she is—being a teenager, hanging out with her friends. I told her I was coming to Bible study, and her only response was to ask that I give you a hug, so I guess I'll consider that delivered."

Both women laughed. Eleanor picked up a handout from one of the chairs and situated herself in a seat at the far end of the circle, exactly opposite from where Shiloh and Jade would be seated. She shifted and squirmed until she got comfortable. "Me and these wide hips, I tell you!" she said and laughed.

Shiloh shook her head. "Don't get me started on mine. At least they're 'in' now. The kids say it's old school slang these days, but I'm still calling myself 'phat' instead of 'fat.'"

They enjoyed another laugh as other women filled the room. Many of them greeted Eleanor with welcoming hugs when they realized she was visiting the class for the first time. The group settled into seats, and one of the women volunteered to open them in prayer. Shiloh encouraged anyone who wanted to give testimonies or share other good news about God's faithfulness during the prior week, to do so, and several ladies took the offer.

When they were done, the Bible study members looked expectantly from Shiloh to Jade, trying to gauge what was coming.

Shiloh glanced at Jade, who nodded to indicate that she was ready to start.

"Well, ladies, we first want to welcome Sister Eleanor, a new St. Stephens Baptist member who is visiting our Bible study for the first time."

Eleanor waved, and the women responded with a round of applause.

"We also want to welcome back Sister Jade, this lady sitting here next to me," Shiloh said. "She has been missing in action for a while, getting ready to compete in the Mrs. Wisconsin pageant, coming up in two weeks. Welcome, Jade. I am honored to have you back, and serving as my co-teacher."

The women stared and some of them delivered polite applause.

"We realized earlier this week that just as God led our husbands to ministry at St. Stephens Baptist, we've been led here, too," Shiloh said. "Two very different women, with different personalities and ways of seeing the world, and different ways of connecting to the one true God. It has taken us a while to realize that God wants us to celebrate and find value in our differences, rather than judge or criticize what we can't appreciate, or don't understand, in the other person.

"Take these chairs that Jade and I are sitting in," Shiloh said. "One is black, one is white. But they're both chairs; they both serve a vital function. I could go on and on, but my point is, they don't have to be the same, or mirror each other, to fulfill their purpose as chairs. These chairs are a metaphor for who each of us is as a woman, and as a vessel of Christ. So that is what will enable Jade and me to teach this Bible study together. Each of us is bringing our uniqueness, our varying levels of spiritual maturity, and our love for God to these meetings. You'll find that one of us will resonate with you more sometimes than the other, and vice versa. But in both of us, we hope you'll see a reflection of God, and our desire to share what he has placed in our hearts."

The women nodded and seemed to soften. A few openly smiled at Jade, and Sister Adelaide was among them.

Jade peered at Shiloh, and Shiloh wanted to give her a thumbs-up, but knew that would let everyone in the room know how nervous Jade was. Instead, she nodded to let her know she had the floor. Jade cleared her throat and pulled out the worksheet Shiloh had distributed earlier.

"If you'll look at your handout for the night, you'll see that we're going to spend tonight, and actually the rest of this year, studying the book of Isaiah," Jade said. "Isaiah is a long book that covers a span of history. He starts out by warning the Israelites of God's wrath and judgment, then in the middle of their years of exile, gives them hope by urging them not to fear, and to remember that whatever they are facing, they won't do so alone. That's the section we're going to focus on for the next few weeks: Where is God when we are in the middle of our stuff? On the outside, we may look happy or like we have it all together, when World War III might be raging on the inside."

The room rang with laughter.

"You better tell the truth!" one of the sisters called out.

Jade grinned, and Shiloh knew she was on cloud nine.

"Isaiah's words written all those years ago still stand today, because just like the Israelites, we can get so caught up in our personal drama that we forget that we don't have to figure out everything on our own. We don't have to hide our truths for fear of others condemning us, when we know that the one who gives us life and breath is always walking with us, no matter what. Sister Davis, would you read Isaiah 41:13 aloud?"

The thirty-something woman nodded and found the passage of Scripture in her Bible, and stood. "I'll be reading from the New International Version, and it reads, 'For I am the LORD, your God, who takes hold of your right hand and says to you, Do not fear; I will help you.'"

Jade thanked her, then took a deep breath. "I read that passage on Monday morning, during my devotion and prayer time with God, and I realized I needed to stop hiding."

The women sat up straighter, and some frowned.

"I got on my knees and prayed for the courage to do what I needed to do, and then, while the kids were still sleeping, I nudged Reverend

Vic awake and told him something important that I had been keeping from him for about four months. I'm going to tell you ladies what it was, in a moment. But first, I have to tell you, I had to cling to Isaiah 41:13 because I wasn't sure if my husband was going to look at me differently, tell me to figure it out on my own, or simply laugh in my face. I just didn't know. But like we often do, I had been so busy trying to fix things and figure them out on my own, that I hadn't given him a chance to do any of the above, or to prove my fears unfounded.

"So I sat him down on Monday morning, and I . . ." Tears welled up in Jade's eyes, and Shiloh reached into her shoulder bag and handed her one of the tissues she always kept handy for Wednesday nights.

"I told him that the reason I entered the Mrs. Milwaukee pageant was not because I wanted the attention or needed to prove something to myself; I did it because I needed the money."

"Huh?" Some of the women looked incredulous. Shiloh's reaction had been similar when Jade had shared these details during her visit on Monday.

"I guess I shouldn't say I needed it," Jade clarified. "I wanted to win the prize money so I wouldn't have to ask Reverend Vic to help me with an expensive, but necessary purchase. And the reason I didn't want him to help me, or give me permission to take the funds from our savings, was because then he'd know I was . . . I am . . . defective.

"You see, I am gradually losing my hearing in both ears. I am mildly deaf." Jade let the tears slide down her cheeks without staunching the streaks of mascara crisscrossing her cheeks.

The women gasped, and Jade raised her hand to silence the murmuring that arose. Shiloh realized she was doing her best to make it through the story before she lost her courage.

"I realized something was wrong about eight or so months ago, when I couldn't clearly hear Nicholas's cries. I'd be down in the kitchen and think he was sound asleep, but when I moved to another room, his cries were muted, but fierce enough that I could tell he'd been wailing for a while. Sometimes by the time I'd get to him, he'd be angry because it took me so long. Or, my sweet Naima would talk to me from the back seat of the car as I drove her home after school, and I'd misunderstand or completely miss part of the conversation, and when she would bring it up later and remind me that she'd already said something, I'd draw a blank. At first, I thought I might have memory loss; but as I put two and two together, I realized I should probably get my hearing checked. My visit to an audiologist revealed severe nerve damage in both ears, leaving me with little recourse except to wear hearing aids."

Sister Rubilene slowly rose from her seat and hobbled over with her cane and gave Jade a hug.

"That's okay, precious. I've been wearing aids for twenty-five years, and you get used to 'em."

Jade smiled and squeezed the elderly lady's hand. "Thanks, Sister Rubilene, you are right, and I appreciate that."

"What's the big deal—isn't it just like buying a pair of glasses? People who can't see—like my blind self—have bifocals, trifocals, and everything in between to see straight and read; we all have something wrong with us."

Jade smiled at Sister Erlanda. "You're right, Sister Erlanda, in some ways it's the same, but you have to admit, there is a stigma attached to losing your hearing, to becoming deaf. It's a full-fledged disability, and in some ways, it makes you feel—at least it made me feel—defective."

Sister Rubilene, who was still standing next to Jade, nodded. "She's right," Rubilene said. "Even though my hearing loss was mostly due to age, I felt self-conscious and ashamed that I had to put a device over my ear to do something as basic as hear a bird chirp, or hear the beep of my microwave, or to watch my favorite TV show. I know folks who wear glasses and can't see a thing until they put them on. They feel lost without them. But Lasik surgery can sometimes cure that, or you can get all kinds of fancy contacts and change your eye color. You don't have as much flexibility with your hearing. If I take these devices out of my ears right now, I'm missing a whole part of the world. I'm at a loss."

Shiloh tried to understand what Jade and Sister Rubilene were describing, but it was difficult.

Monica's grandmother, Sister Eleanor, raised her hand. "I'm beginning to grasp how losing your hearing can affect your sense of self; but why the secrecy? Why didn't you want your husband to know, and why did you need to borrow from your savings?"

Jade nodded. "He asked me the same questions on Monday. The first one is hard to articulate, other than what I've shared. I didn't want him to feel like he had this wife who wasn't perfect anymore."

The room fell silent, and Jade nodded. "I know, I know; I'm not perfect; never was. I see now that God is using this condition as one way of reminding me that only he is perfect, and only in his strength could I expect to come close to that level. But in my human 'foolishness' I guess you could call it, I wanted to be his perfect little wife, with no issues. Just fabulous and fine and all put together.

"Because I was trying to hide my condition from him so earnestly, that meant when the audiologist informed me that the kind of hearing aid that would serve me best would cost a minimum of twenty-eight hundred—for each one, and yes, I need two—I nearly flipped out. Here I was, with a toddler I needed to be able to hear at all times, for safety reasons alone, a daughter I couldn't always hear, and a hearing issue that was destined to get worse if I didn't do something to use the nerve capacity I had.

"The audiologist wanted to fit me that day, but I didn't have almost six thousand dollars in 'fun money' lying around to use, and I wasn't ready to share this with Reverend Vic," Jade said. "Now that I think about how loving and supportive he's always been, I know I was being silly. But guess what? Even we beauty queens can be insecure. That night, as I fretted over what to do, a news segment came on about the Mrs. Milwaukee pageant and the winner receiving dozens of prizes, including cash. I thought if I couldn't do anything else, I could win that pageant; pay for the more expensive, high-tech, and super-tiny hearing aids; and none of you would be the wiser. That was my grand plan, and I was sticking to it."

"But what if you hadn't won Mrs. Milwaukee, and what if you don't win Mrs. Wisconsin?" another woman in the study asked. "What is your plan B? All of this time you've devoted to the pageant has meant time away from your family, and it has meant more time that you haven't been able to clearly hear your children. Wouldn't that have been resolved by now if you had just asked your husband for the money?"

Jade nodded and shrugged. "Too bad I didn't have the courage to do just that from the beginning, or to even bring my fears and pain to this safe space and share with you women, so you could help me brainstorm solutions, and pray for God's will to be done in my life. Truth is, that thought did cross my mind. That's why I started coming to Bible study. But in my first night here, it was clear to me that I couldn't compete with our First Lady. You ladies' love for her was obvious, and I felt insignificant. So, as usual, I decided to fix everything. I decided that my way was best, and that in addition to registering for the Mrs. Milwaukee pageant, I would use these Bible study meetings to prove that I was more than a pretty pastor's wife— I was a godly woman that all of you could relate to and care about. When I pulled this off, you all would respect me, I'd be able to purchase my aids and hear again, and all would be well."

"Except," said Sister Carolyn, who was seated next to Jade and reached over to pat her hand, "you would have been sinning all the way to that pageant crown."

Jade frowned.

"We are studying the book of Isaiah, you say, but what you've described tonight is an Esther experience," Sister Carolyn said. "Remember when her uncle Mordecai came to her and insisted that she go before the king to save the Jewish people from the death and destruction the king's right-hand man, Haman, was planning? When Esther resisted the idea of standing up to the king because she feared for her own life, Mordecai challenged her by asking her, 'Who knows but if you were born for such a time as this?'

"I say the same to you, Sister Jade," Carolyn said. "You're young, beautiful, well-to-do, and able to pretty much do and buy what you please. But here's something that you can't control—your health, the loss of your hearing. And in finding out that the only way you're going to be able to function is with hearing aids, this may be your opportunity to help thousands of other younger Americans across this nation who may be struggling with hearing loss and with trying to pay for hearing aids."

Jade's eyes filled with tears. "None of that crossed my mind. This could be bigger than me."

Sister Rubilene, who had returned to her seat, chimed in again. "My aids were covered by Medicare, but you mean to tell me that your insurance won't take care of these devices for you?"

Jade shook her head. "Many insurance companies across the nation don't cover them. They cover cochlear implants for those who are hearing impaired, or even surgery for those whose hearing loss can be corrected that way; but few of them consider hearing aids a necessity for adults, unless you've purchased a bells-and-whistles plan that includes these kinds of 'extras.'"

Eleanor sat forward. "But how is a medical device that helps you maintain your safety and other folks' safety an extra? What if you can't hear an emergency vehicle while you're driving, or the beep of a horn that could help you avoid an accident? What if you can't hear your child and he's in danger? How is that an extra?"

Shiloh loved the passionate support that Jade was receiving.

"You know, Jade, you should call your insurance company again, or write a letter asking them to cover these aids for you, because they are medically necessary," Shiloh said. "We are going to pray with you tonight that God grants that request, so you don't have to worry about taking anything out of your bank account to cover them, other than possibly a co-pay, and maybe insurance on the wear and tear of the aids.

"But since you've gotten yourself into this pageant, Mrs. Milwaukee, I'm thinking you need to play your Esther role to the finish," Shiloh said. "What if you stood on that stage in a few weeks, in front of a televised, statewide audience, and told them all that you were there to represent the hard-of-hearing citizens of this state who need help affording hearing aids, and in removing the stigma around hearing loss?"

Jade's eyes grew wide. "Are you serious? You think I should do that? Tell the world about my . . . issues?"

Rubilene shook her cane at Jade from across the room. "Isaiah 41:13, my dear—do not fear; God will help you!"

Shiloh pointed at Rubilene. "Do you think any differently about her now than you did half an hour ago, before you knew she wore hearing aids?"

Jade, who remained wide-eyed as she consumed all of the advice, shook her head. "Of course not; she's the same sweet, wonderful person she has always been. I just know a little bit more about her now, and in fact, her willingness to share something so personal to encourage me, has endeared her to me all the more."

Someone tapped Jade on the shoulder and she turned and looked up, into her husband's eyes.

"That, Jade Devereaux Smith, is exactly how I feel about you," Reverend Vic said, to the hoots and hollers of the women witnessing this exchange. "Don't ever think you are just a cover girl to me. All that ever has been is icing on the cake. We are going to get your hearing aids tomorrow, regardless of what our insurance carrier says, so that when you take the stage in the pageant in two weeks, you can hear everything loud and clear, and you can speak up for what is right."

Shiloh was overwhelmed. She had called Randy on the way over tonight and told him that he might want to send Vic into their study instead of keeping him in the men's Bible study. She wasn't sure how long Vic had been standing outside of the classroom or how much he had heard, but Jade got his message loud and clear tonight, as did the other women. His actions spoke louder than words, but Sister Carolyn had nailed it. Jade's entering the pageant may have originally been for the hearing aids, and trying to take over Bible study may have been a stab at improving her self-worth, but now this pageant, and her return to the study, were about something much bigger: the women in this class needing to see God's glory through Jade's vulner-ability, and Vic's unconditional love. And if Jade chose to address her hearing issues at the pageant, maybe this would be about helping a whole group of people suffering in shame and silence.

Thirty-seven

The St. Stephens Baptist youth choir always sang on the first Sunday of the month, and seeing Monica perform with them for the first time this morning made Shiloh's heart swell like a proud mama.

Monica readily acknowledged that flute playing was her first love, but she was enjoying the choir because it helped her become friends with some of the other teens at the church. She bounded over to Shiloh after service today, with her long hair pulled back into a ponytail. Shiloh had been tempted to ask if she was officially done with the afro, but as had been the case at Sherman Park, the boys were drawn to her, and Shiloh suspected the afro would not be resurrected as long as that remained the case.

"Hey, Mrs. Griffin," Monica said and hugged her neck. "How are you today?"

"I'm doing great. Any word yet on the summer music program?"

Monica's smile faded for a few seconds, but she quickly bounced back. "Not yet, but any day now!"

"What are you hiding?" Shiloh put her hand on her hip and leveled her eyes at Monica.

Monica frowned. "What do you mean?"

"I saw that look skate through your eyes. You sure you haven't heard yet and just don't want to tell me?"

Monica sighed and hugged Shiloh again. "I promise you will be the third person to know—right after Daddy and Grandma E, okay? I guess I'm just nervous about what it will all mean . . . and what if I don't get in anyway."

Shiloh stood back and put her hands on both of Monica's shoulders. "If you don't get into this program, that means you keep trying until the one that's right for you opens a door. If you get into this program, then you'll go, you'll shine, and you'll have at least one path set to your dreams. At your age, you have nothing to lose; you are in a win-win situation."

Doubt shimmied across Monica's visage again, and Shiloh questioned its source. She had been gone from Sherman Park for just one week; what could have happened in that time that left Monica feeling unsure of herself?

"I'll be at the school recital tomorrow night, and I'm bringing my private flute students."

Monica perked up. "Really? That's so sweet. Everyone will be excited to see you."

Monica hugged her one last time before being called away by Kourtney and Brendan, two of her friends in the choir. Shiloh watched her flit away and again, felt like this was the daughter she wanted to hold onto, to protect and keep on the right track.

Eleanor appeared at her side and watched Monica, too.

"Are you feeling the same way I am?" Shiloh asked. "I've only known her a few months, and I can tell that she's special. God has his hand on her. Trouble is, I don't know if she sees it or feels that way about herself, and that's the danger that will make her want to fit in and be part of the crowd."

Shiloh didn't normally speak so candidly to others about their children, but she truly loved Monica and wanted the best for her. She hoped Eleanor wouldn't be offended.

"It does my heart good to know that somebody else cares about Monica like her daddy and I do," Eleanor said. "I try to look out for her, but I know she thinks I'm old fashioned and overprotective, especially when it comes to her friends from school, all those little boys that want to call now and everything. I tell her and Phaedra they have plenty of time to worry about boys, but you know how girls are at that age—all giggles and goo-goo eyes.

"Her mama's been gone for two years and Monica misses the connection they had. I know you aren't trying to be a replacement, but Monica needs you. God sent you to her at the right time, and I'm grateful. So if you see something that I don't, that we need to address to keep her on track, you get her in line, or let me know, and Claude and I will handle it."

Shiloh smiled at Eleanor. "You've got a deal, Grandma E."

thirty-eight

The letter Lem placed in Shiloh's hand Monday afternoon was just bulky enough to give her hope.

"Thanks, son," she said as nonchalantly as she could.

He sat on a stool in front of the kitchen island and smirked. "You ain't fooling me, trying to act all calm," he said. "Go ahead and rip it open. That's what I would do."

"That's what you will be doing next year around this time, when you're waiting on your college acceptance letters." Shiloh paused and peered at him. "That's a thought . . . maybe I should wait another year, so we can go to college *together*."

Shiloh burst into laughter at the stricken look on Lem's face.

"I'm not worried," he finally said. "First of all, you're going to be stuck at a university here in Milwaukee, or maybe online. I'm probably going far away."

"Oh?" This was a first; Shiloh wondered what schools had finally piqued his interest.

"Yeah; Lia and I are interested in Georgia Tech; Virginia Tech; Alabama U, of course; and maybe Spelman and Morehouse."

Now she needed to sit down. Shiloh walked around the island and sat on the stool across from him. "Lem, you and Lia live in two different parts of the country and spent two weeks together this summer. How can that constitute a relationship on which you'll base your college decisions, son?"

Shiloh laid the unopened letter from Marquette University on the granite countertop and awaited his reply.

Lem shrugged and looked into her eyes. "Mom, I know we're just sixteen and don't see each other every day, but she is special. We really hit it off this summer, and we can't help how we feel."

"Because you are just sixteen, Lem, you need to make sure you're dating and having fun with your friends here. There will be plenty of time to get serious about one girl."

"I do have fun with my friends—guys and girls. We go on group dates, chat, text, all that. It's just that Lia is my girl. I'm sure Grandad didn't let you and Aunt Dayna and Aunt Jessica date all that much, as stern as he is!"

Shiloh pursed her lips. It wasn't so much that Daddy had banned them from dating as it was being the prominent preacher's daughter that turned off the boys, and even some of the girls who could have been her friends. They either thought having her around would cramp their style, or they mistakenly assumed that she didn't want to come around, because she was "the quiet one." Dayna and Jessica had both been more outgoing, and as a result they had had more luck at sustaining friendships and dating relationships and being included in social outings. But as the "holy sister," she'd had few opportunities and had spent most of her free time perfecting her flute skills and dreaming of her future in the arts. To this day, Shiloh had to admit, she wasn't one to have a lot of girlfriends. The benefit to that, though, was the time she had been able to devote to her family, and she had learned the difference between feeling lonely and being alone. She didn't necessarily mind being alone, because she enjoyed her own company. But how did one explain all of that to a love-struck eleventh grader?

Shiloh knew she couldn't. She just had to trust that it would all work out in its own time. She slid off the stool and kissed his cheek. "You're a good young man, and Lia is lucky to have you."

Lem rolled his eyes, then they landed on her mail. "Are you going to open the letter or not?"

Shiloh grinned and picked up the envelope. She sliced it open with a fingernail and silently read the enclosed letter.

"Well?"

"Looks like I can start school anytime I want, and they'll accept all but a few of my credits from Birmingham-Southern."

Lem hugged her and she wept.

"Aw, Mom. Congratulations."

"Thanks, babe," she said.

This was just one hurdle, though. Putting him and his brothers through college was the priority; she needed to find some scholarship funds in order to resume her education, or it could wait a while longer. Right now, she decided to bask in this sweet victory. It put her one step closer to reclaiming the dreams she once held at age sixteen.

Thirty-nine

Minutes after entering the Sherman Park High recital hall later that evening, Shiloh knew she had two lovesick teenagers on her hands— Lem *and* Monica.

Monica hadn't seen Shiloh enter the recital hall foyer with six of her young flute students, but that was because she'd been distracted by Trey Holloman. He walked past Monica without acknowledging her, because he was holding hands with someone else, a cheerleader named Sheree, if Shiloh's memory was correct. Monica and Phaedra exchanged glances, and she saw Phaedra tell Monica to forget about him. But Monica trailed the smiling couple with her eyes, and rather than appearing angry, she seemed hurt.

Shiloh did a quick headcount, to make sure everyone was still with her. She grabbed Naima by the hand and asked her older students to stick close by. They crossed the foyer and approached Monica, and when she looked up and saw Shiloh, a smile reshaped her furrowed brow.

"Mrs. Griffin! You came, like you promised!"

Shiloh hugged Monica and Phaedra, and a few other band members who were nearby and excited to see her.

"Of course I did," Shiloh said. "And I brought some of my private flute students, so you all could inspire them."

Naima and Timony and the others had eyes as large as saucers, watching all of the teenagers flitting about, getting ready to perform. Shiloh wanted to whisper in Monica's ear that she had seen the exchange with Trey and tell her to get him off her mind. If he had decided to date the next cute thing he saw rather than follow through with dating her, then better for her to recognize his lack of loyalty now instead of later. Monica was going to have to learn that the cliché was true: When people showed you who they were, it was always best to believe them. She made a mental note to take the girl to lunch soon, or maybe her and Phaedra, and share those words of wisdom.

"We're going to go and grab seats now," Shiloh said, and turned to her young students. "Girls, wish them good luck."

The chorus of "good lucks" from the kiddie voices filled the foyer. When the principal saw that the girls were with Shiloh, she came over and shook her hand.

"Are you grooming another generation of Sherman Park High musicians?"

Shiloh chuckled and shrugged. "You never know. These young ladies are pretty dedicated. I promised the band before I left that I'd come back and support them at the recital. Then I got the bright idea to bring along these students, so they can see where staying with their instruments and practicing faithfully can take them."

The principal nodded. "You've got the gift, and you're using it, Mrs. Griffin. We're glad to have you back with us. Enjoy the recital."

And enjoy it, she did. Shiloh wasn't sure it was so much the performances of her band students and Kris's orchestra students that got to her, as it was watching Naima, Timony, Joy, Sasha, Sage, and Eboni soak it all in. As far as they were concerned, they were watching an elite group of performers, and they were wowed.

Shiloh found herself humbled when Mrs. Helmsley took her turn at rendering remarks after the program and asked Shiloh to stand.

"I have to say I'm thankful not only to my students for practicing so hard and giving their best, but also to the person who served as their shepherd and their encourager, as well as their instructor during my absence this fall. Shiloh Griffin was my long-term sub, but I have to tell you, I returned home to this school with some pretty big shoes to fill. Mrs. Griffin, you not only taught them well, you helped them understand the power and the impact of the music they play, and for that I salute you this evening."

"Yeah!"

Shiloh wasn't sure which student broke decorum to yell out his approval, but she suspected it was her favorite drummer.

The band students responded to Mrs. Helmsley's comments by giving Shiloh a standing ovation, and many of the parents followed suit. Beaming, she scanned the crowd and saw Monica's dad and grandmother in the balcony. Claude gave her a thumbs-up, and Eleanor blew her a kiss.

Shiloh waved, then took her seat before she lost her composure. She thought about the Bible study lesson that she and Jade had taught last Wednesday that had led to a discussion of Esther's biblical purpose and Jade's. Shiloh had no doubt that one of her pivotal Esther moments had sprung from her brief tour of duty at Sherman Park High. A lot of seeds had been planted in eight weeks, and, at least in her own life, the beginning of some healing.

forty

An 8 a.m. cell phone call from Monica on a Saturday morning could mean only one thing: Her letter from the summer music program had finally come.

Shiloh opened both eyes after peeking to check the caller ID and sat up in bed. "What's up?" She was too excited to render a formal hello.

"Good morning, Mrs. Griffin, can you meet me for breakfast, or maybe for lunch?"

Shiloh paused. "Okay . . . ," she said, drawing out the word. "That's all you got for me? Did your letter come? What's the word?"

Monica's laugh was tinny. "Don't make me tell you on the phone . . ."

"You're killing me, little girl."

"If I tell you, will you still meet me for breakfast or lunch?"

Shiloh sighed and checked the clock. "I have to meet Mrs. Smith, Reverend Vic's wife, at ten this morning to help her prepare something for her pageant. It's eight now, and I'm not dressed. It will take me half an hour to get to the Sherman Park area, so if we meet before ten, it will be rushed. Can you tell me what the letter says and plan to have lunch with me? I will come by your house and pick you up. You're a church member now, not my student, so we aren't inappropriately fraternizing."

Monica giggled. "Well, I got in . . ."

"Yes!" Shiloh squealed and pumped a fist in the air. She was glad

Randy was already up and gone to a Boy Scout outing with David and Raphael; otherwise she would have wakened him.

"Congrats, my dear! You are on your way."

"Thanks, Mrs. Griffin," Monica said.

"Why don't you sound happy? Isn't this what you wanted?"

"I'm very happy. And proud," Monica said. "It's just that . . . well, that's why I'm asking to meet you. I need to talk to you about it all."

Shiloh was perplexed, but knew she needed to be patient. She had to ask just one more question, though. "Did Phaedra get in?"

"I don't think so," Monica said. "I texted and called her several times yesterday after I got my letter, but I didn't hear back from her. That makes me think she wasn't accepted; I hope she won't be mad that I was."

"She's your best friend; she'll be happy for you. Just give her some time, she'll come around."

They ended the call with Shiloh agreeing to call Eleanor to let her know she'd be coming by to swoop up Monica around noon. Shiloh's thoughts turned to Phaedra, and she was tempted to call the girl to see if her and Monica's assumptions that Phaedra hadn't been accepted were correct.

If that were the case, it was a reality that Shiloh could accept more easily than Monica's not being chosen for the program. Monica clearly had both a gift and a passion for the flute; she lived it, breathed it, ate it. Phaedra, on the other hand, was a great saxophonist, but a music career wasn't her heart's desire.

Shiloh had been praying for Phaedra to find one or a few things that lit her fire, something she could get excited enough about to pursue after high school. As a tenth grader, she had a few more years to figure it out. In Monica's case, the earlier you were identified and placed on track to hone your gift, the better chance you had of becoming a professional musician.

Shiloh climbed out of bed and strolled to her walk-in closet to decide what to wear for her first meeting of the day, with Jade. Though her "Second Lady" had thawed some hearts in the Bible study and had proven that there was a real, God-loving person beneath the hair, makeup, and designer clothes, Shiloh still felt the need to show up at Jade's place looking like more than a slug. So even though it was Saturday, she put on her dressy black jeans and a cute top instead of her faded and worn T-shirt. Truthfully, she had to admit that after taking a little extra care with her attire, she actually felt better.

Nearly four hours later, after leaving Omari and Lem with a list of chores to complete before they could get together with friends, and helping Jade craft the speech about hearing loss that she wanted to deliver at the looming pageant, Shiloh was still feeling cute when she pulled up to the stucco, one-story house in North Milwaukee that Monica shared with her dad and grandmother.

Eleanor peeked out of the front door and waved hello as Monica trotted out to the car and climbed in. Before they drove away, Shiloh leaned over and gave the girl a hug.

Monica grinned. "Thanks, Mrs. Griffin. I wouldn't have accomplished this without you. You told me I could do it, you helped me find audition pieces, you cheered me on. Thank you."

Shiloh beamed and squeeze Monica's hand. "You are more welcome than you know, Monica. I'm proud of you. I didn't know your mother, but I'm guessing that she's looking down from heaven, smiling on you with a proud heart, too."

Monica turned away and peered out of the window, and Shiloh worried that she had upset her. When the girl turned back toward Shiloh, her cheeks were wet.

"I still miss her," Monica said softly and wiped her tears with the back of her hand. "And I wonder what she would say about all of this."

Shiloh didn't know how best to respond, so she prayed. *Heal her heart, Father. Let her feel her mother's love even from afar, and let her know that you are here and that you love her, forever and ever.*

"Where to, Miss Monica? What do you have a taste for?"

Monica attempted a smile. "A burger is fine."

Shiloh frowned and started to protest that this occasion called for something more special and celebratory, but then she had an idea. "You know, I've been wanting to try this place downtown that my two Sherman Park teacher buddies were always raving about—let's go to Stack'd Burger Bar." Shiloh would have to call or text Eva and Kris later, and brag about finally visiting one of their favorite dining spots without them.

Monica nodded. "I've heard of it. They have gourmet burgers, and veggie burgers, and all that kind of stuff. Let's give it a try."

Fifteen minutes later, they were in downtown Milwaukee, in the Fifth Ward, waiting to be seated. For a Saturday around lunchtime, the place was quieter than Shiloh had expected. She was sure that on this unusually mild weekend in early November, people were outside raking leaves before the weather turned cold, or finding fun things to do. She and Monica would benefit by having fewer people to talk over, as they mapped out her future as a professional flutist.

They ordered and enjoyed their delicious burgers on pretzel buns, along with the restaurant's specialty—fried pickles and onion rings. They also chatted about the school recital held at Sherman Park earlier that week. Shiloh took this as an opportunity to share the concerns she'd had that night about Trey Holloman.

"I saw the look you gave Mr. Football Star when he walked by with one of the cheerleaders that night," Shiloh said and took a sip of water. "Don't let him worry you; guys like that blow through girls like nothing. Just like he was in your face and now he's in hers, he'll be hitting on someone else next week."

Monica seemed sad, but she agreed. "I know; you're right."

Shiloh decided not to dwell on it and switched subjects to the real reason for their meeting today. "Tell me about the summer program. When do you leave? How long will you stay?"

Monica finished her half-full glass of soda, sat back in her seat, and sighed. She seemed overwhelmed.

"You okay, Monica? I thought you were excited."

She sat forward again and perched her elbows on the table. "I am, it's just that . . ."

Monica's voice quivered and Shiloh glanced around to make sure they hadn't drawn anyone's attention. Even though they were in the clear, she signaled for the waitress to bring their check, so they could head out and find a private place to talk.

Monica took a deep breath and continued. "I have something to tell you, Mrs. Griffin, and I don't know what it will mean for this summer."

Shiloh tried to remain expressionless, like she did when one of her sons was baring his soul about something that freaked her out, but she didn't want him to know. She stayed silent, so Monica would keep talking, and reminded herself that though she felt it, the girl could not hear or see the anxiety causing her heart to thump faster and louder.

"What is it, my friend? You can tell me anything."

"Mrs. Griffin, I want to go to the summer program, and I guess I will. But first, first I have to get rid of this baby."

Shiloh's eyes bulged, but she caught herself before the shriek left her throat. In one breath, this gifted, sweet child had zapped Shiloh back to her own youth, to that summer in France, when she had sat with herself, by herself, and come to a similar conclusion about a baby she was carrying. She had made a decision that devastated her.

Shiloh inhaled and pulled herself back to the present, to this conversation. "Monica . . . are you telling me that you are pregnant, sweetheart?"

Monica's eyes swelled with tears and she lowered her head, unable to make eye contact with Shiloh. Her shoulders shook with her silent sobs. When the waitress returned with their check, she peered at Monica in concern.

Shiloh shook her head, indicating that the woman shouldn't bother her. "She's upset so we need to go. Let me give you cash for our bill, and you can keep the change."

When the waitress was gone, Shiloh gently grasped one of Monica's wrists and led her out of the restaurant, to the car. She wanted to weep, too. This girl had become her daughter, and her heart was broken that Monica was so scared and broken.

The van was parked a block away, in front of an empty warehouse, and after unlocking it with her keychain fob, Shiloh decided that rather than get behind the wheel, she and Monica should sit on one of the passenger rows, so they could talk. When the van door whizzed open, Shiloh ushered Monica inside, then climbed in behind her. She locked them inside, reached for the box of tissues she kept in the section between the driver's seat and the front passenger seat, and handed one to Monica. She gave the girl a few minutes to compose herself, hugged her, then waited.

When Monica's tears were spent, she looked at Shiloh with red eyes that conveyed a palpable fear. "I'm sorry; I've let you down."

Shiloh reached for Monica's hand. She wanted to tell the girl she had let herself down, but she knew that would be hurtful. She also wanted to ask who and what had happened, but in her heart, she already knew.

"So Trey Holloman had his fun, then decided to flaunt his new girlfriend in front of you." Shiloh stared past the driver's seat of the van, through the windshield. "Now I understand why you were angry at the recital. Does Phaedra know?"

"She knows what happened between me and Trey, but that's all," Monica said. "I got the letter in the mail yesterday right after school. Before Grandma Eleanor came home, I went to one of the neighborhood drugstores where she doesn't shop and got a pregnancy test, because my stomach had been feeling funny and I was two weeks late. The double blue line came up really quick . . ."

Shiloh sat up.

"So you just found out all of this yesterday? You haven't been to a doctor yet?"

Monica shook her head. Now Shiloh understood the 8 a.m. call and the girl's urgency to see her today. The poor girl probably hadn't slept all night.

"I didn't know what to do. I figured you would know," Monica said.

But Shiloh didn't. She was still living with the consequences of her long ago secret decision; how could she advise someone else what to do, with two lives hanging in the balance?

"Monica, I'm in this with you no matter what. I hate that you fell for what Trey was after. Did it happen just once?"

Monica looked away, embarrassed. "Yes. It happened on our third date, and then he stopped calling and wouldn't answer my calls. He told me that he was going to come to the recital, and I thought it was because he wanted to see me. Then he showed up with her, Miss Prissy, and walked by me like I didn't even exist. I guess that was his sick way of letting me know it was over."

Monica shook her head, as if to erase the memory. "I believed it when he told me he was falling in love with me. I should have known better."

"How would you have known better?" Shiloh asked.

She recalled that day at Sherman Park in September when she had seen Trey flirting with Monica and asking for her phone number. She should have warned the girl then, instead of staying out of it. Eleanor was a wonderful grandmother, but Monica needed her mother there to be overprotective, to tell her how boys think, and to help her see past their sweet words and promises and kisses. She rubbed Monica's hand.

"When you know better, you can do better," Shiloh said. "One thing I hope you are planning to do is to accept your spot in the summer music program and participate."

Monica looked at her and frowned.

"For what? Either I'm going to be a candidate for that TV show, *16 and Pregnant*, give up the baby for adoption, or do what I said in the restaurant. My dad and grandmother are going to team up on me, and make me decide. And whichever way I choose, my punishment is going to be staying home with them all summer, not going to some fabulous program for gifted students."

"But you *are* gifted, and this is a great chance to jump-start your plans for college," Shiloh said.

Even as she uttered the words, though, she knew college and otherwise planning for the future were the last things on Monica's mind right now. What could she, or should she, tell this girl about how to proceed? She knew Monica's relatives fairly well from spending time with them at church, but not well enough to know how they would react to Monica's situation. But Monica needed to tell them, and soon.

"I take it you haven't bothered to call Trey and share this news?"

"I sent him a text and asked him to call me about something really important," Monica said, "but I haven't heard from him, and I don't really expect to."

Shiloh didn't say more; she pulled Monica into her arms and hugged the girl. She was frustrated at Monica for putting herself in this position and wanted to scold her and shake her. On the other hand, Monica's revelations had thrust Shiloh back in time, to her own youth, when as a girl much older than Monica was today, she had made some similar naïve choices that left her terrified and tortured.

She couldn't and wouldn't make any decisions for Monica, because she knew that someday Monica would be her age, looking back over her life and assessing both the powerful and painful decisions she'd made. Monica would need to discuss her options with her family and make her decisions based on their counsel and guidance, not Shiloh's. One thing was certain, though: Shiloh knew she was going to have to break a promise to herself to never tell another soul what she had done in France that summer. In order to save Monica, she would have to step into her Esther moment and at some point tell the truth about her past.

forty-one

Monica seemed dazed, but when Shiloh asked to pray with her, she agreed.

"Dear Father, we're coming to you this afternoon with both gratitude and heavy hearts, with fear and doubts. Monica has shared something both personal and life-changing with me. She has made some choices that have led her here, and here we are, seeking your will and your guidance. We don't really know what to pray for, God. We are grateful for the acceptance into the summer music program, yet this other news . . . Lord, we don't even know what to say. You know I am speechless and heartbroken. Monica is afraid and in search of answers. Speak to her heart, Lord, and give me wisdom as well, so that I can nurture her in a way that pleases you. Allow her father and grandmother to show compassion when she tells them her news, and let them respond with wisdom and with a solution that honors you. Help Monica to know that no matter what, she is not alone; I am with her, as are you. In Jesus' name, amen."

Shiloh thought of the Scripture in Isaiah that Jade had shared in Bible study not too long ago, about not fearing and trusting that God was with you. She needed to believe that right now, and she wanted Monica to believe it as well. In the short term, she might have to help carry the girl through. Her silent prayer was that Monica's father and Eleanor would do the same.

Monica lifted her head and wiped the fresh round of tears streaming down her cheeks. "What now?" she asked.

Shiloh reached for her purse on the floor and dug around inside until she found her cell phone. When she had it in hand, she answered Monica's question.

"I think we should call your dad and grandmother to see if they're both home, and if so, I'll go in with you to tell them what's going on."

Monica looked like she'd rather get hit by a bus. "I know what they're going to say, after they kill me. I can't face them; I can't. This will tear them up, they'll be angry . . ."

Shiloh sat in silence and let Monica have her moment. When she was calmer, Shiloh still waited. And finally, Monica slumped her shoulders and relented. "Call them." She whispered her surrender, but Shiloh could tell she knew it was inevitable.

Instead of calling, Shiloh texted Claude to ask if he and Eleanor were there, because she and Monica needed to have an important talk with them. He responded seconds later and told her they would be waiting for her and Monica to return.

Shiloh squeezed Monica in a tight hug, as if doing so would transfer strength from her heart to the girl's. Ten minutes later, they both had moved to the front seats of the van, and were riding in silence to Monica's home. The radio was turned down, and although she wasn't certain, Shiloh had a pretty good idea of what Monica had on her mind. Shiloh alternated from praying for Monica's future, to praying for Claude and Eleanor to offer their support regardless of the heartbreaking circumstances, to praying for this whole experience to somehow shape Monica for the better and draw her closer to God.

When they pulled in front of Monica's house, her father Claude was standing on the porch, hands on his hips, waiting for them. His furrowed brow told Shiloh that her text had set off a round of worry. His eyes locked on Monica and stayed there while Shiloh parked. He didn't appear angry or sad, just resolute.

Shiloh stepped out of the van first and walked around to the passenger side, where she opened the door for Monica, who had begun weeping again. Shiloh helped her out of the van and to the porch, where her dad waited. Eleanor emerged from the house and embraced Monica.

"It's alright, baby, whatever it is."

"You know and I know," Claude said, without looking at his mother, Monica, or Shiloh. Instead, he turned his eyes heavenward. "She's pregnant."

forty-two

Monica looked at her father, both stricken and surprised.

Shiloh wasn't, though. If one of her sons had come home in a similar situation, she would most likely be able to surmise or detect the source of their angst, or at least narrow the possibilities.

Claude still didn't look at his daughter, but when she answered him with a timid, "Yes, Daddy," his eyes filled with tears, and Shiloh saw the first hint of anger.

"That sucker!" He punched at the air. "I knew the first time he came around here sniffing for a date that he was up to no good. I don't care how good he is in football, a jerk is a jerk."

Shiloh looked from Monica to her father. She hadn't realized that Trey Holloman had met Claude, taken Monica on at least one formal date, and still had found the nerve to take advantage of her.

"Then he walks you up to the house and pecks you on the cheek like he's a gentleman." Claude was speaking now through clenched teeth. "He knew I was watching from one of the windows and wanted to leave a 'good impression.' Jerk. Where is he now, huh?"

He punched at the air again, and Monica disengaged from her grandmother's embrace so she could approach him. She stood tentatively nearby, waiting for him to acknowledge her. When he didn't, she spoke again. "Daddy, I'm so sorry. I didn't mean for this to happen. I didn't mean to hurt you."

He looked at her and the tears spilled down his cheeks. "What would your mother say? I've done the best I can by you, even getting your grandmother to move in with us to keep things as normal as possible. And you didn't have enough sense to tell that knucklehead boy to go on about his business?"

"Claude!" Eleanor stepped toward the two of them and touched her son's arm to calm him. "Let's take this inside. Everyone is upset, and we need to sit down and work through this."

Claude shook his head and set his jaw. "Sorry, Mama. There's nothing to discuss. My baby is not ready for a child. She's just in tenth grade."

He looked at Monica, who still stood to his side, facing him, and enduring his tirade.

"Someone from Columbia College Chicago called yesterday about that program you were selected for, to congratulate you. You were one of twenty-five students selected nationwide, out of three hundred and fifteen applicants. Should we call them back and ask if they offer childcare?"

Monica flinched and lowered her head. "I'm so sorry, Daddy. I know I've messed up."

He exhaled loudly and slowly, and then grabbed her, and gave her a hug. "We're going to fix this so you'll still have a future, but promise me you won't do this again."

Monica's eyes widened as she leaned into her dad's embrace. Eleanor frowned, and Shiloh's heart sank.

"Claude . . . ," Eleanor said again. "Let's go on in and sit down and get some idea of what Monica is thinking, what she has to say about all of this. Mrs. Griffin is here . . . she can pray with us, and help us process all of this."

Shiloh nodded at him, to indicate her willingness to help. "I can call Pastor Randy as well, if you'd like him to come over."

Claude hesitated, then shook his head. "Prayer alone won't fix this—not any more than it helped my wife when she was dying," he said. "Thank you for your support, Mrs. Griffin, and thank you for being here for Monica. I think the three of us will figure it all out from here, but thank you for everything."

He turned toward the house with Monica, who was still gripping his waist, to lead her inside. She glanced at Shiloh but followed her father's direction. Shiloh saw a mixture of fear, helplessness, and desperation in the girl's eyes. Shiloh did the only thing she knew to do: prayed for God to take control of the situation in the way that would be best.

forty-three

This wasn't the first time Shiloh wished she could sit on the back pew or in the balcony at St. Stephens Baptist, but today that desire was immense.

She wanted to sit and watch the door, to see if Monica and her family would come strolling in fifteen or so minutes before service, as they had done every Sunday for the past five weeks. She prayed they would. She needed them to. And regardless of whether Monica knew it, she needed them to bring her, so she could spend a few hours in God's presence, basking in his unconditional grace and love, no matter what the future held.

Shiloh hadn't heard from Monica since leaving her in her father's care yesterday, and as a result, she was a distracted mess. She had sent a text to the girl around 10 p.m. the night before, simply asking if she was okay, and after receiving no response, she hadn't slept much. After asking several times what was wrong, Randy finally seemed to get the message that she wasn't ready, or able, to talk about it.

"Is it Monica?"

Her simple nod and rush of tears yielded the response she needed from him. A hug, a promise to pray for Monica, and an offer to listen, or visit with Monica himself, if and when needed.

Shiloh sat in service now, fretting that she couldn't turn around in her first-row pew without being conspicuous. She tried to calm herself and lose herself in the present, knowing that worry wouldn't change a thing, and that she was honestly in the best place to help Monica, if Monica couldn't be here herself.

She clutched her Bible and stood as the young adult choir rendered a beautiful version of Stephen Hurd's "Lead Me to the Rock."

When my heart is overwhelmed, my prayer is, lead me to the rock . . .

She contained her tears by lowering her head and closing her eyes to utter yet another prayer for Monica, Claude, Eleanor, the baby she was carrying, and even Trey Holloman. The choir continued singing, and the lyrics comforted her. God *was* her firm foundation, and Monica's. He *was* their solid rock.

The song reminded Shiloh that she wasn't in control of any of this, and while she needed to pray and be vigilant in waging war against evil and doubt on Monica's behalf, she also had to surrender Monica and her destiny to God.

Shiloh lifted her head and opened her eyes to find Randy staring at her. She gave him a broken smile and he gave her a broad one, reassuring her that he was standing with her, just as God was, and when she was feeling weak, he would be her strength. Shiloh wanted to blow him a kiss or at least wink at him, but even that wouldn't go unnoticed in this setting. She settled for a slight nod, which he acknowledged with one of his own.

She wasn't sure whether Randy did it intentionally, but he helped allay her questions about Monica and her family's presence in service by calling for a period of fellowship earlier than usual.

"Stand and greet at least five people not sitting next to you!" he said. "Tell them good morning! Tell them you love them! Tell them God is good, all the time, and all the time, God is good!"

Shiloh was grateful for the opportunity to circulate and to see if she could find Monica, Claude, and Eleanor in the mingling congregation. They typically sat in the left rear section, and she made her way in that direction. They were nowhere to be found, and while her spirits sank, she had to admit that she wasn't surprised. She had to give this situation to God, and leave it with him.

As that reality resonated with her, a truth struck her core: How could she ask God to help her release her burden for Monica, when she hadn't released the guilt from her own sins that weighed her down? How could she be more concerned about Monica's fate than about her own? As the members began returning to their seats and Shiloh greeted and smiled her way back to the first pew, the truth filled her spirit. This wasn't just about Monica's future, it was about hers, too. Both of them might be delivered, but without one stepping up first, the other might not have a chance. If Shiloh didn't share her experiences, Monica might feel just as alone with her shame as Shiloh had.

Shiloh took her seat and glanced at her husband, who was reviewing a Scripture he would read aloud in a few seconds. Was God really asking her to do the unthinkable and shatter not only her world, but his, too?

forty-four

Shiloh hadn't forgotten the questions or the answers that had consumed her during worship service today, but tonight as she wrestled with how and where to begin the conversation with her family, a call from Dayna removed the sense of urgency. Daddy had suffered what doctors believed was a mild heart attack.

"Mama called me right away to ask my advice about the protocol the doctors are using to treat Daddy. I think it's fine, but she was so upset that I told her I'd take care of letting you and Jessica know," Dayna said. "She rode to the hospital in the ambulance with Daddy and called me as soon as they wheeled him away. I'm taking a late flight out of Orlando to be with her. The deacons from church are with her now, but one of us needs to be with her as she meets with doctors and tries to figure out what's going on. I called an administrator I know at the hospital a few minutes ago and found out that the nursing supervisor in the heart unit was one of my RN classmates at Alabama U. I'll make sure Daddy gets the best care possible."

Dayna sounded efficient and thoughtful, and Shiloh had the feeling her older sister was on autopilot—operating as she routinely did in her workplace. Thank God Dayna had a nursing degree and worked in a hospital setting every day. That would serve Daddy well.

"You'll be getting in late," Shiloh said, still trying to process it all. "Who is picking you up?"

"Deacon Miller offered to come and get me."

"I may need to be picked up, too," Shiloh said. "I'm grateful that you're going and getting there so quickly, Dayna. I'm coming too, though. I'll check flights as soon as you and I hang up."

Shiloh hadn't known what she was thinking, though; Daddy was more than Randy's father-in-law. Before Shiloh could finish explaining what Dayna had shared, Randy had begun texting Vic and a few key deacons at St. Stephens Baptist to let them know he'd be out of town for a few days, checking on his father-in-law in Alabama.

"I can drive through the night and get us there before noon tomorrow," Randy said.

"But you preached two services today," Shiloh said. "You are worn out. You can't drive through the night like this."

"I'll be fine," Randy said. "Who can you get to come and watch the boys while we're gone? Lem will say he's fine staying here and looking out for them, but he's just sixteen and David's just nine. We need a mature adult keeping an eye on all of them."

Lem entered the family room just as Randy made that declaration and seemed miffed. "Didn't hear why you're trying to line up a babysitter for your eleventh grader, but no thanks, Dad."

Randy gave Lem a Cliff Notes summary of what was going on with his grandparents, and the teen's attitude shifted from indignation to concern.

"Is Pawpaw going to be okay? I just talked to him yesterday," Lem said. "He called me on my cell to chat for a few minutes."

Shiloh was surprised and touched. The father she had grown up with didn't have time for that kind of emotional outreach to his daughters; he dispensed it all to his congregation. It was nice to see that beneath his tough exterior, he was understanding the benefit of connecting with family. He and Lem must have bonded over the summer in the same way he had once bonded with Randy. The fact that he'd withheld that level of attentiveness from his daughters was bruising, but Shiloh decided to focus on the fact that he was at least trying with his grandson.

"Your mom and I are going to leave as soon as we can get somebody to come over and stay with you guys," Randy said.

"I'll call Sister Stanley from church," Shiloh said. "She's watched the boys before and she's retired; hopefully this won't be too much of an imposition for her."

Lem stuck his hands in his pockets and looked from one parent to the other. "I hope she can come and stay, too, because I need to go with you."

Shiloh almost snapped at him in irritation. "This isn't about facilitating your and Lia's love connection, Lem," she said after taking a deep breath. "Daddy is sick, and we are driving down to get to his side as soon as possible. No time for anything else."

Randy glared at him. "Your mother's right. You need to get your priorities straight."

Lem turned away and then turned back toward them. "Please let me go, please. Maybe if Pawpaw sees me, that will help him. I'm not asking you to drive me to Lia's, but I want to go."

Shiloh was a knot of helpless emotions. Her thoughts see-sawed from Monica and her choices, to her father and his health. It was all too much, and she didn't have the strength to fight Lem. She looked at Randy and lifted her palms in surrender. She couldn't make this choice; she needed to focus her prayers and energy on Daddy and Mama right now.

forty-five

Mrs. Stanley arrived at 10:30 p.m., and after waking the younger boys to tell them where they were going and why, Randy and Shiloh loaded their luggage in the back of their van and headed for Alabama.

Lem had won the fight. He settled in the backseat and turned on his headphone-ready iPod. Shiloh was certain that he was also texting Lia to let her know he'd soon be in her state. She wasn't sure how she'd felt about Randy's decision to let him go, but she decided not to fret or complain. Lem had packed his textbooks and emailed his teachers to request his assignments for the next few days so he wouldn't fall behind. To his credit, Randy had warned Lem that a slip in grades would mean no phone, no iPod, and no access to Miss Lia, or any of his friends when they returned.

"I'm letting him go because if we don't, this crush of his will only intensify," he'd told Shiloh when they were in their room alone, getting ready for the trip. "Sometimes you have to let them have their way to teach them a bigger lesson. Let him come. I guarantee you he's going to figure out a way to see this girl while we're in Atchity, and maybe it will help both of them calm down."

Shiloh wasn't so sure, but these days, she wasn't sure of much. Texts from Dayna reassured her that Daddy had indeed suffered a mild heart attack and would have two stents inserted into his arteries in the morning. Her texts to Monica continued to go unreturned. It made Shiloh angry, because she'd done nothing but support Monica and stand with her through thick and thin. And yet, her rational side understood; this was a family crisis of gargantuan proportions. Her father may have warned her to keep quiet about everything, or he may have even taken her phone. Anything could have happened. Still, Shiloh decided that if she hadn't heard something from the girl by tomorrow evening, after she had made it to Alabama and ensured that Daddy was okay, she was going to call Eleanor for an update, to make sure Monica was holding up.

Shiloh felt guilty for following her son's lead, but after checking to make sure Randy was wide awake, she slightly reclined the seat of the Lincoln and closed her eyes.

"Hmmm, sweet dreams, princess," Randy said sarcastically, but patted her thigh.

Shiloh woke at 2 a.m. to drive until five. She napped in the early morning, then drove again from seven to nine. Finally at 11 a.m. they crossed the Alabama state line. Shiloh glanced at Randy, whose eyes were glued to the road as he sang along to a gospel CD. She peered in the backseat and saw that Lem was knocked out. A quick check of her cell phone revealed that she had voicemails from Jessica and Jade, and a text from Monica.

Shiloh sat up straight and started with the latter. The message from Monica was brief, but reassuring all the same.

I'm okay. Going to school today as usual. Will call when I can.

Shiloh had tons of questions, but unless she was going to force herself into the girl's space, it was clear answers weren't going to be forthcoming right away. She'd have to keep praying and waiting. She sent a quick text to tell Monica where she was and to invite her to call.

Jessica's voicemail message came through first. "Hey, Shiloh. I'm traveling from Texas and will land in Alabama around ten a.m. I've left a message for Dayna, too, but wanted to let you know I'm on my way. Hope you're holding up okay."

Shiloh appreciated Jessica reaching out. At a time like this, she needed all the sisterly comfort she could get.

Jade's call had been last. It hit Shiloh as she prepared to listen to the message that this was Jade's big week. The pageant was this Friday, and a big group from St. Stephens Baptist had bought tickets to attend and cheer her on. Shiloh's own ticket was in her purse, she remembered—a complimentary one from Jade. If she was going to be here longer than expected, she might need to find a way to quickly mail it back, so Jade could share it with someone else and it wouldn't go to waste.

"Hi, Shiloh, Vic told me last night what was going on with your dad, and I'm just calling to let you know that I've contacted the women in our Bible study and we are bathing you and your father and your entire family in prayer. Fear not, my friend. God is with you, and so are we . . . Love you."

Love you?

Shiloh shook herself to make sure she'd heard correctly. Those words flowing from Jade Smith? To her? There was indeed a God. Despite her longstanding cynicism, God had been softening her heart toward her "Second Lady," and obviously he'd been doing the same work on Jade's attitude toward her. He was something else, and Shiloh realized she was thankful. She'd never be beauty queen material herself and truthfully, had no desire to be. It hadn't hurt, however, to have someone in her world who saw beauty as a ministry of sorts; not a way to just paint the outside with flair, but a means of allowing the outside to reflect the beauty within. Jade had explained that concept to her last Saturday, while they worked on her pageant speech, and since then, Shiloh had seen Jade in a new light. Maybe she had really seen her for the first time, and she'd left their morning meeting wondering if the delay had been her own fault.

Shiloh texted Monica back with the very words Jade had used:

Love you. Call me as soon as you can.

She'd shared that sentiment with Jade as well.

Thanks for the call and prayers. In case I don't make it back
before you leave town on Wednesday to head to Fond du Lac,
all the best getting ready for Friday's pageant. You are a winner,
and God is going to use you!

They reached the city limits, and Randy drove straight to Atchity
Regional Memorial Hospital. Shiloh had forgotten to ask Dayna for
Daddy's room number, but Randy assured her it didn't matter.

"This hospital has an information desk like all others—at least
we hope," he joked. "One way or another, we'll get to Dad's room
okay, even if we have to knock on each one until we find him."

Shiloh hadn't received an update from Dayna in the past few
hours. She hoped that meant all was well. She and Daddy had never
been super close, primarily because he'd always been busy with his
parishioners. But he was her daddy, and she loved him, and in case he
didn't realize that, she was looking forward to telling him in person.

forty-six

Finding Daddy's hospital room became a simple game of follow the church members.

Shiloh, Randy, and Lem boarded an elevator to reach the third-floor cardiac unit and found themselves surrounded by Riverview Baptist members who had come to check on their pastor. They were thrilled to see the family.

"Ya'll been gone two years, but you look the same! Sister Shiloh, you done got a little thicker! Lookin' good back there."

Shiloh glared at Randy, even though the frisky, seventy-year-old deacon who always had a comment that should be kept to himself deserved her visual wrath. Randy pursed his lips to contain his laughter and fixed his gaze on the climbing elevator floor numbers. Shiloh wanted to kick him for not defending her, even though she knew a response would cause more drama.

They stepped out of the elevator before she could think of a respectful, yet pointed comeback, and the opportunity was lost, as all attention shifted to trying to reach her father's room. It meant walking down a hallway full of more Riverview Baptist members, and having a mini homecoming "meet and greet," which was the last thing Shiloh had anticipated or wanted. She was surprised that doctors hadn't shooed some of these people away, or that Dayna hadn't asked them to leave or take shifts. That would have broken every rule in the Southern hospitality guidebook, though. These folks were here to show their respect and love for their pastor; Daddy wouldn't have wanted it any other way.

By the time she found his room, she had to identify herself to a nurse stationed nearby. The woman agreed to let her, Randy, and Lem enter, and the minute Lem pushed the door open for her, Shiloh began to tremble, unsure of what to expect. Randy grasped her hand and led her inside.

Daddy was hooked up to several beeping and pulsing machines, but he seemed to be sleeping. He looked frail and older than Shiloh remembered. Mama sat in a chair near the head of his bed, dozing. Shiloh approached her and touched her arm.

Mama startled awake, but a smile swept across her face when she raised her head and saw Shiloh. "You made it!" Mama stood to embrace her and Randy and gasped when she saw Lem standing behind them. "You brought one of my grandbabies, praise God!"

At five feet seven, Lem was her height. That didn't stop her from gathering him in her arms and rocking him back and forth in a pendulum-like hug for several minutes. When she released him, Lem looked embarrassed, but understanding.

Mama took Randy's hand and led him over to the bed, where they stood side by side gazing at Daddy. Left in the background with Lem, resentment filled Shiloh's chest. Now was no time to seemingly throw a tantrum, though. She moved to the other side of Mama, opposite of Randy, and peered at her father. She said a silent prayer for a quick recovery, just as Randy uttered one aloud.

"Father, thank you for allowing Dad's condition to be caught as soon as it was so this wasn't worse. Please heal him completely, restore his energy, and let him continue to serve you as you see fit. Amen."

Randy hugged Mama. "Does Dad know he's a rock star? The hallway and elevators are filled with Riverview Baptist members."

Mama's eyes widened. "Lord have mercy . . . I didn't know! I need to go out there and thank them for coming . . ."

Shiloh touched her shoulder and shook her head. "This is no time for social niceties, Mama. Just take care of Daddy, and yourself. They'll understand."

Mama paused to consider Shiloh's advice. "You are right; they will understand. I can thank them all during an upcoming service." She turned and hugged Shiloh. "I'm so glad you're here, Shiloh. Times like these cause me to miss having you and Randy here with us, at church. You two were our backup team."

Randy smiled at Mama. "I know it's probably too soon to have this figured out, but any idea who's going to preach this coming Sunday?"

Mama's eyes gleamed with hope when she peered at him.

"No, Mom, I don't think so," Randy said. "Shiloh and I have to get back to the younger boys, plus Lem is missing school to be here, so we'll be heading out in another day or so. We just had to come and lay eyes on Dad for ourselves, and to pray for him and with him."

Mama nodded. "I understand, son. I'm sure the deacons will fig-ure something out for us this week."

She looked toward Daddy and her expression softened. Shiloh saw a tenderness in Mama's eyes she'd never noticed before. This wasn't just a First Lady doing her "job" of honoring her preacher husband; Mama loved Daddy. Serving him, being his helpmate, was her life's calling—her contribution to the building of God's kingdom.

That realization made Shiloh want to weep, because for the first time she understood the mother she had sought to emulate all these years. In some ways, she had been going through the motions—playing the part of the good daughter, the good wife, and the good mother, when for Mama, doing those things were a passion. Shiloh didn't love her family or her husband any less; but it was clear she had to walk her own path and carve a niche of her own, while Mama may have been led to her role by the Lord.

Part of her purpose was to teach; that was something Shiloh could no longer deny. How that would mesh with the life she had established with Randy, she didn't know, but she was thankful that Randy was supportive in helping her figure it out. The same look of love she saw Mama bestow on Daddy was what she felt for her husband.

Mama kissed Daddy's forehead, and motioned for Shiloh, Randy, and Lem to follow her out of the room. Shiloh kissed him, too, before moving away from his bed. Daddy didn't stir, but she quashed her fears by reminding herself he was heavily medicated.

"How are you going to get out of here without stopping to speak to all of those waiting church members?" Shiloh asked Mama.

Mama looked to Randy for a solution. He looked to Shiloh, who shrugged.

"Where's Dayna?" Shiloh asked.

"She and Warren stepped out to get something to eat. They said they'd be back shortly. Why don't you call her? She'll know how to handle them," Mama said.

"No . . . ," Shiloh said, trying to devise another solution. Dayna and Warren had moved heaven and earth to get there as quickly as they could after finding out Daddy was sick; they needed what little down time they had taken.

Shiloh poked her head out of the door and motioned for a young nurse at the station across from Daddy's room to come. "Can you help us get out of here without being mobbed by our well-wishers? My mother can't handle that right now."

The nurse returned to her desk and shared the request with another nurse, who appeared about ten years older. The woman reviewed some notes on a chart, then rounded up everyone in the hallway.

"If you're here for Reverend Wilson, I can tell you that he's doing fine and a full recovery is expected. However, what he needs most right now is some rest, and of course, your prayers. His family also needs some breathing room. So if you'll give them the space to come and go, that would serve Reverend Wilson best right now. They can't talk or visit right now; so please keep them in your prayers, but allow them to have this private time as a family."

Riverview Baptist members gathered their purses or coats and slowly left. Others, like the flirtatious deacon who had arrived at the same time as Shiloh and her family, didn't budge. Shiloh was about to instruct Mama to paste on a polite smile and wade through the congregation as best she could, when a handsome, red-headed doctor wearing an official white coat came through and cleared his throat.

"Good evening, saints! I'm sure Reverend Wilson would be grateful to know you all are here; but as his physician, I must ask you to give him time to get better. The best thing you can do for him and his family is pray for his healing, and their strength. We have to keep the hallways clear. If you are unable to find a seat in the waiting room, please come back some other time."

Within minutes, everyone was gone.

Shiloh turned to her family. "Didn't the nurse say almost the exact same thing?"

Randy grinned. "A doctor in a white coat is revered second only to God. You know that."

"Whatever works," Shiloh said. "Come on, Mama; let's get you out of here for a while." She turned and looked at Daddy. "You sure he's going to be alright?" After asking Mama the question, she kicked herself for possibly planting a seed of doubt.

"In the name of Jesus, I declare that he's already alright, Shiloh," Mama said. "Your daddy has a lot more living to do; he just needs to rest right now, and slow himself way down when he gets out of this hospital. He's got a hard head, but maybe he'll listen to the doctors, if not to me."

Shiloh opened the door for Mama, then led her from the room. They had almost reached the elevators when a young lady carrying a potted plant and wearing a vivid blue sundress turned the corner, striding as if she were on a mission. The teenager looked past Shiloh and Mama, and her eyes lit up. Shiloh heard Lem gasp, and she knew. Lia had come to Atchity.

"You're here," Lem said, awestruck.

The girl nodded. "I came as quickly as I could—all by myself. My grandfather allowed me to drive, as long as I promised to stick to the speed limit and not stop anywhere along the way. Is your grandfather okay?"

Lem seemed flustered now that he was in the presence of the girl he raved about every chance he got. If the circumstances had been different on this first meeting, Shiloh might have been amused to see her son so tongue-tied. Today, however, she watched with mild interest.

Lia turned toward Shiloh and Mama. "Hello, forgive me for being rude," she said, and extended her hand to Mama first. "You must be Lem's grandmother. I'm so sorry to have to meet you under these circumstances. My family and I have been praying for Reverend Wilson. He's well known in Birmingham, too, you know."

Shiloh couldn't help but be impressed. "Nice to finally meet you in person, Lia. Skype and OoVoo don't do you justice; you're lovely. Did you say your family knows my father?"

Lia nodded. "Nice to meet you, too, Mrs. Griffin. And yes, ma'am, we know of Reverend Wilson. Our pastor, Reverend Floyd, is good friends with him, and Reverend Wilson has preached several revival services at various churches in Birmingham."

"What's your name again, baby?" Mama asked.

"Lia—Lia Hamilton."

Shiloh stopped breathing, and if her head could have swiveled on her neck, it would have. This girl couldn't be part of *that* family. Shiloh took a closer look at her light brown skin, long hair, and thin nose. Forget might be—she was.

forty-seven

Lem wasn't the only one smitten with his friend; so was Mama.

She couldn't stop talking about how mannerly and pretty Lia was, and how impressed she was that the girl took time to travel an hour from Birmingham to Atchity to see Lem, and to check on his grandfather. But Shiloh couldn't think straight.

She'd left one secret ready to ripen back in Milwaukee, with her young friend, Monica, who still needed her. Now Shiloh had traveled home to Alabama and discovered that all summer, her son had been falling for a girl whose life was likely borne from Shiloh's other sin. Lia had joined Mama and the Griffin family for an early dinner before driving back to Birmingham, and the entire time Shiloh worried that she would do or say something that tipped her hand. Speaking very little had been her way of making it safely through the meal, but Shiloh knew she'd left Lia and Lem with the impression that she didn't care for Lia, which wasn't the case.

Two hours later, Shiloh sat on the bed in Mama's guest room, which had once been Dayna's girlhood haven, and waited for her sisters to arrive, so they could discuss a change in plans for Thanksgiving, which was just over a week away. She was certain they were going to move the family gathering back to Atchity, since Daddy wouldn't be able to travel; but the three of them needed to make it official. It seemed a given that the family cruise Jessica had in mind would be postponed. A family vacation could wait until Daddy was well, and truthfully, it would be appreciated more, when they could celebrate his return to health.

Allowing those logistics to creep into her thoughts hadn't been part of tonight's plans, which had included preparing and freezing some meals for Mama and Daddy to eat when he returned home, and taking a nap while Lem and Randy followed Lia part of the way back to Birmingham, so she wouldn't drive the whole way after dark alone. Mama was at Daddy's bedside again, awaiting the last visit of the night from his doctor, and Dayna was with her, so she could sit in on the discussion. Warren had driven Jessica to Birmingham to meet Keith at the airport. Since everyone else had come with their spouse in tow, Jessica had decided hers should be here, too.

Shiloh was frustrated that instead of relaxing as she had planned, she found herself wrestling with God. She felt like she was being pushed against a wall, with no choice but to push back and fight her way out—by baring her soul. That was the last thing she wanted to do. Some people managed to receive forgiveness and still take their secret shame and lies to the grave; couldn't she be one of them?

You can win. But only with the truth.

The response God spoke to her heart left her hopeful that she could be released from the shame and guilt that had burdened her for so many years; yet she also felt a tremendous fear of releasing the façade that all was right in her world. She wanted to worry about the inner Shiloh later, in her private time, when she could sort through everything at her own pace. But God wasn't having it.

He wanted her to do the unthinkable and tell it all to her family and friends and to whoever else needed to hear her testimony. As that reality sank in and Shiloh considered the consequences of obedience, she felt sick to her stomach. But how could she turn down this request from God? He had been so gracious and good to her all of these years. If this was the one thing he was requiring of her, she had to relent.

With that silent surrender came another pivotal truth: She was tired of running, hiding, and occasionally trying to explain away her behavior. When all of this was said and done, she knew none of that would matter anyway.

Shiloh slid off the bed and onto her knees and put her palms together. She bowed her head and opened her heart to God, because if he was going to require all of this from her, he had to tell her what to say, and prepare her for what was to come.

forty-eight

The decision to leave for Milwaukee Tuesday evening bought Shiloh a little more time to think everything through.

A great distraction, and blessing, occurred that morning, when Daddy woke up. With him now alert and already getting stronger, Mama feeling confident about his progress, and a promise to return with the entire family for Thanksgiving, Shiloh, Randy, and Lem departed just after 6 p.m. The ride home improved when, two hours into the trip, a text from Monica blazed across her cell phone screen.

I will call you soon. Dad is calming down.

Praise God. She had finally heard from her daughter. The message was cryptic, but at least Monica was communicating again. Shiloh texted her back to let her know she was happy to receive that message and that she would look forward to talking whenever, and however soon, Monica could.

Other texts began flying between Shiloh and women in the Bible study group, many of whom who were eagerly planning a caravan to Fond du Lac on Friday to support Jade in the Mrs. Wisconsin pageant. Shiloh chuckled at how the ladies had moved from what her students would have called "hater-ation"—wagging their fingers at Jade for being so superficial—to waving their hands in support of her.

Ya'll don't go out and break your banks, trying to get all fancy.
The camera and lights will be on the ladies on stage—not you,
St. Stephens Baptist divas! :)

Shiloh laughed out loud as she sent the group text to everyone on her Bible study list who was planning to attend the pageant. The ladies would get a kick out of her teasing, and she was glad to have this harmless outlet for her stress. If Daddy continued to improve and she didn't have any emergencies the rest of the week, Shiloh might make it to the live program after all.

Shiloh glanced at the clock on the dashboard and saw that with the time they were making, she would reach Milwaukee early enough to send her youngest three off to school Wednesday morning, and to get some rest before Bible study. She still might be too exhausted to lead it, but she could sit in. With this being the week before Thanksgiving and no Bible study scheduled for next Wednesday, maybe they could have an open faith discussion and gratitude reflection period, rather than a formal lesson.

She leaned over and patted Randy's shoulder. "Thank you for doing most of the driving, babe," she said. "And for taking time to get us to Atchity so quickly; love you."

He frowned at her. "You know I love your dad like he's my own, Shi, and in many ways, he has been. So why are you thanking me? Isn't this what we're trying to teach our boys—God first, family second? There was never a question that we needed to drop everything and be there for Dad, and for Mom."

She smiled at him. He was right; she knew there'd never been a question of whether they'd go to her father's bedside. It was more a matter of how soon, and how many of the boys they'd take with them.

Lem cleared his throat dramatically.

Randy copied him. "'Ahem,' back to you, sir," Randy said. "We haven't forgotten you're rolling with us."

"Can ya'll chill with the mushy stuff, then?"

"I'll be sure to tell you that, the next time I see you and Miss Lia making goo-goo eyes at each other," Shiloh retorted.

Lem blushed, but kept his eyes on Shiloh. "We weren't doing that," he said. "For real, though, what did you two think of her?"

Shiloh turned in her seat and faced Lem. "She is a lovely young lady, Lem, and I can see why you care for her," she said, remembering that her silence at dinner had probably led him to assume that she disapproved of the girl. "I knew you were planning to find a way to see her from the moment you jumped in this car with us, but it was commendable of her to drive down to see you and meet us on her own. I can tell that she really cares about you, too."

Lem nodded and seemed on the verge of speaking.

"What is it, son?"

"She thinks you have issues with her because she's being raised by her grandparents."

Before Shiloh could respond, Randy chimed in. "Why would she think that? Life happens. She can't help how she got here or who took on the responsibility of caring for her. Her grandparents were delightful. I enjoyed meeting them yesterday when you and I drove halfway to Birmingham. It said a lot about them, being willing to meet us at a halfway point to follow Lia the rest of the way home. In the brief time I was around them, and her, I could tell they care very much about her, and that they've raised her well. That's what matters."

Shiloh nodded. Soon, she would have to explain to both of them how Lia's family circumstances were indeed coloring her new relationship with the girl, but for now, Randy's explanation was sufficient.

"Your dad is right, Lem," she said. "We don't want you getting too serious about anyone right now. Both of you have your whole lives in front of you, and through its various twists and turns, you are going to change and grow. It isn't ideal or wise to settle so firmly in the middle of all of that morphing and stretching on who you want to be with long-term. If you are concerned about the fact that I didn't have much to say over dinner yesterday, that was all about me, not Lia. I apologize if I made you two think otherwise. At the same time, I ask that you continue calling each other just 'friends,' and consider dating other people, as you two get to know each other."

Even as she uttered that advice, however, Shiloh sensed that Lem was going to do what teenagers throughout the centuries did when their parents rendered wisdom in the context of a romance: hear it, and forget it, in the same breath with which it was spoken. Her eldest born gave her a tolerant smile and she turned to face the front again, marveling at where life had taken them.

She truly didn't hold a grudge against Lia; still, who would have known that allowing Lem to spend a few weeks in Alabama with his grandparents this past summer would lead to a serious teenage romance that could inadvertently put a chink in her personal emotional armor? She knew better than to question God or his timing, yet still wondered why he had so much faith in her ability to handle it all.

forty-nine

"You guys just got home after a fourteen-hour drive from Alabama and you're going to Bible study tonight? I'm impressed."

Her sister Jessica's teasing didn't bother Shiloh this morning, and besides, she had all day to rest. "Don't try to talk about me—if you had returned home to an audience waiting to hear your next speech, you'd pull out a dress and a pair of your fabulous heels and be there with bells on, baby girl."

There was a long pause.

"Yeah . . . you got me on that one. Guess I better bless you and send you on your way," Jessica said and laughed. "I'm just calling to let you know that Daddy came home about an hour ago. He is resting well, but he's another Christian that needs his mental capacity checked. The first thing out of his mouth when he crossed the threshold into the house was, 'Thank God.' The second was to ask Mama to fry him some catfish. And she had the nerve to seriously consider honoring the request! Dayna told Mama she was going to call PPS—'Preacher Protective Services'—on her if she cooked him anything in grease in the next twelve months."

Shiloh laughed until her sides hurt. She wished she had been there to see Mama's face as her oldest child reprimanded her. But Jessica's well-honed storytelling abilities helped Shiloh imagine the scene. She understood why her sister got paid the big bucks—and the call from Oprah.

"I'm glad Dayna was willing to move our Thanksgiving celebration back to Atchity," Shiloh said, changing the subject. "It's the best thing, with all that Daddy has gone through, and we really do have a lot to be thankful for."

"Yes, we do," Jessica said. "Dayna understands. Since we won't be taking the family cruise anytime soon, maybe we can all visit Florida in the spring, around Easter."

They chitchatted while Shiloh finished unpacking her bag and started a load of laundry. Jessica had called just after Shiloh had shooed Omari, Raphael, and David off to the school bus stop, and sent Lem and Randy to bed. When she wrapped up this call, she intended to join the Griffin men in napland.

"Easter sounds good," Shiloh said.

"I'll mention it when we're together next week, sis," Jessica said. "I'm signing off now, to check on Mama and Daddy again. Talk to you soon."

That one word—*sis*—sent a rush of joy through Shiloh that she hadn't expected, or felt before. She was grateful to hear Jessica use the term of endearment, and grateful for the direction in which their relationship was headed; but the timing was bittersweet. What would happen when Jessica found out about the real Shiloh?

fifty

Tonight's Bible study class had a third fewer attendees than usual, despite Shiloh's text to the members that she was back in town and eager to gather. She suspected some of them were out this evening searching for the right outfit for Friday's pageant. Or maybe they thought she'd be too tired to teach. Shiloh noted that the murmuring and soft conversations of those who were present ceased when she entered the meeting room. She took her seat at the top of their circle and confronted them.

"Good evening, ladies, what gives?"

They looked from one to another, without responding, until Shiloh prodded them again. Sister Adelaide finally spoke up.

"Sister Griffin, you and Sister Smith have really helped us grow recently in how to love and accept others, including those who may be lost, hurt, or different from us in some way. We think one of our new members fits this category—your former student, Monica, and we don't know how to help her."

Another Bible study member, Dora, interjected. "I'm just going to put the truth on the line, and tell it like it is. You don't see Sister Eleanor here tonight because the word on the street is that her granddaughter, your student Monica, is pregnant. Now, I don't know how true that is, but that's what has been circulating around the church, and even out in the community, because the boy who apparently knocked her up is some sports star."

Shiloh tried to mask her emotions, and her breath caught in her throat. How on earth had word gotten out? She wondered if Monica knew that rumors were circulating. If so, she had to be devastated.

Shiloh willed herself to return to the present, and saw that the women were watching her intently, gauging her reaction. She didn't want to give away what she knew, but she didn't want to lie, either. Protecting Monica was the priority.

"I haven't talked to her since I left town to check on my father," she said, after releasing a long sigh. "I will call her first thing tomorrow. She is a wonderful and talented young lady. All I can say is, all of us have sinned and fallen short of the glory of God. I know I've messed up over and over again, and I'm thankful every day for God's new mercies. If what you all are hearing turns out to be true, then Monica is hurting and scared, and she and her family will need our support now more than ever."

That comment was followed by an awkward silence.

"Our support for doing something she had no business doing, something that's wrong in the eyes of God?" Sister Adelaide asked the question that seemed to be on all of their minds. They didn't utter their agreement or nod, but their eyes were fixed on her as she spoke, and they all seemed to be saying, "Amen, sister!"

Shiloh leaned forward. "But you don't know that what you've heard is true. Rumors are rumors, and until we are able to find out what's really going on with Monica, and with Sister Eleanor, I think it's best to withhold judgment and pray for the family, especially for this young girl whose mother died just two years ago. Even if it is true, that she made an unwise decision—and yes, committed a sin, since she had sex outside of marriage—if we allow her to deal with a pregnancy and then teenage motherhood alone, are we any less wrong?"

Some of the women glanced at Sister Adelaide to see how she would respond, but others hung their heads as they considered her position.

"Sister Griffin is right," Sister Dora said. "We can sit here and condemn this girl, or even Sister Eleanor when she returns, but what good will that serve? What will be the purpose behind that? We'll be no better than the Pharisees who sat watching Jesus healing and ministering to people, and all the while mocked and judged him for doing so on the wrong day of the week, or with the wrong kind of people, instead of understanding that he was effective precisely because he met people at the point of their need and accepted them for who they were. Pastor Randy is always talking about putting our faith into action. If these rumors are true, and Monica has done this thing, how can we help this young girl heal?"

Shiloh remained silent. She wanted the consensus on how to proceed to come from the women, not from her, since she was so close to Monica. Finally, these women were getting it. What would they say, though, when she shared her skeletons? She knew she couldn't focus on that; she had to simply do what God was compelling her to do when the time was right.

In the meantime, she would focus on tonight's pressing needs, and that meant leading the ladies in a prayer of support for Jade and the upcoming pageant. "Bless Jade, Father. Give her the opportunity to speak out and the courage to do so when she can. Permit her to go as high and as far as you desire in this pageant, even taking home the title. Allow her efforts to yield major blessings, for Jade and her family, and for all of the lives she touches as a result of this opportunity."

The women wrapped up the study by deciding who would reach out to Sister Eleanor to chat with her about whatever may be on her mind, and to invite her back to Bible study. They agreed that anyone who called or encountered her would focus on her potential needs and not mention Monica or the persistent rumor. If Sister Eleanor brought up Monica and requested prayer, they would comply. Otherwise, they would bathe the Garrett family in secret prayer and allow God to minister to their needs.

Shiloh agreed to the plan, but also asked God to give her the faith to believe they could pull it off. The church sisters' hearts were in the right place, but they were human. She prayed that God would block anyone who couldn't handle this appropriately from running into Eleanor, Monica, or Claude, and that he would send the right people at the right time to the family. She prayed that she was in the latter number, because she missed Monica, and she knew in her heart that Monica missed her. Monica's brief message last night gave Shiloh the impression that Claude was monitoring the girl's phone, or giving her limited access to it, especially since Monica hadn't kept her promise to call. The more time passed, the more anxiety Shiloh sought to keep at bay.

fifty-one

Shiloh left Bible study with Monica on her mind. The minute she settled into the passenger seat of the car to wait for Randy to lock the church doors, she decided she couldn't hold off any longer. Her heart pounded as she dialed the girl's number.

It didn't surprise her at this point when she didn't get an answer, but she left a message again, urging Monica to call. After what she'd heard tonight, she needed to talk to Monica, and soon.

Randy climbed into the car, buckled his seatbelt, and cranked the engine. A familiar Marvin Sapp song filled the airwaves: *So glad I made it* . . .

Shiloh's insides felt like jello. Before she changed her mind, she touched Randy's arm to stop him from putting the car in drive and heading toward home.

"Babe . . . I need to talk to you about something really important. Right now."

Randy's eyes filled with concern and Shiloh's filled with tears. "Don't worry—I'm not sick or dying and neither are the kids. But what I have to share may leave me wishing I were dead."

Randy responded by turning off the car. He shifted in his seat to face Shiloh, who wondered how just enough moonlight could be cast through the windshield to allow her and Randy to see each other's faces.

"Whatever it is, I'm here."

Tears fell as Shiloh grasped for the right way and the right words to begin. Reality hit her, though: There were no right words, and no right way. She just had to tell him the truth, and after all of these years, allow it to set her free. She didn't know what would happen after she made her revelations, but there was no turning back. She would be sharing all of herself for the first time in their seventeen-year marriage, and giving Randy a chance to decide which Shiloh he loved—the pretty and perfect Christian trophy wife, or the "good girl gone bad," who at one time had been selfishly willing to save her reputation and her future by any means necessary. She hadn't counted the steep cost back then, but as she thought about the recorder tucked away in the family room, near her two flutes, the melody of "Her Song" floated through her mind. After tonight, there would be no more private commemorations.

"I'm listening, Shiloh," he said and reached for her hand. "Let it go."

Let it go?

That's what God wanted her to do. Randy was asking the same. But that also was the source of her deep shame and pain—letting "it" go.

Shiloh fixed her eyes on her hands in her lap and blurted the truth that had held her hostage for nearly two decades.

"Eighteen years ago I had an abortion, Randy."

The silence that followed caused a chill to crawl up Shiloh's spine, and she was afraid to look his way. After a few seconds, however, she peeked at her husband. His face was contorting, with emotions ranging from disbelief to sorrow to disgust to horror flooding his eyes and his features. Her heart hurt, but she kept going, because if she didn't, she might not get another chance, nor the courage, to tell him everything.

"It happened the summer I went to France for my flute fellowship. I spent the bulk of those ten weeks dating a student from Spain who was there studying with harp professionals, and I got pregnant. Of course we broke up before the program ended, but by then, I was . . .

knocked up. I discovered it a few days before it was time to come home, and because I knew the relationship wasn't going anywhere, I didn't even bother to tell him. My future hung in the balance—the chance to finish college, my opportunity to shed my middle-sister status and shine with my flute, my reputation and even my father's, with his congregation. I felt like I had no choice. I took the so-called abortion pill, which was legal in France back then, but I still wound up in a medical clinic when I suffered severe cramping. One, or both, of those actions led to me murdering my unborn child."

There. She'd said it out loud. For the first time ever.

Shiloh lowered her head and wept. And she waited.

It felt like an eternity, but what must have been just a few minutes later, Randy squeezed the hand he was still holding. He didn't speak, but the pressure of his touch let her know he was there, and apparently he wasn't going anywhere. Dare she tell him the rest?

I am with you, my daughter.

God's sweet reminder gave her the courage to finish what she had started, and to ignore her pounding heart, accompanied by an overwhelming desire to crawl away in shame. Randy hadn't spoken yet, and she wasn't sure what he was thinking, but she kept talking.

"There's more . . ."

fifty-two

The ride home was long and quiet.

Shiloh finally stopped crying, and Randy released her hand so he could drive. He turned up the volume on the radio, but switched to a jazz station, which played nothing but instrumental numbers. No lyrics were necessary with his mind likely reeling from the unspeakable, Shiloh surmised.

Randy turned into their driveway and pulled the car into the garage. As the garage door lowered, he sat there, staring into space. Shiloh wasn't sure whether to go inside or wait for his direction on when to leave the car. Given all that she'd just dropped on him, the latter seemed wisest. So she turned her eyes forward as well, and prayed that her husband wouldn't leave her.

"When you agreed to marry me, were you in love with him?"

Randy's question took her aback. It was a legitimate query, though. Shiloh had selfishly failed to realize how he would be affected by the timing of her decisions, as well as by the decisions themselves. That same summer of her fellowship, Randy had decided to stay in Atchity to pursue his calling to the ministry. When she came back from France, Randy had asked her on a date, picking up where they'd left off before she traveled to France. Before that summer, Randy had seemed more taken by their occasional outings over the past eighteen months than she was, but Shiloh always went out with him when he asked, and usually ignored his romantic overtures. When she had returned home, broken and ashamed, and realized Randy was growing seriously fond of her, she took his deepening interest as a sign that God wanted her to devote her life to ministry, by serving as a helpmate to Randy. So when he asked her to marry him only two weeks later, before school started, she said yes.

Shiloh thoughtfully considered his question tonight: Had she been in love with Armando? She didn't think so. They hadn't known each other long, and were just excited to be on their own in a foreign country, flirting with someone different. She was disappointed when they broke up, but at the same time, they both knew it was inevitable. They lived in different countries and different cultures. Their summer together was a momentary season in their young lives—one they would remember, but not necessarily long to repeat. Armando had swooned over her and given her the kind of attention from a guy that she didn't know was possible. Being swept off her feet had led her to lose all reason, and the sense of morality she had clung to since her childhood days at Riverview Baptist. In fact, she had willfully decided to forget the rules and even particular tenets of her faith, in order to embrace all that was possible that summer in France.

"No, Randy, I didn't love him." Shiloh uttered the statement with finality and reassurance. She hoped he believed her.

"It was a summer fling that shouldn't have happened, but nothing more. I made the unwise decision to do what I did, because I couldn't afford to get off track with such a promising future. Thing was, I didn't anticipate the guilt and regret that have haunted me every day since I made those poor choices. I came home that summer and rededicated my life to God, after asking for forgiveness and a second chance. When you wanted to resume dating me soon after my talk with the Lord, I thought it was God showing me what he wanted me to do next. Marrying you was not a mistake or afterthought, Randy. You have been supportive in every way a husband should be . . . You've been very good to me, and I truly love you."

His gaze remained fixed as he kept facing forward, and Shiloh knew he was deeply hurt.

"And that other thing . . . where did that idea even come from? That doesn't sound anything like you. How could you be so . . . so calculating?"

Shiloh stared at him without responding, because she had no acceptable answer. There was no excuse for her behavior back then, and after all these years, she still hadn't been able to formulate a sensible explanation.

"I don't know, Randy; I was scared. I didn't know what else to do. I was thinking only of myself, and it was wrong. That's all there is to it. And one of the biggest consequences is having to sit down with you, and with Lem, and confess that I did this."

Randy finally looked at her. Rather than accusatory, his gaze was sorrowful, as if part of him had died with her revelation.

"You need to tell all of the boys, not just Lem. Especially if you're planning to share any or all of this with Monica, as you've mentioned. Your sons need to hear it first—from you."

Shiloh nodded. What was going to come of all of this? Her stomach was still in knots, but even so, she knew it had been the right time to come clean. She just hoped that Randy, and their boys, would be able to forgive her, and continue to love her.

fifty-three

Shiloh's hands gripped the steering wheel. It was Friday afternoon and she was heading to Fond du Lac, an hour's drive away, to join other church members to support Jade in her bid for Mrs. Wisconsin. The plan was to enjoy an early dinner together at the hotel before the pageant began at seven. Needing some alone time, she had decided to drive by herself rather than carpool with the other ladies.

The quiet time gave her an opportunity to process all that had happened over the past few days: Daddy's sudden illness, her confession to Randy, the shedding of her perfect façade. She realized she felt simultaneously grateful, awful, and free—grateful that Daddy's heart attack was mild enough for him to be going home today; awful for the shame and disappointment she'd seen in her husband's eyes every time he'd tried to look at her the past two days; and free that she didn't have to hide the truth anymore. She had bared her soul, and despite the present pain, her heart was still beating. Somehow she'd survive this; God wouldn't fail her.

Randy had chosen to stay home with the boys this afternoon, because they couldn't afford to leave them alone again so soon after their trip to Atchity, plus he had a lot to do before their trip back to her hometown for Thanksgiving next week. Besides, she knew he could use some alone time himself. Since Wednesday night, he'd been quiet and withdrawn, and she had tried to give him the space he seemed to need. They had agreed that she would tell Lem, Omari, Raphael, and David about the sins of her youth sometime tomorrow afternoon. That would give the boys the weekend to process what she shared, and ask any questions they may have, during their private family time.

She looked at the clock, which registered 4 p.m., and pressed on the gas to pass a slow-moving truck. The clouds were low today, and the fields, already harvested of their corn and wheat, looked wind-swept and bare. The landscape and the weather matched her gloomy mood.

Half an hour later, as she drove at a slow, but steady pace, a ray of light pierced the gray sky, highlighting one of the naked trees in a roadside field. Shiloh knew the setting sun was the source of this beauty, and the scene took her breath away. *Thank you, God, for reminding me you are here*, she silently prayed as she peered through the windshield. *Your light shines even during the darkest of times. How great you are.*

Shiloh continued her internal dialogue with God, thanking him for giving her the strength to share her past with Randy, and asking him to allow Randy, and eventually the boys, to move forward with her. Besides Randy, Lem would have the hardest time, but God could make everything alright. She clung to that belief. Even so, it didn't remove the dread of having to alter her sons' view of her tomorrow, or her sorrow over the wall her confession had formed between her and Randy. She silently pleaded again with God to remove it.

Eventually, her mind was spent from tossing around various scenarios about how the conversation with her boys should unfold, as well as potential ways to regain Randy's respect and trust. Shiloh finally gave up and turned up the volume on the car stereo, so the gospel songs on the radio could fill the car, and hopefully her, too.

The soothing, biblically based lyrics had calmed her by the time she pulled into the parking lot of the hotel hosting tonight's pageant. She made her way inside the historic hotel and found its quaint restaurant, where she and the members of St. Stephens had agreed to meet. A buffet line snaking around the wall was indication that many pageant-goers had decided to arrive early and dine. Several groups of St. Stephens Baptist members were seated at the small round tables, already sharing their meals. Each of them waved a greeting. Shiloh took her place in line and chatted with ladies around her.

She was surprised when Reverend Vic entered the restaurant a few minutes later with Naima. The girl lit up when she saw Shiloh, and she dashed over for a hug.

"You came, too? Wow—everybody's here!"

Shiloh laughed at the girl's excitement and hugged her again. "I don't know about everybody, but a lot of us are here to support your mommy. I'm glad you're happy to have our company. Where's your little brother?"

Nicholas was living up to the behavior expectations of a two-year-old these days, and Shiloh had wondered how Jade and Vic were handling his attendance at the pageant.

"My grammy is here from California," Naima said. "She's watching him now and she's going to stay in our hotel suite this evening and keep him while we are at the pageant."

Shiloh was surprised. Jade's mother was going to miss seeing her daughter live on the stage tonight? That was quite kind of her.

The woman strolled in a few seconds later, holding a squirming Nicholas in her arms. She searched the room for Vic, and headed in his direction when she saw him standing at a table, talking to some of the church members. Before they reached him fully, Nicholas's hands were outstretched toward his daddy. Vic shook his head at the boy before taking him. Jade's mother left father and son together and walked toward Shiloh and Naima with a smile on her lips and in her eyes.

"You must be Mrs. Griffin. I'm Melba Devereaux—Jade's mother. She's told me a lot about you."

Shiloh returned the smile and leaned forward to embrace her. "Nice to meet you, Mrs. Devereaux," she said. "I know Jade is glad to have you here with her, for this special occasion."

Mrs. Devereaux beamed. "My baby in another pageant—I wouldn't miss it for the world! I'm going to be in the room with the baby, though, watching by TV." She pouted for a split second. "That's okay. We can't have Nicholas there live, trying to sit still and making noises, especially when he sees his mommy on the stage. He and I will have snacks in the room and dance around to the songs and enjoy ourselves whenever Jade comes on screen."

Shiloh imagined the scene and smiled. She had been tempted to offer to stay in the hotel room and keep Nicholas, but after that description of their evening plans, it was clear this was a night Mrs. Devereaux wanted to enjoy with her grandson.

"Have you all talked to Jade today? Is she nervous?"

"She didn't sound so, but I'm sure she is," Mrs. Devereaux said. "They are just so busy getting ready for everything this evening that she hasn't had a chance to really think about, or allow herself, to be nervous."

Vic slid into line with the ladies and with Naima, and they collected their food and found a table big enough to seat them all.

"So how are you feeling about all of this, Vic? What if Jade wins the crown?" Shiloh posed the question before taking a bite of her lasagna.

Vic, who was holding and trying to feed his bouncing son, shook his head and looked at Mrs. Devereaux. "First thing I'm gonna do is convince Grammy to move to Milwaukee from Long Beach!"

They all laughed.

"If the price is right, son, I just might help you out," Mrs. Devereaux quipped. "Convincing Jade's step-dad to move might require a little more negotiation—some pro football season tickets, a golf club membership . . ."

Shiloh raised an eyebrow. "Vic can pull it off, I'm sure. Better get ready, just in case, Mrs. Devereaux . . ."

fifty-four

Shiloh had viewed many a pageant via television, but seeing all of these beautiful women strut their stuff on stage live was an entirely different experience.

All of the hearsay was correct—TV did add ten pounds, because these ladies were rail thin, including Jade, who had been eating nothing but salads and lean meat for the past month, and she looked as tiny as the other contestants. The other amazing thing was how every strand of gorgeous hair was in place, every smile was perfect, and so was every set of teeth. Colgate, Crest, and others who produced whitening products would have been proud.

Shiloh had great seats, near Vic and Naima, not far from the stage. Over the course of the evening, whenever Jade Devereaux Smith's name was called or she was asked to comment or present, a section of the audience in the rear left balcony erupted into cheers and applause.

"You need to teach your congregation how to behave in public, Rev," Shiloh whispered to Vic and laughed.

He gave her a wry smile. "How do you know those are my— our—people? That could be a whole 'nother fan base."

Shiloh was delighted to hear him use the word *our*, but didn't have time to reply because the names of the top five finalists were about to be called.

Mrs. Green Bay. Mrs. Kenosha. Mrs. Milwaukee.

Shiloh heard "Milwaukee" and tuned out the rest of the finalists. She stood to her feet and cheered, along with Vic and Naima.

Naima looked as if she wanted to cry and scream with excitement all at once. Vic picked her up and hugged her. He pumped a fist in the air and high-fived Shiloh. She returned the gesture, then turned her attention back to the main attraction of the night—the ladies on the stage.

After the tumult had died down, the MC asked each woman to come forward and answer a question about how she would serve the state as Mrs. Wisconsin. This time, they went in reverse order, with the fourth and fifth finalists—the ones Shiloh had completely missed—going first.

Mrs. Appleton would focus on child abuse prevention by creating a statewide public awareness campaign that promoted positive parenting education as the best antidote to abuse. Mrs. Brookfield would encourage Wisconsin residents to do a better job of going green, and caring about the environment, from the youngest citizens to the eldest. And then, it was Jade's turn.

Shiloh thought she looked nervous, yet confident when she stepped out of the soundproof box all of the contestants stood in as they waited their turn to answer the question. She walked the two or three steps forward, where the MC was waiting, and clasped her hands together in front of her. Her shimmery, beaded sea blue and green dress fit her perfectly, and the drop diamond earrings looked gorgeous with her swept-up hairdo.

"Mrs. Milwaukee," the MC began, "you indicated early on in the pageant that you would consider spending your tenure as Mrs. Wisconsin championing education. However, fairly recently, you updated that to something else. Please tell us what your platform would now be, and why you made the change."

"Thank you for this opportunity to share about a cause that's personally meaningful to me," Jade began, and then faced the audience. "Education is still a very important topic, because without it, our dreams and often our efforts to succeed, can be limited. I was fortunate enough to graduate from college, but these days, that's almost equivalent to a high school degree. I was planning to advocate for higher education counseling and funding, but also for Wisconsin citizens of every age to continue learning however they can—through local community college courses, by reading more books, or by other creative means—just doing something to stay aware of the world around us and to remain abreast of life's most pressing issues.

"However, as the pageant neared, I experienced several meaningful exchanges with a group of women friends about the power of perception, and about the importance of being true to one's inner beauty. That will be my platform."

Shiloh was taken aback. She had expected a speech about insurance companies needing to cover hearing aid devices; this was going in a whole new direction.

"These women saw me as this beauty queen diva, and you know," Jade chuckled, "I guess I have to own that. That's how I portrayed myself and how I wanted to be seen. But over a period of time, I realized that my need to always be perfect kept them from seeing the real me, and from relating to the fact that just like them, I had fears, doubts, and unfulfilled dreams. When I took the time to share with them that I entered this pageant for vain reasons, a wall tumbled down. They saw the real Jade, and I found out what it means to be authentic, and to open one's heart without worrying about being judged or gossiped about or ostracized. Actually, what happens is that you find out who your real friends are, and you come to understand that you are meant to be loved no matter what you look like or whether you wear designer clothes and shoes, or what you drive or where you live. I told these women the truth—that I entered this pageant because I was losing my hearing."

The audience gasped. Jade's voice quivered and trailed off for a split second, before she regained her confidence. The MC seemed stunned into silence, so Jade continued.

"I learned that my hearing was diminishing in a manner that cannot be cured through surgery, and I'd need two hearing aids to compensate," Jade continued. "Problem was, my insurance company didn't cover them, and the cost would be at least five thousand dollars. Out of pocket."

Another gasp from the audience led Shiloh to turn and survey the people around her. Some were sitting on the edge of their seats as Jade continued. Naima's wide eyes were glued to her mother and she sat forward, as if she were afraid she might miss something.

"I'm blessed and fortunate enough that my husband and I could have paid for the aids from our savings, but my pride wouldn't let me go that route. In trying to explore my options, I discovered this pageant and thought I'd enter to see if I could take care of the hearing aids through success here. But I also discovered how few insurance companies actually cover these devices, and I realized not everyone has the option of entering a pageant or finding a potentially quick source of income to help cover the cost of devices that are often a necessity—not a cosmetic option.

"I'm not sure how insurance companies have gotten around paying for these important devices for most patients. In some instances, they'll cover surgery when the hearing aids are more economical and more prudent. I don't know why. They serve a vital function that keeps people safe. If I can't hear my crying baby, he's at risk. If a hearing impaired person is driving and can't hear an emergency vehicle's siren signaling that she should pull over, that is dangerous. So all that said, it took my diagnosis with this mild disability to wake me up out of my 'vanity fog,' I call it, to help me realize that unless there is something of substance on the inside, and unless I'm willing to be real about who I really am, the pretty package doesn't really matter. Therefore, my platform as Mrs. Wisconsin would be to help girls and women own their true beauty—physical flaws, disabilities, weight issues, or whatever—and embrace who they are so they can grow and mature in ways that lead them to purposeful lives."

The MC held the microphone as the convention center exploded in applause. Shiloh glanced at Vic, who stood gazing at his wife with a level of love and respect that made Shiloh want to cry.

"Wow," the MC finally said. "What a powerful story to explain a wonderful platform. Thank you, Mrs. Milwaukee. You have inspired us all tonight."

After another thunderous round of applause, the next finalist emerged to share her platform. Shiloh listened intently to the rest of them, but her mind and heart kept returning to Jade's message and testimony. God had used the Bible study group to help Jade find her voice and her inner confidence. Would that have happened if she had stopped coming? Randy had been right all along: God had a reason for bringing Jade to Bible study, and because of the influence of the women there, Jade now felt free to educate and touch thousands.

fifty-five

In the end, Jade was the biggest winner, at least in Shiloh's mind.

An hour after sharing her intended platform, Jade was one of two women left on stage, with one prepared to don the crown and sash of Mrs. Wisconsin. When Mrs. Kenosha was declared the winner, Shiloh's heart sank. She was so certain that Jade had wowed the crowd and won. Instead, Mrs. Kenosha, who seemed like a perfectly nice and lovely lady, would represent the state and spread a message of healthy eating and the importance of organic food during her reign.

The minute contestants were ushered to a backstage room where they could meet the press, Jade was swarmed by reporters who wanted to hear more of her story. One informed her that #insurehearingaids had become a trending topic on Twitter, and news stories were surfacing in media statewide about the challenges faced by the hearing impaired who can't afford hearing aids. Half an hour after the new Mrs. Wisconsin had been scooted away, Jade was still answering media questions. Finally, one of the pageant organizers escorted her out of the press arena, so she could go to her dressing room and change. Shiloh decided to wait with Vic and Naima to see her and congratulate her, and many of the St. Stephens Baptist members came backstage as well.

When Jade returned to the room, wearing jeans and a Mrs. Wisconsin contestant T-shirt, church members burst into applause.

Shiloh, Vic, and Naima joined in on the standing ovation, and Jade beamed.

"You didn't take home the crown tonight, Jade, but you are clearly a winner. No doubt about that."

Shiloh's words made Jade tear up. "Thank you for being here, everyone," she said. "This means so much. I don't know what to say."

"That's okay," Sister Dora said. "You honored all of us, and God, on that stage tonight. No need to say anything else—except where you want to have dessert, our treat."

Everyone laughed, including Jade.

"How about I take a rain check on that?" she asked. "My mom is here from California, and she's been holed up in our hotel room with Nicholas all evening. I'd like some time to celebrate with her, too."

Once they finished congratulating her, the St. Stephens members departed, leaving just Shiloh, Vic, and little Naima.

"Well, I don't know what to make of all of this," Jade said. "I'm overwhelmed."

"You did great, Mommy," Naima said and hugged her waist. "You made me proud."

"Me too, honey," Vic said and winked. "And between your two pageants, you got help paying for the hearing aids!"

Jade punched his arm, then hugged him. She looked at Shiloh and explained. "As first runner up tonight, I'll receive a two-thousand-dollar cash prize and a few other goodies," Jade said. "You see where his mind is, don't you?"

Vic kissed her cheek. "My mind is on you, and how proud you made me tonight. You can do whatever you want with your winnings. I'm paying for the hearing aids in another way, and don't argue."

Jade stepped out of his embrace and looked into his eyes. She didn't say anything, but all that she was feeling was evident. She hugged him again before releasing him and approaching Shiloh.

"Thank you for becoming my friend, and for being here. I can't tell you how much it meant to not only have church members come, but to have you here, Shiloh. You've been a great blessing to me."

Shiloh hugged her tight. "Likewise, Second Lady, likewise."

fifty-six

The ride home on Friday night was lighthearted, as cars filled with St. Stephens Baptist members caravanned down Interstate 94 toward Milwaukee. Shiloh traveled alone, as she had on the way to the pageant, but it was heartwarming to see all of the members socializing with each other and laughing and chatting in their individual cars. Jade, Vic, their kids, and her mother would stay overnight for a final pageant breakfast, and return later on Saturday.

Shiloh arrived home well after midnight and went directly to bed. She didn't wake Randy, since he was still recovering from the long drive to Atchity earlier in the week.

Hours later, Shiloh awoke in good spirits, although the looming conversation with her boys filled her mind. Thankfully, they had nowhere to be this early on Saturday, and would sleep in. Randy, who joined her for breakfast, was in a surprisingly good mood, too.

"That was an awesome way for the church to support Jade," he said, after she described the evening. "She deserved to win. But God knows what he's doing. No worries about how it all turned out."

Shiloh nodded. "Yeah, the kids are still kind of young for her to be obligated to traveling the state and all of that now, anyway. Maybe this will encourage her to try again in a few more years, when they are older."

Randy shook his head. "I don't know. I think the media attention she's getting from her platform—at least her intended platform—will resonate in ways that are going to open other doors for Ms. Jade. She's on her way."

"Good for her," Shiloh said.

Just as she was about to take another sip of coffee, her cell phone pinged. She picked it up, wondering who would be calling so early on a Saturday, and was delighted to see a text from Monica.

> Saw Mrs. Smith from church on tv! Tell her I said congrats!! Call me when u have time.

Rather than chance missing her by responding later, Shiloh dialed Monica's number immediately. Heart pounding, she prayed Monica would answer. When Monica picked up on the third ring, she wasn't sure what to say.

"Mrs. Griffin, is that you?"

"Yes, Monica. How are you, sweetie?" Shiloh wanted her to know she had been worried about her, but she didn't want to start off the conversation with words that might be taken the wrong way.

"Hanging in," Monica said. "Sorry you haven't heard from me until now. My dad . . . I . . . I'm sorry it couldn't be avoided."

"You okay?" Shiloh wondered whether she was aware of the rumors that had been circulating. Randy turned down the radio, and Shiloh was grateful that the distraction was reduced.

"Not really, but I guess I will be," Monica said. "Can I see you again?"

"Will your father allow it?"

"I think so," Monica said. "He's calmed down a lot."

"I have a commitment today," Shiloh said, thinking of her errands and her plan to talk with her sons. "I'm not sure I'll be able to get away . . . Are you coming to church tomorrow? Will your dad and grandmother be there?"

"I think so," Monica said. "If they don't come, I think one of them will drop me off."

"Okay," Shiloh said. "Either way, let's plan on spending some time together after church. You can come over for dinner, and then maybe we can go somewhere to talk."

"Sure," Monica said. "Thank you, Mrs. Griffin. You don't know how much I appreciate you."

Shiloh smiled. "Oh, I think I have some idea. I hope you know just how mutual the feeling is. I've missed you, little girl."

fifty-seven

Shiloh spent the rest of the morning grocery shopping and running errands. With Thanksgiving looming, the stores were packed. Shiloh was glad she needed to buy only a ham and enough food to get them through the next five days before they headed back to Atchity.

When she turned into their neighborhood just before noon, she discovered she needed to park on the street. David, Raphael, and a few friends were playing basketball in the driveway, using the hoop hanging in front of the garage.

Omari sat on the porch stoop with an iPod in his hand and earphones dangling from each ear, bobbing his head and half watching the game.

"Playtime, huh? Their rooms better be clean," Shiloh muttered.

Her motherly frustration was a futile attempt to ignore the knot of tension returning to her stomach, because she knew their carefree demeanors would soon change. How did one tell the children you wanted to look up to you, and cherish you, that you'd done some very wrong things? How did you go on to serve as those children's role model, and to urge them to make good and godly choices?

Randy appeared in the doorway. Shiloh could tell that he was feeling anxious, too. His lips were pursed, and his words to the boys were terse. "Wrap up your game and come inside, boys. We have to have a family meeting."

"Just ten more minutes, Dad, okay?" Raphael called.

Randy responded without looking his way. "Not today, son. Come on in."

Randy unloaded the groceries and Shiloh wandered into the kitchen. She sent Lem a text to let him know she was home, and told him to come downstairs. Shiloh glanced at the clock and saw that it was 12:30. She washed her hands in the sink and quickly pulled together a light lunch for the boys. She'd tell them at the table after they ate, she decided, since there was never going to be a perfect time.

Lem trotted down the stairs just as Omari, Raphael, and David tumbled in from outside. Shiloh wrinkled her nose.

"I can wait ten more minutes, so you smelly basketball players can at least take off those sweaty shirts," she told David and Raphael. "As a matter of fact, go ahead and wash up a little, too. Twenty minutes won't kill us."

Shiloh saw that Lem wanted to roll his eyes, but didn't want to get in trouble. "I was on ooVoo with Lia; can I go upstairs and get back online until those two are ready? Or can we eat without them?"

"No, we aren't eating without them," Shiloh said. "Fifteen minutes max on your video chatting. I want you down here when they come down."

Lem headed back to his room, but Omari settled onto one of the stools parked at the kitchen island. "We watched the last hour of the pageant last night. That would have been so cool if Mrs. Smith had won. I told you she was a winner."

Shiloh glanced at him and tried not to show her amusement. If he thought he was hiding his crush, he was doing a very poor job.

"Did you watch the whole pageant, or just the end?"

He swiveled around on the stool before answering. "I watched most of it. The other guys joined me for the last hour."

"She did great, right? Did you see me on TV?"

"Nah, I didn't see you. But she was awesome. I never would of thought someone like her would need hearing aids, though."

"What do you mean, 'Someone like her'?"

Omari shrugged. "She's so pretty and young . . . I thought that was for old folks."

"But that was part of her message," Shiloh said. "We have to look past the surface, into one's heart and into their character, to really see them and understand them. Her having to wear hearing aids doesn't detract from her beauty or her role as a pastor's wife and mother; it's just another detail, another piece of information about her, just like it would be if she had to wear glasses."

Omari pursed his lips as he thought about it. "I see your point."

By the time everyone had reconvened in the kitchen and chitchatted over lunch, Shiloh was reluctant to have her heavy conversation. But Randy gave her the eye, and she knew she had to move forward. She cleared her throat. "Guys, settle down, I need to tell you something, and I need your full attention."

They stopped talking and peered at her. She surveyed the remains of their lunches on the table and pushed her chair back from the table.

"You know what? Let's move into the family room. I think that would be better."

Randy gave her a look that warned her to stop stalling. She ignored him, and led the way out of the kitchen.

When everyone was settled on a sofa or a chair, staring at her like they knew more chores or a lecture was coming, Shiloh opened her mouth to begin. But instead of words coming forth, tears spilled from her eyes. David furrowed his brow and dashed over to hug her.

"Don't cry, Mama. What's wrong? Are you okay?"

Realizing that she was scaring them, Shiloh took the tissue that Lem had trotted to the bathroom to retrieve, and wiped her eyes and cheeks. She took a deep breath and squared her shoulders, then looked each of her sons in the eye. The fear she saw in return saddened her, but what made her sadder was knowing it would soon be replaced by anger and shame.

"I'm fine, David," she said and hugged and kissed him. "I just have something very hard to tell you."

He stayed next to her, and she let him.

"I have to tell you boys about a couple of things that I did a long time ago, that I've held inside for a very long time, nearly twenty years," Shiloh said. "Your father was the first person I ever told, and he just found out a few nights ago."

The boys looked at Randy, who was doing his best to remain expressionless. He left his seat on the sofa and moved closer to Shiloh, and grabbed her hand. She was grateful, and struggled to stave off the fresh round of tears that sought to erupt. Instead of looking at her sons, she stared at her hands.

"I did some things when I was twenty years old that I've been ashamed of ever since. One of them is really personal, almost inappropriate to share with you. But with the world we live in, it's probably not something you've never heard before.

"The summer after my second year in college, I won this great fellowship." She looked at David to better explain. "That's like a special opportunity to do something unique or different, and it's an honor to be chosen."

He nodded, and she continued. "My goal was to someday be a professional flutist, and to travel the world sharing my music. So I won this fellowship, which allowed me to spend a summer in France."

All of the boys looked surprised.

"You've been to France? And you never told us?" Omari was stunned.

Shiloh gave him a wry smile. "Yes, son, I had a life before marriage and motherhood, and in one season of it, I had a wonderful opportunity to study abroad. I went to Paris for ten weeks. I lived in an apartment with a French family, and I studied and practiced with some of the best flutists in the world, at a university based there."

Lem sat back on the sofa and shook his head. "Wow, Mrs. Smith almost winning that pageant last night has nothing on you."

Shiloh smiled at him, but continued. "There were also other college musicians from around the world studying that summer, and I became special friends with a young man from Spain named Armando. We really liked each other, and we wound up dating exclusively the whole time we were there. He had never dated or even been friends with a black woman, and I hadn't dated much at all, maybe once or twice before that. Anyway, I thought he was something special, and I thought what we had together was special, so . . . after a few dates when he wanted to . . . go all the way . . . I agreed."

Lem turned his head and Omari and Raphael wrinkled their noses.

"Mom, please," Omari said.

"I know, son," Shiloh said, "but I have to tell you all everything. Long story short, I wound up pregnant, but by the time I found out, the summer program was about to wrap up, and Armando and I had already said our goodbyes. I decided that I was too young and had too much going for me to keep a baby, especially a biracial one that would have to be raised in Alabama."

Shiloh took a deep breath and Randy squeezed her hand in support.

"Boys, I set aside all I knew about how God cherishes life, and I thought only about what I wanted at that time, at my age. I killed that baby before I left France, as if it was no big deal. I had an abortion."

Silence engulfed the room, and David, who was still standing next to her, peered at her, as if in shock.

"Did you understand what I just tried to explain?" she asked him.

He nodded and stepped back. "You said it: You killed your baby."

"Because it was inconvenient," Raphael said. "Oh, wow, Mom."

"So I'm really not your first child," Lem said and glared at her. "At least I shouldn't be."

Shiloh nodded. "If I'd had the baby, it would be seventeen years old now—a year older than you, Lem. I think about that often. Who or what would he or she be doing; how would he or she have turned out?"

"That might have been the daughter you've never had," Lem said. "What were you thinking?"

Chills ran through Shiloh. She hadn't known what to expect from her boys, but Lem's third-degree interrogation was unsettling. How would he handle the rest of what she had to share?

"And you never told the guy?" Omari asked.

Shiloh shook her head. "There was nothing to tell after I had taken care of it."

"But it was a baby, Mommy, a person," David said. "I can't believe you did that."

Shiloh peered at him for a long while before speaking. "I can't believe I did it, either, David, but you know what? Lots of people do it every day, and it's legal. I'm guessing a lot of them believed like I did that if they just 'took care of it' and moved on with their lives, it would soon be forgotten. Truth is, it hasn't been that way at all. There's not a day that I don't ask myself 'what if'; and every time I enter a hospital, I remember how terrible and disgusting I felt when I did that in France."

She almost told them about the annual commemoration of that child's life that she held every year, on the date of her abortion, but she hesitated. Doing so might come across as her making an excuse, or trying to show how she had redeemed herself. But telling them about her sin wasn't for the purpose of justifying her actions or making herself look better; she had to let the truth out, and let them chew on it and process it however they needed.

"So why are you telling us this now? What gives? Did Armando show up in Milwaukee or something?"

Shiloh tried to smile.

"No—at least not to my knowledge. I'm telling you because . . . because just like Mrs. Smith stood on that pageant stage last night and shared one of her truths, I might need to share this information with the St. Stephens Baptist congregation, to help some people in the membership."

Lem grew angry. "This is about that Monica girl getting knocked up, isn't?"

Shiloh's eyes grew wide. How had he heard about this? Monica attended school in Sherman Park, in the city, and Lem was in the Mequon school district thirty minutes away. Was the rumor started and spread only at church?

"It's all over Facebook and Twitter, Mom. They say Trey Holloman got her pregnant and then dumped her. He's going to get a big college scholarship to play football, and he doesn't want to be tied down with any baby mama drama."

Now it was Shiloh's turn to be stunned. Social media was danger-ous. If that's how the news was circulating, Monica surely knew what was being said.

"Monica's having dinner with us tomorrow, Lem; please don't tell her what you've been seeing about her online; none of you boys say anything about her, or her circumstances, you hear me?"

The grim-faced boys nodded, including Lem, who looked angrier than she'd ever seen him.

"So now you've got to do a tell-all confession in front of the church," he said. "That's just great. Next thing you know, all my business is going to be all over Facebook and Twitter, and I didn't even do anything."

He stood up and headed toward the door to leave the family room, but Randy called him back. "Son, I know this is hard. It's hard for your mother to even tell you all this, let alone the world. You need to be respectful and come back and sit down, though. You have to hear her out. You need to know what she has to say."

Lem reluctantly returned to his seat on the sofa across from his parents, but hung his head.

Shiloh felt numb by this point, but continued. "I am just as uncomfortable as Lem with the thought of standing up at St. Stephens as the First Lady, and putting all of my business on Front Street," she said. "But when God puts something on your heart and challenges you to be obedient, you have to honor that call, or you're sinning again. I have to do this, boys, to honor how far God has brought me, in spite of that grave sin, and to help someone else who may be struggling.

"When I came back, your daddy and I started dating seriously, and got married. I dropped out of college because I felt so guilty. I believed that if I gave up everything earthly that mattered to me, God would know I was truly sorry, and he would forgive me. I feared that like some people who've had abortions, I would never be able to have children, and yet he soon blessed me with Lem, and then the rest of you.

"Your dad has been gracious in allowing me to take the lead in naming each of you. It's by design that, put together, the letters of your first names spell LORD," Shiloh said and smiled at her sons. "And as you know, each of your names—Lemuel, Omari, Raphael, David—means something biblically significant. I haven't taken for granted that God has smiled on me and granted me unusual favor with four healthy sons. So I need to share this painful and shameful part of my past so others can see how God can move them forward, whatever they've done, even if it's something as murderous as this."

"You keep calling it murder," Raphael said. "But it's legal, right?"

"It's legal in the eyes of many countries, Raphie," Shiloh said, "but I try to live by God's principles, and I knew way back then that

God considers even the seed of life sacred. So the minute I got the idea in my head to do this get-rid-of-it-quick scheme, I knew I was premeditating something that wouldn't please God. The fact that it was so easy, and so affordable, made me feel okay about it, leading up to the act. And even as I cried my way through it, I couldn't help feeling that I was snuffing out a life, just because I could."

Shiloh took another deep breath.

"So I'm going to share this soon in church, and I wanted you to know so you can ask me whatever questions you need to, and so you'll have time to prepare yourselves for whatever may happen after I tell everyone."

"I'm not going to be able to show my face," Omari said and hung his head.

"Yes, you will, son," Randy told him. "If someone tries to make you feel bad or says something negative about your mother, you tell them to go home and sit down with their parents, and ask them to share details about the things from their youth that they're most ashamed of. We've all got something. Just do that and see if that won't shut them up."

Shiloh wanted to hug Randy. As hard as he was taking all of this himself, he was standing with her. She looked at all four of her handsome young men, each of them miniature versions of Randy, with different haircuts, shades of brown, and heights.

"There's more, boys, and it's just as bad."

Lem sat back and groaned. "Mom . . . really?"

She looked at him and her heart ached. This was going to tear him to pieces.

fifty-eight

Shiloh dove right in, before she lost her courage, and before the boys could ask another question about her first transgression.

"That fellowship I mentioned, the one that allowed me to go to France? Well . . . I stole it."

Lem sat forward again and frowned. He looked pained. Omari, Raphael, and David exchanged glances.

"Are you going to jail?" David asked.

Shiloh was grateful for the comic-relief question. "I guess the only good news of the day is, no—I'm not going to jail. But again, this is another case of me feeling like I committed murder."

She released Randy's hand and walked over to the sofa on the other side of the coffee table and sat next to Lem. She wanted to hug him, but he radiated anger and hurt. So she sat there, close, but not touching, and spoke directly to him, but loud enough for the others to hear.

"Lem, I had a college roommate at Birmingham-Southern named Leslie Hamilton, and she was a gifted flutist."

Lem sat up and stared at her. "Hamilton? You're kidding me."

Shiloh shook her head.

The other boys frowned.

"Can you stop talking in 'Lem language,' Mom; we don't get it," Omari said.

Shiloh continued. "I had a roommate named Leslie Hamilton, who was from Birmingham, but lived in the dorm as part of her music scholarship. She was from a well-to-do family and respected throughout campus because of her good looks, athleticism, and of course, her ability to play the flute. We were often competitors, with the two of us routinely flip-flopping between first and second chair in our classes," Shiloh said. "It was often a toss-up between the two of us when community groups or organizations on campus wanted a solo musician to play for an event, and it got to the point where if I couldn't make it, I'd recommend her, and vice versa.

"Well, when the flute fellowship opportunity came around and we found out there was only one spot going to a Birmingham-Southern student, the competition was on. It put a strain on our friendship as we sought to find the best song to impress the judges and practice nonstop so we'd each be ready for our audition. It was hard, because it meant we couldn't practice in our room after hours, since we'd hear each other's piece, and also how good each other was.

"One weekend, I went home to Atchity to practice the song I had selected, and I was feeling pretty confident about it. But that Sunday, when I returned to campus and stepped off the elevator onto my dormitory floor, I heard the sweetest sound flowing from our room. It was absolutely beautiful. Leslie had discovered a breathtaking melody that I'd never heard before, and she was playing it with heart-wrenching power. I was blown away. I sat there in the hallway and listened to her play it over and over, until she nailed it without flaws. I knew if I went into the room she'd stop practicing and put everything away, so I wouldn't know. But at this point I did know, and I knew if she played that song with that level of skill and emotion, I could forget it; the fellowship was hers."

The boys were riveted, even Lem. Shiloh got up and walked over to the piano in the corner of the family room and sat on the bench, with her back to Randy and her sons.

"I heard the phone in our room ring and while I couldn't hear the entire conversation, I heard Leslie tell someone she would take a break and come down for just a few minutes, so she could get back to practice. I trotted down the hall and hid in the bathroom until I felt like she was out of the hallway, then I went into our room, and there was her music, splayed on her bed. The title of the piece and its author were there in plain view.

"I thought about taking it and tearing it up, but realized how silly that would be; she'd just get another score, and she'd know I was the one who did it. But something came over me and I decided that I would perform that same piece, but do her one better. I'd figure out how to play it on both of my instruments—the flute and the recorder. I'd have to figure out how to smoothly transition from one to the other, but if I pulled it off, I could win this fellowship over her.

"I told myself I needed it more," Shiloh said and turned toward her family. "I was the middle child of a preacher, who cared about his church more than his children, it seemed at times. Maybe winning something big like this would make him notice me."

"Pawpaw?" Lem asked incredulously. "He's so caring; what are you talking about?"

"That's another story for another day, Lem," Shiloh said. "I'm glad that you and your grandfather have a wonderful relationship, but it was different with us girls back then."

"Back to what you were saying." Randy gently nudged her.

Shiloh nodded. "I told myself that Leslie was well off enough that if she really wanted to study with flutists abroad, her parents could pay to send her, and plus, I just needed the recognition of winning, of doing something different and better than my smart older sister and pretty, outgoing younger sister. I was tired of being the bland, invisible one."

"That sounds so lame." Raphael's disgust was palpable.

"I agree," Shiloh said. "You've never been a young, insecure woman, so I can't and won't even try to explain where my head was. Even so, all these years later, I know how silly and self-centered that explanation sounds. But back then, it was real, and it was serious, and I just wanted to escape my life and travel to a world where I could be special. When I heard Leslie play that piece, I felt my chance slipping away."

"So you stole her song and played it yourself, in a better, more unique way and won the scholarship?" Lem almost spat out the question.

Shiloh looked him in the eyes. "I did, son. I did."

"Why is he so angry?" David asked, looking from Lem to Shiloh.

"Because Leslie Hamilton is the name of Lia's drug-addicted mother," Lem said between clenched teeth, glaring at Shiloh. "The mother who gave birth to her, then dropped Lia off on her parents' doorstep so she could return to a life on the streets, playing her flute whenever she's not strung out. Sounds like our mother had something to do with that."

Shiloh dipped her head to her chin and let the tears flow. "I told you, I murdered twice, in the same year."

"I don't understand, Mommy," said David, frowning. Shiloh appreciated his nine-year-old innocence, and his effort to connect the dots. She had to finish the story for his sake—and for Lem, who seemed to feel he already knew the answers.

"On the day of the audition I arrived before anyone else so I could sign up to be the first to go in. The rules were we had to bring two pieces to play, so if we saw our original piece on the list, we had to move to our second piece of music. The judges would give us a chance to play both pieces, but the initial one had to be their first time hearing it.

"I got there first, signed up, and wrote down the name of the piece I'd be playing on the sign-up sheet. When Leslie arrived fifteen minutes later and saw the selection, she knew I had somehow found her music and betrayed her. That piece was so obscure, she'd convinced herself no one else would have it, so she'd poured herself into learning it and practicing it, and had only skated the surface on learning a second piece.

"Truthfully, if I hadn't stolen the piece from her, she would have been right; no one else would have discovered it. It was truly unique. But I did what I did, and she was hurt and furious and in her opinion, doomed. For whatever reason, she didn't rat me out, like she could have and probably should have. She went in and played her second song, which by all accounts was good but not earth-shattering. She went on to play her original choice as her second piece, but I had blown them away already by playing it on two instruments; she couldn't top that, and I knew it."

Shiloh tried to reach for Lem's hand, but he pulled away.

"We got back to the room that morning and she said she knew I'd land the fellowship, due to the music she had hunted high and low for, and that when I arrived in France that summer, I should . . ."

Shiloh looked at David, wondering if he needed to hear this part, but decided to barrel through.

"She said while I was in France, I should think of her, in her Birmingham home, all alone with a relative who was abusive while her parents were away."

Shiloh's revelation sucked the air out of the room. Even Randy, who had heard this earlier in the week, seemed stunned. Shiloh felt like she was having an out-of-body experience. She couldn't be talking about herself, and her actions.

Lem was pale. "What did she say?" He whispered the question, as if it pained him.

Mindful of her three youngest boys, Shiloh didn't want to say too much. Some of the answers Lem sought would have to wait until later, for a one-on-one conversation.

"Apparently Leslie worked hard in school and won a flute

scholarship that allowed her to stay on campus to get away from her abusive relative. She never felt like she could tell, because this person held the family's purse strings. He was the one with the wealth, and her father worked for his company. He had always threatened that if she shared their secret, the whole family would be ruined. Her parents were loving and trusting and had no idea that she was being mistreated. So when she made it to college and got a chance to live in the dorm, she said she had peace and safety for the first time in six or seven years, and she needed to do whatever she could to avoid having to go home for the summer and allowing the abuse to resume."

Retelling Leslie's horrific revelation made her shudder.

"When she told me, I pleaded for her forgiveness, and I offered to go to the fellowship committee and tell them what I had done, so she could have another chance. I should have done that anyway, regardless of what she said," Shiloh said. "But I was scared at that point that if I told the truth, I'd be kicked out of college and I'd never get my degree or recover from the shame.

"Leslie told me she'd figure something else out. She'd never speak to me again, but she would find a way to do what she needed."

Shiloh looked heavenward. "God forgive me, but I listened to her. I heard what I wanted to hear, and I moved on and let the school praise me and honor me and do all of this great stuff for me for landing this prestigious fellowship, and Leslie watched from the wings and never said anything.

"On the last day of the spring semester, before school ended for the summer, she left a note on my bed and told me to find a new roommate for junior year, and good luck in France. I never saw her again after that day, but I left her a note on her bed that simply said 'I'm sorry.'

"I don't know if she ever got it," Shiloh said. "I went on the fellowship, made the stupid mistake with Armando, and came home grieving about that. Your dad and I started dating soon after, and one weekend we went to Birmingham for a music festival. When we drove through downtown . . ."

Shiloh began to sob and dropped her face in her hands. Randy walked over to her, rubbed her back, and continued the story for her.

"We drove through downtown that evening, looking for a place to eat, and when I stopped at a red light, your mother looked over at a woman sitting on the corner," Randy said. "I didn't know who the woman was, but I noticed that she had a flute in one hand, and a bottle of liquor in the other. She was barely clothed, and she looked out of it. Your mother took one look at her and got sick in the car. I asked her why later, and she just played it off as being a stomach virus."

"That lady was Leslie Hamilton, wasn't it?" Lem asked.

Shiloh nodded. "It was, and I realized that night that I had ruined her life. She had chosen to live on the streets rather than go home to her big pretty house with her loving parents, because she dreaded further abuse."

Lem broke down in tears, and turned away from his mother. Shiloh could barely breathe. But when she looked up to console Lem, she saw that all of her sons were crying, and so was Randy.

This . . . this moment here was her ultimate penalty, the most painful consequence for what she had done all those years ago. If she'd had the ability back then to see into her future, and witness how following temptation down a path she knew was wrong would affect those she loved the most, she would have moved heaven and earth to make everything right. How shameful that she hadn't moved heaven and earth anyway, knowing all along what was right.

"I don't think Lia knows," Lem finally said, in a small broken voice. "She doesn't know all of this. She thinks her mother just left her because she was a young college student interested in the party life, which led her into drug addiction. You have to tell her, too, Mom. She deserves to know."

Shiloh's heart sank. The ripple effect of the pain she had caused was unfolding before her. She had planned to wrap up today's confession by asking her sons to forgive her, in their own time, and to learn from her mistakes. But she realized just now that this wasn't going to be the end of it. She would have to face Lia and ask her forgiveness, and maybe Leslie too.

fifty-nine

The entire family moved through the rest of the afternoon in a daze, not watching TV, answering calls, or even gathering for dinner.

Everyone had eaten leftovers from the fridge, including the pizza they'd almost devoured the night before. Finally, at bedtime, Shiloh had mustered enough strength to corral the younger three boys, who had settled on the sofas in the family room to watch ESPN with little commentary or interest, and get them into bed.

"We have church tomorrow," she reminded them.

They hadn't argued or delayed, as they usually did on Saturday evenings. Shiloh wondered what they were thinking of her, and whether they hated her, but she was afraid to ask.

As she tucked David in and told him to say his nightly prayers, he stared at her, as if she were a stranger. "Mom, were you afraid to talk to God after you did all that stuff that summer? Do you think he still heard you?"

Shiloh sighed and a lump filled her throat. "I think he heard me, David, but yes, I was very afraid to talk to him. And I felt like I needed to do something drastic to show him how sorry I was. So I didn't finish school . . . I dedicated my life to serving him as a good wife and mom, and I hope I've done that."

David stared at her for a long time before answering, then he stroked her face. "You're a good mommy, and even though you did some very bad things, I still love you. I guess that's how Jesus felt when he was hanging from the cross for us."

With that, he rolled over and closed his eyes. Shiloh let the tears fall, but caught them before they dripped from her chin and drenched her baby boy's arms. She'd taken her family through some tough stuff today, and it was going to take a long time to heal. The only thing she could hold onto was the nugget of blessing David had tucked within his comment: he still loved her.

She left his bedside and made a pit stop in Raphael and Omari's room. For the first time ever, they'd turned out the light without a third or fourth reminder. She wasn't fooled; she knew they hadn't yet succumbed to sleep. But she didn't move past the doorway.

"Omari and Raphael, just want to say that I love you, and I hope you can find it in your hearts to forgive me. I'm sorry I've dumped all of this on you at once, and I hope you don't think I'm a horrible person."

Next was Lem's room. His door was closed and she started to knock, but she'd never done so before and decided against it now. She cracked it open and found him sitting on his bed, scowling at the wall across the room, rather than video chatting on his computer, as usual. Shiloh eased into the room and closed the door behind her. She stood at the foot of his bed with her arms folded, not sure what to say, but knowing she couldn't go to bed without having a final conversation with him.

"Are you being blackmailed?" he finally asked.

Shiloh frowned. "What? Why would you ask me that?"

"Why else would you tell us all of this crazy stuff all at once, about your days back in college? You had us thinking you were the perfect little Christian all these years, and here you were, having sex, killing a baby, stealing and cheating your way into a program. Who are you?"

Any other time, that bold backtalk would have landed Lem in punishment for the rest of the school year, and it was just November.

She would cut him some slack, because what she had shared was heavy for an adult to wrap his mind around, let alone a sixteen year old.

"Lem, I'm your mother. And I'm human. I've made some horrible decisions and some bad mistakes and the time has simply come to tell the truth. I didn't know someone at church was going to wind up in a situation that might mirror my own and need a mentor," Shiloh said, trying to tell her son what she needed him to know without completely giving away Monica's issues. "And I didn't know that you were going to go to Alabama for the summer and fall in love with the daughter of the woman I had betrayed. When I saw her at the hospital this past week and learned her last name, I knew right away who she was, and I knew that it would be wrong of me to allow you to continue a friendship with her without telling you the truth. That's all—no blackmail; just God telling me to finally stand in my truth and take off my masks so that someone else can be healed."

"I might be able to see how your first revelation can help some people at church, but how is this news going to do any healing in Alabama? Doesn't sound like you're willing to tell Lia all that you know about her mother."

Lem still wasn't looking at her, but Shiloh moved closer to him and perched on the end of his bed.

"Lem, I've done enough 'favors' for Leslie Hamilton. In her own way and time, she'll tell her daughter what she wants her to know about their family dynamics and what led her to a life on the streets. I do take the blame for that, and I can share that with Lia, but I'm not comfortable repeating the part about the abuse, because that's not my place. I'm sorry, son. And I don't know why God has allowed all of this to happen. He wants me to learn something for sure; I'm just not sure why I've had to crush all of you in the process."

Lem shook his head and lowered it.

"I haven't called Lia tonight because I just can't face her. She'll know something is wrong with me. I can't tell her that stuff about her mother, or that you helped drive her mother down that path. She'll never speak to me again."

"Can you keep it to yourself? At least for a few days? We're going to Atchity for Thanksgiving now, since Daddy has been sick."

Lem's eyes lit up. "For real? When did you decide?"

"Actually before we left Atchity earlier this week; I just forgot to tell you," Shiloh said. "I'm not asking you to keep a secret, I'm just asking you to hold off on telling her if you can. It's hard stuff to hear on the phone or via video; I just don't know if that's the right thing to do. But I wanted you to know, because I can't continue to keep secrets and have them eat away at me. I'm not perfect, Lem—far from it. But I do love you, and your brothers and your dad. And I'm grateful God gave me the chance to be your mother, despite all of the terrible stuff I did. I hope you can find a way to forgive me someday, and to see beyond the ugly stuff I've done, into the heart that God has cleansed. That's who your mother is, not the person I was at twenty."

Lem peered at her, but didn't respond.

She finally stood up to leave, but instead approached him and kissed his forehead. "Good night, son. I love you."

Shiloh closed the door and leaned on it once she was on the other side.

Dear God, let them all still love me, like David said, with the compassion of a forgiving Jesus.

sixty

The somber faces that had climbed into the van with Shiloh this morning transformed the minute they arrived at St. Stephens Baptist and the boys connected with their friends.

Once again, they were the chatty, playful Griffin boys she knew. She wondered, however, if they were worried that she'd spill the beans about everything in service today. Shiloh wasn't sure when she'd share her testimony. Just as God had put it on her heart to release her secrets, she was certain he'd tell her when and how.

She strolled into the church this morning, greeting members along the way as usual, and tried to stay grounded in the moment. Dwelling on how the boys were reacting to her news wasn't going to make them accept it and move on any faster; she had to press forward herself, and show them by example how to trudge through challenges with faith and hope that God would give her another chance to correct her wrongs.

She was doubly surprised this morning when she entered the sanctuary. Not only was Monica and her grandmother seated in the middle section of pews on the right, so was Eva, her teaching colleague from Sherman Park High. Shiloh trotted over to greet all three of them with kisses and hugs.

"Was this planned?" Shiloh asked Eva.

"No," Eva said and grinned. "I told you I was going to visit your church one Sunday, and I just chose this one. Plus, I missed you and I knew I'd find you here, if nowhere else!"

Eva seemed oblivious to the sideways glances and outright stares she was receiving from St. Stephens Baptist members, and Shiloh was glad. Didn't they have any manners? She wanted to stare them down until they got the message, but she had to remember her role as First Lady, and behave.

"Why don't you come sit with me, near the front?" Shiloh glanced at Monica, who was sitting next to her grandmother. "Do you two mind?"

Eleanor shook her head, and so did Monica.

"That's fine, Mrs. Griffin," Monica said. "Am I still coming with you after church?"

Shiloh grinned at Monica, who didn't look any different than she had several weeks ago. Shiloh asked herself why she was surprised. Most teens didn't show until the fifth or sixth month of pregnancy.

"Absolutely," Shiloh said, and peered at Eleanor. "As long as it's still okay with you?"

Eleanor seemed less chipper than usual, but was receptive to Shiloh, as always.

"That's fine," Eleanor said. "She needs to be home no later than seven, to wrap up the homework she hasn't finished, but I know she's in good hands."

Shiloh wondered where Monica's father was this morning, but decided not to ask.

She returned to the end of the pew, where Eva was waiting, and escorted her tiny friend to the front of the church, where she usually sat.

Eva slid into the second pew on the left, and watched with interest as the choir filled the loft behind the pulpit. Shiloh sat next to her and instantly felt like the jolly green giant, given that Eva's head barely reached her shoulder.

"What is this—a full-fledged professional choir? You've got men, women, drums, a sax, an organ, and a guitar?"

Shiloh smiled. "Welcome to the black Baptist church, my dear."

Eva chuckled. "When you visit me and my Korean friends, don't talk about our harp. That's all we're working with now."

Shiloh peered at her, waiting for Eva to declare that she was joking, but Eva shook her head. "No joke. We make sweet simple music to the Lord. It's all good!"

Shiloh grinned and patted her hand. "You and your slang."

"Don't hate," Eva said with a straight face.

Shiloh giggled, appreciative of the lighthearted banter, after what she had put her family through yesterday.

The choir launched into gospel renditions of several hymns, and Shiloh was surprised not only by how well Eva knew the songs, but also by how lovely her voice was.

"You've been holding out on me!" Shiloh whispered. "Your voice is gorgeous."

Eva blushed. "Thank you . . . First Lady."

A few folks had come by and addressed her that way, and Eva hadn't been able to contain her amusement.

The morning was eventful, with Jade's return from Fond du Lac and the standing ovation she received from the congregation.

"And here's the latest news," she said as she stood in front of the church this morning to thank them for their support. "I've been asked to testify before Congress from a layperson's perspective about why hearing aids should be covered by insurance companies, without families having to write special letters of appeal. Sometimes they are granted the coverage, but just as often, they are denied. I'll travel to Washington in early February to have my say."

"Amen!"

"Go 'head, Sister Jade!"

The chorus of approval rippled through the church, and Jade beamed. Shiloh's heart smiled. She was happy for Jade, and proud of her, too.

When Randy asked the congregation to turn in their Bibles to Ephesians and announced that he would be preaching on grace, Shiloh found herself near tears again.

"For it is by grace you have been saved through faith, and this is not from yourselves, it is the gift of God, not by works, so that no one can boast."

Shiloh had memorized Ephesians 2:8–9 as a teenager, at the insistence of a Riverview Baptist Sunday school teacher in Atchity, but not until this very day had those words registered in her heart as relevant to her life. It struck her that she'd been trying to work her way into God's grace for the past eighteen years, by getting married and serving as the good preacher's wife, by volunteering in church, and by holding her annual commemoration every August—even though she knew this wasn't how it was supposed to work; grace was already free and didn't have to be earned. She'd heard Daddy declaring that truth for as long as she could remember, and her husband asserting it for nearly twenty years.

Yet she kept giving the same burden to God every year on that date in August, which meant she was never really releasing it to him. When would she stop taking back the guilt and shame and finally accept his offer?

Her family was still furious with her; she needed to talk to Monica about her experiences; and she needed to deal with whatever fallout would come from her eventual conversation with Lia; but for now, in this moment, she truly felt for the first time God's indescribable peace, and the reality that he had forgiven her a long time ago—the moment the plane from France had landed in the U.S. and she had gone into the airport bathroom, entered a stall, and cried her eyes out and told God she was sorry. He had heard her. He had forgiven her. She just hadn't allowed herself to receive it.

Randy lowered his head to pray before beginning the sermon and when he said "Amen" and opened his eyes, a beam of sunlight streamed into the sanctuary.

"Well, alright then," he said, surprised, and the congregation chuckled. "I couldn't have planned that if I wanted to, but clearly grace has entered this place with the Spirit of the Lord."

Shiloh smiled through her moist eyes. Whoever the sign was for, it was right on time.

sixty-one

The tension during dinner had been thick enough for Shiloh to carve a sculpture.

She could tell Monica was uncomfortable and knew she'd have to reassure her later that the frostiness had nothing to do with her. They were leaving the house now, heading to a neighborhood ice cream shop. Few people would be there on this chilly fall afternoon, but Monica had requested it, and Shiloh didn't mind complying with what might be a craving, or simply a teenage request.

They settled into their spots with their mint chocolate chip and birthday cake ice cream and enjoyed their treat and the sunny day.

"I told Pastor Randy I enjoyed his sermon today," Monica said. "That grace stuff he talked about is what I need right about now. Good to know I'm still eligible."

"Always," Shiloh said, reflecting on her own worship service revelations. "Don't be like me and think that it applies to everyone but you. It's a gift that's granted the minute you repent, and turn toward God."

She hated to change the subject, but she couldn't wait any longer for an update. "So how are you doing, and how are things with your dad?"

Monica shrugged. "I'm the talk of the town, I guess. It's all over Facebook and Instagram that I'm pregnant by Trey, and everyone is saying horrible things about me. It's insane, and I can't believe I'm being trashed this way. The crazy thing is, I think he's the one spreading the rumor, even though he's like my father—demanding that I get rid of the baby."

Monica's stoic revelations threw Shiloh for a loop. "Come again? Why would Trey mess up both of your reputations like that?"

Monica gave her a "Let's get serious" look. "It doesn't mess up his reputation, Mrs. Griffin. Especially if I get rid of the baby like he wants. It builds him up as a guy who can have any girl, and keep rolling along. And I guess that's exactly what he's doing. Meanwhile, everyone is shunning me like I have a disease."

There was still some ice cream left in Monica's cup, but she rested it on the table as if she were full. Shiloh leaned forward, so she could peer into the girl's eyes. Now seemed as good a time as any to share her own experiences, if Monica wanted to listen. "So what are you saying, Monica . . . are you going to get rid of the baby?"

The girl shrugged and sighed. "I don't know, Mrs. Griffin. My dad is insisting that we make an appointment as soon as possible; my future is hanging in the balance here. But Grandma Eleanor is saying not to do that, because I'll regret it for the rest of my life."

Shiloh decided to tread carefully. "What do you think?"

"I think there are going to be regrets whatever I do. If I become a teen mom I'll miss college altogether, or go somewhere local that won't allow me to study music and become a professional musician. If I give the baby away to be adopted, I'll always miss him or her, and wonder if my child is being cared for the right way. And if I get an abortion I'll wonder for the rest of my life who or what my child might have been."

Shiloh nodded. "I get it; I've been there."

Monica's eyes widened as she soaked in what Shiloh was saying. "What do you mean? Did you . . . ?"

"I had an abortion when I was in college, and to this day I remember exactly where I was and how it felt before, during, and after. Those memories are etched in my spirit forever."

Monica was taken aback. She didn't speak for several minutes, and Shiloh allowed the silence to fill the space between them, as the girl thought about, or prayed about, what she wanted to know next. When Monica finally spoke, she still didn't have much clarity.

"Well, if you were me, what would you do? I'm just so torn . . ."

Shiloh sat back in her chair and shook her head. "I'm sorry, sweetheart, I'm not going to make this decision for you, like Trey, your dad, and your grandmother want to do. As much as I have my own set of beliefs and experiences, I need you to talk to God and follow his lead. You have to live with yourself, and with your decision—not Trey, not your dad, and not your grandmother.

"We parents can become frantic sometimes in our efforts to ensure that our babies get all the right breaks and opportunities in life, but we don't realize the power in allowing you all to see us being authentic, and sometimes afraid. You will face a consequence for your intimate relationship with Trey, whatever you decide. The question is, which choice is going to honor God more. You have to go into your secret, quiet place with God—or create one if you don't have one—and tell him what's on your heart and mind. Then you need to find the courage to follow where he leads, Monica. That's the only thing that's going to give you peace."

Monica fixed her eyes on her melting ice cream, but didn't speak. Shiloh knew she was wrestling with everyone's voice swirling in her head, with what she knew of God's truths, and with how her own heart might feel about all of this. She saw a reflection of herself in the girl, whose dreams still rested with the summer flute program that she hadn't mentioned this afternoon.

"I know this seems hard to imagine, Monica, but twenty years from now, God willing, you'll be about the age I am, looking back over your life and the choices that loomed before you. If you can visualize it, try to ask yourself what you would tell your fifteen-year-old self."

It sounded so Oprah-like that Shiloh wondered whether Monica would even grasp what she was trying to say. And in some ways, she felt hypocritical sitting here trying to minister to a teenager, when her own house full of them was angry with her.

Monica sat back and peered at Shiloh. The poor girl looked miserable. "I can't talk to an older version of myself when I can't connect to the current version—sorry, Mrs. Griffin."

Shiloh thought about the anniversary commemoration she had held in secret all of these years and wanted to shout "Don't do it!" She also thought about Monica's musical gift, and what her father was likely demanding of her in regard to staying on track. She wouldn't interfere with another parent's reasoning; she wouldn't want someone doing that with one of her sons, especially someone she entrusted her child to.

What she could and would do was pray for God to give clarity to both Monica and her dad. She also would continue to be part of Monica's support system, however all of this turned out. That's what grace was all about.

sixty-two

The short drive back to Shiloh's house was quiet, as Shiloh and Monica lost themselves in thought.

When Shiloh pulled into her driveway and parked, Monica turned toward her. "I just texted my dad and told him you'd be bringing me home shortly, but he said he'll come and get me."

Shiloh was surprised. "Okay; that's fine. Is everything alright?"

Monica shrugged. "Who knows? He's been acting weird ever since he found out. For all I know, he was at church today, sitting outside in his car listening to the live sermon on the radio instead of coming in to sit with me and Grandma."

Shiloh frowned. "Is he upset with me? Or with Pastor Randy?"

Monica shook her head. "No, Mrs. Griffin, I think he's mad at God. For taking my mom instead of healing her cancer. And now for letting his baby girl be stupid enough to fall for a cute boy's whispered lies."

Shiloh understood. Grief could lead your mind down strange tunnels. She made a mental note to have Randy reach out to Claude when he arrived, and invite him for coffee.

They got out of the car and strolled to the edge of the lawn to admire Ms. Betsy's lush indoor plants, which were visible from her bay window facing the street.

"They're beautiful," Monica said. "She must have what you call a green thumb, to keep her plants looking so good."

"It takes a lot of time to maintain, but Ms. Betsy loves it," Shiloh said. "I guess anything worth having in life does—flowers, gifts and talents, relationships."

Monica looked at her. "I'm glad you make the effort, especially with me. Since my mom has been gone, I haven't had anyone to talk to like I really need to, because both my dad and grandma have been grieving and overprotective. Thank you for being here for me, Mrs. Griffin, and for always being honest with me. I know you can't tell me what to do about the baby, but at least you're not judging me, or running from me."

Shiloh touched Monica's arm. "You're welcome, sweetheart. I'm grateful to be here to listen and to offer my friendship. And did you hear me at the ice cream shop? I can't run from you or judge you if I've been in your shoes, which I have. But even if I hadn't, no one has the right to judge another so harshly that we can't reach past our beliefs and assumptions and love them. None of us is perfect and none of us always gets it right. Why do I get to judge my sin as less problematic than yours? We Christians do that all day long, but that doesn't make it right. I'm glad you still consider me *your* friend, despite my flaws and imperfectness."

They hugged and walked toward the house. They were about to go inside when a horn beeped, and Shiloh turned to see Monica's dad pulling into the driveway. He gave her a slight wave, and motioned for Monica to join him.

"Just a minute, Daddy—I left my Bible in the house," she called to him.

Shiloh pushed open the door and told Monica to go on inside and find it. She strolled over to Claude's pickup truck and tried to muster a smile. He remained expressionless, but nodded hello.

"Hi, Claude. It's so nice to see you. Thanks for letting me spend some time with Monica this afternoon—I've really missed her," Shiloh said. When he didn't respond, she continued. "We missed you in service this morning, but I was glad to see your mom and Monica."

More silence led to more chatter from Shiloh. "I won't ask how you're doing, because I know you've got a lot on your shoulders right now. My heart hurts for you, Claude, and for Monica. But you can trust God with this. Ask him to guide you."

He looked at her with questioning eyes.

"Trust him? Like I did with Sheree? I didn't even make it to the hospital in time to say goodbye before she passed. I begged God on the way there to have my wife hold on, so I could at least tell her goodbye. Didn't happen. Now you're saying I should trust him with my daughter?"

Shiloh was grasping for a response when Lem's panicked shout caused her heart to clench.

"Mom! Come now! Monica just passed out in the kitchen!"

sixty-three

Claude flung open the door to his truck and reached Shiloh's front door before she had even moved.

Shiloh yelled, "Call 911, Lem!" and followed Claude inside.

When she reached the kitchen, however, Randy was there, with a 911 operator already on the phone, following the woman's instructions about how to revive Monica. He knelt beside the girl and placed a cold wet dishcloth on her forehead, and Monica came to.

"Don't try to move, sweetheart," Randy instructed the groggy girl, in a soothing voice. He cradled her head on his lap and the phone in the crook of his neck. Monica's skirt and legs were soaked in blood, and Shiloh knew what had happened. She looked at Claude, who stood just inside the kitchen, peering at his daughter in shock.

"Daddy."

When Monica uttered that single word, he sprinted across the room toward her, knelt on the other side of Randy, and held her hand.

"I'm here, baby, I'm here," he said, his voice thick with tears. "God, please don't let me lose her, too. I need her."

His prayer sent a shudder through Shiloh, and she realized that this man was still reeling from his wife's death more deeply than she had realized. She wondered whether he, Eleanor, or Monica had received grief counseling.

"She's going to be fine, Claude," Randy said. "But I think she's lost the baby."

Monica was alert enough to hear that pronouncement, and as the words sank in, her pain ripped the air from the room. With her head still on Randy's lap, and her father caressing one arm, she released a guttural howl, a scream of loss so primal that the hairs on Shiloh's neck stood on end. Before she could control herself, Shiloh fell to the floor where she was, a few feet away, and let her own pain tear through her body. She heard herself howling too, releasing all the pent-up anger, guilt, shame, and loss she'd felt all these years for the child she had intentionally chosen never to know.

When paramedics arrived, they were initially perplexed about who needed care—the woman or the girl. But the moment they saw the bloody lower half of Monica's body, they shifted into action, staunching the flow of blood, then lifting the girl onto a stretcher to carry her out of the house and load her onto the ambulance that would take her to Froedtert Hospital in the city.

Her father trotted alongside the stretcher, still holding her hand. "I'm not going anywhere, baby," he told Monica. "I'm right here with you. Pastor Randy, my keys are still in the truck!"

Claude and Monica disappeared into the ambulance, and Randy dashed back into the kitchen, to check on Shiloh. She lay crumpled on the tile, and he gathered her in his arms.

Her tears had finally abated, and she was spent. Shiloh realized she hadn't been any help to her young friend; instead, the tables had turned. Monica's instant grieving of her loss had allowed Shiloh to finally grieve her own. It had scared Shiloh, and Randy, and their boys, who stood around her now, in tears, asking their dad if she was okay.

Just as calmly as he had helped Monica, Randy stroked Shiloh's hair as her head lay on his shoulder, and he reassured them that she would be fine.

"God is doing some healing today in his own way, sons. Your mother loves you; she needs you to understand that, and to love her back. I guess you all are discovering earlier than most that Mama and Daddy aren't perfect."

Lem was the first to approach his parents and kneel beside them. He leaned over to peer into Shiloh's swollen, tear-stained face.

"I'm sorry that I've been so mean, Mom. I love you, no matter what. Everyone makes mistakes. I know you're really sorry; that's what matters."

He wrapped his arms around her and Randy, and the other boys came over too, and followed suit.

Shiloh's tears kept flowing, but she didn't mind. They were cleansing, at this point, and she knew if she released them, she'd be able to help Monica heal, and maybe Lem's friend, Lia, too. God's timing was impeccable. Whatever he was doing in Monica's life had intersected with her need and her father's need, too.

sixty-four

By Tuesday morning, Monica was still pale and weak, but her doctor had decided to let her go home, if she ate breakfast and lunch, and walked the hall a few times with no problems.

According to Claude, that prescription had garnered the first smile from Monica since her miscarriage, and she had heartily eaten the light breakfast the nurse placed before her two hours ago. He sat next to his daughter this morning, stroking her hair while filling Shiloh in on how Monica's recovery was going. Shiloh had been taking turns with him and Eleanor in staying by Monica's side, and had come by today after getting the boys off to school, Randy off to the church, and prepping a few things for their drive to Atchity tomorrow.

"I feel a lot better leaving town, knowing you won't be spending Thanksgiving here, my dear," Shiloh told Monica.

Monica, who hadn't said much since Sunday, gave Shiloh a half-hearted smile. "Me too."

The sadness in her voice matched the emotion enveloping her spirit. Shiloh wished she could hug or pray away the girl's pain, and she knew Claude's sentiments were similar, but he was doing a great job of staying upbeat for his daughter.

Shiloh and Randy had chosen not to share with the congregation that Monica had been hospitalized, because of the sensitive nature of her illness; but Eleanor had been surprisingly forthcoming with members of the women's Bible study, and according to Claude, several ladies had come by their home to deliver hot meals and drop off gift cards to area restaurants.

Another group of ladies texted Eleanor this morning to share their plans to prepare Thanksgiving dinner for the family, Claude announced, so Eleanor could focus on caring for Monica when she came home.

"This is a difficult spot to be in," Claude said after describing the women's kindness, "but I tell you, Mom's friends from church have shown us a lot of love. She says they knew about Monica's condition already, and this just gives us an opportunity to receive some grace and unconditional support."

Shiloh smiled, but didn't respond. Love in action always resonated more than words. Randy had informed her that when they returned from Atchity, he would be spending some regular one-on-one time with Claude outside of church, playing golf or tennis or doing whatever Claude preferred. So Claude didn't know it yet, but he was going to have more than enough opportunities to vent, laugh, cry, and see God at work.

Monica struggled to sit up and take a sip of juice.

"You sure you're feeling better?" Shiloh asked.

The girl shrugged. "Everything aches—but what can I do?"

Shiloh knew Monica was talking about her heart and her reputation as well as her body. Before she could respond, an answer came from the doorway.

"You can keep your head up, Monica, that's what."

Shiloh shifted in her seat to find Jade standing there, looking fabulous as always, and carrying a bouquet as big as herself.

"What on earth . . ."

Jade laughed at Shiloh's reaction. "I know. These flowers are on steroids, right? Each pageant contestant received one of the bouquets that graced the stage on Friday night, and since Vic and I are going to California for the holiday, I thought I'd share mine with a very special girl."

Jade sauntered into the room and turned in circles, trying to find a spot large enough to hold the arrangement. Claude left Monica's side to take it from her.

"Tell you what? Why don't I put this in my SUV, since it looks like Monica will be going home later today. There will be plenty of room there, and I'll make sure to put it in a nice spot once we get it home. Thank you, Sister Smith."

Jade gave him a wide grin and a light hug. When he left the room, she offered Monica a hug, too. The girl reciprocated, but looked embarrassed.

"I guess everyone knows I'm here, huh?"

Jade grew somber. "I don't know what everyone knows, sweetheart. But your grandmother is part of our Bible study group, and she shared with us in confidence that you were going through a tough time. I just came by to let you know that like First Lady Griffin, I'm willing to go through it with you. As pastor's wives, we both can tell you it's not easy having a spotlight turned on you, or having your every move and decision judged or scrutinized, and in your case, maybe the choices you've made in private. It's tough.

"But you hang in there, and know that everybody has a story. You might not know what's going on with your classmates or your friends, or everybody else who seems to know your business, but they've got issues, too. We all do. So never let anyone make you feel less than worthy."

Shiloh couldn't believe it. This was a side of Jade she hadn't known existed. This was a real person, with a heart. This must be the woman Vic knew and loved. Shiloh was glad Jade was finally warming up to sharing herself with everyone else.

"That means a lot, Mrs. Smith; thank you," Monica said softly. "Thank you for coming."

Jade rubbed the girl's arm and smiled at her.

"This too shall pass, my friend. Just keep telling yourself that and keep your head up. It's one of God's promises, so it will happen."

She turned on her heels and gave Shiloh a light peck on the cheek before heading toward the door.

"I didn't come to stay long. We're packing for Cali and I have tons to do before we leave, but I wanted to come by and see Miss Monica, and you too, First Lady, since there's no Bible study tomorrow night. Have a safe trip to Alabama, and thank you for all you did to help me have a successful run in last week's pageant. Your support meant more than I can really express."

After blowing a kiss to Monica, she was gone.

Shiloh looked at Monica and shook her head. "If wisdom can come from a Christian in diva form, it can come from anyone, my friend!"

Monica actually laughed, and Shiloh's heart lightened.

"Mrs. Smith and I have had our issues, but as different as we are, God has found a way to bring us closer and to help each other grow," Shiloh said. "If you had told me four months ago I'd think of her with fondness and actually consider her a friend, I would have laughed in your face. But if God can do that with two grown women, he can do some amazing things in and through you, too, Monica, even after this. You just focus on who you know you are, and do your best, and wait and see how he works. I can't take away your pain and shame, but I hope you won't hold onto it as long as I did. It's a burden you don't have to carry."

Tears welled up in Monica's eyes and she smiled again.

"I believe you, Mrs. Griffin. And I trust him. I'm ready to see what kind of good he will bring out of the mess I've made."

Shiloh walked over to Monica's bed and patted her hand.

"It's called beauty for ashes, my friend, and you don't have to keep calling it your mess. If you'll give it to him, he'll take it and call it his own. All you'll have to do is hold onto his grace." Shiloh paused before continuing. "I've been saying that for a long time; if I'm going to ask you to live it, I guess it's time for me to do the same."

sixty-five

The boys were asleep in the back of the van and the radio was playing softly when Randy proposed. "Shiloh Ann Wilson Griffin, will you marry me?"

"Excuse me?"

Shiloh swiveled her head toward her husband, whose eyes were fixed on the dark road. It was nearly midnight on the day before Thanksgiving, and they were about eight hours from Atchity.

"I know it's not appropriate to do this while I'm driving, but we have four rowdy sons who have finally given us some privacy, and sometimes you have to seize the moment," Randy said. "So forgive my informality, and the unromantic nature of this request, but will you marry me?"

Shiloh giggled. "I think this late-night drive is getting to you, but um, sure, honey. I will marry you. Want to pull over so I can drive for a while?"

Randy didn't respond, but as he approached the next exit off the interstate, he made the right turn, and minutes later was sitting in a well-lit gas station/convenience store parking lot. Rather than pull up to one of the pumps, he parked along a row opposite the tanks and across the parking lot from the twenty-four-hour convenience store. Shiloh was surprised; usually when she offered to drive at night, he declined.

Instead of getting out of the car to trade seats with her, however, he turned to her and reached for her hands. "We've been through a lot in the past two weeks—a whole lot," he said, sounding more like the twenty-something man who proposed the first time around, rather than the esteemed pastor he now was. "And you haven't heard me say much."

Shiloh's heart beat faster. She didn't know where this conversation was leading, but he was right; she'd been wondering where his heart and mind were ever since she'd shared her dangerous secrets. He had continued to go through the motions of a good husband, but there had been unusual and uncomfortable periods of silence between them, and what felt like a wall had formed, causing her to tiptoe around him like she never had before. Randy's coolness had only reinforced her fear that maybe she had been little more to him than a convenient and appropriate wife for the preacher role he was ready to assume, and that maybe now, she was no longer worthy. She hadn't wanted to believe that, but she also hadn't wanted to question him about it. His answers might shatter her.

"I've been praying a lot and processing a lot, Shiloh," Randy said. "And truth be told, I've been shell-shocked by all that you've dropped on me and the boys. You're not who I thought you were. You're not who I thought I married. And honestly, I've been angry; I felt betrayed, which I expressed by pulling away from you. I have to admit that I was scared, too. Scared that you would stand in front of our church family and tell them your ugly secrets and bring shame and judgment on us all."

By now the tears were falling. Shiloh couldn't hold them in. But she prayed this show of emotion wouldn't stop Randy from sharing. She needed to hear what was in his heart. She needed to really know him.

"But every time I would take my anger to God and point out what you had done and what all of this could mean for my ministry, he would back me in a corner and ask me how I'd managed to be so perfect along my entire life's journey. He showed me that truthfully, maybe I chose to date you and to marry you because you fit the preacher-wife mold: pretty, musically inclined, already well-entrenched in the church, and familiar with the protocol. You fit the bill, babe—every criteria I could outline."

Randy lowered his head and sighed. "God asked me, though, if it had been that criteria that had held me and prayed with me when my dad overdosed on his anxiety medication after another Vietnam flashback; or if that criteria had birthed me those four healthy boys in the backseat, or nursed me back to health after my gallbladder surgery, or prepared meal after meal for me, or prayed with me and for me whenever I needed it, and sometimes before I could ask."

Tears filled his eyes as he peered at Shiloh. "I realized that I had been a boy with my own plan when I married you and wanted everything to go my way. But being your husband has shown me that God's way is better. Nothing you've shared about your past has been a betrayal of me or our vows. You betrayed yourself, and the gifts God placed inside you; but can't you see, he has even redeemed that, by putting a passion for teaching in your heart, and by knitting you and Monica together? If I had to choose all over again, Shiloh, even knowing the grave sins you've committed, I'd have to look at my own sins and shortcomings and ask myself if I was worthy enough to be your husband. So I'm asking you tonight, in this gas station parking lot, with our sleeping sons snoring in the back seats, if you'll consider me and my faults worthy enough of your company and your love, and share the rest of your life with me."

Shiloh's heart was so full of joy it ached. She pursed her lips and nodded, because any effort to respond would lead to sobs. She hugged Randy and thanked God over and over. And finally she was able to say the three words that mattered most, but meant more now than they had when she married him seventeen years ago. "I love you, Reverend Randolph James Griffin; I love you. And yes, I will marry you, all over again."

sixty-six

By the time they made it to Atchity, the sun had risen and it was Thanksgiving morning.

The only good thing about arriving the day of the holiday was Shiloh knew she'd be spared any heavy cooking. It wasn't Dayna's forte so she'd only do a dessert or two, and Jessica wouldn't even bother. Usually it was Shiloh and Mama at the helm, but this year, Shiloh's long-distance trek gave her the privilege of arriving with the ham she had already prepared and put on ice, and with assorted beverages.

The Griffin family poured out of the van at her parents' house and stretched their legs before climbing the steps to the porch. Seconds after she rang the doorbell, Dayna's husband Warren greeted her. This was a first. Mama and Daddy were becoming progressive if they were allowing the son-in-law they liked to keep in the shadows to welcome guests. What if she had been one of those less than open-minded Riverview Baptist members?

"Warren!" Shiloh gave her handsome, dark-haired brother-in-law a hug. His blue eyes radiated warmth, as did his smile, and Shiloh's affirmation of Dayna's choice of a second husband remained unchanged: Dayna had really good taste.

"Come on in, sis," he said, with an eyebrow raised. She laughed, knowing he was thinking the same thing that had just run through her mind—amazement that he, of all people, was being given the opportunity to usher everyone inside.

"How've you been?" Shiloh asked. "Where are the twins, and Dayna?"

"Let's see, let me handle those questions in order," Warren said. "I've been doing great, especially now that the house is built and we are settling in. Michael and Mason are in the family room playing the Wii and waiting on your boys to arrive, and Dayna is in the kitchen with Tamara and Naomi, helping your mother put the finishing touches on the meal."

Shiloh stopped in her tracks and stared at Warren as if he had two heads.

"Come again?"

Warren smiled. "You heard me right: Tamara and her mother Naomi came to Atchity with us to celebrate the holiday; it's all good."

Shiloh wanted to settle in a chair in the living room and get the full scoop on this one. She knew that Dayna and Warren had been heavily involved in helping create a scholarship foundation for Tamara's late husband Brent—the man who had been Dayna's college sweetheart and first husband. But to invite the woman who had once been her nemesis—Brent's mistress during their marriage—to dine with her family for the holidays? Dayna obviously had grown in ways Shiloh hadn't imagined possible. This was the side of her sister she wanted to know and love better.

Jessica strode into the living room wearing an apron and a grin, with her arms open for a hug, and Shiloh decided she was in the middle of a dream.

"The hug I'll take, but what are you cooking?" she asked and laughed.

Jessica paused and put a hand on her hip. "You better take this hug while I'm offering it, Miss Thang, and this dish I'm cooking up, too. Once my show starts on Oprah's network, the fans will besiege me, plus my first splurge is going to be a personal chef."

Shiloh laughed and pinched Jessica's cheek. "Why did I think you already had a personal chef? And I don't care whose network you are on, you'll always be my little sister and required to deliver hugs or whatever else I want."

Jessica grinned. "Glad to know who I can call to help keep my feet on the ground."

Jessica stepped around Shiloh and hugged the rest of the Griffins as they flowed into the living room, going from Randy to Lem to Omari to Raphael to baby-of-the-family David.

Mama and Daddy finally appeared, and the round of hugs and kisses continued. When Shiloh's turn came with her father, she held onto him and hoped he could feel every ounce of affection in her hug. How thankful she was to have this chance to be in his arms again, and to tell him that no matter what they'd been through over the years, she loved him.

Daddy stood back and surveyed the bustling room filled with his family.

"Praise God—all my children under one roof, and their families too. God has been good to me."

Dayna stepped into the room at that moment and hugged him from behind. "He's been good to all of us, Daddy, and you're the cherry on top."

Shiloh couldn't have said it better herself.

sixty-seven

It was almost time for dinner, but Shiloh couldn't find Lem anywhere.

Finally, something told her to check the van. Maybe he had gone there to call Lia and have a private conversation. She trotted outside and sure enough found the front passenger door of the van partially open.

When Lem noticed her, he lowered the cell phone from his ear. "Mom, would it be okay for Lia and her family to stop by later this evening, after dinner? Or can you take me to Birmingham tomorrow to spend some time with her?"

Shiloh's first inclination was to say no on both counts, but she knew that response was stemming from her personal discomfort with all she had shared with her son. She had come too far in the past week to regress. She needed to show Lem, and the other boys, that she could face the music her truths would render.

"Yes, Lem, either of those options is fine."

He raised the phone to his ear, with an air of confidence. "My mom says it's cool, Lia. I'll text you the address. Let me call you back, okay?"

Lem ended the call and climbed out of the van. "Thanks for that," he said, without looking at Shiloh.

Shiloh tilted her head and folded her arms, curious about his response. "You're welcome, Lem. Want to talk about what's eating at you?"

He kept his eyes fixed on his phone. "You already know."

"Then why did you invite Lia to come here? With her grandparents, I assume?"

"Actually, she's bringing her mother."

A chill coursed through Shiloh. "Leslie's coming? Lem, how could you?" She leaned against the van. "I don't know about this, Lem. You might need to call her back. I thought her mother wasn't part of her life anymore. I had no idea . . ."

"She's been in a treatment center for the past year trying to pull her life together, according to Lia. She's at home today and tomorrow, for the Thanksgiving holiday."

Shiloh's mind was racing. To tell the truth was one thing; to face it was another. Was Lem doing this to hurt her?

"Lem, son, we need to talk about this."

"About what? There's nothing to talk about. You've told it all, haven't you? It is what it is."

He'd never raised his voice at her, so Shiloh tried to keep her cool. "It's easy to say 'It is what it is,' but not really easy to live." His fustration was palpable. "Let it out, Lem. I can take it."

He turned away and stalked to a pine tree near the side of his grandparents' house. Within minutes, the tree felt his full fury. Lem pummeled the trunk with his sneakered foot over and over, until Shiloh worried that he would sprain or break one of his toes. Instead of intervening, she held her tears at bay, and she prayed.

Help him release the anger, God. Help him forgive me. Help him feel no shame for my mistakes.

The fact that her disappointing revelations had brought him to this point devastated her. Yet even as she hurt, she knew without a doubt that she had done the right thing. She needed to tell the truth for her sake, for Randy's, and for Lem and his brothers.

In this horrifying moment she understood that while she could have easily taken the secret of her abortion to her grave, but doing that wouldn't change the consequences her long-ago decision had yielded. It had shaped who she was as a person and even as a wife and mother. It had led her to make decisions based on guilt and on feeling required to live a life of penance and perfection, functioning as a people-pleasing saint.

How could she tell her wounded son that the very actions causing him anguish—her admissions of guilt—had been the ones to fill her with a sweet freedom she hadn't known was possible? How could she tell him that for the first time ever, she fully understood the meaning of and power of grace?

Even as she quaked inside at the thought of meeting her former college roommate face-to-face, she had a peace that just as God had brought Leslie's daughter into her son's life, he was orchestrating a reunion at the time he knew was best. It wasn't going to be pretty; Shiloh had to steel herself for that. But as much as she wanted to resist and flee, she had to trust God's heart.

Shiloh didn't know how to take her son's outburst, however. Was he angry with her or ashamed of her, or both? Either way, he was justifiably so. She remained by the van and waited for him to collect himself. At some point, he slid to his knees, then sat under the tree, with his head bowed. Shiloh closed her eyes and prayed again.

Minister to him, Lord. I know he's young, but help him forgive me and see your hand in this.

Shiloh wasn't sure how much time had passed, but when she saw Randy poke his head out of the front door and frown when his eye caught Lem, she motioned for him to go back inside. He complied, and she stood there, continuing to watch and wait, until she thought her legs would fall asleep. Finally, he raised his head and pushed himself up off the ground.

He looked toward the van and seemed surprised that she was still there. He walked toward her, and she thought her heart might thump right out of her chest. When he reached her, he gazed into her eyes, as if searching to see who or what lay inside. Eventually, he spoke.

"I've been wondering what kind of person you were back then to have done the things you did," he said, with little emotion in his voice. "It's hard to believe that you, the mother who taught me to always tell the truth, do good to others, and treat people like I want to be treated, could do something so mean to someone who considered you a friend."

Shiloh had no rebuttal; all she could do was nod. His perception of her had been shattered, and she had to let him deal with this in his own way, and in his own time. She wanted to tell him that no one was perfect, not even his beloved Lia. She wanted to ask him to consider the many times she had scolded him or punished him, while forgiving his transgressions. Those words danced on her lips, but she knew this was a matter that could only be resolved when Lem was ready to receive that wisdom. In the meantime, she would continue to love him and do what she could to prove to him that while she may be less than perfect, she was still his loving mother, and he, her beloved son.

She extended her hand.

"Truce? At least for today?"

Lem hesitated, then grasped her hand. They walked toward the house and entered to find everyone sitting around watching each other. Shiloh knew they had been peering out of the window, and before they left the dinner table today, she might have to share some uncomfortable truths with them.

Lord, tell me how much to share, and when.

She released that prayer, then turned her attention to the aromas floating from the kitchen. Whatever she decided to do could wait until after dinner and certainly dessert.

sixty-eight

Shiloh had temporarily forgotten they had guests for dinner this year, and she wasn't sure she should put her business on front street, with Tamara and Naomi there. But Lia and her family would be visiting in a few hours, and she didn't know what to expect. It was only fair to prepare the family, just as she needed to prepare herself.

After everyone had feasted on turkey, dressing, greens, yams, and other traditional holiday fare, Mama and their guest Naomi, the mother of Dayna's friend Tamara, had taken turns bringing in one dessert after another from the kitchen to place on the long dining room table. This year there were three cakes—caramel, coconut, and pound—a sweet potato pie, key lime pie, apple cobbler, and a variety of ice cream flavors.

"I feel like I'm in a restaurant," Naomi said after she settled in her seat and prepared to dive into a slice of pound cake and key lime pie. "Dayna, please feel free to invite Tamara and me to Thanksgiving dinner every year!"

Dayna had just taken a bite of sweet potato pie, but paused to give her a thumbs-up.

Tamara shook her head. "How are you going to invite yourself to dinner next year, in the middle of eating this year's meal, Mama? I can't take you anywhere!"

The family erupted in laughter.

"You're both welcome to join us anytime," Mama assured them. "Now, enjoy that dessert!"

The food and conversation flowed until Daddy cleared his throat and tapped his fork against the side of his plate. Shiloh, Dayna, and Jessica exchanged glances and tried to stifle their giggles. Thank goodness they had eaten and satisfied themselves before he decided to speak—it looked like they were in for his annual sermonette. But with all that Daddy had been through in the past few weeks, Shiloh decided she'd be willing to sit here the rest of the evening, just to hear his slow Southern drawl punctuate the air.

"I can't say often enough how thankful I am to be here with my family this year," Daddy began. "I want to thank my wife—my partner in life—for taking such good care of me since my heart attack. I must say I will miss my fried catfish and okra, but she can make anything taste good, so I will learn to eat healthier and enjoy the meals along the way."

Daddy nodded at Mama, who was blushing and beaming simultaneously, then scanned the faces of his three daughters and his sons-in-law.

"I also want to thank my children for running to my bedside when I was in the hospital. I hear that members of Riverview Baptist were lining the halls, and I'm grateful for that, but it's a true blessing to know that your family will drop everything at a moment's notice and come to be with you in your gravest time of need. Even though I was out of it most of the time you were there, I just know your presence helped me heal. This crisis was a wake-up call on many levels, but one important consequence was to remember that nothing is more important than family. God has given us to each other for a purpose. We are each other's gifts, and gifts are meant to be treasured and taken care of. So I urge you all to continue taking care of each other and loving each other. Doing just that is a form of praise to God."

Randy squeezed Shiloh's hand under the table, and she repeated the gesture with Lem, who was sitting on the other side of her. She saw Jessica and Keith, and Dayna and Warren, trade smiles. Tamara leaned toward Dayna to give her a light hug. Daddy acknowledged the gesture.

"That's right—some friends become family too, often in the most unusual circumstances."

"Amen, Reverend Wilson," Tamara said. "I see Dayna maybe four times a year, when the foundation Brent launched before his death needs to meet with the board of directors. And occasionally we'll call each other to check in. We aren't in each other's daily lives or up to speed on every twist and turn, but I know that if I ever need anything, she'll do her best to help, and vice versa. I don't know why God took us on the journey he did to bring us to this place, but our ability to sit around the same table at a board meeting, let alone over a Thanksgiving meeting, is nothing but God."

"Hallelujah, young lady," Daddy said. "Nothing but God is right—in every situation. I loved my son-in-law Brent, but . . ." He paused and looked at Warren. "Had it not been for Brent moving on, my daughter would not have the benefit of helping raise these two handsome and bright young men sitting at the table today, or of experiencing love in the selfless and sincere way I see that Warren loves her. Thank you, son."

Daddy's use of that term of endearment with Warren left him, and everyone else, speechless. Warren seemed stunned, but acknowledged the compliment with a smile.

Daddy nodded at Keith, who as usual was quiet and taking everything in. "Keith, you're a man of few words, but it takes a strong man to stand with and care for my strong-willed, on-the-go baby girl."

Everyone laughed and Dayna and Shiloh clapped, while Jessica scowled at them.

"I know you're a good man, son," Daddy continued. "Keep doing what you're doing to keep you and Jessica on track, and I'm

284 / LEAD ME HOME

looking forward to the day God blesses you two with some grand-babies for me."

"Daddy!" Jessica seemed shocked by her father's brazenness, but Keith looked hopeful.

"What? As the kids say, 'I'm just sayin'!'" Daddy uttered the comment with a straight face, but pretended to wipe his mouth with his linen napkin to mask his grin.

Lem and Omari exchanged glances and nearly lost their composure. Their grandfather winked at Raphael, who gave him a thumbs-up. Shiloh shook her head. Raphael had probably charged Daddy five dollars for that tutorial on the best slang to use during dinner.

Daddy turned toward Randy. "You've been like a son to me since you first started spending your summers here when you were the same age as Lem is now," Daddy said. "Then you gave me the privilege of serving as your father in the ministry. It's been wonderful watching you grow in faith and leadership, and as the head of your family. I've been praying a lot about what I should do, after having this health crisis, and I know that I need to step down as pastor of Riverview Baptist sooner rather than later."

The collective gasp around the table interrupted Daddy's speech, but after giving his initial declaration a few minutes to sink in, he continued. "Yes, I know what I'm saying and I mean what I'm saying. I love preaching and leading God's people—you all know that. But as the book of Ecclesiastes declares, there is a time for everything under the sun, and while I'm still able to do some things and enjoy myself, I want to do just that, with my girlfriend."

"Reverend!" Mama's embarrassment caused another round of gleeful laughter.

"Careful now—ya'll better use some protection," Jessica said, and Keith shook his head.

Dayna swatted her sister's hand and reminded her with a few motions of her head and eyes that the boys were also around the table. Jessica looked sheepish and mouthed "Sorry" to Dayna and Warren and to Shiloh and Randy.

Daddy chuckled. "Now, ya'll are getting out of control. I'll wrap this up by saying to Randy that I would love for you to pray about possibly coming back home, to lead Riverview Baptist. I'm hoping to retire in six months."

That news lit everyone around the table afire. Shiloh looked at Randy, and he looked like a deer caught in headlights. What did he think of this offer, she wondered. Would he accept it, or refuse to leave his Milwaukee congregation?

"Daddy, you won't be able to retire and sit in a chair all day doing nothing, and you know it," Jessica said.

"You're right—I can't do that, and that's not my plan," Daddy said. "But I feel like God is calling me to step away from the formal role of pastoral leader and to minister in a different, more subtle way, through the various experiences he puts in my path. We'll talk more later, Randy, but I wanted to share that with you, with the entire family present, and ask that we all pray for God's will and wisdom in this situation, both for me and for Randy. I would love to see Randy leading Riverview Baptist as senior pastor, since he was the assistant pastor there for so long, before the move to Milwaukee. But if God has something different in mind, so be it. Now, where was I?"

Daddy turned toward Shiloh and Lem this time. "There's nothing like a parent's love, you know. So whatever issues or challenges that occur between a child and a parent—outside of abuse—should usually remain in that safe and loving space between them," he said. "You two seem like you have something to work out, and that's okay. That happens during the teen years sometimes. Just know that your mama has your back, Lem, and Shiloh, just know that the love you've poured into him will always rise to the surface, in its own time."

A lump filled Shiloh's throat and she swallowed hard. "Lem and I are going to be fine, but does that apply to fathers and daughters, too, Daddy?"

Now it was Daddy's turn to be speechless. He peered at her, waiting.

"I have something to tell you, Daddy and Mama, and I guess I'll tell you in front of everyone. I've been learning these past few months how important it is to be honest and authentic in every area of your life, and sometimes that requires you to take a step back in the past, look at who you were then, accept that, and tell the truth about it, so you can move on."

Shiloh saw Dayna and Tamara look at each other, and she knew they were acknowledging the pain and betrayal that had occurred between them, over Brent.

"I'd like to share something with you that's shameful and hard. I've already told my boys, but Warren . . . you might want Michael and Mason to leave the table for a few minutes."

Warren shook his head. "If you're okay with them being present, I don't mind them hearing, but that's up to you."

While Shiloh paused to ponder that, Tamara and Naomi pushed back their chairs and began clearing plates and dishes of food from the table, to carry into the kitchen.

"You all go on and have your family discussion," Naomi said. "We'll be in the kitchen, tidying up."

Shiloh appreciated their gracious offer to give the family some privacy. She clasped Randy's hand and he patted hers, in reassurance.

"Eighteen years ago, the spring I was a sophomore at Birmingham-Southern . . ."

sixty-nine

Before Shiloh could say more, Daddy raised his palm to stop her. Stunned, and already nervous, she paused midsentence.

"Shiloh, you are about to share something that's obviously very personal and very painful, that happened almost two decades ago—before you were a wife or a mother or a full-fledged adult. Before you go on, let me say something, and ask you something."

Daddy sat back in his chair and folded his arms across his protruding belly. "First, if you've already shared this information with Randy and your sons, that may be enough. Your immediate family may need to know your particular truths, to help them learn from it and to help them understand you better, and that's all good. But ask yourself before you continue if there's a purpose in sharing what's on your heart with the rest of us.

"Now, we are your family and we'd certainly like to know and understand you better, too. We love you. But will what you share help us do that? Or will it help our family as a whole in some way?"

Shiloh lowered her eyes, thinking, and wrestling with herself, to see what answers were honestly surfacing.

"If the only purpose in sharing is just so we'll know, only do that if it's going to make you feel better or stronger in some way," Daddy said. "If you're telling us just to get it off your chest, it should still fit the two prior criteria. Or, if telling us allows us to take some sort of action or become aware of a larger issue that all of us might need to address, please tell us. Just don't do it out of obligation or guilt or because someone said you had to. Do what's best for your heart, mind, spirit, and soul, sweetheart. We love you, either way."

When Daddy was done, Shiloh was, too. What a gift he had just given her. For the first time in her entire life, she didn't feel the need to measure up, to explain herself, or explain away a behavior or attitude. She could just be, and in doing so, just be loved.

She felt like saying, Wow. Or crying. Or leaping for joy. But she was so overwhelmed by this side of her father that she'd never known, she also just wanted to sit and soak in this moment.

Everyone around the table sat silent, with their eyes on Daddy, waiting for what would come next.

Randy leaned toward Shiloh and gently kissed her lips.

This public display of affection from him was unusual, at least in front of her parents, but she knew he was sealing the vows he'd made earlier, in his interstate marriage proposal, and letting her know that he stood with her, whatever she decided. She looked at her four sons, and wondered what was racing through their minds. When she realized they were looking back at her with love, even the hurt and broken Lem, it didn't really matter and neither did the ghosts from her past.

Leslie might come today with Lia, and if so, she could take her aside and apologize for her hurtful and horrible actions all those years ago. But Daddy's words had echoed what God must have been trying to tell her all along: His grace was sufficient. He had forgiven her the first time she'd said she was sorry—for both offenses. Just as she'd promised Monica he would, a few days ago.

Shiloh sighed and made a decision. The next time the anniversary date of her abortion rolled around, she wouldn't hold her usual commemoration. She would pull out the recorder on that date and conjure up memories of today's family gathering and conversation, and play a new song, to honor God's graciousness, and her season of new beginnings.

seventy

Shiloh looked from her father to Randy and back again.

She took the time to peer at everyone seated around the table—men, women, and boys, who had known her as little as the four years Dayna and Warren had been a couple, and as long as the day she entered the world. Michael and Mason, whom she knew the least, stared at her curiously. That same perspective, coupled with compassion, seemed to fill Keith and Warren's eyes. Dayna and Jessica seemed perplexed. Shiloh wasn't sure how to respond, then God spoke to her spirit.

It's already settled. I have taken your burdens upon me. You have the victory.

Suddenly, peace flooded her spirit, and it was indescribable. Shiloh sat back and smiled.

"Thank you, Daddy. All I have to say is, eighteen years ago I was a young, Christian girl who had heard since childhood that God was a God of grace and that there was no sin he wouldn't forgive. I heard those words, and I recited the Scriptures reflecting those messages, and I believed them. But then . . . when I became the worst sinner of all sinners in my eyes—a liar, a thief, a hypocrite, even a killer, from the way I saw it—I forgot all those truths; at least, I didn't believe they applied to me. I thought because I knew right yet did wrong anyway, I owed God greater sacrifices than most. I actually thought about becoming a nun."

Mama gasped before she could collect herself. Shiloh smiled again.

"I know—shocking. But when Randy began courting me and I saw what a committed man of God he was, I knew God was leading me in a different direction. Another way to be connected to him as a pastor's wife and ministry helpmate. And that's what I've done all of these years to the best of my ability. But this year . . . this year, God has shaken me out of my comfort zone. It's like he said, 'Enough is enough. No more guilt, no more playing the martyr.' He wants me to use my experiences and my shame to help others heal, and to bring his name glory. Thank you, Daddy, for helping me understand I should only share my experiences when they serve a purpose. I don't think it's necessary to go into all of the gritty details after all. I just ask that you all pray for me, and for Randy and the boys as we learn a new way of communicating and loving each other."

Shiloh sighed and lowered her head. Dayna pushed her chair back from the table and walked around the table to Shiloh. She stood just behind Shiloh and opened her arms for a hug. Before Shiloh could react, Jessica jumped out of her seat and trotted around the table to extend her arms as well. Shiloh couldn't withhold the grin as she scooted back her chair and joined her sisters in a group hug.

"Doesn't matter what it is—or was," Jessica whispered in her ear. "We've got you."

Dayna quoted Ecclesiastes 4:12. "'Though one may be overpowered, two can defend themselves. A cord of three strands is not quickly broken.' We know you; we know your heart. Every single one of us has fallen short of God's best, either intentionally or by mistake. You are a loving, giving, encouraging, and inspiring woman of God. Nothing and no one will ever change that."

She paused and peered at Shiloh. "I love you, sis."

seventy-one

When the food and dishes were put away and the kitchen was clean, everyone settled in the family room to watch movies.

As one action flick ended and Keith added another to the DVD, Lem, who had been stretched out on the floor, scooted over to Shiloh. "Lia just called. Her parents think it may be too late to come tonight—how about tomorrow?"

Shiloh leaned toward her son and stroked his cheek. "Tell you what, son. Why don't we save them a trip? I'll drive you to Birmingham in the morning, and we can stay as long as you want."

Lem's eyes widened. "Really, Mom? Thank you."

She smiled. What she didn't say was that she'd even go sit in the mall or walk around Wal-Mart if necessary, if it turned out to be too tense between her and Lia's mother. All Shiloh could control was her apology, and she was ready to render it, as forcefully and as often as Leslie needed to hear it.

By midnight, Shiloh was one of the last family members to crawl into bed. She snuggled in close to Randy, asked God to bless her journey to Birmingham and her reconnection with Leslie tomorrow, and then she wept. The tears woke Randy, who startled awake, his face awash with concern.

"What's wrong, Shiloh? What is it?"

She swiped at the tears, but they kept coming. Finally, she gathered herself enough to reassure Randy that nothing was wrong—everything was finally falling into place. She knew she was loved, simply because she was Shiloh. How beautiful that felt.

The secrets that had held her hostage for all these years only had the power she had given them. Her shame didn't serve anyone, and especially not God. She was finally free. And in that freedom, she could love others like never before—those who were broken or lost or lovely or seemingly perfect, or obviously sinful. She had been all of those at one time or another, and never once had God let go of her. Shiloh was ready now to hold onto God. These tears were her baptism, of sorts, her new beginning.

Randy couldn't read her mind so he didn't know that transformation was taking place, but the inner joy he must have read in her tear-stained expression seemed to calm him. He pulled her close, and held her, until they both fell asleep.

seventy-two

Shiloh and Mama were the first to stir in the morning, as usual.

They met in the kitchen just minutes apart. Shiloh was measuring coffee for the coffee maker when Mama joined her at the island with ingredients she had pulled from the pantry and refrigerator to make a memorable family breakfast.

"Homemade biscuits?" Shiloh asked.

"Yep," Mama said. "Like always. Even Michael and Mason have come to love them."

Shiloh peeked at Mama. "And how are you feeling about *them*—about adding them to your brood?"

Mama worked in silence a few moments while she kneaded the dough. Finally she said, "Let's put it this way: When the photographer from Cedaric Photography comes tomorrow to shoot our family portrait, Michael and Mason will be surrounding me, along with your four boys." A mischievous gleam filled Mama's eyes. "Can't wait to show off that picture and see the faces of the ladies in the women's missionary society!"

Shiloh couldn't believe it. Mama used to care so much about what those ladies said and thought. *What was going on?*

She saw Shiloh's quizzical stare and laughed. "Yes, I can poke fun at them and at myself." She stopped pounding the dough and turned toward Shiloh. "I want to know your secrets, if you're willing to share them with me."

Shiloh's breath caught in her throat.

Mama touched her hand. "Your father was absolutely right in the position he took yesterday. You don't have to tell any of us what happened all those years ago. You were young, you were a different person. I will love you the same no matter what. But I can't get your twenty-year-old face out of my mind, and I keep wondering what was going on behind your air of confidence and pretty smile that I didn't see, that somehow crippled you or burdened you all this time. I feel like I failed you as a mother because you held onto whatever happened and didn't feel like you could come to me and trust me. That means you thought I'd judge you."

Shiloh looked away. It was the truth, but she wouldn't hurt Mama by confirming it.

Mama gently grabbed Shiloh's chin and turned Shiloh's face toward hers. "You thought I'd judge you, and truthfully, you were probably right," Mama said. "I would have cared what the people at Riverview Baptist would have to say. I would have been appalled that whatever it was led you to forget your Christian upbringing. I would have been hard to live with, and it would have made your burden greater." A sad smile crossed Mama's face. "It's unfortunate, but true. That's the good, Christian First Lady I was back then, and have been, for way too long. Your Daddy's heart attack shook me into reality: what really matters is loving each other unconditionally, not with strings attached."

Shiloh didn't know if Mama's change of heart would stick, but this conversation was certainly throwing Shiloh for a loop. Maybe she had such a fixed image of who her mother was that she didn't believe Mama could change. But this was the same lens of judgment that she had used to view Jade, she suddenly realized, and she was learning that she could not truly assess a person's heart or character.

"I can't blame you if that's the only mother you know—I guess that's the only side I've shown you," Mama said. "But it's way past time that I get to know the true Shiloh, and you have the benefit of knowing all of me. That's why I want to know, sweetheart. Not so I can make you feel worse. I want to stand with you and pray with you when the doubts creep in and the shame tries to reclaim its spot in your mind, as it inevitably will. I'll always be your mother, but I also want to become your friend."

The plea was evident in Mama's eyes as much as it was in her voice. Shiloh was undone. Could she trust Mama with this? Would it come back to haunt her? That voice, unbidden, filled her spirit again with an answer. *Trust me.*

Shiloh silently replied. *Yes, Lord.*

She grabbed Mama by the hand and led her to the kitchen door.

"Where are we going?" Mama asked.

"Outside, to the porch, where we'll have some privacy," Shiloh said.

She pulled Mama along. They walked around the side of the house to the front, and climbed the stairs to the porch where they settled in the swing.

Mama scooted close to Shiloh and turned to face her. "Before you begin, I want to answer a question you asked me a few months ago. You asked me whether I had a dream of my own, outside of my marriage and family, and I gave you a flippant, yet appropriate answer for the First Lady of an esteemed church. That's because I wanted to shush you before you awakened those dreams. Truth is, I wanted to dance, Shiloh. Professionally, in New York. So it's no surprise to me that you had artistic musical tendencies, and Jessica has a public speaking, motivational platform. I see myself in both of you, and even in Dayna's desire to touch others through her administrative and nursing gifts. I was a talented dancer, and my teachers growing up always said so. I moved audiences. I lifted their spirits with my performances. I saw it and I felt it.

"But my father wasn't having it. He was a church deacon and die-hard Christian who stayed angry with my mother for years for even putting me in dance classes. So when I graduated from high school and had a chance to audition for a prominent dance company in Washington, DC, that could help pay my way to Howard University, Daddy wouldn't buy me a ticket to go. He used that money to take me along to a church convention in Memphis with him and my mother. I met your father on the second day of that weeklong conference, and truthfully, I fell in love the minute he took my hand and kissed it, before he even said hello. We courted long distance for about six months, and, well, you know the rest. I became his wife, he was hired to lead a small Tennessee church, and eventually got the call to come to Atchity.

"I shared all of that to let you know that yes, I had dreams, and some of them did die. But your father became a new dream, and you children were a blessing. So even when life doesn't take the path you believe is best, God can give you beauty from ashes in every situation. I've asked myself 'what if' about dancing; but if I had gone that route and never met your father, I'd have a whole other set of 'what ifs.' Please share with me what you will, and even before you begin, know that I love you and I'll stand by you, no matter what."

"Even if it ain't pretty?" Shiloh asked, grateful to know more about Mama—finally.

"As ugly as it can get, I'm ready." Mama took Shiloh's hand in hers and kissed it.

Shiloh took a deep breath, and began. "Eighteen years ago, the spring that I turned twenty . . ."

seventy-three

The ride to Birmingham later that morning was filled with laughter and singing and remembering good times from the past. But when Shiloh pulled up to the mini-mansion that bore the address Lem had punched into the GPS system as Lia's, they fell silent.

"Wow," Lem said from the backseat. "I had no idea."

Shiloh looked at Mama, who sat in the passenger seat, staring at the brick Georgian-style home situated on what must be three acres of land.

"God is good," Mama said. "His blessings come in all shapes and sizes, but he loves us all the same. This house is beautiful, Lem, but you know as well as your mother and I do the problems and issues this family has faced, despite the material trappings. Don't go in there feeling insecure because of what they possess or drive; Lia cares about you because you're you. That hasn't changed, so don't you go changing."

"Yes, ma'am," Lem said.

Shiloh found herself grateful that after hearing the details that morning, Mama had invited herself along. "Leslie is going to be there surrounded by her family. You need a prayer warrior with you, to show them that no matter what, someone has your back," Mama had said. "What time are we leaving?"

And here they were, about to face down Shiloh's final demon together, and release Lem to love this girl if he loved her, but to also see his mother accept responsibility for her actions.

"Let's go," Shiloh said.

Lem stepped out of the van first and opened the door for his grandmother and then for Shiloh. He squeezed Shiloh's hand before releasing it, but didn't utter a word. Again, she found herself grateful.

Lia came out to greet them before they made it up the winding, cobblestone sidewalk. "You're here!"

She trotted down the lane to meet them, and took turns embracing each of them—starting with Mama, then Shiloh, then Lem. Shiloh wasn't sure what, if anything, Lem had shared with Lia, but she didn't seem upset or uncomfortable. That made Shiloh uncomfortable, wondering if now she'd be breaking news to this sweet girl that would shake her confidence in Lem. She stole a quick glance at Lem, and he gave her a thumbs-up. Shiloh didn't know exactly what that meant, but she knew she had to stay on mission, no matter what.

Lia led them inside, and the foursome paused in a breathtaking foyer that featured a twelve-foot ceiling and a gorgeous chandelier. This time she wanted to utter, "Wow," as Lem had upon their arrival, but she held it in.

A gray-haired man with long white sideburns appeared from a doorway off to the side and approached Mama and Shiloh with his hand extended. He was wearing a collared shirt and slacks with suspenders, and looked as if he were ready for a day at the office, although Lem had informed Shiloh that both of Lia's grandparents were retired.

"William Hamilton," he said and shook the ladies' hands first. "Welcome. So nice to see you." He turned toward Lem and shook his hand, too. "Young man—nice to see you again."

A few seconds later, his wife joined them. "Well, hello and welcome!" She was petite and stout, and also silver-haired, though it was in a stylish bun. She hugged the ladies and Lem. "I'm Marian Hamilton. Lia, William, why do you have these folks standing in here? You all come on in and make yourselves at home. Follow me."

She led them to an expansive sitting room that housed two sofas, a baby grand piano, and floor-to-ceiling windows.

"You have a beautiful home, Mrs. Hamilton," Shiloh said, accepting that they must not recognize or remember her from their visits to Leslie at Birmingham-Southern. She didn't know whether to remind them now, or just let it be. After a few minutes, she decided the latter choice would be the wisest course, for the time being. "Thank you for allowing us to visit today, so the kids could spend some time together."

Marian showed them to their seats and offered them iced tea. "I'm glad we could get them together," Marian said as she poured the beverages. "Thank you for offering to bring Lem; that gives us more time to spend with our daughter, Leslie, before she has to leave."

Shiloh looked at them again to see if there was any hint of recognition, and Marian smiled at her. "Yes, dear, I remember you from Birmingham-Southern," she said and sat across from Shiloh. "Your name is so pretty and unusual—how could I forget you, or that pretty face? After all that happened that summer . . . with Leslie and all . . . we just lost track of everything and everyone."

Her candor surprised Shiloh. There was no guilt or shame in her voice, just an acceptance of reality. Shiloh wondered how long it had taken her to get there. Before she could reflect on it further, a tall, thin, copper-brown woman with high cheekbones, deep-set eyes, and hair that flowed past her shoulders strolled into the room, her hands tucked casually in her pockets. She looked photo-shoot ready in her fitted jeans, white collared shirt, and cowboy boots.

Shiloh's thoughts and words left her. Looking at Leslie took her back to the last time she'd seen her at Birmingham-Southern, sitting on her bed in their dorm room, defeated, distraught, and hopeless about her future. This woman was beautiful, but she looked older than her thirty-eight years, and her eyes held a sadness that looked unshakable. Shiloh flung herself back into the pit of shame that Mama warned her would resurface.

Shiloh hadn't expected it to happen so swiftly; then again, there should have been no expectations at all. She didn't know what Leslie would say or do, or how she would respond to Shiloh being in her home or her presence, after all these years. She just didn't know.

Everyone seemed to be waiting with bated breath to see what would happen next. Leslie finally sliced the roomful of tension with her quirky humor. "Why so somber? So silent? Ya'll act like I'm going to pull out a machete or something."

No one laughed.

"Okay, a water gun?"

Marian sighed, and Lem and Lia looked away. Marian said, "Leslie—let's not behave this way."

"Mother, can't you take a joke? I didn't mean anything by it." She pulled her hands from her pocket and sat on the sofa near her mother, staring at Shiloh.

"So your son and my daughter just happen to meet at camp and just happen to fall in love," Leslie said and barked a laugh. "First, you stole my life, now your son wants to steal my daughter's heart. You Wilsons gotta be watched. Lia, keep an eye on him!"

Marian frowned and pursed her lips, but she didn't try to stop her daughter. Lia peered at her clasped hands in her lap. Shiloh remembered two things as she tried to remain calm: Leslie was still in rehab, only home for the holidays, so she still had a lot to work through, and secondly, she had stolen this woman's music, and in doing so, killed Leslie's dreams and hopes for a safe summer right along with it. How had she expected to be greeted?

Leslie seemed curious about Shiloh's level of calmness.

"Where did life take you, Shiloh Griffin? I'd expected to see your name in lights somewhere by now. Did motherhood slow you down?"

Shiloh ignored the taunt just so she could say what needed to be said first, and most: "I'm sorry, Leslie. For everything."

Leslie's eyes grew wide. "Everything?" she whispered in almost childlike wonder, and the depth of her former roommate's illness filled Shiloh with sadness.

"Everything, Leslie. Stealing the music, taking the fellowship knowing I had cheated, and how it could have saved you. Not coming to your rescue that summer when I saw you on a street corner you should have been nowhere near. I am sorry for being the deceitful, selfish person I was, and taking what should have rightfully been yours. I don't know if you can, but I'm asking you to forgive me. I'm not that person anymore, but I own that she was me, and what I did was absolutely wrong."

Leslie bowed her head, and when she looked up, into Shiloh's eyes, her own were glistening.

"Do you know how long I've waited to receive that apology? I thought it would never come, and now that it has . . . it still isn't enough."

Shiloh's heart sank. She didn't know what else to say, or do.

Mama reached for her hand, while addressing Leslie. "Sweetheart, I don't know if you remember meeting me or seeing me a few times when we visited Shiloh at Birmingham-Southern," Mama said. Leslie's soft shrug was neither a yes nor a no, but Mama continued. "Dear, I'm so sorry for what my daughter did to you. She was wrong—plain and simple, no excuses. And if she didn't have the strength of character to do the right thing back then, I wished you would have had the courage to turn her in. It would have been a huge embarrassment for her, but it might have saved you, and your need to win that fellowship."

Mama looked at Marian, and Shiloh knew she was pondering whether Leslie had told her mother about the abuse she declared her grandfather was inflicting upon her at the time. If Leslie had, Marian seemed unfazed. Leslie looked away, and Shiloh suspected that the secret still thrived. Knowing how freeing it had been to share her past with her husband, and just yesterday with Mama, she realized in large part, that might be what had prevented Leslie's full recovery all this time—those demons that still haunted her from the abuse, as well as Shiloh's betrayal. Shiloh wished she could have a private moment with Leslie to share that, but it didn't look like they'd have the opportunity.

Lia broke the silence that had engulfed the room by clearing her throat and standing. "Um, Lem and I are going to go outside for a walk, if that's okay," she said.

Marian nodded. "Don't go too far, Lia. Stay near the perimeter of the property, where someone can still see you."

"Yes, ma'am."

When they were gone, Marian retrieved the tray of tea from the coffee table. "I'm going to go and refresh our beverages." She looked at Mama. "Want to join me?"

Mama leapt from the sofa. "Be happy to."

When the mothers were gone, Shiloh and Leslie stared at one another for the longest time without speaking. Shiloh saw hurt, envy, pain, sadness, anger, and regret in her former friend's eyes, and it made her want to cry.

"Leslie, I am truly sorry for my part in bringing your life to this point—I can't tell you how much I regret what I did. I've lived with the guilt and shame of it all these years, and I should have found you and told you long before now. I have no excuse. I. Am. So. Very. Sorry."

Shiloh didn't think she had any tears left, but the waterfall erupted and she couldn't control it. She wept into her hands, not for herself but for Leslie. She wanted Leslie to forgive her, not for her own selfish reasons anymore, but so that Leslie herself would be free. She wanted Leslie to stand in whatever her truths were, and she wanted to help her.

Shiloh knew she had to pull herself together before she could do anything. She dug around in her purse and found a tissue. She wiped her eyes, blew her nose, and took a long, deep breath. She looked up at Leslie, who had been watching her this whole time, without moving. Her eyes still held contempt and anger.

"I know I can't turn back time or do anything to restore to you what you fully deserve, Leslie, but I'll tell you this: You have a beautiful daughter who loves you, and who needs you. You have parents who seem to love you. I sense . . . have you not told them about the abuse you shared with me?"

Leslie looked away.

"Ah, I see . . ." Shiloh wanted to reach out and grasp Leslie's hand, but she knew Leslie wasn't ready. "I've spent the past week spilling my guts, telling my family about the sin I committed against you, and about some other pretty terrible things I did, and it was the hardest thing I've ever done. But you know what, Leslie? Telling them freed me. Freed me to forgive myself. And to come here today and apologize, like I should have done all those years ago.

"I need to tell you what I didn't have the maturity or the knowledge to tell you way back then, but what happened to you wasn't your fault. You were a young girl, and you didn't do anything wrong. You have to forgive yourself for being young and vulnerable. Grant yourself some grace. And if you have the courage—no, *when* you gather your strength and courage—you have to speak your truth. I can tell you from experience it will heal your heart, Leslie."

Leslie looked at Shiloh as if she were confused. "It's not too late for all of that?"

"Of course not," Shiloh said. "If you think it's too late, why are you in rehab? It's never too late, as long as you have breath in your body. Every day you awake is another chance to let Lia know you love her, and you're here for her."

Leslie sat up straighter, and she looked past Shiloh. Shiloh turned to see what had captured her attention, and caught herself before she gasped. It was a photo of a years-younger Leslie seated next to an older man who resembled her father. Her parents stood behind the two of them, smiling.

"Every time I come here to visit, I have to see that picture, and it makes me sick," Leslie whispered.

Shiloh turned and faced her again. "It's not the photo that's making you sick, Leslie. It's the secret you're harboring about the man in the photo. Have you told your therapist, or your counselors at rehab? Until you do, you will never truly be able to heal. You have to take care of Leslie, and those around you will eventually come around."

"It sounds so easy, but it's complicated."

Shiloh nodded, and this time, she did make a move. She left the sofa she sat on and perched on Leslie's, so she could grasp her hand. "If you want me to tell your parents that part of your story, at least in the context of what happened between us at Birmingham-Southern, I'm willing to do that."

Shiloh's heart was beating wildly. She hadn't come here to get entangled in Leslie's affairs, but she could see Leslie struggling, and a sliver of a breakthrough on the horizon. She'd be just as guilty as she was last time if she left her hanging on the precipice today, without offering to serve as her safety net. But Leslie shook her head, and looked into Shiloh's eyes.

"You know, you always were special. You cared more than normal. You gave more than anyone else. You didn't mind showing and sharing your heart. I think that's why when you betrayed me like you did, I let it slide. Something in me believed that if you, of all people, had been desperate enough to stoop that low, you must have had a need greater than mine. That's why I didn't report you, Shiloh. And in some sick way, I rationalized that this had happened between us because you were better than me anyway—kinder, smarter, more giving—and I was too weak to tell my grandfather no, and to tell on him. You didn't drive me to the streets—my own cowardice did, and my desire to forget everything and drown out the pain."

Shiloh didn't know what to say, so she simply responded with a hug. She held Leslie in her arms for a long time, and Leslie didn't resist. At some point, she rested her head on Shiloh's shoulder.

"I'm going back to the rehab center tomorrow," Leslie said, her voice muffled by Shiloh's thick sweater. "My counselor there is wonderful. She'll be the first person, besides you, to learn the truth. We'll see what happens from there."

Two hours later, when Shiloh, her mother, and Lem were preparing to head back to Atchity, Leslie reached for her, to give her a hug.

"I don't know what's going to happen—if I'll be able to be successful after rehab this time or not, but thank you for coming, and for helping me see some things today," she said. "I forgive you, Shiloh. Now I have to figure out how to forgive myself, so I can ask my daughter, and my parents, to forgive me too."

Shiloh pulled away and looked into her eyes.

"The biggest lesson I've learned over the past few months—including in the past few days, Leslie, is the power of standing in your truth. You have to do that for you, and to teach Lia how to do the same. That's what will bring you back home—to your family and to yourself, whoever you want yourself to be in the here and now."

Leslie nodded.

"Thanks for the challenge. I think I'm ready this time. I'm going to give it my all."

On the ride home, Shiloh, Mama, and Lem immersed themselves in their thoughts. When they reached the Wilson home, Shiloh had to wake Lem and send him to the guest room he was sharing with his brothers.

Mama walked toward the house with Shiloh, but stopped her before she entered.

"Thank you for letting me come along, Shiloh, and for allowing me to share this journey to healing with you," Mama said. "You are an amazing woman, and I'm honored to be your mother."

Shiloh leaned down and clung to Mama.

"Don't buy me anything for Christmas this year. You just gave me my gift."

seventy-four

Now that Thanksgiving was behind them, the nation was barreling toward Christmas. Shiloh, Randy, and the boys saw signs of the commercial emphasis on the holiday throughout the route back to Milwaukee.

Even so, instead of using the drive time to plan for the holiday and the gifts she needed to buy, Shiloh spent it pondering how far she had come this year and how everything she'd experienced had been life-changing. And with Daddy's request of Randy, she sensed more changes were on the way.

"What are you thinking about Daddy's plea for you to come back to Atchity?"

Randy didn't answer for so long, Shiloh thought he hadn't heard her.

"I'm waiting to see what God says," he finally responded, and glanced at her. "How do you feel about it?"

Shiloh shrugged. "It's funny how I'm just getting settled in Milwaukee, making friends in and out of church, developing a bond with Jade, preparing to return to school and get my teaching license, and now this. Makes me wonder what God is doing. I feel like we have a solid ministry in Milwaukee. We're helping people, the church is growing, I'm mentoring Monica . . . and yet, home is home. We'd be there to help Mama and Daddy as they get older, you know the congregation at Riverview Baptist and they love you, and as senior pastor, you could implement some of the things you're already doing in Milwaukee. I agree that we need to pray about it; God may have to reveal the answer on this one."

Randy nodded. "A year ago, I would have readily and immediately said yes to your dad; but we are in a position now to elevate St. Stephens Baptist to new heights. The members are engaged, and even Jade and Vic are on board, working alongside us rather than with a different agenda. God is up to something; I just don't know what or where he really wants me—at least not yet. I've already asked, though, and I know the answer will come."

Shiloh reached for his hand. "I'm with you, wherever he plants us."

"Sounds good to me, babe. Team Griffin, at God's beck and call."

By the time they reached home, it was Saturday morning. They had arrived in time for Randy to prepare his Sunday sermon, but they were exhausted. After helping unload the car, the boys scattered in various directions—Lem went to his room to video chat with Lia; Omari and Raphael climbed into bed and went back to sleep; and David, happy to have the TV to himself, turned to one of the cartoon channels that showed all of his favorite action shows and relaxed on the sofa. Shiloh made sure he was comfortable before curling up in the chair across the room from him and dozing off; unpacking the suitcases and washing the dirty laundry could wait.

Two hours later, she woke up refreshed, and headed up to her bedroom to start on the tasks she had deferred. Randy was stretched across the bed, snoring lightly. Shiloh giggled and checked the clock. She'd let him sleep two more hours if he needed, then she'd wake him to see if he wanted to get started on his sermon.

The doorbell rang as she was loading the whites in the washer, and it took her a few minutes to answer. Already breathless when she reached it and pulled it open, she was speechless when she saw the beautiful spray of flowers the deliveryman held.

"Shiloh Griffin?"

"Yes, that's me."

"Special delivery for you, ma'am. Please sign here."

Shiloh frowned, but complied. Who had taken the time to send her flowers? Randy usually did so once or twice a year, but it wasn't her birthday or their anniversary today. After signing for flowers and wrapping her arms around the oversized bouquet, she kicked the door closed with her foot and headed to the kitchen. She set the glass vase on the table and reached for the card.

"Thank you. For everything. I'm on a journey, and my head is in the game. Will keep you posted. Leslie."

Shiloh sat on the chair and sighed. As Daddy would say, God was still in the miracle-working business. She bowed her head and uttered a prayer for her college friend. *Help her father. Show her the way. Let her forgive, and shed her secrets. Let her live, really live, Lord, to your honor, and for the benefit of her entire family, especially her parents and her daughter. Amen.*

Shiloh finished the laundry, started dinner, and was reading a magazine when Randy strolled into the family room and laid his head on her shoulder.

"Aren't you supposed to be in your study, working on tomorrow's sermon?" she asked.

He nodded. "Normally, yeah. But Vic and Jade are back in town. He sent me a text and asked if he could preach tomorrow—part two of a message he started a few Sundays ago when he preached. Says he thinks it's fitting for the weekend after Thanksgiving. If he's ready and willing with a word that can bless the members and visitors, so be it."

Shiloh couldn't believe her ears. This was a first. He considered it a tradition to preach holiday weekend sermons. She wondered if he had relented so easily because of travel fatigue.

"We're still going to worship service, though, right?"

"Wouldn't miss it. We'll see what God says tomorrow. I'm going back to bed."

seventy-five

"Tomorrow" came quickly for all of them.

Shiloh spent the morning nagging the boys to shower, get dressed, eat breakfast, and pile into the van so they could make it to Sunday school. Randy had already left to attend the eight a.m. service. They somehow made it on time for Sunday school at nine forty-five, and Shiloh was surprised to see Jade, Naima, and Nicholas there as well.

"Yes—there's a first time for everything," Jade said and laughed. "Nicholas is two and I'm finally getting into a routine on Sunday mornings that actually works for getting both kids ready and out of the door on time. So here we are."

Shiloh chuckled. "I hope it didn't require as much yelling, threatening, and cajoling as it did in my house this morning, with four boys well past their babyhood, and with my youngest easing out of elementary school. How was your Thanksgiving?"

Jade shared that the family's brief visit to her mom and stepdad's place in California had been wonderful. They returned late Friday, and on Saturday had enjoyed a second Thanksgiving feast with Vic's family.

"Usually I'm the butt of all the cooking jokes since I show up with something very simple, like cookies or cupcakes," Jade said. "But this year, the Mrs. Wisconsin pageant and all the notoriety surrounding my advocacy for hearing aids caused them to cut me some slack. Thank God for our nation's obsession with celebrity!"

Shiloh swatted her arm. "Don't start praying for foolish stuff, now. You've been doing well."

Both women laughed and wound up in Randy's study, where they played catch-up on the past week in each other's lives. When Shiloh glanced at the clock and saw it was nearly eleven a.m., she stood and stretched.

"Service will start shortly," she told Jade. "Do you need to get Naima?"

Jade shook her head. "She's with her little friends. Their teacher will lead them to the sanctuary and probably sit near them to keep them quiet during service."

"Charlene is really great with them, isn't she?" Shiloh asked. She was a fairly new member, but she had jumped right in and started helping out however she could around the church.

They left Randy's office and headed to the sanctuary. When they entered and were near the front of the church, Shiloh felt a tap on her left shoulder. She turned and was greeted with the look that had caught her eye on her first day of teaching: petite little Monica wearing a mile-high afro. Shiloh grinned and hugged the girl.

"It sooo good to see you, my friend. I hope you had a nice Thanksgiving."

Before Monica could respond, there was a tap on Shiloh's right shoulder.

"Don't I get one, too?"

Shiloh turned toward Phaedra. "My other band student baby! Come here!"

She enveloped both of them in a hug, and asked them to sit with her and Jade during the service. Eleanor, Monica's grandmother, was watching the lovefest from across the sanctuary, and she waved and blew Shiloh a kiss, which Shiloh reciprocated.

Jade and Shiloh sat shoulder to shoulder when service began, and Monica flanked her on the other side, with Phaedra next to her. The choir launched into a familiar gospel tune, and Shiloh's head nearly did a 360-degree turn on her neck when Monica began belting out the words with fervor in a beautiful soprano.

Monica's voice was so moving that her flute playing almost paled in comparison. Yet she wanted to go on and become a professional flutist. Shiloh was perplexed, and knew she'd have to get answers later.

When it was time for the sermon, Randy stood in the pulpit and explained that Reverend Vic would be preaching this morning instead of him.

"He's got a word for us today," Randy bellowed. "Prepare your hearts and minds to be fed!"

And fed they were, by Vic's message of thanksgiving, redemption, and purpose in the midst of trials.

"If you want to have a story of victory, you have to go through the beginning, the middle, and the end," Vic declared. "Stopping before you get started well gives you little to work with. Stopping in the middle, just after the crisis point, means you're only halfway through. You have to resolve the conflicts and journey on to the end. But you can't just go through, you have to come out on the other side, maybe bloodied, but not bowed. Maybe messy and less than perfect, but still standing, still fighting for the Lord, still ready to give him your heart and receive his grace!"

By the time he was done, twenty-four people had come forward to join St. Stephens Baptist or to rededicate their lives to Christ. When Monica stirred next to Shiloh and stood to make her way to the front, Shiloh was surprised. Monica patted her hand and smiled, but kept going. When she reached the front, Reverend Vic seemed puzzled too, knowing that she and her family had joined the church just a few months earlier.

Sitting in her usual seat, on the second row of pews, kept Shiloh from seeing the congregation's perspective on this outpouring of connection to God this morning, but she knew some of the ladies who had murmured about sweet Monica in the Wednesday Bible study in recent weeks were likely making comments now about her decision to rededicate her life to God, so soon after joining church in the first place. But instead of joining the group of men, women, and children who had come forward to join St. Stephens Baptist, or the group that was rededicating their lives, she whispered in Reverend Vic's ear. He paused, as if contemplating how to respond, then nodded, giving his consent to whatever her request had been.

Monica stood just behind him, with the other worship attendees who had come forward, until the formal altar call had ended. Once the music wound down and Reverend Vic had shared the names of everyone who stood at the altar and had given them an opportunity to speak, he turned toward Monica and motioned for her to join him.

"Many of you in the women's ministry know Eleanor, this young lady's grandmother," Vic said. "Sister Monica here is a high school sophomore who joined St. Stephens Baptist on the same day as Eleanor and her father, about a month ago. Wave your hand if you're out there, Brother Claude."

Monica's dad stood and waved. Shiloh turned to see where he was seated, and recognized the surprise in his eyes over Monica's going to the altar.

"Well, Monica is here," Reverend Vic said, "because she wants to bless us with a song God has placed on her heart. I've heard many times from First Lady Griffin that this young lady is a gifted flutist—one who is going places. But I didn't know that she could also sing. She tells me this afternoon that she's ready to use this other gift, too."

Reverend Vic motioned for everyone else at the altar to take their seats and handed the microphone to Monica. He went over to the pianist and whispered something in his ear, and Shiloh guessed it was the name of the song that Monica planned to sing.

All of a sudden, Monica looked nervous. Her eyes flitted from Shiloh to Phaedra to her grandmother, since her father was sitting too far back in the congregation to find. Suddenly, though, a smile brightened her lovely face, and Shiloh turned to see that Claude had stood up, in a sea of sitting parishioners, to lend his daughter his support. He nodded at her, and she brought the microphone to her lips.

"Good morning, church," she said tentatively. After their swift reply, she continued. "I . . . my mother used to always tell me that my voice was so sweet it made her cry. And after she passed away, almost three years ago now, I kind of stopped singing, because it reminded me of her too much. I threw myself into my first love, playing the flute, and I just didn't sing much at all, until I joined the youth choir. Lately I've been going through some things. Some tough things. And I'm finding that what is seeing me through are my family, Reverend Griffin and First Lady Griffin, my closest friend, Phaedra, and most of all, God. I'm realizing more and more that Philippians 4:13 is right: I can do all things through Christ who strengthens me, even when I feel like I've failed God or I'm at my weakest. He still forgives me and loves me, and I'm grateful.

"So, my grandmother had her CeCe Winans CD on the other day, while we were cleaning the house, and you know, it's a CD I've heard her play a million times. But last week when one particular song came on, it just stopped me in my tracks. I realized that it is my story. And because CeCe Winans is singing about it, it must be the story of other people, too. So on this Sunday after Thanksgiving, I want to give thanks to God by honoring him and you, and everyone who needs to hear this, with 'Alabaster Box.'"

The full band of musicians began to play, under the direction of the pianist, and as the music swelled, Monica closed her eyes, put the microphone to her lips, and seemed to be transported to another place, as she sang the lyrics from her heart.

Shiloh let the tears fall, unchecked and unabated. She raised her hands in praise. Today, she didn't care who saw her. Monica's voice was so lovely it touched the soul. But the song itself wasn't just Monica's anthem in this trying season; it was her own. She realized, yet again, that God's love was more than enough to cover her sins, and she was truly thankful.

"You did not feel what I felt when he wrapped his loving arms around me. And you don't know the cost of the oil in my alabaster box."

When Shiloh, still weeping, opened her eyes, she was stunned to see that Monica wasn't standing by herself anymore. Jade had joined her, and so had her grandmother Eleanor, and Sister Adelaide from Bible study class. Shiloh left her seat just as the song wound to a close, and opened her arms to envelop the girl in a hug.

The church erupted in praise. Randy had been standing in front of the pulpit, watching Monica sing, clearly awestruck. When he saw the reaction of the congregation, he took his seat and let the church have its way. Shiloh motioned for Phaedra to join her at the altar, with Monica, who was still in her arms. She asked the girls if they had been obedient to the message she'd given all of her students throughout her substitute teaching stint—to carry their instruments wherever they went, because an opportunity to perform could arise at any time, in any place.

"Yes, we brought them," Phaedra said. "Want me to go to the car and get them?"

"Yes—please," Shiloh said, and Phaedra trotted down the aisle to Monica's dad to ask him for the key to the car.

"Mind if I borrow your flute?" Shiloh asked Monica. Monica, who seemed dazed by the reaction her singing had rendered, nodded. "I have one of my own, in Pastor Randy's office, but it's easier to just use yours, if you're okay with that. I'd like to have you sing that beautiful song again, sweetheart, and Phaedra and I will accompany you on the instruments. I can't speak for Phaedra, but you've validated my alabaster box, too, this morning."

Monica smiled and Shiloh kissed her cheek. When Phaedra returned with the instruments, the two of them quickly set up and tuned them, and Shiloh motioned for the musicians to launch into "Alabaster Box" again. This time, the flute and sax combined to play the opening melodies, and Monica, waiting for the perfect timing to chime in, did so at the chorus, reminding everyone present not to count the cost of someone else's gift to God, or the cost of their journey to faith. Only God knew, just as only God had the power to heal, restore, and bless.

seventy-six

By Wednesday, Shiloh knew the answer. She would wait, however, for Randy to reveal their destiny.

Shiloh made that decision as she pulled into the parking lot of St. Stephens Baptist for Bible study. There were more cars than usual, and she wondered whether some of the women had invited friends. She gasped when she entered the room and saw Monica helping Sister Eleanor set up an extra row of chairs. Monica properly positioned the chair she had been holding, then paused to hug Shiloh.

"Surprise!"

"Surprise indeed," Shiloh said. "To what do we owe the pleasure of your company this evening, young lady?"

Monica shrugged. "Grandma said it would be okay for me to come, even though I'd be the youngest person here. I just want to keep growing in wisdom, and in faith, Mrs. Griffin. This seems like a good place to start."

Shiloh smiled. "Well, I'm happy to see you, as always. If you get tired of hanging out with us old ladies, you know you are welcome to attend youth Bible study on Tuesday nights, even if you decide not to participate in choir rehearsal. And just know that I'm always here to talk—just a phone call away—if you ever want to work through something you're studying in the Bible, or if you have a spiritual question you're wrestling with."

"I know—and I will," Monica said. "You have been such a blessing to me, Mrs. Griffin. I think God sent you to Sherman Park just for me this year. I couldn't have gone through all of this hard stuff without you, and your family."

Shiloh's eyes grew misty. How was she going to leave this baby behind if God had other plans for her and Randy and their family? How would she break the news to Monica? She squeezed the girl's hand.

"Well, since we're family and all, and I'm not teaching at Sherman Park at the moment, please stop calling me Mrs. Griffin or First Lady Griffin. I'm just Shiloh to you, okay?"

She wanted to offer up the name "Mama Shiloh," but knew it might be too soon. In some ways, three years was a long time, but when a young girl lost her mother, it was just as if it happened yesterday.

"And I promise you this, no matter where life takes us, I will always consider you my daughter in spirit, and part of my extended family, got that?"

Monica grinned and hugged her. "So that means you'll come to my end-of-summer recital, when I complete the music program in Chicago?"

Shiloh broke into a grin. "You're definitely going? Good for you! Absolutely, Monica. I will be there and so will Pastor Randy. We wouldn't miss it."

Jade strode in and captured the room's attention with her fitted jeans, wide-brimmed straw hat, stiletto boots, and celebrity-style shades.

"What?" she asked, hand on hip, as she posed in the doorway. When no one responded, she did. "Look, God didn't say we couldn't be faithful and fabulous. I've been trying to tell ya'll that. You better recognize."

The women burst into laughter, and Sister Adelaide shook her head. "That woman . . . gotta love her."

And love her they had learned to do. Shiloh saw it that night, as Jade led them through a study of what it means to be transparent yet obedient, by reviewing Ruth's life and her faithfulness to her mother-in-law, Naomi.

"Ruth could have returned to her homeland and presumably found another husband," Jade said. "But she clung to this woman who had shown her a love like no other—a love that mirrored God's own love. And when that woman—Naomi—reached a point of despair so deep that she thought God had forsaken her, God used the presence and faithfulness of Ruth to prove that he was steadfast, and that he was right there with her, in the middle of the darkest nights. When Ruth had her baby, whose child did they call it? Naomi's! The village celebrated the fact that Naomi had a child, although Ruth had given birth. This is another sign of God's faithfulness to keep his promises. His blessings don't always come in the package or in the presence we expect; he sends them in ways so out-of-the-box that we're often left speechless."

Jade pointed to herself when she said this, and the women who had been in the Bible study the longest and remembered her first blundering attempts to teach them, smiled or chuckled. Then she reached into her ears and pulled out two caramel hearing aids and held them in the air. The room rang with applause.

Shiloh grinned. She understood now why Jade had dressed like a diva tonight: Her outfit had been part of the lesson—a visual example to help the women see that what they often understood or interpreted a certain way wasn't always wise; nor was it the way God saw and operated in the world.

Thank you for using her, Lord. She's even helping me.

When she reached home that night, after Randy as usual, she searched the house to ask if he wanted his evening bowl of ice cream, and finally found him in his study, on his knees. She was about to tiptoe away when he lifted his head and saw her, and motioned for her to join him. She complied, and he reached for her hands. She placed her palms in his, then lowered herself to her knees, so that she was eye-to-eye with him.

How was it possible that the older they grew, the wider they spread, the grayer they turned, the more she loved this man? She didn't know the math of the heart, but she was grateful. Shiloh looked into his eyes, already knowing what he needed to tell her.

"God says go, babe. Go back to Atchity, to Riverview Baptist, and assist Dad in his final months as pastor, so that we can lead the church that he and your mother took from its toddler years to amazing heights."

Randy paused. "How do you feel about that?"

Shiloh smiled. "I say, 'Yes, Lord.' He told me the same thing earlier today."

"Vic and Jade are ready to lead St. Stephens Baptist," Randy said. "I have no doubt that the congregation will embrace them, and that they will serve well and minister to those in need—yes, even Ms. Jade."

After seeing Jade connect with the women tonight, including those who had come to Bible study for the first time, Shiloh agreed that Jade would be up to the task. She was going to do wonderful things in both the secular world and through ministry—Shiloh could see it all over her. Whatever had been holding her back had lost its grip; she was on fire for God, and it was evident in every aspect of her being, even when she wasn't talking about her faith, the ministry, or anything related to religion. Her light just shone.

Shiloh and Randy embraced, then Randy led the two of them in prayer, asking God to direct each and every decision and step they'd make from here to there—from Milwaukee back to Atchity.

"If God says so, we'll work toward making the transition in late spring, after the boys are out of school," Randy said. "That will give you time to explore a way to complete your bachelor's degree at Alabama U, or maybe at a satellite campus of Birmingham-Southern. If you want to teach, I'm going to support you in that. You need to be using your gifts just as well as the next person, and I can see how God has used you in Monica and Phaedra's lives."

Shiloh kissed him.

"Thank you for that, babe. I do want to finish my degree, and it would be wonderful if I can do it at Birmingham-Southern, since I started there. I'll check and see. And about Monica . . . I've already let her know that she's our surrogate daughter. If we move in early June, like you're suggesting, we're going to have to come back this way in August. I've promised her that we'll attend the wrap-up concert for her summer music camp in Chicago. It means a lot to her for me—for us—to be there."

Randy gave Shiloh a thumbs-up. "Done," he said. "She is a special and gifted girl. If she stays on the right track, she is going to have some awesome opportunities come her way. We'll call your parents in the morning and tell them what we've decided, okay? If we call tonight, Dad won't sleep."

Shiloh laughed. "Then you better wait and tell the boys tomorrow, too. Lem will have dates with Lia on his mind, but the rest of the boys will be happy just to go back to their former schools and friends."

Shiloh left Randy in his office, staring out of a dark window, much like she did in the mornings, when she stood or sat in the sunroom, playing her recorder, her flute, or simply praying. She strolled past the family room, where David and Raphael were watching the scrolling credits on a Nickelodeon TV show.

"Turn it off, now, boys. Gotta get ready for bed and school tomorrow," she said.

Shiloh ignored their groans and made her way to the sunroom, where she leaned against the doorway. Had it really been just over three months ago when she rolled out of bed before anyone else was stirring, to go through the annual commemoration of her season of transgressions? So much had happened in such a short period, that it seemed like a lifetime ago.

She moved into the room and decided not to turn on the light, because the glow from the hallway provided just enough of a beam for her to navigate the room. Shiloh retrieved her recorder from the corner, and the three-by-five picture frame that she pulled out once a year from its hiding place in the room. She strode to the sofa, where she cradled it in her palms and read it one last time.

Remember this day, the mistakes you made.

Now she understood why she'd been stuck for so many years. She hadn't really been commemorating her loss, or truly seeking peace on the anniversary of the act she committed in France all those years ago; she'd actually been using that date to dredge up old feelings of guilt and shame, and to remind herself why she needed to be so good for the rest of her days. Through her own might, she'd held herself in bondage all of these years, when God only required repentance once. No more.

Shiloh laid the frame on the sofa next to her, pulled the recorder out of its case, and softly began playing "Her Song," for what she knew would be the last time. Just ten notes into it, however, she stopped. There was no need to play this original piece all the way through, ever again. It was a reflection of where she had been, not who she was today, or where God was taking her. Someday, when she felt a new song in her heart, she would pull out the recorder again, and play until her heart was content. Or maybe she'd devise a melody for the flute. For now, she would tuck away this instrument, and along with it, the song that had chronicled a loss that had been deeply wounding.

Shiloh picked up the frame again and slid off the back. She pulled out the typewritten note that she had used to condemn herself for nearly two decades. When it was in her hands, she read the phrase aloud, but changed it to what would be her new commemoration going forward, on that particular date in August: "Remember this day; God's grace is always sufficient."

Shiloh wished she had a pen so she could scribble those words on the back of the note, then she decided that wasn't necessary. Her life would reflect this phrase every day of the year going forward, not just in August, because this truth finally had a home—in her heart.

DISCUSSION QUESTIONS

1. What themes resonated most with you in this book?
2. What did you think of Shiloh? Was she likable?
3. Was it realistic for Shiloh to be so self-conscious about not having her bachelor's degree? Do you know women who have felt a similar level of insecurity about a particular issue, or have you, and how was it resolved?
4. Do you think Shiloh was wrong for keeping such a significant secret from her husband?
5. Do women of faith routinely mask their true selves? If so, is this appropriate or harmful?
6. Why was it important for Shiloh and Jade to share painful parts of their life's journey with others?
7. What did you think of Jade? Was she innately a showy person, or were her actions a sign of her insecurities?
8. Were the women in church justified for judging Monica?
9. Do you believe Shiloh took the right approach in addressing Monica's difficult choices?
10. Was Shiloh right to share her secrets with her young sons? Should she have been more concerned about the impact of those secrets on her husband and family?
11. What did you think of Shiloh's relationship with her sisters? With her mother?
12. How did you feel about Randy's initial reaction to Shiloh's secret?
13. Randy acknowledged that his motives for choosing to marry Shiloh weren't so innocent. How would that have made you feel if you were Shiloh?

14. How did you feel about Lem's reaction to Shiloh's revelations?

15. A lot of judging took place among these characters. What did you learn from the experiences of those being judged, as well as those rendering judgment?

16. Was this story an accurate portrayal of "church folk," and if so, in what way?

17. In this era where there's much talk about people leaving or avoiding church, should regular churchgoers change how they interact with each other, or operate in ministry, and if so, how?

18. What did you take away from reading this book that may help you better relate to people who are different from you in personality, values, or otherwise?

Acknowledgments

I have many people to thank for walking with me, pouring into me, cheering me on, and lifting me up with prayers and other tangible support during the writing of this novel. My book ministry thrives because you have in some way been an "armor bearer," or sister or brother in heart and spirit. I sincerely thank my son and daughter, Jay and Syd, for continuing to be my biggest cheerleaders, and for your unfailing love. I consider it a privilege and blessing to be your mother. I thank my siblings, Dr. Barbara Grayson, Henry Haney, Sandra K. Williams, and Patsy Scott, and my extended family in Arkansas, Texas, Iowa, and beyond, especially Larry Armstead, Lisa Armstead, Pamela Williams, and members of the Adams family. I'm grateful to my spiritual mentor Muriel Miller Branch, my dear friends and first readers Carol W. Jackson, Teresa Coleman, Cheryle Rodriguez, and Maya P. Smart; my pastors and spiritual leaders Rev. Drs. Micah and Jacqueline Madison-McCreary, and special friends Bobbie Walker Trussell, Comfort Anderson-Miller, Charmaine Spain, Connie Lambert and family, and Sharon Shahid. I sincerely thank: my loyal crew of friends Gwendolyn Richard, Otesa M. Miles, Robin Farmer, Karen Shell, Nancy Lucy, Joe and Gloria Murphy, Margaret Williams, and Danielle Harne Jones; my awesome colleagues at Collegiate School, including Amanda Surgner, Elizabeth Cogar Batty, and Dianne Carter; my author buddies, Rhonda McKnight, Tyora Moody, Tia McCollors, Fritz Kling, Booker Mattison, Tiffany L. Warren, Adriana Trigiani, Roger Bruner, Reshonda Tate Billingsley, Victoria Christopher Murray, Kim Cash

Tate, Bonnie Calhoun, Dr. Linda Beed, Gigi Amateau, Meg Medina, Lillian Lincoln Lambert, Michelle Sutton, and Carol Mackey.

Gratitude is also extended to my agent, Steve Laube; my speaker agent, Patsy Arnett; my editors Becky Philpott, Sue Brower, and Becky Monds; and Alicia Mey and other members of the Zondervan and Thomas Nelson marketing and sales team. I also sincerely thank Dr. Debra Ogilvie and her colleagues at Richmond Hearing Doctors for your generous hearts and inspiration, members of Spring Creek Baptist Church for your support and prayers, and readers and book clubs across the nation (and around the globe) for reading, and for sharing this book with others.

In closing, I invite you to consider, who among us hasn't made mistakes, intentionally committed a wrong, or suffered the consequences of a foolish act, brazen decision, or circumstances dealt us by life? In some form or fashion, we've all been there, and in the pages of this book, I hope you, the reader, discovered themes that helped you realize it takes all of a person's being—the high notes and the low, the woundedness and the wellness—to make one who he or she is. If we're willing, we can use all that we've journeyed through to become a blessing to others.

Thank you again for reading!

All My Best,

Stacy

NOTE TO READERS: FACTS ON HEARING LOSS

I chose to tackle the issue of hearing loss in this novel, and specifically focus on a character who believed she couldn't afford hearing aids, because some form of hearing loss is a growing condition among Americans of all ages, and few insurance companies in the United States treat hearing aids as necessary medical devices, thereby refusing full or partial coverage for their purchase. Having been personally diagnosed with mild hearing loss six years ago, I know firsthand how challenging it can be to secure hearing aids—something as critical to a person with mild, moderate, or severe hearing loss as eyeglasses are to a person with impaired sight.

Currently, a majority of Americans who need hearing aids must petition their insurance companies for coverage they may or may not receive, or pay out of pocket for the pricey devices (typically $1,000 to $5,000 per aid). If hearing loss is considered a disability and/or a medical condition, it is disturbing that these devices cannot be secured with insurance, leaving those who can't afford the aids or obtain special approval from their insurance companies to miss important conversations and sounds, or learn to read lips.

If you don't suffer from hearing loss, someone you work with or care about likely does. And whether those individuals are able to fully experience the world around them, or in some instances, maintain appropriate safety, often depends on whether they have personal funds readily available or access to a charitable organization that will help them cover the cost of an aid. You can help by contacting the Hearing Loss Association of America (www.hearingloss.org) or the National Association of the Deaf (www.nad.org) to lend your support. You also can contact your leaders in Congress and ask them to support policies that will nudge insurance companies to cover hearing aids as necessary medical devices, when surgery or other forms of treatment aren't ruled effective. By taking the time to advocate for others, you not only will have enjoyed a fictional character's journey, you also will have made a difference.

—Stacy

If forgiving your ex-husband was easy, everyone would do it. In *Coming Home*, Stacy Hawkins boldly explores the limits of loyalty and unconditional *Love.*

DON'T MISS THE NEXT WINDS OF CHANGE NOVEL

FINDING
home

AVAILABLE IN PRINT AND E-BOOK JUNE 2014